Know your enemy...know yourself...

treason's edge

THE TYON COLLECTIVE BOOK THREE

Susan M. MacDonald

WWW.BREAKWATERBOOKS.COM

LIBRARY AND ARCHIVES CANADA CATALOGUING IN PUBLICATION
MacDonald, Susan M., 1962-, author
Treason's edge / Susan MacDonald.
(The Tyon Collective ; book 3)
ISBN 978-1-55081-728-7 (softcover)
I. Title. II. Series: MacDonald, Susan M., 1962- . Tyon Collective ; bk. 3.
PS8625.D7725T74 2018   jC813'.6   C2018-900375-8

Canada Council   Conseil des Arts   Canada   Newfoundland
for the Arts   du Canada   Labrador

We acknowledge the support of the Canada Council for the Arts, which last
year invested $153 million to bring the arts to Canadians throughout the
country. We acknowledge the financial support of the Government of Canada
and the Government of Newfoundland and Labrador through the Department
of Tourism, Culture, Industry and Innovation for our publishing activities.

PRINTED AND BOUND IN CANADA

Breakwater Books is committed to choosing papers and materials for our
books that help to protect our environment. To this end, this book is printed
on a recycled paper that is certified by the Forest Stewardship Council®.

MIX
Paper from
responsible sources
FSC® C004071

For Caileigh, Jamieson, and Margot

Dedicated to my husband, Christopher

ocks as large as soccer balls dropped from the ceiling. Crashed around her feet. Tremors shook the very ground. She toppled. Caught herself. Held the wall for a second. The cave was collapsing. The cave was under the ocean. She had to get out. But where was it safe?

She was panting. A stitch in her side. People were screaming in terror. Jostling her, leaving her behind. Where was the ship? Where was Darius Finn? Why couldn't she find him? It was almost too dark to see.

Running, running. Heart pounding. Breath ripping at her throat. Terror and death behind her. She dodged another falling boulder. Scraped her outstretched hand. Cried out.

The sound of roaring water. Getting closer. Oh God, the sea had broken through.

Run faster.

Run *faster*.

Run...

1

Riley Cohen exploded into awareness. She took a deep breath of cool, unscented air as her brain moved into first gear. She was lying on her back on something firm. Everything around her was a white haze. Riley blinked several times. It took a moment for her to realize that her lack of visual clarity was not her eyes but a warm, scentless mist that floated between her face and the opaque glass window a hand-span above her nose. Raising her hand to touch the glass was beyond her abilities, but she could clench her fists and flex her wrist. Her fingertips brushed her thighs and instantly she knew what she was missing. Clothes.

"Hey," Riley tried to shout. It came out as a feeble croak but someone must have heard it. The light around her brightened and a face, features indistinct, leaned over the glass window directly above her.

"Relax," a woman's voice ordered. "You are inside a meditube. I will open the covering once I've checked your vital signs."

The face moved out of view. Riley licked her dry lips. What the heck was a meditube? Why was she in one? Where were her clothes? There was a faint flicker of multi-coloured lights around her but Riley told herself to stay calm and focus.

Images careened through her mind as if someone were rapidly changing channels on a TV. The devastation of an underground bunker. Running in a rock-hewn tunnel. A blond woman holding a crystal on a chain; a lanky boy with melting chocolate eyes reaching towards her. A narrow metal hallway bathed in blood-red light. Dear God, she *remembered*. It hadn't been a dream. That high-ranking Tyon operative, Anna, had tried to kill her. Almost succeeded too, if the way she was feeling was any indication.

The glass above her face slid back. Cool fresh air wafted over her and she breathed deeply. The face returned and Riley recognized it. Unfortunately.

"What symptoms are you experiencing?" asked Martje, the chief medic of the Tyon Collective, Earth mission branch.

"Where am I? Why am I naked?" Riley rasped.

"You are on board the intergalactic vessel *Nui*. You will receive a uniform once I determine your fitness to leave the meditube," Martje replied in her clipped, no-nonsense voice. "Debriefing will commence at that time."

"I feel fine. Let me out." Riley tried to lift herself upwards but fell back the couple of millimetres she'd managed. "I have to…"

"Your musculature is still compromised. You require a stimulant. Wait."

"Yeah, whatever," Riley muttered. Speaking to Martje had always been like conversing with a wall.

"Regeneration time is variable," Martje continued as if Riley hadn't spoken. "Terrans are slower to recover from this type of trauma. However, you display fortitude and considerable strength." Her face disappeared and Riley could hear her picking up something and putting it back down, just out of sight. The lights inside the glass tube flickered again.

So, she was on one of the Tyon ships. An intergalactic vessel too, which meant they'd probably left Earth. *Oh my God, was she in outer space?* Riley struggled to sit, if only to look around, but again her weakness defeated her. Don't think about it, she ordered herself. There were more important issues to consider; like where was Alec, and what was that creepy Anna up to? She'd worry about getting home later.

"How are you feeling, Riley?" A familiar young man with pale blue eyes and almost translucent skin suddenly appeared directly over the opening above her face.

"Hi, Dean. Get me out of here." Could he see down the tube? Tyons had no concerns about nudity—Riley knew that from her previous enforced stay—but she did. She felt the blush stinging her face.

"There will be a debriefing once I have determined she is strong enough to participate. Limit your discussion," Martje ordered from somewhere out of sight. Riley pulled a face.

"You have been unresponsive for six cycles." Dean lowered his voice. "I have been concerned."

"I informed you that she was past the point of succumbing to her injuries. There was no need to repeatedly

9

visit to supervise my care of this Potential," Martje scolded.

Dean straightened up. From Riley's perspective it looked like he was smiling at Martje, but that was highly unlikely as even Orions like Dean seemed to keep their emotions under tight wraps and Martje was hardly a laugh a minute. "I'll be back when you are ready to leave Med Ops to assist your acclimatization to space flight."

"Yeah, but I need to..." Riley began. The weakness that flooded her limbs made even finishing the sentence impossible.

"You will recover shortly. Do not fret," Dean advised before he moved out of view.

Yeah, right, Riley thought, easy for you to say.

Riley heard the two of them talking quietly and thought for a second that Dean laughed before deriding herself for such a silly idea. She'd stayed with these aliens for weeks before, and other than Darius Finn, none of them laughed. *Darius*. Instantly Riley's gut clenched. Darius had been gravely ill. Several days had passed, according to Dean. He hadn't died, had he? Anna hadn't done him in while everyone's back was turned, had she?

"Martje," Riley rasped. She tried to slap her hands on the bedding but it made no sound.

"Relax, I am here." Martje's stern face came into view.

Riley couldn't speak past the huge lump in her throat. A tear streamed out of her left eye, ran down her temple and into her hair.

"He's recovering well," Martje said briskly. "Like Dean, Darius has been monitoring your recovery and making a nuisance of himself by getting in my way." She left with an impatient sigh.

Tears of relief streamed unnoticed into the padding beneath Riley's head. Darius was alive. He was here. He cared about her. Riley tried to relax but her brain, now awake, was determined to get up to speed. So much had happened while she was unconscious. The questions kept flowing. Was she in orbit around Earth or on her way to some other planet? What had happened to her friends? Darius and Dean were here, but what about the others? Peter, Alec's older brother, had been seriously injured while trying to use his genetic gift— the one the Tyons had given them, without any training. Was Peter with the Tyons now or was he still in Kerry's apartment in Australia, his mind in pieces? And Kerry? Was he still a prisoner of the Council? And dear heavens above, what about Alec? The last thing Riley remembered was standing in the submarine hallway with Alec and Anna. Anna had been planning to take Alec somewhere and leave the rest of them to die on that tiny ship. Riley remembered arguing. Then there had been a blast of light from the weird crystal around Anna's neck and that was it. Riley had no idea how she'd survived that *and* the imminent danger they'd all been in. The little submarine they'd been on had been surrounded by rips in the fabric of time and space and seconds away from complete destruction. What had happened? Who had saved her? Where in the world was she?

Martje returned, fiddled with something just outside Riley's field of vision and a second later, energy and a feeling of well-being flooded Riley's entire body. "I will remove the upper portion of the meditube and assist you to a sitting position."

Riley bit her tongue and focused on gathering her strength. "Are we alone?" she asked, suddenly remembering her lack of clothing.

Martje pursed her lips but didn't answer. The glass slid back entirely without sound. The air was cool and goosebumps sprang to life all over. Riley covered herself as best she could with her hands. A rapid glance around the small Med Ops station indicated no one else but Martje. Martje, and three other body-sized glass tubes, all filled with swirling white mist.

It didn't really look like a space ship, Riley noted. The

windowless room was small, maybe six metres in both directions. The walls were the same brown metal as the bunker under Toronto, and other than the four medi-tubes and a long counter that ran along one wall, there was nothing to indicate it was a medical centre. Any cupboards holding sophisticated technology were hidden away and, Riley figured, took an orb to access.

A firm grip on her upper arm and a heave effortlessly pulled her upright and into a sitting position. The hated grey uniform was thrust into her arms without comment. Riley quickly slid her legs into the trousers and shimmied herself into the rest of it in record time, despite fingers that trembled so badly she could hardly bring the material's folds together for them to seal. She started to roll up the sleeves—there wasn't a Tyon outfit small enough for her—and looked up as the door straight ahead of her opened.

Darius.

Riley had only a second to see the dark circles under his eyes and note that his cheekbones were more pronounced before she was enveloped in a bear hug that threatened to crack all her ribs. "I thought you were dead," she gasped. She could feel the pounding of his heart and it seemed to be beating as hard as hers.

"I'm not that easy to kill," Darius murmured into her hair.

"Me neither," Riley breathed in the familiar scent of him and closed her eyes for a moment of bliss.

Darius pulled back abruptly. He held her at arm's length and peered down into her eyes. "Can you remember what happened? Anything at all?"

"I—" Riley got in before Martje interrupted.

"Debriefing will take place once the Commander is present. Not before, Finn. Withhold your questions."

"I want to talk to Darius," Riley snapped. "I don't want to discuss anything with your Commander."

"What you want is immaterial," Martje replied frostily.

"You would be wise to obey me."

Darius touched a forefinger to Riley's lips and frowned slightly as she took in a sharp breath. "Use caution, Riley," he said quietly. "There's nowhere to go now if you don't like the rules. Remember this."

Riley glanced at Martje's stern face and back at Darius. He looked older and worried. Perhaps he wasn't completely over his pneumonia? "Are we really on a space ship?"

Darius nodded.

"In space?"

He nodded again. The corners of his lips turned up as he felt her rising excitement.

"Cool," she breathed.

"Remember that when you start complaining how bored you are." He winked.

The door slid open behind them. Riley felt the temperature plummet and didn't need to turn around to see that Logan had entered. Seeing the shutters drop over Darius's eyes had been enough.

"Let the Terran Potential go." Logan's deep bass brooked no argument.

Darius said nothing but instantly dropped his hands from her shoulders. Riley turned and stared upwards. The Tyon Commander's face could have been carved from granite.

"Potential, you were found unconscious and transported to this vessel," Logan began with no preamble. "Report all knowledge of that situation. What happened immediately before you were injured?"

Riley straightened her spine and raised her eyes to Logan's icy stare. "We were on one of your little submarines, leaving the Base. We were surrounded. Tyrell and the other pilot, I don't know his name, were trying their best, but it was looking desperate. Ty thought we should abandon ship but your boss, Kholar, said we couldn't. Ty thought we were all going to die if we didn't. Kholar didn't care."

Logan leaned in closer. "Kholar would never endanger the lives of his crew."

"Yeah, well he did," Riley snapped. Honestly, this guy was so rigid it was a wonder he didn't crack in half when he bent over. "You guys may think the world of him, but *I* know he didn't care about the crew. He was only interested in saving something important. Something he and Anna had. I was touching him and I felt it."

"What was so important to Kholar?"

Logan's expression was unreadable. Riley couldn't tell if he was angry, suspicious, or satisfied. Or all three. "Alec," she said.

"I have scanned the complete list of personnel who were on board. Our records show neither Anna nor a Terran male by that name were on that list."

"Your records are wrong then." Riley crossed her arms. "They were both there. Alec was acting all weird and everything. Anna was her usual b—," she changed her choice of words at the last second, "her usual bossy self. She didn't want me. She was going to leave me to die."

"Anna wouldn't do that," Darius said quietly from behind her left ear.

"I'm not mistaken, Dare. She's the one who blasted me with that crystal she wears around her neck. She was taking Alec and making a run for it. They were going to let the rest of us drown."

Darius stepped away. His face was set in an expression of cold seriousness that seemed foreign to him. "You're mistaken, Riley."

Riley turned to face him, momentarily ignoring the looming commander. "No, I'm not. And I'm not lying either. Kholar told her to and she agreed. The only one worth saving was Alec. They snuck off down a side corridor. If I hadn't followed them, she wouldn't have blasted me." She turned back to Logan as another thought came to her. "Just how did I get on board this ship? We

14

were seconds away from getting creamed by Rhozan."

Martje forestalled any response by Logan. "You were brought here by Dean. He found you unconscious in a connector corridor behind the main compartment of the transport shuttle. He transported you with another two Tyons, at great personal cost. His report indicates limited similarities to your comments."

"Who else got off that ship?" Riley asked as she broke eye contact with Darius.

"The pilot and co-pilot. Several Tyon Operatives and two other Potentials," Logan replied.

"What about Anna?"

"Logan has already answered that question," Martje interjected. "There was no indication in the ship's records that Anna was aboard and no one else remembers her there."

It was Riley's turn to frown. "That makes no sense. She was there. She's the one who hurt me."

"Your injuries have impaired your memory. The ships records do not lie." Martje's tone was reproving.

Riley held onto her temper but her hands curled into fists. "Well then, what about Alec?"

Logan regained control of the conversation by answering before Martje could. "There are no records of anyone by that name on board."

Riley turned back to face Logan. "He was using a different name. Called himself William for some stupid reason."

"I remember him. A sulky undisciplined child. We considered that he was controlled by the Others. He was not listed as aboard that vessel either."

"Then where is he?" Riley asked angrily. "You must have records from the other ships. Where did he go if he wasn't on my ship?"

"Anna and William are among several missing individuals. We suspect they didn't make it out of the tunnels alive. All occupants of Home Base, including all

Terran Potentials, are now safe aboard this ship."

Riley pressed her lips together and fumed. She knew otherwise. This was somehow part of Anna's plan. How she'd managed it, Riley had no idea, especially as things had happened so quickly. Anna was behind it—Riley felt it in her bones. But Logan was going to refuse to believe her memory over the proof in their records, no matter how much she argued. She'd have to take a different tack with him. "What about Kholar?"

"Commander Kholar is dead," Logan replied curtly. "Tyrell and Ennis are currently in lockdown for their failure of duty to the Commander. Their priority was to save his life."

Riley nearly reeled. She glanced at Darius for confirmation. She took a deep breath to launch into her questions but Logan beat her to the punch.

"Nothing you have said can be corroborated. Why do you lie?"

"I'm not lying. You don't have to probe my brain with that thing to prove it," she said, nodding towards the orb he held in his massive hand.

"Terrans often tell untruths," Logan stated.

"If you treat everyone with this tell-me-or-I'll-punch-your-lights-out mentality, I'm not surprised people don't go around sharing their innermost thoughts with you," Riley snapped. "Honestly, bullying people only turns them against you. Or don't they teach that at Tyon Command school?"

"Silence." Logan raised his eyes to pierce Darius with his icepick gaze. "Don't deny that you've told this Terran to lie to me, Finn."

"He hasn't had the chance," Martje pointed out. "He arrived immediately before you did. They have not had time to organize any response to questions."

Riley swallowed her surprise and strove to keep her expression neutral. She could feel the waves of distress emanating from the man directly behind her and the waves of dislike from the one in front.

Logan took a step back. The frost hadn't melted from his features but the anger was fading and something softer was replacing it. "Your memory is faulty. The injury you sustained has impaired you. Anna and William are most probably both dead. Complete your debriefing, Martje. Finn, report for duty." He turned his back and strode from the Med Ops without another word.

For a second no one said anything. Darius's relief was palpable but there was still anger simmering just below the surface. Riley didn't need to touch him to feel it.

"You had better go," Martje said to him as she inclined her head towards the still open doorway.

Riley turned back to Darius and grabbed his arm. She needed him around for a while longer. He'd believe her, she just needed time to convince him.

Without meeting her eyes, he peeled her fingers off his sleeve. "Obeying his orders is the last thing I want to do right now," he said quietly, "But there's nowhere else to go and I'd rather not give Logan an excuse to throw me out the nearest airlock. We'll talk about this later." Without a backwards glance he strode quickly from the room. The door slipped silently back into place.

"Whatcha mean, nowhere?" Riley called after him.

"Don't get too attached to him," Martje cut her off as she pointed to a small chair almost out of sight behind a meditube. "Sit down."

Riley crossed to the chair on slightly shaky legs and sat down gratefully. "Why not? He's Terran."

"He's incapable of constancy or commitment. I have had many in here plagued with their feelings for that man and unable to focus on their duties. The Tyon Collective does not support pair bonding during active duty years, and you still have years of training ahead of you before that."

"You can't stop young men and women from falling in

love," Riley scoffed. What a stupid idea. "We're biologically primed to *pair-bond* at this age. Anyway, I know Darius is a horrible flirt. Don't worry about me."

"You care for him but the overriding feeling is one of physical attraction. It is not a lasting emotion and you would be well advised to focus on your future role with the Collective." Martje went over to the counter and with a wave of her orb created a computer screen. Instantly her attention was absorbed by the symbols flickering across the translucent screen.

Riley crossed her arms again and turned her face away. If Martje thought she could dig into Riley's brain and get at her most personal feelings, she had another thing coming. Besides, love was a stupid emotion. Look at her parents. They'd said they loved each other and her father had an affair and her mother hadn't loved him enough to be able to forgive him. Both of them claimed they loved her, too, but neither of them was around to save their daughter when all this started.

Martje was wasting her time giving Riley advice. She was *not* some stupid, vapid teenage girl drowning in her own hormones and unable to worry about anything but herself. There were far more important matters at hand. A twinge of uncertainty shivered through her. Was there a possibility that her memory was really a dream? Maybe she'd been hurt some other way and her injured brain had created the memory of what she'd wanted. She'd never trusted Anna and casting her as a villain could end Darius's ridiculous desire for her. Maybe Logan was right and she was lying to herself.

She gave her head a shake as if to clear it from those troubling thoughts. She felt well. She remembered what had really happened.

The part about Kholar dying was worrying though. That didn't make sense at all. The Kholar she'd stood next to was oozing with Tyon power. How in the world had he not transported off in time? Even if he was one of those Tyons unable to teleport, one of his minions should have been able to whisk him away in an instant. This whole thing wasn't making any sense. It was giving her a headache.

Dean walked through the door and startled her out of her reverie. "I'll take her now to her quarters," he said to Martje. "Let her settle in. We start the jump in one cycle."

Martje turned to Riley and said, "Let Dean help you acclimatize to this environment. Space travel is outside your planet's experience and can be unsettling for many. Should you require sedation, return to Med Ops and I will provide it."

Riley said nothing as she got to her feet. Martje's advice wasn't a bad idea. She needed a breather, time to herself to go over her memories and figure out what was real and what wasn't. Then she'd figure out what she had to do to get back home, find Alec, and get her life back on track, the way it should have been before she met all these lunatics.

She followed Dean out into the corridor, completely unprepared to have her mind blown away.

2

"A re you hungry?"

Alec looked up from the orb he was holding and smiled warmly at Anna. She was so good at knowing his needs. He reached up and took the cup of hot broth from her hand and sipped gratefully. Anna took his orb and slipped it into her pocket. They never let him keep it after practice time was over, but he didn't mind. She sat down on the sofa beside him, her hand automatically coming up to stroke his forehead while she held the crystal around her neck with the other. The soothing sensation of her fingers wove a deep contentment into Alec's soul. He was so lucky to have found her.

"Have you been practicing?" she asked.

"Yeah," Alec sighed. "But the telekinesis thing is impossible. It's like the more I concentrate, the tougher everything is."

"This is common," Anna reassured him. "Focus and practice overcomes the mind's barriers once it awakens to Tyon power. Time is all it takes."

"Do we have enough time?" Alec asked, looking towards the shuttered window for a moment.

"Hopefully." Anna abruptly got up and walked over to the window. She unclasped the shutters and pulled them back. Glorious sunshine streamed through, causing Alec to blink. The worst heat of the day had long passed but the room would be stifling if she kept them open for much longer. Still, they usually kept the house in darkness and a glimpse of the outside world was not to be missed. Alec hopped up, careful not to spill his drink, and crossed to her side.

The tiny farmhouse was tucked in a valley of rolling high hills. There wasn't another dwelling in sight. Alec hadn't been able to explore since they'd arrived several days ago, but he hadn't seen or heard any other people and he assumed they were alone. The hills were covered in scrubby vegetation with the occasional stunted tree breaking up the monotony. It was a barren yet beautiful place, particularly with the partially ruined, ancient wall perched high on the crest of the hill directly ahead. When the sun went down, the crenellated bastions of the towers to the far left and right seemed majestic.

The house, on the other hand, was anything but. There were only three rooms, no running water and the toilet was outside in a stinking hovel that Alec avoided until inescapable. The main room held a few chairs, a sagging sofa, a desk and a long countertop where they prepared meals and ate. Two bedrooms, one so small you could barely turn around in it, completed the dwelling. Who owned it wasn't clear to Alec and no one had mentioned anything to him. But it didn't matter. They wouldn't be here long.

Outside the sun blazed overhead and the parched earth shrivelled.

"I wouldn't mind hiking up to the wall. It's famous," Alec ventured quietly.

Anna shook her head. "We've discussed this Alec. You're hunted. I won't take the chance on anyone seeing you."

"C'mon," Alec sighed. "I've been stuck inside for ages. You told me this is an out-of-the-way location and tourists hardly ever come here. The farthest place on Earth from where they'll be looking, you said. Almost the other side of the planet. What are the chances?"

"Low," Anna agreed. "But still there. We look quite

different from the locals and will stand out. We must remain hidden. You can magnify the Great Wall with the orb, Alec. I've showed you how."

"And I suck at it," he replied gloomily. He'd been good with an orb. He had memories of it. Sure they were faint and hard to hold onto, but he felt in his bones he'd once been a natural with Tyon power. He had glimpses of it, could sometimes almost touch the wild electric *something* inside him, but he couldn't hold on to it. And time was running out.

"You will improve," Anna reassured him.

The door opened and a blast of heat surged ahead of a small man with a clipped goatee and hard eyes. He was followed, as always, by the tall, muscular hulk who shadowed him and did everything he said.

"Shut the door quickly, Paran, before this shack becomes unbearable," Kholar muttered irritably. He wiped at his forehead with sharp movements, then addressed Anna. "The signal continues to transmit but no response is detected."

Anna shuttered the windows and the room returned to its twilight gloom. "They are not looking for us and are likely quite far away."

"Hmmph." Kholar kicked off his shoes and sat on a chair. Sweat stained his grey overalls and several days' growth shadowed his cheeks. Paran wordlessly stood behind the chair and crossed his arms.

"Any movement?" Anna addressed her question to the bodyguard.

Paran shook his head. "Peasants in the distant hills. A tour bus passed on the road last evening but nothing today. No one has tripped the alarms."

"And the *Nui*?" she asked.

"Still orbiting. Shrouded but visible on our sensors. The Terrans will have missed it."

Anna gave a brief nod and sat down on the sofa. She

absently patted the cushion beside her and Alec instantly obeyed. "Logan will not leave until he is sure there is no sign of us. It will take time for our counterparts to ensure he comes to the desired conclusion. Once he does, we can amplify the beacon."

"Why do you want Logan to take your ship?" Alec asked. He could vaguely remember the huge Tyon Commander, knew the farther he was away from him, the better. "We could be on it and out of here already."

Kholar was rubbing the sole of his left foot angrily. "It is part of our plan that Logan is fooled into thinking we are dead. My ship is collateral damage. I can hardly take my vessel, slip away *and* convince him I am no further threat. Losing my ship is a necessary hardship, as is staying here in this remote backwater. Necessary to protect you."

Alec ducked his head. It was hard to live with the sacrifices they all made to keep him alive. Someday he'd pay them back.

"Darkness won't fall for an hour," Paran said. "I can leave now and hunt game for a proper meal."

"Bank the fire in the pit before you go so it is ready for your return," Anna instructed.

"I'll go with you," Alec offered.

Paran didn't even look at Alec as he left. Arguing with the colossal guard was pointless, especially when all he generally did was ignore him. Alec heaved himself of the chair and began to pace. Sometimes the urge to get out and just *move* was overwhelming. He knew he couldn't though. Anna had been through this many times. Logan was looking for him. Logan wanted him dead. The entire Tyon organization was convinced by the lies spoken by some Terran girl named Riley and a turncoat Operative called Darius. They'd have his guts in a jar before he could protest his innocence.

If only he could remember what exactly had happened, what he'd done to piss off the Tyon Commander so much the entire Collective was out for his blood. Anna said the head injury he'd sustained would eventually heal and his memory would likely return, but the days were passing and if anything, his memory was worse. She refused to tell him how it had happened or what memories his brain was hiding; obviously, it was pretty horrific. He kicked at the leg of the desk as he passed.

"Perhaps some concentration exercises would help," Anna suggested.

Alec shrugged and continued to pace. It felt like something was building inside him. Sitting and staring at an orb wasn't going to help.

"The boy needs a physical release," Kholar said as Alec passed. "I can take him out along the roadway. There are ample alarms along that route and I will be alerted to any approach."

"I won't leave his side," Alec added before Anna could refuse. He knew she didn't like him exercising after his injuries. "I promise."

Anna frowned. "It is unwise."

"I won't run very hard, just jog a bit," Alec argued.

"At the first sign of danger—" Anna began.

"Yeah, I'll be right back." Alec wrenched open the door before she could change her mind.

Outside the air was like an oven. It was going to be another miserable night for sleeping. Kholar followed him to the tiny, barren yard. The cooking fire inside the stone chimney was pouring out a thin trail of smoke that spiralled upwards in the still air. Above, the cloudless sky went on from hilltop to hilltop, empty of birds and sounds.

24   He could smell the outhouse.

Kholar pointed to the rutted track that meandered drunkenly through the bushes towards a distant gap in the hills directly ahead. "Run to the gate that blocks this path and straight back. I will monitor."

Alec grinned and bolted.

His eyes rose to the unfamiliar landscape around him. He'd never travelled to China before, he was certain of it, but where else he'd gone was unclear. So many of his memories were fuzzy—like watching television at his grandfather's place in Jamaica where there wasn't cable and the aerial didn't work too well. He stopped at the broken gate to catch his breath. Beyond the rusting latch and chicken wire the path met a dirt road, which wound its way around the side of the closest hill. There was no one there and not even a distant car to break up the scenery.

In the stifling heat, there wasn't enough air, but the blissful pumping of blood through his muscles with every jarring step was worth it. Alec couldn't remember the last time he'd run like this. For a second he almost stumbled. He used to run like this all the time; it was as much a part of him as breathing. The memory flashed into his brain, clearer with every step he took.

He turned around and raced back to Kholar's side. He skidded to a stop. "Again," he gasped and turned to race back down the path again before Kholar could forbid him. This time he ran slower. Sweat poured down his back and under his arms. He wiped the drips from his forehead. He remembered little things now. His favourite pair of cleats, the winning goal in a nail-biting tournament last summer, the cheap medal designating him MVP hanging on its ribbon over his desk at home. But he couldn't picture his parents; Anna said the accident that had killed them had been long ago. He knew she must be right, so it was funny how that felt so wrong.

He arrived at the gate and stopped for a moment to rest. He rested his forehead across his arms, leaning on the flimsy fence. The wooden slats were broiling under his bare skin but the feeling of being truly alive again felt good. Anna had to let him do this more often. He was straightening up for the return jog when a flash of grey caught his eye.

Someone was on the road, just at the turn where it curved around the hill. Alec squinted. More than one someone. Without thinking, Alec ducked under the fence and hid himself behind a bush. He peeked around the prickles.

Paran was holding someone up by the neck. Alec couldn't tell if it was a man or a woman, only that he or she was likely local, judging by the small stature and straight black hair. Paran gave the figure a slight shake and dropped it to the ground. There was a bright orb-flash and the person lay still. Alec muffled his gasp as Paran bent down and grasped the figure by the ankles, pulled the body off the road and up into the scrub-covered hillside until he was lost from sight.

Alec dashed back under the fence and headed back to the house with careful, measured steps, giving himself time to think. What the hell had just happened? Was the local person one of their enemies? Had Paran overstepped his instructions or did Kholar tell him to kill? Mind buzzing in a way it hadn't for days, Alec was unsure what to do. Kholar was waiting with a frown plastered over his face. He looked like he'd been for a swim despite the fact he hadn't even run anywhere.

"Back into the house. Anna has water warmed for bathing."

Alec nodded and brushed past the older man. Even at only fifteen, he was taller than the Tyon Commander. Kholar immediately fell into step behind him. "Did you practice your exercises today?"

"Yeah."

"Yes, sir," Kholar corrected.

"Yes, sir," Alec parroted.

"It is imperative that you be ready."

"It would help if I knew what I'm supposed to get ready for." Alec slowed to walk beside Kholar.

"Anna will tell you when the time is right, Alec. Not

before. There is no need to worry."

"I'm not worried," Alec replied. The annoying voice at the back of his head said he should be, but he ignored it. They were silent all the way back to the dismal little house.

In the doorway, Anna was holding her crystal in one hand and had a bucket of water in the other. Alec's heart lightened at the sight of her. "How do you feel?" she asked as she exchanged glances with Kholar.

Alec smiled. "I feel a million times better. I can think clearly too." He instantly realized he'd made a mistake as he saw Anna's frown.

She placed the bucket on the ground and reached out and clasped his upper arm. "You don't need to think any more clearly than you already do, Alec. There is nothing wrong with your memory. Everything is under control."

"Sure." Alec felt immediately calmer. The questions on the tip of his tongue melted into nothing the instant she touched his skin. He gave her a soft smile, then carried the bucket over to the chimney and yanked off his jumpsuit. As he washed, he tried to remember what exactly he'd seen earlier, but he couldn't picture it, not at all. He'd wanted to ask Anna something, but now the thoughts had evaporated like mist in bright sun. Shrugging, he dumped the dregs of the water onto the ground, picked up the bucket and headed inside.

3

Riley squeezed her eyes shut and forced herself not to throw up. The shifting of realities and the overlaying of one visual image onto another was nausea-inducing at best, totally freaky at worst. She couldn't trust her eyes to tell her where to put her feet and worse still, the thought that nothing on this ship was actually real and that any second she might plummet through the floor and into the vast freezing nothingness of space was almost paralyzing. Where was the *Enterprise* and its cool Holo deck and why couldn't these stupid Tyons even do space travel properly?

Dean pulled her hand through the crook of his arm. "Everyone reacts the same way, the first time they travel in space on one of our ships."

"I'd be better off with a blindfold," Riley muttered.

"You'll get used to it," Dean said.

"Why exactly are there three floors and how can I manage to see all of them at the same time?"

"Interstellar distances are huge," Dean began. "Travel by propulsion, in the same manner we use in our underwater vessels, is inefficient for space. Tyon engineers managed to shift the ship temporally in space and using boosted Tyon power we can slip through distance without having to travel through it."

"That made no sense at all," Riley muttered.

"Once we leave orbit and speed up, it will settle down and there will only be one floor."

"Really?"

"No. But hopefully you'll just *see* one floor. If you don't, I'll have Martje give you something for it."

"Gee, thanks."

"You're welcome."

As usual, Dean didn't get the sarcasm. Riley rolled her eyes. "How come Med Ops wasn't all twisted and stuff like the rest of the ship?"

"It's stabilized. Same as the bridge."

"I bet space travel isn't all that popular if everyone gets sick like I do," Riley said.

"The visual distortion only applies to Tyon ships."

"Why?" Riley asked without thinking.

"Only Tyons have the ability and are trained to use the orbs. You know that. It's only a very small percentage of any population that has the gift."

The genetic gift that was bred unscrupulously into those populations by the Tyons themselves, Riley mused wryly.

Dean propelled her around another identical three-layered corridor. Another wave of nausea rose into the back of Riley's throat.

"So, everyone else lets you guys drive them around the universe? That must make you very popular. And probably rich."

"Tyon gifts are secret, as you well know. The rest of the universe travels using standard propulsion and fusion generators. It's slower and extremely expensive. If they knew about our method of travel, or even that we exist, there would be a massive revolt and chaos." He stopped walking. "You probably won't like your new quarters. We're short on space on these interstellar vessels and sleeping accommodations tend to be tight. Still, it's not for long."

"Where are we going?" Riley had a sudden over-whelming wish to look out a window and see the blue-green Earth below, before it was gone, heaven knows for how long. "When will we be back?"

"The trip to Celes takes fifteen cycles, more or less. You can spend most of that sleeping if you want."

"And the return trip?"

There was a pause. Riley planted her feet on what she hoped was the floor and managed to swing Dean around a bit. He stopped. She opened an eye and stared at him, determinedly ignoring the walls that seemed to be moving around them. "*And the return trip?*"

"There isn't any plan to return," Dean said slowly. "While you were unconscious, the number of rips on Earth exponentially multiplied. It's the fastest we've ever seen. Rhozan has been very busy with his interdimensional booby traps and spreading discontent and malice. A war has broken out in the desert region. We expect nuclear weapons at any time."

Riley's heart literally stopped beating. She grabbed onto Dean's arms and her eyes flew open. "You have *got* to be kidding."

"No. Why would I?"

"I have to get off this ship, Dean. Right now." Her mother was in Africa and likely out of danger for the time being, but Canada was directly adjacent to the United States and if the Middle East was already at war, it wouldn't take long for some extremists to get involved and blast the Americans. Nuclear bombs would be next. Or worse. "My dad is down there," she gasped. "My sister too. I have to get them."

"You can't," Dean said.

Riley wasn't listening. There had to be some transporter to get her off this ship right now. Either that or an escape pod. She struggled against Dean's hold. "Let me go."

"Riley, you have to stay with us. You can't save them."

"I have to!" Riley screamed.

The pain hit with lightning speed. Her brain was on fire. She dropped to her knees and grabbed her head. She was going to be sick. She was going to die.

"Riley, what's wrong?" Dean crouched down beside her.

She couldn't speak. Something inside her head was screaming but it wasn't her. There was a flash of something bright, the image of torture, misery and pain, then nothing but white-hot agony and sudden realization. Riley shuddered violently as it began to reduce in severity.

Kerry. She'd forgotten all about her mission for the Council.

She rubbed her head where the implant was doing its work. She'd been unable to further her investigation for four days. That was ninety-eight hours that Kerry had been tortured and ninety-eight hours Riley hadn't been getting to the bottom of the Council's mystery.

The Council wouldn't care that her world was on the verge of annihilation. They wouldn't care that her entire family would probably perish and she wouldn't have a chance to tell them she loved them. The knowledge the Council had placed inside her mind was sure and unwavering. She'd have to forget her parents and her sister. The planet was beyond saving.

"I feel sick," she murmured, barely able to get the words past her frozen lips.

Without another word Dean scooped her up in his arms and strode back the way they had come. Riley buried her face in his chest while the tears burned tracks down her cheeks and soaked into his uniform.

Her despair prevented further thought. She didn't notice entering Med Ops or Dean's quiet conversation with Martje. Curled up on the mattress of an open medi-tube, she sank deeper into desolation. She was sobbing so hard she wasn't aware of the glass dome slipping over her or the sudden swirling mist. Only the deep soothing sensation of nothingness, of the drug-laden air, penetrated her abject misery. Without a fight she fell back into a deep and dreamless state.

"Are you planning to snore your way across the universe?"

Riley cracked open one eye. Darius was sitting on a chair across from her open meditube. His arms were leaning on the edge next to her shoulders. As usual, his hair needed combing. Riley lifted a finger to run it through his golden-brown spikes and gave him a lopsided smile. "If I get up I'll have to see the ship."

Darius raised an eyebrow. "Nope," he said reaching down to pick up something at his feet. He handed her a narrow circular band of navy, clear plastic.

"And this would be for?"

"You wear it," Darius said as he took it back from her and slipped it over her head so that it rested on her nose, like glasses. Instantly the Med Ops was coloured greenish-blue.

"It helps with the visual distortion. You'll be able to walk around the ship now," he explained.

"If you say so," Riley muttered. She sat up slowly. The anguish had dulled to a background despondency; whether because of the medication or the implant, it was impossible to tell. She felt back in control, although joyless and empty. With the clarity of thought came other, more pressing concerns.

There were things inside her head she couldn't let anyone see, not if Kerry was to live. Darius was adept at telepathy. Martje would have been an impediment to Darius getting too close or Riley dropping her guard, but there didn't appear to be anyone else in the room. Worse still, Darius didn't seem to be annoyed with her anymore. "Aren't you supposed to be at work?"

Darius leaned back in his chair and swung his feet up onto the edge of the meditube. He gave an insolent shrug. "The big boss man's put me on sanitation duty. There isn't much to do on a ship this size. It's all pretty automated."

Riley dangled her legs over the edge of the tube's bed. "Guess he thought you'd hate it."

"I've done worse things." Darius smiled. "How are you feeling?"

"Okay, I guess." Riley feigned an interest in a loose thread on her overalls.

"Want to tell me what's going on?"

"What do you mean?"

"The meltdown in the forward corridor. Dean said you collapsed. Martje couldn't find anything wrong. So, what happened?"

"I was overcome," Riley said

"Overcome with what?"

"Grief."

"Pull the other one, kiddo. I know you too well."

Riley hopped down and wandered over to an open panel of instruments. She leaned over to peer closely at one, keeping her back to him. "It's true. My parents are in danger and so is my sister. I freaked out thinking about how they're gonna die."

Darius got up and padded silently behind her. She startled as his hands gently gripped her shoulders. He spoke quietly into her ear. "You and I know that's not what I'm feeling now. There's something more. I can help. You know I can."

Riley mutely shook her head.

Darius moved his hands, starting to massage her shoulders and neck with firm, soothing movements. She felt the tension start to melt away. The man was certainly gifted in this department, she sighed to herself. Suddenly she jerked away. Touch was a direct conduit to her mind. "Stop it."

"There isn't anything you can't share with me, Riley," he said softly.

"Please, Dare, don't. I can't."

She felt his sigh as much as heard it. "Don't push me away," he said. "I'm on your side. Maybe the only person on this whole ship who's on your side. Remember that."

Riley didn't trust herself to speak. There was a long silence.

"If you change your mind—" he started.

"I won't."

"Maybe you'd prefer talking to Dean?"

She almost laughed at the sulky tone. She clamped down on the smile and mentally kicked herself for the words she had to speak. "Yeah, maybe I will."

Darius straightened and the tone of his voice was coolly impersonal. "I see. Well, if that's what you want to do, I can live with it. I just thought after all we'd been through together—and how I thought we felt about each other— things were different. I guess I was mistaken."

She didn't see him leave. She kept her back to the door and heard him pause, waiting for her to call him back. After a moment the door *swooshed* closed behind him. It was only then that she could breathe again.

Martje returned some time later and after scanning Riley, permitted her to leave Med Ops. Dean was summoned from his work with the other two Potentials. He escorted Riley with frequent sideways glances as they silently made their way to her quarters.

Riley forced herself to focus on figuring out the layout of the ship now that she could see it without vertigo. She had her despised assignment to accomplish and although she felt emotionally bereft and hollow, her brain was actively planning. Millions and millions of people might be dying right now, she had no way of knowing, but she was damned if Kerry's life would be on her conscience. And when this stupid mission was done, she'd explain to Darius why she'd acted this way. Of course, he'd totally understand and would forgive her instantly. She'd had one of Darius's kisses in the past: making up with him would be spectacular.

The ship was much smaller than she'd envisioned. There was only one large chamber for the travellers unless they were on the unseen bridge. The resting quarters were long narrow corridors with upright open closets lined along the wall. Dean showed her how to position herself inside the small space and discussed how the life-support system worked. Riley wasn't sure why Darius had a job with the ship's sanitation when the personal closet Dean called a sleeping pod took care of all the normal bodily functions while the occupant stayed in a state of suspended animation. But she declined Dean's offer of letting her pass the next several cycles unaware. She headed back to the main galley. Too much time had been wasted already.

With its low ceiling and excess number of people, the galley felt claustrophobic. Tyons and Terrans, all in various states of resolve or disequilibrium, spilled off the seats and around the tables, lounged against the walls or sipped hot drinks in clusters, talking quietly. Riley looked around. Darius wasn't there.

Dean led her to a quiet corner and shooed another Potential off a chair. "I'll get you something to drink. Stay here."

There were several Tyons she didn't know but a few looked familiar. She recognized none of the teenagers. She discounted them as possible suspects. If only she had an orb, she could listen in to the conversations around her. The faster she found the traitor, the better.

"Try this." Dean handed her a beaker.

"I need an orb," Riley said as she raised the steaming liquid to her lips. "I need to start working on mastering it."

Dean surprised her by handing over a pale pink crystal, the size and shape of a golf ball. "I knew that you would want one. Another has never used this one. I think it will suit you."

Riley took it gratefully and instantly felt the soothing sensation an orb always gave her. Pretending interest in her drink, she gripped the orb tightly and focused as hard as she could on the Tyons across the room. It was nearly impossible to hear anything. There were too many people nearby and their thoughts crowded her mind. Someone was angry with their work partner, at least three others were annoyed they were travelling on such a small ship, and one was having very amorous thoughts about another Operative. Riley rapidly backed away as the thoughts became uncomfortably explicit.

"Why are you listening in to others' thoughts?" Dean asked quietly.

Riley nearly dropped her drink. "Who says I'm—"

Dean slid his back down the wall until his face was level with hers. Looking straight ahead he replied conversationally, "I am responsible for your training. That gives me access to your orb."

Riley racked her brain for a suitable response. "Just curious I guess."

"Privacy is an important concept in a society where we can knowingly intrude on others' personal thoughts. I would ask you to restrain your natural curiosity and desire to utilize the fascinating power of the orb and respect the limits I impose."

Riley nodded. She couldn't look at him.

"Who taught you to do that?"

"Darius," Riley said.

"You're a remarkably good pupil. You had only a few days with him."

"He's a great teacher." Riley forced her thoughts away from the truth that she and Darius had spent much longer together than anyone but Anna knew. She could not afford to let their time-travel secret get out.

36   Dean stood up. He was looking at Martje, who had just entered the galley and was striding across the crowded room, unerringly in their direction.

"I think she likes you," Riley observed dryly.

"She should," Dean replied. "She's my mother."

Riley startled. She would never have guessed that they

were related. It did explain the level of familiarity they had with each other, though. "I thought Tyons didn't pair bond until after their tour of duty was over?"

"She re-enlisted," Dean replied.

"I see you are using the Ulat band," Martje said without preamble. "Does it facilitate visual perception?"

"Yeah, it helps," Riley said.

"I scanned you several times during your stay in Med Ops," Martje began. Riley's heart sank. "You have an implant. There is no record at Home Base that you underwent the procedure."

"There isn't?" Riley stalled.

"No."

"Must be a mistake. Anna arranged it the minute we arrived."

"Anna would have discussed it with me. Potentials undergo extensive aptitude testing prior to implantation. If their power is insignificant or they are deemed unable to adapt we do not waste one."

Riley scuffed her toe along the floor. "You'd have to ask her why she didn't leave a record of it."

"Unfortunately, Anna is no longer alive. Asking her anything is out of the question." Martje frowned.

"Why are you so certain?" Riley turned to face Martje. "Just because you can't find her doesn't mean she's dead."

"Her implant is non-responsive. That only happens when there is no brain function."

"She was on the ship with me." Riley watched Martje's eyes' narrow, but continued anyway. "And I know what Logan thinks and what the ship's records show, and I'm telling you, I think they're wrong. Somehow she's managed to turn off her implant or stop you from getting a readout."

"There's no method of turning the implant off," Dean interjected with a frown. "They're supposed to be permanent."

"If it can be turned on, it can be turned off," Riley said.

"I'm telling you, she was with me on that ship."

"You are the second person to make such a statement." Martje replied slowly. Her brow was furrowed. "You have a relatively high level of Tu quotient. It is rare and could be useful to the Collective. I noted it on the preliminary scan. This is an indication that you may be using it."

"What does a Tu quotient do?" Riley asked warily.

"Prevent mental influence and outside control. It's a requirement for training as a pilot," Martje replied.

"So, I can't be brainwashed, is that what you're trying to say?"

"I am unfamiliar with that term, but it does mean that you are far more resistant to having your mental function interfered with than most."

Riley's brain did a few intellectual somersaults. "So, Tyrell has it, if he's a pilot. He remembered the same thing I did. About Anna."

"I wish to discuss this with Logan." Martje's lips were pursed. She didn't look too happy, but then, she never did.

Riley didn't move as Martje turned and headed for the door. There was no choice now. She was going to have to question Tyrell despite him being in lockdown, whatever that was. She *had* to find out exactly what he remembered about the last few minutes they were on the ship. If Logan found her talking to him he'd probably have her tossed out of the nearest airlock without a spacesuit. She'd have to take the chance. Too much was at stake.

She'd just have to avoid getting caught.

Alec lay awake. It was too hot to sleep. He'd defied Anna's instructions and cracked open the window above his head in the hopes the cooler night air would find its way into the stuffy bedroom. So far, no such luck.

He clasped his hands behind his head and stared at the ceiling. The unexpected crunch of gravel outside the hovel caught his attention. Was that one of the locals come to spy on them? Alec got to his knees silently and peered out through the slight space between the thin drapes. The side yard was empty. Silver moonbeams traced tracks in the pitiful clumps of weeds and threw the distant outhouse into a tangle of shadows. He heard the voices before anyone came into view.

"There is still no sign of it." Kholar's voice made Alec jump.

"They will be here. The message was received."

The second speaker was Anna. Her voice was getting louder; they were walking towards the window. Alec leaned back so they wouldn't see him.

"There will be punishment for this tardiness."

"Just so. However, the plan is not jeopardized. If they arrive within the next two cycles, and Paran and I boost the speed, we can make the Council Senate in time and destroy them without having to wait until the next grand conference."

Alec's heart leapt in his throat. What was that again?

"I would much prefer to complete our mission

4

on this rotation. The following Council session is on Iqib—far too distant to make a serious impression."

"Agreed. However, with Alec's ability, even if we miss this meeting, we will succeed."

There was a long moment of silence. What was Anna talking about? His orb ability was terrible.

"My change in plans is now acceptable to you, correct?" Kholar asked. They had stopped walking and were close enough that Alec had no trouble hearing.

There was a moment of silence before Anna responded. "We would have been successful with Darius too."

"Are you regretting your sacrifice?"

"Darius was an amusing companion," Anna replied. She must have turned to face the other way because her voice was less distinct.

"He was growing wary, Anna. Surely you realized this."

Anna didn't reply. Alec bit his lower lip. Who was Darius and what was he suspecting? The name was ringing bells inside his head, loud and clear, but the mental picture was nothing but static.

"Logan is right, you are sentimental for this race." It sounded like Kholar was laughing. "Once we are aboard, I will send Paran to Ehra to prepare the safe holding for our commodity."

"Ensure the shields are at maximum. He will eventually rebel. The hold I have was too quickly established and won't last forever."

"Agreed." There was another long moment of silence. Who was going to rebel and against what? Alec's brow furrowed with concentration. He had the feeling that Anna was talking about him, but it couldn't be so. What hold? Why the need for shielding?

"If Darius Finn has managed to live, he could be trouble." Kholar had returned to the previous subject. "Your Kira was extensive and lasted years. He might pursue you. Raise all sorts of unanswerable questions. I have changed my mind. I think he should be destroyed. We only need the one to accomplish our mission."

"I still feel that two combined are better than one alone, but I am willing to consider this."

"And the brother?"

"His power was a fraction of Alec's. The Council must have terminated him because the incomplete teleportation was not repairable. When I returned to kill the female, he was already dead and the dwelling still emanated miro particles. I had missed them within hours."

Alec's heart gave a funny spasm and a sick feeling washed over his skin. He didn't have a brother—*did he?*

"Indeed. This indicates that the Council suspects. The fact they took the female and returned her confirms my theory. She has likely been programmed to subvert any conspiracy. You should have killed her in the Base. There is a minute possibility she survived."

"Impossible. Destruction was seconds away. We are safe." Anna's voice faded as she moved out of range but the tone of her voice indicated the subject was closed. Alec shimmied over to the edge of the bed and peered outside. He could make out Anna's blond head, almost glowing in the moonlight, as she walked out of sight. Alec sat down on the pillow. He rubbed his forehead. If only this concussion would heal. His brain felt like someone had encased it in cement and he couldn't even chip away at the walls. And, while that should have been frightening, it wasn't. He didn't feel *any* emotion.

He sat for some time, thinking about the conversation he'd just heard. Most of it didn't make any sense. He couldn't remember any girl, or this Darius person, so it was unsurprising that he didn't feel anything about their fates. But a brother?

He heaved himself to his feet and padded barefoot out of the bedroom. The main room was glowing with a greenish yellow light from Anna's monitor. She had created the transparent screen in midair and was waving her fingers in front of it. Symbols flitted across but Alec couldn't read them.

"Can't sleep?" she asked without taking her eyes off the rolling script.

Alec shrugged and pulled out a chair next to the counter, resting his elbow on it as he watched her. It crossed his mind to mention that he'd heard her talking but at the last second, he reconsidered. He'd been ordered to get some sleep and she'd be annoyed at his eavesdropping. He picked up a grain of rice off the counter and rolled it between his finger and thumb. "It's too hot. What're you watching?"

"Violence reports," Anna said. "Several continents are in serious trouble."

"Which ones?"

"North America, six European countries, all of the Middle East and this country."

"Canada too?" Alec asked.

Anna nodded.

He should at least be concerned—this was his home planet after all—but there was nothing there but apathy. "How close is the violence to us?"

"The capital of this country is two hours away by motor vehicle. There is rioting and widespread fighting among the citizens. The army has been deployed. This countryside is still relatively quiet."

Alec smothered a yawn. "Any sign of our ship?"

Anna's attention returned to the screen and she waved her fingers again. Frowning, she answered, "No."

The door opened and Paran walked in. Cold, wood-smoke-stained air followed him like a shadow. "There is a small village two hills over. Two of the villagers have murdered family members tonight and there are rumours abounding that evil spirits are on the rise."

"The villagers are correct."

Paran snorted. "Ignorant savages."

"Sheep, ready for the slaughter," Anna agreed.

Alec sat up straight. He'd heard someone else say the same thing not so long ago and it had bothered him then, too. Who had said it and why did it unsettle him so much?

Paran stopped by the counter. He pulled a bowl of nuts closer to him and dug into the contents. He dropped the handful into his mouth and chewed quietly for a moment.

"I will want you to continue to patrol. If there is violence, there are rips. We must monitor their locations and frequency to determine when we must leave," Anna said.

"Any message from the *Rua*?"

"No. Out of range. The beacon is still functioning."

"Has the *Nui* left?"

Anna shook her head.

Paran looked satisfied. "The *Rua* won't move into Sensor range until the *Nui* is gone. Torraz won't take a chance on Logan spotting his ship."

"Agreed," Anna said. She dropped her hands and the screen dimmed. "Logan is taking an unusually long time to leave." Paran looked at Alec, then back at her. "It is not possible he is suspicious," Anna answered his unspoken question. "Kholar and I erased any record of my presence, and Alec's, on the submersible. With my signal gone, he will assume I am dead. Alec has an implant but I removed its code in the central bank. Logan can't use it to trace Alec, either."

Paran took another handful of nuts. "He will search for your body."

"Not for much longer. Protocol dictates he must leave within two more cycles. Attend to your duties."

Paran left and the room seemed much larger with him gone. Alec popped a nut in his mouth and rolled it around with his tongue. "The *Rua* is the ship we're going on?"

Anna nodded.

"I hope it arrives before there's serious trouble here."

Anna agreed. "That is another reason I wish you to stay

within the confines of this house, despite the fact doing so makes you feel restless. When the *Rua* arrives and we transfer aboard there will be more to occupy your mind."

Alec stood up and ran his fingers through his hair. He walked over to the window and pulled up the shutters for a moment. There was nothing but blackness outside. Sighing, he dropped the shutters back into place.

"Would you like me to sedate you?" Anna asked.

"No," Alec replied.

"You are uneasy and unable to rest. This is unacceptable. Let me help you."

Alec avoided her eyes and headed back to the bedroom. He didn't want anything that would dull him any more than he already was. "I think I'll go lie down," he said.

He crossed past her and re-entered the tiny bedroom. He paused on the threshold. It was weird to feel this uneasy. Goosebumps were gathering across his shoulders and his neck. He felt like running somewhere, but of course, there was nowhere to go.

He climbed onto the bed and shimmied across to the far side, plumped the pillow and repositioned it. He straightened the thin bedclothes and pulled the blanket up to his chin. He stared upwards.

The moonlight was temporarily diminished as a cloud passed in front of it. Alec raised his eyes to the window. The silver-grey mass moved ever so slowly, its darker centre obscuring the moon entirely before wisps of cloud-edge let filtered slivers through. Was Logan's ship up there, near the moon?

The last of the cloud passed by and the beams once more illuminated the bedroom. Something caught Alec's eye, just on the edge of the beam, where it came through the window. Curious, he sat up and peered closely.

How odd. A little cloud of sparkling dust.

Alec watched the sparkles silently glitter for a long time. Inside him, a strange feeling grew stronger with every heartbeat. He *knew* this. He could hear the distant echo of a girl's scream and had a vague sense he should flee.

The sparkles didn't do anything. After a while the moonbeams shifted as the moon slid inexorably on its nocturnal arc and the sparkles lost their brightness. The niggling feeling he should escape was getting stronger. Alec flung off the blanket and slipped out of bed. He opened the door and stepped into the main room. Anna was still on the couch, the glowing screen bathing her face in a sickly green light. She glanced up at his silent presence. "What?"

5

"I don't know," Alec said. He jerked his head behind him. "Something odd. I can't remember what it is."

Anna was immediately on her feet. She brushed by Alec and illuminated the room with her orb. She immediately backed out and closed the door behind her. "That is a rip."

While he'd heard that term before, its meaning eluded Alec.

"They're dangerous segues from here to somewhere else in the universe," Anna replied to his unspoken question. "Once you go in, you can never come out. Come and sit on the couch."

Alec did as she requested but his frown deepened. She was wrong about something, but he didn't know about what.

Anna went to knock on the flimsy door of the other room and a rumpled Kholar immediately opened it. "It's started," she said.

Kholar gave Alec a dark look before replying. "Has contact been made?"

"It doesn't appear so. Monitoring only. He doesn't have an orb."

They rarely talked about him if he was paying attention. Alec turned to the screen hanging in the air in front of him and used his index finger to trace the moving symbols across the air while listening intently.

"Do not give him one," Kholar ordered quietly. "I'll monitor for others, just in case. You set up shielding."

Anna nodded and returned to Alec's room. A moment later she returned holding his dry overalls. She handed them to him.

"Dress and be ready to leave," she instructed as her attention returned to the screen.

"Why?" Alec said as he automatically donned the grey one-piece. "Are we going somewhere?"

"There is the possibility we will have to vacate this property. Rips are highly dangerous, Alec, and we cannot take the chance that they may impede our function here. Kholar will monitor the rip and I will set up defensive shields around us to reduce observation by the Others."

"Who are the Others?"

"Enemies." Anna didn't look like she was inclined to say anything further and Alec was well used to her refusal to elaborate. He ran his finger up the main seal of the uniform to close it and searched under the couch for his shoes. One was easily grasped, but the other was missing. He dropped to his knees and peered under. The darkness made it difficult to see, but he thought the dark object under Anna's end of the sofa was the other. He reached in.

Suddenly Anna grabbed the back of his neck and

hauled him away. He landed on his butt with a thud.

"Ow! What did you do that for?" he gasped.

"Rip." Anna pointed to the screen where a glowing red hexagon pulsed. She then pointed down to the sofa. "There."

His heart rate zoomed upwards and a cold, clammy feeling settled in his legs. "I need my shoe."

Anna's orb flared into brightness and she peered under the sofa. A second later his runner sailed across the air. He snatched it without thinking and immediately put it on. He wasn't going anywhere in bare feet.

Kholar poked his head out of Alec's bedroom. "Another?" He looked surprised.

Anna glanced at the screen. "Two in the last minute. One inside and another near the fire pit."

"Unusual."

"Agreed. But not without precedence," Anna replied.

"No," Kholar drawled thoughtfully. "But the second time with him."

"And with us. *And* the pilot. There is no conclusive proof."

Kholar's expression soured. "True."

Anna waved her hands over the screen and her orb flashed brightly twice. The room was heavy with silence. Alec could hear his heart beating. He stood in the middle of the room not quite sure what to do or where to go. Was there any way of knowing where the next rip would appear? Where were they coming from and why had so many appeared?

Paran entered the house in a sudden rush, slamming the door behind him.

"Emissaries?" Kholar asked as he pulled his orb from his overall pocket.

"Eight."

Kholar and Anna exchanged a dark look.

"What's an Emissary?" Alec asked.

"A human controlled by the Others," Anna said.

"What are they going to do?" Alec asked. He looked from one Tyon to the other. The foreboding expressions made the clammy feeling increase tenfold.

"Paran, are these farmers or military?" asked Anna slowly.

"Peasants. All unarmed."

Anna looked at Kholar. "The power has been markedly dormant. This may be the best opportunity to remove the impediment imposed by my hurried Kira." Kholar frowned and Anna continued. "We must take this chance if we are going to use him." Kholar slowly nodded and Anna turned back to Alec. "There are several people outside who intend to harm us." She withdrew Alec's orb from her pocket. "You will go outside and remove the threat."

"How?" Alec stammered. "Aren't they dangerous?"

"Alec, listen to me," Anna said. The orb was pulsing slightly and Alec found himself unable to look away. "You will go outside. You will take this orb and face the Emissaries. You will kill each one of them."

Alec gasped. "I can't kill anyone. That's crazy."

"Alec, you will do as I tell you. We are in danger. *You must protect us.*"

"But, Anna—I don't know how."

"You will use the power of the orb. It will come when you focus. Do as I tell you."

"I don't know how to use it," Alec said weakly. The compulsion to obey her grew as the pulsing strengthened.

"Kill them," Anna said firmly.

"Please," Alec whispered as the glowing orb became all he could see.

"This will make you one of us. It is required to show us you are worthy of our risk in saving your life." Alec heard Kholar's voice from far away.

Kholar and Anna were right. They had risked a lot to protect him. He owed them his loyalty, even if something

48

in his heart urged him to disobey.

Alec turned towards the door and headed reluctantly towards the yard. Paran followed immediately behind him. Passing clouds had blanketed the moon and the yard was bathed in darkness. Inky shadows moved restlessly just outside of the pool of light from the doorway. Paran's orb flared into brightness, followed by Anna's and Kholar's.

There were eight peasants clustered together. The two women were in the middle. None had weapons. All looked poorly nourished and cheaply dressed. Their eyes were blank but Alec felt they were watching his every move. Without comment, he took the orb from Anna's outstretched palm. He gripped it tightly in his right hand and racked his brain for what to do. It was so hard to think clearly.

"Choose one and kill him," Anna prompted from behind.

The compulsion to obey was overwhelming. Alec took a step forward, then another. The Emissaries shuffled their feet, seemingly afraid to step forward and engage in combat. Somewhere a bat squeaked and the rustling of leathery wings overhead seemed unnaturally loud in the silence. Alec felt the blood singing through his veins and the nervous fear boiling in his stomach. Surely Anna would step in if he started to get hurt.

"It is time to play." The words came from the closest man's mouth but Alec instinctively knew it wasn't his voice. He'd heard that voice before. Alec took a step backward. What did he mean, *play*?

Before Alec could open his mouth to ask, two of them rushed him without warning. A knee hit his solar plexus. Two hands grabbed at this throat. Someone kicked him in the kidneys. Alec dropped to his knees as his stomach and back exploded in pain. He let go of the orb. The others joined in. He was hit so rapidly he lost count. Pain sprung to vicious life in his head, neck and chest. The hands around his neck tightened. He couldn't breathe. He tried to hit back, to pull the fingers away from his windpipe, but there were too many of them. His nose was bleeding. His lip split as his face hit the ground.

He was suffocating. Bright shards of colour danced in front of his eyes.

Why wasn't Anna stopping them?

Help, he cried—but he didn't have enough breath to make a sound.

Somebody help me.

Riley's plan to find Tyrell and get to the bottom of things was almost immediately scuttled. Dean's hand came down on her shoulder unexpectedly and Riley skidded to a stop, blanketing her thoughts immediately.

"He's out of bounds," Dean said.

She hadn't been fast enough. "He knows if Anna was there or not. You heard mommy dearest."

"Tyrell is off limits to everyone until the hearing. I cannot permit you to wake him and ask any questions."

Riley's hands went to her hips. "There is one thing you need to understand, Dean, if we're going to get along. Telling me not to do something is like waving a red flag at a bull."

"What do symbolic pennants have to do with Earth-based ruminants?"

"Nothing," Riley muttered. She pulled out of Dean's grip and headed down the hallway, shoving her slipping Ulat band back into place. She turned the corner and suddenly came to a full stop. A huge window took up almost all the space on the wall to her right. There was no mistaking the massive blue-green planet below. "Oh my God," Riley breathed in wonder. Almost in a trance, she walked over to the window, reaching her hands up to touch the warm glass-like substance and leaning her forehead against it. The astronauts were right. It was unbelievably beautiful.

"That's my country," she said softly as Canada

rolled beneath them. "I never realized just how big it is. Hardly anyone lives up north."

Dean leaned over her shoulder.

"I would have been a lot more interested in geography if I had seen this before," she breathed. "It's amazing. Look at the size of the ocean. It really is bigger than the land. And the atmosphere is so thin. Hard to believe that's all that protects us from cosmic rays, isn't it?"

"Seen from this distance, the delicate balance of your planet is much more obvious."

"Hmm," Riley agreed. "See that little bit sticking out into the ocean? That's where I grew up. You can't see it from here but there's a cove where we had our summer home. I used to dig for clams so much my fingers were always blistered."

Something caught her attention. "What was that?" She pointed to a bright flash lower on the North American continent. Several other bright flashes followed.

Dean didn't answer.

"Look, over there too." She pointed towards Europe. "Is it some kind of weird weather or—" Realization hit her hard. Her throat seemed to close over. She couldn't get any air.

Multiple flashes covered central Europe and moved east rapidly.

"Riley," Dean gripped her shoulder again and pulled her away. "Do not look any longer. It will not do any good."

A*nna, help.*

Alec was dying. He couldn't breathe, couldn't move and the blows were coming harder with every second.

This was so *stupid*.

His face was mashed into the dirt. A stone ground into his cheek.

That was it. He'd had *enough*.

His fingers scrabbled in the dirt with the last of his conscious thought. Something was rapidly building inside him, like an electrical charge. His fingers touched something smooth and familiar. He pulled it into his palm, tightened his hand convulsively around the orb. The electricity exploded through him.

7

All the Emissaries flew off him as if yanked by invisible wires. They landed with dull, heavy thuds and didn't move.

Gasping, Alec pushed himself to his hands and knees. Every part of him hurt yet the pain was the least of his concerns. He squinted at the bodies around him and felt suddenly, profoundly sick. He crawled over to the closest peasant and with a finger touched the unmoving chest. There was no response. Heart in his mouth, Alec shook the man. Please don't be dead, he pleaded to himself. But the peasant's head only lolled towards him, his eyes staring sightlessly at Alec's shoulder.

Bile rose in Alec's throat. His heart tried to claw its way out of his chest. Somewhere inside his head he could almost hear a woman shrieking in disappointment at him. Totally horrified at what he'd done, he crawled away and curled up into a ball. *Oh my God. Take it back*, he moaned, *I didn't mean it.*

Two feet planted themselves in front of his face. Alec's hand tightened on his orb again. The power thrummed through his blood.

"Hand over the orb, Alec," said Anna. She sounded distant and colder than ever before.

Alec's stomach heaved again. He shook his head mutely. The orb was his.

"I am ordering you to return the orb to me. You cannot disobey me."

He swallowed and tried to look up. His neck hurt too much and he could only see her knees. The words barely formed in his swollen mouth. "It's mine."

"The orb belongs to me. It is too dangerous for you at present. Eight people are dead because of your misuse. In the future, I will permit you to use it once I am sure you have learned control. Currently, we must return to the house and prepare to leave. The sensors indicate increasing violence and a number of rips. It will not be too long before the rips zero in on you."

He needed to obey her. Every word she spoke hammered the nail of despair further into his soul. "Anna, please. I need it."

A second pair of shoes stopped beside Anna's. Two massive hands grabbed him under the arms and hauled him painfully to his feet. The moment Alec was upright, Paran yanked Alec's orb effortlessly from him and handed it to Anna. Alec winced but said nothing.

Anna was holding her orb in one hand and the crystal around her neck with the other. "Obey me, Alec," she said. She brushed her orb across his forehead.

Alec shivered as the compulsion to do her bidding slipped through him. He reeled unsteadily as Anna turned and walked away. Paran and Kholar silently flanked her. They were probably too ashamed of him to even look in his direction. He limped painfully across the yard behind her, pointedly ignoring the bodies he had to step over. They entered the house in a silent single file. Paran lit the room with his orb and Anna held hers out, swinging it in an arc to take in the entire room.

"Only the one under the sofa," she said to Kholar as he closed the door. "Alec, sit down in this chair. Paran, fetch a bowl of water and a clean rag."

Alec shuffled to the chair she'd indicated. It even hurt to sit.

"You murdered eight innocent people, Alec." Anna reached down and stroked his forehead. Each of her words tore at him, splintering him into raw, bleeding pieces. "That is unacceptable to Earth law. You will be punished if anyone from this planet finds out." Alec's nausea increased tenfold and he started to shiver. "You are a fugitive from justice here on Terra. Only Kholar and I can protect you. You must obey us in all things." Alec couldn't help the moan that escaped from his lips. What was he going to do? "Do you understand me?"

He weakly nodded.

Paran returned to the room and slopped water onto the floor as he handed the wooden bowl and a small torn cloth to Alec. Alec received it wordlessly and began to wash his face with shaking hands. His lip hurt even more as soon as he touched it.

A sudden flash of light lit the entire room as if the yard had been hit by lightning. The image of Anna and Paran standing before him was seared into Alec's retinas. For a moment he was utterly blind.

"Protective stance," Kholar yelled.

Anna grabbed Alec and hauled him, unseeing, to his

feet. The bowl of water tumbled to the floor, splashing his legs. Kholar pushed Alec into the centre. They all turned to face outwards, towards the walls, keeping Alec inside and protected. Around them a sudden shimmering appeared out of thin air.

"Nuclear?" Anna shouted.

"Two," Kholar yelled back.

Outside, the roar of a locomotive fast approaching split the silence. Alec clasped his hands over his ears. The sudden pain in his ears became almost unbearable just as his vision began to return.

"Hold," Anna yelled.

The shock wave hit with an unbelievable force. The walls splintered apart like matchsticks and the windows tore from the framing as if there'd been no nails. Everything around them was picked up and whisked away so fast Alec barely saw it happen. Dust, debris, trees, rocks: gone. Inside the shimmering bubble, Alec watched in stunned horror. He'd seen this before. Somewhere. Something told him to wait for the heat.

It struck a second later. The remaining floor underneath them burst into flame. The very air was on fire.

Terror seized him. He knew what this was. They were all going to die.

The pressure grew. Alec gasped. He couldn't breathe. The air was boiling.

He reached out and clasped his hand around Anna's arm. Hurry, he thought. *Get us out of here.*

Riley wiped a tear from her cheek and tried to stop trembling. It was over. There was nothing she could do about the fate of the billions below now. She could do even less about her own family. She wanted to go back to her pod and scream until her throat was raw, but she couldn't. The numbness inside her was almost paralyzing. The only emotion she felt was anger—at the Councilor, at the Tyons, and at herself. And even that was muted.

"I must spend some time with the other Terrans," Dean said as he got up from the chair beside her and plucked the empty beaker from her unresisting hand. "Have you recovered from your distress?"

Riley nodded. She didn't trust herself to speak.

"It is entirely normal to experience such emotions. I can have Martje give you something to help the worst of the sadness, if you wish."

Riley shook her head.

"I want you to return to your pod and enter sleep mode."

She stared at the tabletop.

"I will wake you once we are within transport distance of Celes. Everyone will transport to our base there."

She nodded.

"You and the other Potentials will stay there for further training. It is a pleasant planet and you will find it invigorating. Logan and his crew will leave again for their next assignment. I will stay with you."

"And Ennis and Ty?" Riley forced the words out through frozen lips.

"They will be interviewed by the Council and their punishment determined."

A spasm of anxiety ran down Riley's back. The last thing she wanted to do was run into any member of the Council.

"Stay away from Tyrell, Riley. There is punishment for interacting with him."

"He's a friend of yours," Riley reminded him. Suddenly, the words poured free. "You've worked with him for years, haven't you? He must have had a good reason for doing what he did. Why don't you find out? At least let him know you haven't turned your back."

Dean rubbed his forehead wearily. "You do not understand. The rules are here for good reason. I cannot use personal feelings to subvert them."

"Some friend you are," Riley muttered.

"You are emotionally compromised at the present. We will converse on this subject later. Please get some rest." Dean reached out and somewhat awkwardly squeezed her shoulder before he crossed over to the other Potentials. Riley watched. His other two charges were younger than herself by several years and had a deer-in-the-headlights aura that was off-putting. The chubby girl's mouth of metal braces caught the overhead lights with every move of her head and probably made speech impossible, Riley thought uncharitably. Her name was Serena Something-or-other. And the skinny boy with knock knees and more pimples than skin was no great prize either. Riley didn't know his name. So much for a representative sample of Earthlings. The other Potentials that crowded the gallery weren't much better—not a super model or Olympic athlete among them. Dean seemed unfazed by their mediocrity. He ushered them out of the room without a backwards glance.

Riley sat at the galley table for a long time after he

left. The enormity of what had happened had yet to sink in completely. Her school, her friends, her way of life; all destroyed, or at least they would be shortly. Riley prayed that those she loved had died in the immediate blasts. Even the wisp of an image of her parents stumbling around in a post-holocaust world was too upsetting.

Focus, she berated herself. The faster she found the traitor the faster Kerry was free—and the faster the hold the Councilor had over her was ended. And when it was, the Others were going to pay. And how.

Mind made up, she left the almost empty galley and headed for the pods. She passed several Operatives, although none gave her anything more than an uninterested glance. She was sure Tyrell wasn't in her section but then she hadn't peered in every pod. Riley glanced furtively back down the corridor. Several sleeping pods were half open, indicating their emptiness. Most were occupied. She tiptoed along, aware that even the slightest step made too much sound. The pods weren't numbered and only the shadow through the hazy glass window set in each pod gave any indication of the occupant. It was kind of creepy, she mused as she rose on tip-toes to see through the glass. Like walking through a waxwork museum. She passed Tyrell's co-pilot, Ennis, before it twigged who he was. She backed up and peered inside. Asleep or unconscious, it didn't matter. Either way he wasn't in any shape to talk to her and it would be a tough conversation considering they had never spoken before. And besides, Martje hadn't mentioned that Ennis had the same recollections; only Tyrell.

She continued her search. Tyrell was in the second-last pod of the third corridor. He was taller than she remembered and even unconscious, he was imposing. Taking a deep and tremulous breath, she waved her palm over the glowing red indicator next to the window, tightened her grip on her orb and pushed the thought at him. *Wake.* Nothing happened. In frustration, she slapped her hand over the indicator.

His eyes snapped open and he pierced her with a look that wasn't even remotely friendly. Riley took a quick step back. The upper portion of the door sunk into the lower and Riley was face to chest with an unclothed and clearly annoyed Tyon pilot.

"Sorry to bother you," she began, forcing her eyes upward.

"Explain," Tyrell barked.

"I have to ask you a few questions. It will only take a minute."

"I am under restriction. Contact with me puts you in jeopardy," he said.

Riley looked at his face in surprise. "It's nice of you to be concerned," she began.

"Dean will be punished," Tyrell cut her off.

"Dean? Whatever." Swallowing a sharp retort, Riley continued. "I have to ask you a few important questions. It'll only take a sec. You can go back to la-la land the minute I'm finished."

Tyrell said nothing.

Riley cleared her throat. "Why did you leave Kholar to die?"

Stone faced, he gave no response.

"What is Kholar like as a person? Do you trust him?"

Silence.

"Is there a plot to expose the Tyon Collective and have it destroyed?"

"Why would I answer such questions?" Tyrell didn't sound curious, merely wary.

"I'm checking things out. I know there's trouble brewing. I just don't know who's at the bottom of it."

Tyrell clenched his jaw. "I have no response."

Riley crossed her arms. "Good one. I can tell you don't like the man. Neither do I. He was planning on letting those people die on that little submersible ship. You know it and I know it. That's hardly admirable and if there's one thing I know about you, it's that you're an honourable man. Abandoning your fellow Operatives is not in your code of conduct."

Tyrell didn't answer.

"So," Riley continued, jumping in with both feet, "you and Dean and Ennis did your own thing. You grabbed a bunch of us and headed for safety. Personally, I'm happy about that. But Kholar didn't die, did he?"

Tyrell's facial expression didn't change but something inside his eyes did. Bingo.

"He's alive, isn't he?"

"I strongly suggest that you stop playing games and focus on your studies. You are entering dangerous territory and someone might not like these questions of yours."

"Is that a threat?"

"Advice."

He didn't look like he was going to come out of the pod swinging but you never knew. "One last question," she said, "and I'll quit." Tyrell merely stared down his nose at her. "Was Anna on that ship?"

Tyrell's lips curled into the faintest of smiles. "Your cleverness will get you killed."

"I don't feel like sleeping, Anna. I'd rather stay up."

Alec knew his argument was falling on deaf ears but he felt inexorably restless and the last thing he wanted to do was enter the creepy transport pod and have someone knock him out. He'd discovered that the corridor that held the pods was circular and he'd hoped that with everyone busy steering and powering the ship, he could build up a good sweat running. He tried to think about something else as Anna leaned in closer to him and peered firmly into his eyes. If she knew what he wanted to do, she'd force him into stasis.

"Are you not bored?" she asked. "There are limited activities on an interstellar craft if you are not involved in its function."

"I didn't say I won't be bored by tomorrow," he began, "just that I'm not now. I'd rather stay awake. I feel like I'm asleep most of the time anyway."

"What are you planning to do?" she asked.

She didn't like him watching them on the bridge, he'd discovered. And besides, it was kind of weird seeing several people all holding large orbs and swaying slightly with their eyes closed hour after hour. The galley was generally empty and there wasn't a game system anywhere on board. "I'll watch outside," he offered. "I was always kind of interested in astronomy."

That was an outright lie. He couldn't have pointed out the Big Dipper if his life depended on it, but lately, with Anna hovering close to him all the time, the inability to do anything on his own was starting to irritate. It was silly. He knew that. Anna was the best thing that had ever happened to him and she took such care of him, despite all the trouble he'd been to her and the danger he'd put all of them in. He knew the others on the little interstellar ship didn't like him, they knew how dangerous he'd made everything, but he'd sworn to himself that he'd make it up to everyone. He just wasn't sure how. So the lie was uncomfortable but also necessary.

Anna glanced over at Kholar, who was leaning against the doorway and frowning. "Let the boy stay awake if he chooses," he shrugged, then addressed Alec. "Do not interrupt us when you are unable to amuse yourself any longer. We have important work to accomplish."

Alec nodded.

Anna straightened with a slight sigh. "I will return for you in half a cycle. At that time, you will consume nourishment and enter your pod without argument."

She was gone an instant later, Kholar behind her, and neither gave any indication they were still thinking about him. Alec followed them down the hall until he saw them enter the bridge of the ship. Sighing deeply, he leaned up against the wall and closed his eyes.

He felt odd, shivery and cold, completely unlike himself. His memory was worse than it had ever been before. He'd been gone from Earth—what, two days now?—and he couldn't remember his family or where he used to live. He even found that the memories of the last horrific moments on Earth, when the conflagration of nuclear holocaust had chased them to the far reaches of the South Pacific, slowly fading. Now he couldn't even remember where they were when the rescue ship had signalled them. What was happening to him?

It seemed like the more he was around Anna, the less he remembered of his life before but the less she was around, the more uncomfortable he felt. It was weird and a little scary. Now that she and Kholar were needed to power the interstellar vessel, they spent considerably less time with him. And that gave him time to think, even though his thinking seemed to make Anna annoyed.

He pushed away from the wall and headed for the circular corridor. Twenty or thirty laps would help to clear his head.

He ran slowly at first. The distortion of space travel hardly bothered him at all and seemed to be lessening with every cycle. His feet slapped against the brown metal floor and echoed eerily, but no one poked a head out of a door to tell him off. With every lap he felt a bit better. Sweat beaded his forehead. He finally stopped at the viewport, the stitch in his side forcing a halt. He leaned into the glass, letting his rapid breath fog the clear material. The galaxy beyond was haloed with condensation.

He lifted a finger and drew a circle. He marked two dots in the upper half and a small inverted semicircle in the lower and stood back. He smiled. He hadn't seen a happy face symbol in ages, not since Mei Ling had spray painted one on the back door of her family's convenience store during her birthday party. They'd sneaked off to make out behind the dumpsters and she'd gotten a bit silly when she found the spray-paint can.

Alec stood up straight and his heart slammed into his ribs. *He remembered her.* Chin's older sister and his first real girlfriend. He could even taste the strawberry lipgloss she used. His finger touched his own lips before he used it to write her name next to the smiling face. She was dead now. Burned alive or smothered with debris or slowly destroyed by the radiation blast that flattened Toronto.

She wanted to be a pharmacist.

He wasn't supposed to remember this. The thought

came out of the blue but Alec knew it with conviction. No one wanted him to remember his life on Earth. Why not? Was it possible that something was interfering with his brain? And if so, how—and why? He wasn't a threat to anyone.

He leaned forward and breathed against the glass, fogging it further. Then, with the tip of his finger wrote a few more words: Mom, Peter, Chin, Riley. The memories were just out of reach. Another minute and he'd have them.

He was so engrossed in his internal dialogue, in the pictures rapidly flickering across his memory like a film on fast forward, he didn't notice their approach. Anna's grasp bit into his shoulder as she swung him around. Paran punched him in the solar plexus. The wind rushed out of Alec's lungs and refused to return. Paran hit Alec on the temple. The blow was brutally jarring.

Alec heard Anna shout, "Don't kill him, you fool," before the floor rushed up to meet him.

Alec awoke when Anna opened the window on his pod. He squinted against the sudden light and forced wakefulness. He raised a hand to gingerly probe at his right temple and winced.

"You fell, Alec, and hit your head on the galley table," Anna said in explanation. "How do you feel?"

"It's pretty sore," Alec replied. His mouth felt gummy and had an unpleasant taste. He took a deep breath and grimaced. "Why's my stomach killing me?"

"Get out of the pod and dress. We are arriving shortly and will transport within the hour." Anna gave him a faint smile that didn't quite reach her eyes and walked away before Alec could take a breath to speak.

He leaned back in the pod and closed his eyes. He felt awful, like he'd been in a kickboxing tournament with twenty ninja assassins. He rubbed his forehead but it was no use. There was absolutely no memory of falling in the galley. He must have concussed himself. *Again*. How come he was so clumsy? It was clearly annoying Anna and he certainly didn't want to anger her. She'd been so kind to him, protecting him against the mob that had bayed for his blood before they left Earth. Alec shivered as that memory surged to the fore of his mind. Thank heavens Anna had been there.

Forcing the unpleasant recollection from his mind he pulled down the grey coveralls. The pods were so tiny he couldn't maneuver properly so he stepped out into the corridor to dress. He slipped on his shoes and headed for the galley. Despite feeling unwell, he was hungry. The hallway was empty but the galley was full. All but three Operatives, the pilot and the two Alec had nicknamed "pushers" as they were responsible for the ship's propulsion, were sitting at tables or leaning against the walls, waiting. Paran was in quiet conversation with Kholar; both had their backs to Alec. Anna was nowhere to be seen. Alec pulled a bowl of nutritional protein from the warmer, got a spoon and crossed to the least occupied part of the room. While he shovelled the goop into his mouth as fast as he could swallow, several Operatives stared openly at him. Alec realized he knew none of the members of the crew by name and hadn't had a conversation with any of them. Or perhaps he had and just didn't remember it. He dropped his empty bowl on the counter and wished Anna would show up.

The door slid open and the last Operatives entered. In their hands, they held the large, unpolished orbs they used to propel the ship. One marched right up to Alec and blocked his view of the rest of the galley.

"Come with me, Terran," the Operative said coldly.

"Where are we going?" Alec asked.

The Operative didn't answer. His hand shot out and clamped onto Alec's wrist. There wasn't much option without an orb. They trudged down the narrow corridor past the observation window, Alec trailing behind like a reluctant toddler. Alec had a glimpse of a bluish sphere spinning rapidly below them before the Operative tugged him past. Was that a new planet? A tiny spark of interest permeated his brain but was quickly extinguished.

The Operative lead him into the bridge of the ship. Only Anna and another Tyon stood in front of him quietly engaged in conversation. The new Operative, a woman of middle years whose grey hair was cut into an unflattering crew cut, held a large reddish crystal rock in her hand. She and Anna looked up and stopped speaking.

"Erim will transport you to the surface of this planet, Alec. You will be shown your quarters and rest until I join you."

Alec's escort withdrew and the door closed behind him. Erim stepped forward. She held her huge crystal out in front of her, balanced in the palm of her large hand. With her free hand she beckoned Alec nearer.

Erim had cold, unfeeling eyes and Alec felt a frisson of discomfort slip down his neck.

"Why aren't you coming with me?" he asked Anna.

"Our plans have changed slightly and I have other duties to perform," Anna said.

"Can't I stay with you?" he tried. "I'll keep out of the way."

"I'm afraid that won't be possible, Alec. Your face is too well known; you have caused significant trouble and are hunted. I am hiding you on Eu Station while Kholar and I try to undo some of the damage you have done."

Alec felt crushed. He nodded, keeping his eyes downcast. Anna walked over and touched his forehead with the gentle stroke that instantly eased the internal pain. Her crystal pendant glowed brightly through her fingers. Alec closed his eyes against the glare. How he wished she would do this forever.

"You will be patient, Alec. You will wait for me on the

station and cause no trouble for Erim or Paran while I am gone. You will not try to exercise or force your memory to repair. You will not try to leave. Do you understand?"

Anna's words wove themselves into Alec's mind and soul. Their grip inside him tightened. Of course he would obey her. She always had his best interests at heart. He loved her.

"Yes, Anna," he whispered.

Abruptly the pleasant sensation ended as Anna stepped back. "You may transport him now," she said briskly to Erim. The older woman grasped Alec's upper arm in a tight grip.

Alec had a last glimpse of Anna's back as she leaned over the instrument panel. If she was aware he was leaving, she gave no sign.

Riley awoke with Dean's face peering in through the glass window of her pod. His hand waved over the indicator and the glass dropped into the door. Riley automatically covered herself with her hands.

"We are transporting off in ten minutes. Dress and meet me in the galley."

Riley nodded but doubted Dean had noticed her response. He was already striding down the corridor, whistling tunelessly under his breath. For a second she closed her eyes. The deep nothingness of stasis had been soothing only in that it prevented any emotion. But now she was cognizant and vulnerable again. *Focus*, she admonished herself. *There'll be time to fall apart when this is all over.*

10

With shaking hands, she pulled her uniform out from where it was folded above her head and awkwardly donned it. She took the blue eye protector from a pocket and placed it over her eyes. No need to upchuck all over the floor on her way out. Double-checking that her orb was in her pocket, she opened the door of her compartment and stepped out.

Two pods down, Darius was doing the same. They saw each other in the same instant. There was a distinctly uncomfortable pause. Riley bit her tongue. It would be even more difficult to have to hurt his feelings by rejecting him all over again. But if she ever needed one of his fabulous hugs, it was now. For a second it seemed he was going to ignore her. "Sleep well?" he asked in an ultra-casual tone.

"Who's asking?" Riley said turning her back.

There was a long pause again. Then Darius cleared his throat. "Enjoy Celes," he said quietly. "Your first planet is always the best one."

She heard his soft footfalls quickly leaving in the same direction Dean had gone. Riley nearly shouted out to come back, but she jammed her lips together and the words remained silent. She took a deep breath and forced herself to swallow past the lump in her throat.

She passed the viewport on the way to the galley and paused for a moment. The entire window was filled with the huge planet spinning below. Riley felt the breath leave her chest in a rush. She pulled off the visor and pressed her forehead against the warm glass. *Incredible*. High jagged peaks, burnished in red, alternated with wide, deep blue oceans. Expansive swathes of green striped the borders between the mountains and the seas. Shifting her gaze to the upper pole of the planet, she noted far less blue or green and far more of the red peaks poking up through thick white clouds.

It was a shame Alec wasn't with them. He'd be so excited to explore a new world; she could almost hear his laughter. A sudden surge of disappointment stopped that train of thought. No one knew where Alec was. He might even be dead, like her family.

Stop it, she told herself. *Don't think about them.* Tamping down the excitement that warred with the grief in her gut, she tore her eyes away, replaced the visor and headed to the galley. The room was filled to the brim. The Tyons appeared blasé but the Terrans' emotions ranged from outright terror to unsuppressed excitement. Riley pulled a mask of nonchalance over her own features. She was not going to appear like a pathetic tourist in front of anyone.

Dean was in the corner talking to his other two Potentials but he noted her arrival and waved her over.

Riley weaved her way through the crowd, surreptitiously scanning for Darius. There was no sign of him. Swallowing disappointment, she arrived at Dean's side.

"We will transport down in pairs," he was saying to the others, "and I will ask that you wait for me to escort you to your new quarters in the training facility."

Both the Potentials nodded. The girl with the braces had a sullen expression that didn't improve her looks. She raised her eyes to Riley as if to say "Are you kidding me?" but her companion merely blushed furiously and stared at his shoes. Neither had orbs, Riley noted.

"How do we get down to the surface?" she asked, affecting a casual stance.

"For distances this far, we use a distinctive type of orb," Dean said. "An Operative with special training will transport you."

"What do we do when we get there? I mean how long will we stay there and stuff?"

"Celes has a Tyon training facility. The planet itself is uninhabited so we have the place to ourselves, so to speak. You will have an orientation session and then begin orb lessons. If you are deemed worthy, further instruction will continue."

"And if we're not?" Riley asked with a sideways glance at the two shivering teens at Dean's side.

"Then memories of your training will be wiped from your mind and we'll integrate you into one of several other planets to begin your new lives there. The possibilities are endless for careers and the opportunity to travel. There is an entire galaxy out there and it is all open to you." Dean finished this little pep talk with a quiet smile. He met Riley's eyes over his trainees and Riley had the distinct impression he was outlining their future, not hers.

"Well, doesn't that sound peachy?" Riley tried for a casual tone but missed as someone walked into the galley and caught her eye. It was Tyrell. The look he gave her could have sliced a bowling ball in two. Riley glared back and was pleased to note that he broke the gaze first. Logan entered a moment later.

"Where's the big chief heading after he drops us all off?" she muttered to Dean.

Dean's expression remained neutral but Riley wasn't fooled. "He will travel on to the next planet scheduled for evaluation and set up a preliminary base."

"Doesn't this get a bit old after a while?" she asked, thinking out loud. "Why not just wipe out the Others? They've proved on Earth they don't deserve to live in the same galaxy."

"Perhaps the Others are merely consuming food and maintaining their existence. Would you suggest that their lives are worth less than your own, that their society has less value than yours merely because you do not agree with how it functions?"

Riley crossed her arms. "*You* might want to veil your argument in philosophical jargon, but *I've* had my entire planet wiped out, not to mention my family, and I'm aware that I'm clearly biased. Nuke the lot of them, that's what I say."

Dean didn't answer and Logan diverted Riley's attention. He had moved to the centre of the room and was holding his hand up. The excited hum dimmed to silence.

"We will disembark shortly. All Potentials will remain with their Guardians until instructed to transport. Arrangements have been made on this planet for your training. Make every effort to master the orb techniques." Logan gazed down his nose and around the room, taking in every frightened face. He paused when he locked eyes with Riley. She refused to look away. The silence grew uncomfortable. Riley's eyes began tearing and she felt the burning stare of everyone in the room turning to look at the two of them.

"I will personally interrogate each Potential to determine

the suitability for training," he said aiming each word at her. "Interrogation starts in half a cycle." Logan smiled tightly and an uncomfortable shifting rippled through the galley as Potentials shivered with concern. Riley ground her teeth together. Arrogant swine.

Without another word, he flicked his hand at Tyrell, turned and strode from the galley. Tyrell left the wall he was leaning against and with a quick look in Dean's direction, followed Logan out. The doors slid silently closed behind them.

"Would you excuse us for a moment?" Dean said taking Riley's arm and pulling her out of earshot of the two younger Potentials. He stopped and leaned close so his words could not be overheard. "You have made an enemy of Logan. Your other companion, William, did so as well. How and why?"

"Logan's a bully," Riley hissed back. "You know it and I know it. He hates to be contradicted and I hate telling something other than the truth. Those two things just don't mesh sometimes."

"Riley," Dean said ominously.

"Maybe it's like Logan and Darius," Riley said. "Why does Logan hate the very air Dare breathes? Come to think of it," she tacked on, "why do you?"

"I don't hate him," Dean said, not quite meeting her eyes.

"Well, they say it's akin to hate," Riley said quietly. "And it'll make you crazy if you don't deal with it in a more constructive way."

Further conversation was halted as the door slid open and several Tyons entered, each bearing a huge reddish crystal. Dean's female Potential was chosen to leave before the male and she clung to Dean's arm in a pathetic display of terror. Dean had to pry her fingers off. The boy went shortly after her, shaking so hard his teeth rattled.

Riley was one of the last to leave the ship. She couldn't

help the quiver of excitement inside as the Operative began the teleportation process, but gritted her jaw purposefully and strove for an uninterested expression. The push/pull, in/out sensation was stronger than usual—but then, she didn't remember the last transfer.

The surroundings winked into existence around her and despite a distinct queasy sensation in her stomach that wasn't nearly as awful as usual, she was forced to abandon her feigned disinterest. This place was *amazing*— like nothing she had ever seen on Earth. Impossibly high above her, a glass and metal dome arced across the sky for as far as she could see in all directions. Sunlight beamed through and lit the wide-open plaza with so much brightness she had to squint. The warm air was subtly spiced with aromas she'd never smelled before. The ground was paved with stone tiles, all in varying shades of red. Here and there, large leafy and very unfamiliar trees grew out of the ground, their remarkably long branches striving towards the sunlight. To her right, there was a series of three-storey buildings, all fashioned from the red stone and without glass in any of the windows. Riley shaded her eyes. In front of her, behind the cluster of Potentials, who all looked as amazed as she felt, was a huge lake that stretched out towards the horizon. There were several small platforms dotting the deep blue water and people standing on them engaged in some activity Riley couldn't make out.

Dean touched her shoulder and she jumped. He pointed to the hexagonal glass roofing, so high above them Riley almost couldn't see the lattice structure holding the panels in place. "The dome keeps out the noxious gases created by some of the vegetation. We live inside for the most part. You'll get used to it in time."

"Did you guys make this dome?" Riley breathed.

"Yes. And the others." He pointed to her left past another cluster of buildings and what appeared to be a forest beyond them. "There are four domes, all connected.

You won't get claustrophobic here. There's enough room."

"Can we ever go outside?" she asked.

Dean nodded. "It's not advisable for long periods of time but there will be training in the later years to prepare you for other worlds. Some of that takes place outside the dome. Let's get Mike and Serena and I'll show you to your quarters."

Riley followed Dean and the two others to the building closest to the lake. She rubbed her hand across the grainy surface of the outer wall as she entered. It felt like sandstone. Tiny, shimmering particles came away in her hand. She brushed the dust off and entered. The inside was typical Tyon construction. Bare and functional, little in the way of comfort or esthetics, and yet the main room was pleasing in a way Riley couldn't put into words. There was none of the horrible metal. The furniture, although simple, looked comfortable enough. Her quarters were on the third floor and she had a lovely view of the water from her bed. Dean's room, however, was right next door, she was disappointed to discover. The lack of window coverings would make any noise in her room easily heard and the thin partitions that covered the doorways would provide only the minimum of privacy. Still, it was better than the transport pods.

She stood off to one side thinking while Dean explained the workings of the protein dispenser and where they would get the rest of their meals. There had to be a way of determining whether Anna had been on that ship, and if so, how the recording devices had been tampered with. The main problem, as far as she could see, was that the little submersible was back on Earth so she couldn't search it for clues, and she didn't understand the Tyon computer system. She'd have to get someone, likely Dean, to hack into it for her and explain what all the stupid symbols meant. Just how she was going to accomplish that she had no idea. A voice spoke sharply behind her, making her jump nearly a foot.

"Riley Cohen, you are to be interrogated."

She whirled around. Logan stood in the doorway, hands on his hips and a look of dark pleasure across his face. "Come with me."

Fu Station was cold and empty and Alec hated it. Of course, the hate didn't start instantly. There was the first day or so of overwhelming awe at the very idea of being on a different planet and the novel surroundings he could feel even through the fog in his mind. But as the days wore on, the limited space, the boring diet of the Tyon nutritional supplement five times a day in limited quantities and Erim's silent companionship fed his antipathy.

Erim kept him confined to a small room that wasn't even large enough to pace. Most of the time she was gone. There was nothing to do. Without an orb he couldn't access the computer system, even if he'd known how. Two windows gave him a view of the watery surface of the planet: the free-floating hummocks of vegetation that occasionally bumped into the floating, metallic station and the pink-tinged sky with at least two moons visible during the frequently occurring night. But hours of gazing upwards at the bazillions of tiny clouds was getting really dull.

The only good thing, Alec decided after finishing his one-thousandth sit-up, was that left alone, hour after hour, had provoked in him a more heightened sense of restlessness. Erim, unlike Anna, paid little attention to him, generally ordering him to spend his time away from her. As a consequence he filled his hours with exercise. He wiped the sweat from his brow and lay back on the metallic floor so he could see outside the window.

He felt better. Stronger, clearer and fit for action. Whatever plans Anna and Kholar had percolating he'd be ready for now. Undoubtedly, he'd be expected to fight and use his Tyon abilities. Why else would Anna have provoked his anger back in China? Sure, killing those people had been an awful thing to do—remembering it made him squirm with guilt and self-loathing—but it had unblocked whatever was jamming access to his power. Over the last day or so, the electricity under his skin had steadily grown with every push-up, jumping jack and squat.

As had his thinking. In fact, he couldn't remember his mind being so clear in ages. With clarity came memories. Scattered, but memories. His family; arguments, happy times, his mom's unconditional love. The world he'd known; the sound of the suburbs, the smell of hot pizza, the elation of soccer games on broiling hot afternoons. Video games—for some reason he could remember those more clearly than anything else, sometimes so clearly he would walk his way through one while he exercised.

Everything else was dimmer. He remembered his brother, Peter, and felt confused about him. He had a vague sense something bad had happened to him, that he'd heard a rumour about it, but there was no way to confirm it. Other memories were hazy and unformed, troubling in their evasiveness. There'd been a girl he'd really liked but hadn't gotten too far with. There was a nagging feeling that something bad had happened to her, too, and a sense of not being able to help, but desperately wanting to. The feeling clung to his skin like mist. Along with the memories came emotion. Sadness, elation, surprise, fear. It was all there—still somewhat muted and sometimes elusive, but there. Like an echo of himself. He rolled onto his side and began a thousand leg lifts. Maybe by tomorrow, if he sweated enough, it would be clearer. And the gaps would start to fill in.

Erim stood in the doorway. Alec came to a startled stop. He hadn't heard her approach. "You should not be doing that," Erim said. "Anna orders rest."

Alec shrugged. "I'm bored. It's something to do." He resumed the lifts, welcoming the slight burn deep within his muscles that the hours of repetitive movement were giving him. He was going to be cut after this enforced stay, that was for sure.

"I said, stop."

"No." He didn't bother to look at her. She'd spoken maybe six words to him since they'd arrived and none of them were friendly. If Anna had something to say to him, she could say it in person.

Erim was across the room fast as he could blink and her grip was remarkably painful. She literally yanked him to his feet, letting go only when he was upright. He jerked away from her, almost unbalancing himself.

"Don't touch me," he snapped.

Erim's eye's narrowed. "Obey me or be punished."

A shiver of apprehension slid down Alec's back. He'd heard those words before and the punishment had been awful. He remembered the feelings of helplessness and terror, even though he couldn't place exactly who had said those words before or what they had done. It was a Tyon though. He knew it. He crossed his arms, backed up against the wall and fought to keep the tremble out of his voice. "I want to go out for a walk."

Erim didn't respond.

"Did you hear me?" Alec's voice rose slightly. "I'm going crazy here. I need to get of this room."

"There is no place to go."

"There's the rest of the station," Alec countered. "Paran leaves every morning and doesn't come back until rest time. You're gone for hours at a time."

"Paran has important work on this station. You do not."

"So?"

Erim cocked her head to one side while she worked out what he meant. "You have no work function, therefore there is no need to enter the rest of the station."

Alec looked down his nose at her and resisted the urge to swear, although barely. He knew he owed these people his life and perhaps more, but the hours and hours and hours of nothing to do were too much. "Look. I'm bored stiff. I'm a teenager. I *have* to move or my brain seizes up. So either let me out of this room and walk around your stupid station, or I do jumping jacks until I drive you up the wall."

Erim gave him a very dark look but he refused to drop his gaze.

"And I want an orb and access to your computer system."

Erim's expression soured. "No."

Alec stepped around her and went to stand by her chair. A cold smile tugged at the corner of his mouth. "I'll just stand here then," he pointed at her seat, "and sweat a bit longer. Hope you don't mind."

"Terran males have an unpleasant odour when they utilize kinetic energy."

"Yeah, we sweat," Alec's smile broadened. "In fact, the entire station will reek if I get going. You'll probably choke."

Erim seemed to agree. She reached for her pocket. "The station is off limits. Exercise is off limits. You will practice telekinesis." She pulled out a bluish orb and a small, flat metal object the size of a pancake. She tossed the object to him and he caught it reflexively. She reached out and handed the orb to him with narrowed eyes. "Place the turis on the table and practice moving it towards you."

Erim turned her back on him, reseated herself and created another computer screen in the air in front of her.

Alec tossed the orb into the air a couple of times experimentally, gauging the weight and size. It felt cold and decidedly alien, but the sense of calm an orb always gave him was still there, though not as complete as usual. Shrugging away his nagging discomfort, he crossed back to his side of the room and dropped the metallic object to the surface of the table before pulling a chair over and seating himself.

He held his orb firmly and focused. Channelling the burgeoning power underneath his skin, he visualized the metal disc moving closer and closer to him. He closed his eyes to minimize any distractions. *Move.*

For almost a minute nothing happened. He could feel the turis on the table, almost taste the power that infused it, tugging at it ever so slightly. The pressure built. He could do this. Once it had been so easy he'd laughed at Riley as she struggled with a simple task.

Whoosh, the turis slid off the table and directly into his chest, knocking the memory of Riley right out of his mind. He grabbed at it and held it aloft, silently fist-pumping in celebration. He glanced at Erim, interested to see if she'd noticed his quick success. She hadn't. Annoyed, Alec rubbed at the developing bruise on his chest and dropped the turis back on the table.

He did it again and again, each time with less and less effort on his part. He tried spinning the turis like a top, increasing the speed and then stopping it in mid-spin. It grew easier. Pleased, he tried something new. Focusing his attention again, he lifted the turis up in the air, let it hover for a moment and then sent it on a circuitous fly around the room. It zipped past Erim's nose without her even raising her eyes.

Alec pulled a face. She was a complete cow; the least she could do was notice his prowess. How many Potentials caught on this quickly, anyway? He bet she wasn't nearly as adept with telekinesis as he was. Time to show her just what he was capable of.

He raised the turis to eye-level and let it hover in front of him for a moment. He lined up his sight with the doorway.

Gathering his strength, he *pushed* as hard as he could, gasping with the effort. The turis left his sight like a bullet from a gun. It rammed through the metallic door as if it was made of butter and disappeared. Almost immediately, there was a second bang as metal collided with metal. Instantaneously an overhead klaxon blared into life and the lighting changed from pale yellow to blood red.

Alec stumbled backwards. What had he done?

Erim's screen disappeared and she jumped to her feet. Without looking back at him she ran to the doorway and peered through the hole the turis had created. Her orb was already in hand and glowing. She turned back to him with a horrified expression.

"You have punctured the outer wall."

Alec bit back a saucy response. He ran over to the wall and gave the startled Erim a slight shove. He peered through the hole.

The corridor was rapidly filling with a pale pink mist as it poured in through the slit the turis had manufactured on its flight to freedom. Erim rapidly waved her orb in a circular motion over the puncture in the door before the mist could cross the expanse of the hallway. The air in front of the hole began to glow red. Erim shoved him backwards as Alec leaned forward for a closer look.

"What is…?" he began.

"The atmosphere of this planet is poisonous to humanoids. I have sealed the door but it will not last long," Erim snapped. She turned and levelled Alec with a frozen stare.

Alec backed away warily. "Then just grab some oxygen masks and we'll leave."

Erim's expression gave the answer before her words did. "There are no masks. The seals never break. There is no method of transporting off this station without an interstellar ship and the closest one is several days away."

Riley forced herself not to show fear.

"Come with me now. That was an order," Logan barked.

"I want Dean with me," Riley blurted out. There was no way she was going anywhere with Logan by herself.

"It is unnecessary." A muscle quivered in Logan's cheek and his eyes narrowed as she crossed her arms.

"You're going to determine my future. I think that should be witnessed by someone who's unbiased."

"Are you questioning my judgment?" Logan growled.

"You hate me." Riley refused to cower even though her heart was slamming against her ribs like it wanted to escape. "Everyone knows it. You'll be accused of ruining my chances with the Collective and you won't be able to argue the point. I'll have my mind wiped so I won't know a thing. But you'll never stop the rumours that your emotions got the best of you."

"The Terran child is right." Martje walked out of the exercise room and into the lounge area. She was tapping something on a palm-sized screen, not even looking at the assembled group. If she was aware of the tension, she gave no indication. "An unbiased witness is always a better option. Rumours are so difficult to dispel once they start."

12

Riley held her breath. Martje was a better choice. She would be seen as impartial while Dean might not be. She was also fairly senior.

Logan ground his teeth together. Then he gave a curt nod in Martje's direction. "Come."

Dean squeezed Riley's shoulder and for a second she connected with his concern and encouragement. "You will be chosen for training," he whispered. "Do not show fear."

Riley followed Logan's wide shoulders out the front door and across the huge plaza. He didn't look back to see if she was following. Martje took up the rear, still absorbed with whatever she was reading. They trouped past several identical sandstone buildings, another wide plaza and a third cluster of buildings. There was little difference between each group of buildings and it occurred to Riley as she walked that it would be easy to get lost in this settlement. The flagstones were a repetitive hexagonal shape as were the panels of glass high above her in the domed ceiling. The air smelled of sunlight and something rather yeasty. Riley inhaled deeply. Maybe there would be something normal to eat, like bread or pizza, she thought hopefully.

They turned right, away from the lake, and entered an area denser with buildings, some four and five storeys high. There wasn't anyone around, Riley realized as they passed through this section. She hadn't seen a soul other than the group that had transported down with her. No animals or birds, either.

"Where is everyone?" she asked Martje.

"Everyone?"

"There's no one here but us," Riley pointed at the empty buildings. "I thought this was a training centre. Where are all the trainees?"

"Domes one and three are full to capacity," Martje said, giving a nod towards the domes that Riley could just barely see in the distance. "This is number four and we reserve it for our newest arrivals. You remain in segregation here until initial training has been completed and we are sure no one carries a contagion."

"That makes sense," Riley replied. Martje went back to reading her screen. Riley had a lot of other questions, but it was clear the doctor wasn't interested in conversation and there was no way she was going to ask Logan anything.

Logan turned to his left and walked through two wide pillars. Riley followed but stopped immediately. Straight ahead, the ground dipped into a hollowed-out amphitheatre, very similar to the ones she'd seen back in Greece. Instead of rows of seats ringing the central hexagonal shape, steps had been cut into the sloping side. The red tiled ground was smooth and looked almost slippery. In the centre of the lowest level, a stone dais bisected the space and several orbs littered the top. Logan was striding purposely down the steps towards the dais. Martje gave Riley a little shove to indicate she was to follow.

Reluctance dogging her every step, Riley obeyed. At least there was no one else around to witness what was about to happen. She squared her shoulders. She knew she was strong enough with Tyon power to pursue the training even if Logan planned to make her grovel to continue. She had a job to do for the Council and getting kicked out of the Collective was tantamount to failure. She had never failed a test before and she wasn't going to start now.

Logan stopped at the dais and reached for an ugly hunk of red crystal. He hefted it in his huge hand and turned around to face them. For a split-second Riley wondered if he was going to throw it at her.

"Stand here," he pointed to a black tile about a metre from his own widely planted feet.

Her features carefully arranged in an expression of blank cooperation, Riley complied. Silently, she warned herself to keep a hold of her temper.

Logan waved the orb in front of her for several minutes.

Riley contained her sudden spasm of laughter. He looked so incredibly serious waving a rock around like an idiot. He placed the orb back on the dais and plucked his own from his pocket. He folded his arms across his chest and frowned at her.

"The Tyon power is of moderate strength and enough to support your continued training," he announced.

Whatever she was expecting, this wasn't it. "Are you sure?" Riley asked warily.

"I have also reviewed your file. Your Tu quotient is well above average and several other parameters are strong. In addition, you are loyal, inventive and brave. Those traits are important for Tyon training."

"Okaaay," she drawled, turning slightly as if to leave. "Then that's fine. I mean, great. I'll just go back and let Dean know the good news and get out of your hair."

"Not so fast, Terran. I have questions for you. This is an interrogation."

Riley raised her eyes to his. Now *this* was what he really wanted to do. "Okay. Fire away."

"You spoke to Tyrell, despite being warned that it was unwise to do so. What questions did you ask him and why?"

"Did Ty tell you this?" she asked. "If so you should ask him yourself."

"The ship is constantly monitored. Your interactions were recorded."

"Why ask me if you already know?"

"To determine your honesty." Logan said. He took a step closer. Riley held her ground. "Why did you ask if Kholar was dead? Why do you think Anna was aboard that vessel?"

He might be able to tell if she was lying if he had the telepathy gift and there were some things she absolutely could not divulge. So, honesty, whenever possible. "I was certain that Anna had been there. Kholar was way too strong with Tyon power to snuff it without a fight. The guy could have transported anywhere he wanted, so for someone to say he didn't get off the ship the instant trouble started sounds like crap. I think Tyrell believes the same thing."

"What memories do you have of Anna?"

That was personal. Riley smiled to herself. "I'll trade you for them," she said.

Logan frowned. "What do you mean, trade?"

"I share what I can remember with you in exchange for information."

"Logan is your commander," Martje piped up. Riley startled. She had forgotten the medic was there. "You must divulge all information to him at request. It is your duty."

Riley pulled out her own orb and held it out in the palm of her hand. This was going to be tricky. "I'm not officially in training yet." She glanced up at Logan's granite jaw. "Am I? So, until I agree to study with you and whatnot, I'm not under any obligations. So. Want to trade info or not?"

Logan gave a sudden tight smile. "Are all Terrans like you?" he said. "Or are you related to Finn and carry the same inability to accept domination?"

Riley shrugged a shoulder. "We're as individual as you Tyons, but we do tend to wait to see if you can prove you're worth following before we jump on board. And no, Darius and I aren't related. At least I hope not."

"Be grateful there is no genetic link," Logan nodded. Riley doubted he was considering the same reasons she was. "Tell me what you remember."

There wasn't much choice. She needed the information and Logan as an ally was far preferable than as an enemy. If she didn't clear him from her list before he and the other Tyons left for their next assignment, she might never find the mole. And that meant Kerry would die.

"I don't think your scans are correct. I can't explain it, but I'm sure that Anna was on board that ship. I know that

Tyrell thinks so too. I can remember her."

Logan peered over Riley's head and nodded at Martje. Riley heard her footsteps and turned to see the older medic climbing the stairs back up the way they had arrived. She strove to keep her worry about being left alone with Logan out of her mind, but either he was adept at telepathy or the flicker of distress across her features gave her away.

"I will not harm you, as long as you speak the truth," he said.

"Where's she going?" Riley asked.

"To summon Tyrell." Logan sat down on the edge of the dais and crossed one long leg over the other. He folded his arms and cocked his head to one side. For a brief moment, Riley was aware of how attractive he could be and what Anna might see in him. "There are two aspects of your supposition that are impossible to repudiate. One, the ship has no record of Anna being aboard. Two, none of the people aboard have memories of her."

Riley chewed her lower lip. "Yeah. I know. It sounds crazy." She racked her brain, inadvertently beginning to pace. "Could the memory banks of the ship be tampered with? You know, erased?"

Logan nodded. "I am not familiar with the term memory bank; however, it is technically possible to manipulate the record. But to do so requires tools that were not available and a very high level of security access."

"Kholar was there. You can't get higher on the totem pole than him, can you?"

"If you mean the levels of Tyon hierarchy, then no. Kholar was the first of us. He trained us all."

88

Riley thought some more. She shoved her hands into her pockets and unconsciously gripped her orb tightly. "It was Kholar's ship we were on, wasn't it?"

"Yes," replied Logan. "One of them."

"So," Riley spoke out loud as the ideas drifted across her mind, "he could have had the ship's records fitted to erase whatever he wanted. In advance. So, he wouldn't need any tools or anything when the time came. Right?" She lifted up her head in time to see Logan's expression. "I'm right. It's technically possible."

"Technically. There is no indication that it was so."

"Okay. So, Kholar *could* have modified his ship to record only what he wanted recorded. The question is, how do you erase the memory of a whole bunch of people, most of whom you didn't want on your ship in the first place and didn't know in advance would be there? Anna did it a lot, right in front of me, so I know it's possible. But can you do a whole group of people at once?"

"Theoretically, it could be done, with the right crystals. But not to Operatives."

Riley stopped mid-step. "You guys are immune to a memory wipe?"

For a second Logan looked a bit uncomfortable.

"What?" Riley pounced on his frown. "You've just thought of something that supports my argument, haven't you? There *is* a way to tamper with an Operative's mind, isn't there?"

"Wiping the memories of Tyon Operatives is very difficult. Even with the correct tools on hand. The training precludes it."

"But it's not impossible," Riley countered. "That's why this Tu quotient thing is important. Coz people with it, like me and Tyrell, are immune to a mind wipe. Right?"

Logan ignored her question. "Kholar is the Quadrant Commander. He is above suspicion."

"Oh please," Riley rolled her eyes. "These blinders you guys wear tie your panties in a knot. 'He's the boss so he's above suspicion.' 'Finn is too emotional so he can't be a good Operative.' 'It hasn't been done before so it can't be done.' How on earth do you manage anything if you can't think outside the box?"

Logan looked decidedly confused by her outburst.

He held up his hand. "What are panties and where is this box—"

The sound of approaching footsteps stopped him. Tyrell was striding down the stairs, followed by Martje. He didn't look happy, but then, Riley thought, he never did.

"You requested my attendance, sir?" Tyrell came to a halt a metre from Logan. He didn't give any indication that he had even noticed Riley.

Logan stood. "Recount your experience on Kholar's ship immediately after the collapse of Home Base."

"I have not changed my recollection, sir," Tyrell said. He was speaking to Logan's left ear.

"Noted. Proceed."

"Multiple sightings of time/space distortions made escape from the gravitational pull of the collapsing island difficult. There was clear evidence that the rips were strategically placed to prevent our escape. Despite evasive maneuvers, we were surrounded. I brought the ship to a standstill and awaited evacuation orders."

"Who was in command?"

"Kholar, sir."

"Did he give the order to evacuate the ship?" Logan continued.

"No, sir."

"There was no ability to fight, you were in danger of destruction and Kholar did not order evacuation. Is this your recollection?"

"Yes, sir."

"Tyrell, Commander Kholar is responsible for the lives of all the Operatives in his quadrant. Are you intimating that he knowingly put Operatives in danger and effectively signed their death marks by refusing to evacuate the ship?"

"I am stating fact, sir. Nothing more."

Riley was impressed. He might be a cold fish but he didn't flinch at all. Her estimation of the pilot rose a notch.

"What happened next?"

Tyrell frowned. It was the first expression of emotion Riley had ever seen him have. "I am unsure, sir. There are gaps in my memory."

"How can this be so?" Logan pushed. "You have extensive training in this area. Your memory cannot be faulty."

"True. I was not physically injured in my escape. I can only believe that my mind was forcibly coerced into the state it is in now."

"I have read your report several times," Logan said. "You indicate that you, Ennis, Dean and Tor teleported everyone you were able to reach, just as the hull was breached. None of the others have any memory of escape. In addition, you believe that Anna was on board and accompanied by a young Terran male. His description fits that of William, the boy I found with an orb. The same boy who is in league with the Others."

Riley startled. Alec wasn't working with the Others. Was he? Had Anna somehow coerced him into turning against his own planet?

"His name is Alec," she said.

Logan turned. "Who?"

"William," Riley said. "He might have told you that his name is William, but that's his middle name. Everyone knows him as Alec."

"How do you know him?" Logan took a step towards her.

"He was on the ship too. With Anna."

"Riley was found in the aft corridor, alone and severely injured," Tyrell stated as he gave her a piercing look. "I remember her following Anna."

Whatever Logan was about to ask was halted. Logan clasped his orb and suddenly raised his eyes to the top of the steps.

"The Council is here," he said in sharp tone. "Prepare yourselves."

Who in their right mind built a station on a planet with a poisonous atmosphere and didn't stock it with oxygen masks? Alec was disgusted. What a bunch of idiots.

Erim stared at the hole in horrified disbelief.

"Call Paran," Alec urged. "Get him to seal the hole."

"He will be locked into the section he was working in. He cannot reach us," Erim said tightly. "Just as we cannot get out of this room."

"Override the locks," Alec argued.

"It is not possible," Erim countered. "We are trapped here until the gas penetrates my shield or the oxygen runs out. My shield is rudimentary and will not last long."

13

This was stupid. There had to be another way. "What if I can break the lock?" Alec asked as he racked his brain for a solution. "If we can get out of here, can't we make a run for it? Head towards Paran or something? There must be a larger part of the station."

"It is impossible to open the door once the seals have been compromised," Erim's voice had dropped to a defeated monotone. "The station was built precisely to react in this way."

"Nothing is impossible," Alec muttered. His fingers tightened around his orb. If he could use his power to punch a hole through the walls, he could overpower a lock. The issue was breathing on the other side of the doorway. Without oxygen masks, he doubted they'd get too far. He stared at the glowing air by the puncture. Unless...?

"I can make a shield around us," he said. "Anna and Kholar did it on Earth, when the nukes blew. If they can do it, I can too."

"Shield work is highly detailed. It takes extensive training. And I cannot produce an effective shield large enough for both of us."

"Yeah, well, I bet I can. I'm not staying here, waiting to suffocate." Alec backed up from the door and held his orb up to his face. "Show me a map of this station. I need to know what direction to run in."

Erim's expression reflected the war between skepticism, loathing and fear that was going on inside her brain. She paused for a second, then waved her orb in front of her in a complicated movement. Instantly a screen materialized between them. The outline of the station was clear, even with the unfamiliar symbols. Hexagonal in shape with an open centre like a donut, the ringed station was much larger than Alec had considered. The small rooms he'd been confined to were on the outside of the ring. It appeared all the rooms branched off a corridor that ran around the inside. His turis had passed through the door, straight across the corridor and out the inner ring wall. Multiple barricades sectioned the inner corridor into air-locks. The ones on either side of their room glowed red.

"Can you show me where the gas has penetrated?" Alec leaned in to observe the detail of the map. "And where Paran is?"

Erim pursed her lips and tightened her fingers around her orb. A tiny circle appeared in a room nearly a third of the way around the hexagon and pulsed in green. The corridor outside their room changed to red and the corridor sections on either side of it were coloured a paler pinkish hue.

"We have to get through three locks," Alec pointed out.

"And when we break the third, some gas will leak through into that chamber, so we really need to go one further, to be safe."

"The gas is heavier than the atmosphere of this station," Erim slowly agreed. "It will diffuse slowly. It may be possible to outrun it." She didn't sound at all hopeful as she waved her hand and the map disappeared. "But the locks are unbreakable and creating a shield for the length of time needed will be impossible."

"It's either try or die, and personally, I plan to live." Alec pointed to his side. "You should stay as close to me as possible. The smaller the shield, the less energy it takes."

"Once this door is opened, there will be no turning back," Erim grimaced. "If you can't get the shield to work adequately…"

"Yeah, tell me something I don't know."

Alec wiped his palm against his pant leg and retightened the grip on his orb. Already the little room seemed warmer and stuffy. There wasn't going to be much time. He took a slow deep breath and tried to calm his pounding heart. He could almost hear the instructions in his ear: stay calm, concentrate. He closed his eyes and focused on the door ahead of him. He let his power do the work for him; inching out towards the door, seeping into the actual metallic frame and door, infusing itself into the locking devices that were surprisingly placed in a circular pattern in the centre of the metal. It took several minutes before he figured out what needed to be done. He was just about to release the key to the apparatus when he realized that the instant he opened the door, the gas would pour in.

He broke his concentration and opened his eyes. "We need the shield first," he said, more to himself than Erim.

"Encircle only our heads," she advised tightly. "Less work."

Surprised, he glanced down at her. She was pale and visibly trembling.

"Good idea," he answered. "Don't worry."

"I am not," she snapped, staring straight ahead.

Alec gave a slight snort and closed his eyes again. Within seconds a pale blue shimmering sphere encircled them from the waist up. Alec could have stretched out his arm and touched it, but decided not to. There was no telling if the protective barrier could hurt him and he had enough things to think about. He focused on the lock again. It took several moments to find the mechanism again; surprisingly it wasn't easier than the first time, perhaps even a bit harder to keep his focus.

The door suddenly slid open. The pinkish gas, now to the ceiling of the corridor beyond, rapidly flowed into their room and almost immediately covered their feet. It was unpleasantly cold.

"C'mon," Alec shouted. His voice was muffled but loud enough for her to hear. He grabbed Erim's arm and propelled her forward, afraid that they'd be separated. He wasn't sure what his shield would do if that happened.

They moved forward quickly. It was much harder to see than Alec had considered and the far walls were indistinct. He forced the fear from his mind and concentrated, maintaining the shield to full capacity. He couldn't afford a lapse, even for a second.

Alec turned right, the opposite direction from Paran's location. The last person he wanted around was Kholar's bodyguard. Erim tugged at his arm but said nothing. She quickly matched her steps to his. It was twelve paces to the next doorway. Alec stopped immediately in front of it and tightened his grip on his orb. Focusing as much attention on the lock as he dared, he searched again for the way to open the mechanism. But this lock was different from the last one. The controls were somewhere else. He couldn't find the key to unlock it.

Alec bit his lower lip. It had to be there somewhere. You didn't build a door and put the lock somewhere else.

"Hurry," Erim said.

Sweat beaded Alec's forehead. Where was the damn thing?

The cold gas pressing against their legs was getting more uncomfortable by the second. The air inside the shield was too warm. At the back of his mind, Alec noticed he was panting slightly.

"The air is running out, you must get through this door *now*," Erim implored him.

He didn't answer. It would break his concentration. Could they have built the release mechanism in a distant part of the ship? He cast his mind further afield, searching the walls, the floor and the rooms on either side of the doorway. Nothing.

"We can't go back." Erim leaned against him. "There are only a few minutes of oxygen left."

He hardly needed her nagging him. He knew as well as she did that if he didn't find it soon, they were both going to die.

everal individuals appeared high up on the edge of the amphitheatre. One by one, the Council ringed the edge.

Riley's breath caught in her throat. What if the Councilor who'd put the device in her head was here? A deep shivering started inside her as she remembered the pain and threats. Without conscious thought, she ducked behind Logan. There was little space between him and the dais but he didn't seem to notice her brushing up against him.

The Councilors stood shoulder to shoulder. Peeking under Logan's arm, Riley counted ten of them. It was hard to tell from this distance if the Councilor she had met in Kerry's living room was there. It was hard to tell men from women. Squinting, she focused on the two tallest at the end. They didn't even look *humanoid*.

14

The members of the Intergalactic Council formed a single file and started down the stairs with slow and measured steps. Martje followed behind at a very respectful distance. Riley couldn't tear her eyes away from the procession. Unlike the Tyon organization they had created, these individuals did not dress alike. They weren't even the same species. Some wore brightly coloured flowing robes, others, tightly wrapped silky one-piece suits. At least three wore only a wide belt around the waist and matching leather-looking boots. The two who were not humanoid weren't those evil Thtkas,

Riley was relieved to see. She was so amazed at the aliens she nearly missed the conversation.

"Commander Logan, we meet again." A short woman with no whites to her eyes and a very deadly looking curved knife on her hip stepped forward. She was bereft of hair and her gleaming skull was patterned with inlaid jewels. That must have hurt like hell, Riley thought.

Logan bowed deeply, crossing both arms in front of him and clasping his shoulders. "Madame Councilor."

"The report was disappointing, Commander. The second planet gone in two partons. We had hope for Terra."

"Agreed," Logan rumbled. "The Others' tactics have changed significantly and we were unable to mount any defense. Only twenty Potentials were rescued before the population was destroyed. Fortunately, we were able to acquire a significant portion of the planet's digital archives."

"The Others grow stronger, Logan." The woman's melodious voice filled the centre of the amphitheatre and echoed around them eerily. "They now decimate entire planets and the efforts of the Tyon Collective are unable to withstand their growing domination. What do you suggest we do?"

Destroy them, Riley thought with sudden unsuppressed anger. *Go on, say it.*

"We must disseminate the resistor more efficiently and move to more planets. Our organization must increase in size to do so," Logan said.

"We have discussed this before and your answer now is the same as before. Kholar thought highly of you. With his death you assume his position, but we of the Council are not convinced you are suitable. New problems require innovative solutions and yet we have heard nothing new, either now or in your report."

"The previous system was sufficient. It will be again."

Logan wasn't as sure as he sounded, Riley realized with a slight shock. His emotions were available to her, though just barely, through the slight physical contact. He's worried but can't think past what he knows, she sensed. The Others had the benefit of Alec's knowledge and extensive experience with video games, she remembered with sudden clarity. Rhozan thought it was real and subsequently deployed strategies that Alec knew. The Tyons had none of that knowledge. They were metaphorically going into battle blind. But how could she let the Council know that without jeopardizing Alec and his dangerous ability?

"There has been no success in finding the time shifter either, Logan. This is of paramount importance," the Councilor continued.

"Agreed, Madame Councilor," Logan replied. "We have compared the power signature at the shift site with all records of Tyon Operatives and there is no match. We correlated the psychic imprints of all new Potentials and none were identical matches either. We have reviewed our records and all but four orbs are accounted for. Some were likely contained in the training bases we had to abandon. We concluded that a Terran found or stole an orb and somehow activated latent Tyon power."

It was a flimsy conclusion, even to Riley's ears.

"This is far too important an issue to be left to premature conclusions," said a voice to Riley's right. The insectoid creature was twice as tall as the woman Councilor and spoke with a voice that sounded mechanically produced.

"While I agree with you, Councilor," Logan bowed to the alien, "there are limited records available and the witnesses have died. The planet is decimated by nuclear war. There is no further opportunity for investigation. However, we are interrogating all Terrans regarding this matter and will review our conclusions. We will also continue to monitor carefully for any evidence of time shift and will evaluate the power signatures of all Tyon Operatives, in the slim chance we have missed some previous clue."

"Were you interrogating this Terran?" The female Councilor pointed to Logan's left elbow.

"I was," Logan said. Without preamble, he turned, grasped Riley's arm and thrust her in front of him.

Riley jerked free the moment she regained her balance. Showing fear and subservience in front of these people, especially the non-humans, was not an option. She raised her chin and met the chief Councilor's gaze without flinching.

"Terran female, you are among the last of your race. You have heard us speak and the questions we pose. Do you have a response?"

Riley licked her lips as her mind moved at the speed of light. If she played her cards right she could move her own investigation forward quickly, keep her knowledge about Alec hidden, and get herself out of Logan's clutches. "I do. First, I commend you on promoting Logan. Kholar was willing to let members of the Collective die for no good reason. Logan would never do that. He'll make a much better Commander." She paused to let that sink in. "Secondly, I don't believe for a second that an orb was stolen by a Potential. We don't have any idea how to use one until we've had some training. If there are orbs missing, then you have someone inside your organization who is working for someone else."

"A traitor?" The insectoid Councilor cocked its head to one side. "Tyon training precludes this."

"Nothing's impossible, with humans," Riley snorted. "There will always be an exception to any rule. It's a mathematical probability. The ship we were on was supposed to record the presence of everyone on board but we've just figured out that someone tampered with the mechanisms and the readings were faulty. Didn't we, Logan?"

Logan gave Riley a sharp glance. "There is a theoretical possibility."

"Who did this?" the female Councilor asked.

"Unclear at present," Logan replied. "Supposition only."

"Witnesses?"

"Two," Logan said. "This Terran female and my pilot, Tyrell."

The entire collection of Councilors turned as one and stared at Tyrell. He didn't flinch, Riley noted, nor did he look at her.

"I think you have a mole," Riley spoke into the silence.

"A what?" asked the insectoid.

"A double agent. Someone working for a completely different purpose that you don't know about," Riley explained.

"Your thoughts are irrelevant," the lead Councilor waved her hand. "You are Terran and untrained."

"She speaks the truth," Logan said. Riley nearly did a double take. She caught Tyrell's shock before he rearranged his features into stony impartiality. "There is someone working against us. I have felt this for some time. Kholar was aware of my concerns. I have found two of his agents within my ranks, both sentenced and removed from service. The third was the Terran boy, Alec. His location is unknown and he is presumed dead."

Riley couldn't prevent the gasp. Alec. Dead? A sudden tightening of her throat prevented speech for a moment.

The Council turned towards each other, but did not speak. Riley saw through her momentarily blurred vision, tiny flashes of light from the palms of their hands, to and fro—some type of communication. The flashing stopped and the Councilors turned to face her again.

"Did you know this Terran male?" One of the older male Councilor's asked her. He would have looked human but for the extra set of arms folded across his patterned robes.

Riley nodded. "I did."

"Who among the Collective, knew this human boy?" the same Councilor asked.

Logan answered. "Dean, our Guardian of Potentials, myself, Kholar, Anna, and Darius Finn."

"I did as well," Tyrell spoke up. "I remember him on Kholar's vessel. He asked me questions about steering the ship."

"He wasn't the mole," Riley interjected. "I knew him on Earth. Darius and I travelled together. Darius didn't train him to do anything special. I was there. I'd know."

"Darius Finn is Terran," the lead Councilor spoke up. "He was acquired long before the protective phase began on Earth. He was noted to be a spontaneous mutation of exceptional strength. He was young when he began training as a Tyon and demonstrated considerable aptitude. I read the reports. Who was his Guardian?"

"Anna," Martje said.

Logan and Riley whirled around to face the medic, who was tucking her handheld computer into the pocket of her uniform. "I supervised his condition throughout the training process. As the first Terran, it was important to ensure he was mentally and physically capable."

"Finn is the agent working against us," Logan spat. "I have never trusted him."

"You just don't like him because he's different," Riley interjected. "And because he and Anna were lovers. Your judgment is clouded by jealousy."

"Silence." Logan's eyes narrowed to slits of silver. Riley backed up, recognizing her mistake. The temporary truce has dissolved as quickly as it had been forged.

"There was no reason to consider Finn as anything beyond an Operative," Martje went on, uninterested in Logan's anger. "He performed well, scored highly on his tests and completed his assignments correctly. His emotional nature is perhaps not in keeping with Orion or Tholan temperaments, which has caused disruption within the ranks, but Anna worked closely with him for years and had no complaints."

"Anna is missing," Riley reminded her. Riley faced the Council and pushed on, despite Logan. "Anna is the key to all of this. She trained Darius and was his lover. If anyone had control over him and could convince him to do something underhanded, it would be her. You won't get to the bottom of this without interrogating her."

"I concur." Tyrell's voice was quiet but resolute.

Logan fumed. "You are out of order."

"Anna and Kholar spoke of some plan they were working on while I was piloting the ship. Neither realized I was able to hear them through the Terran girl." Tyrell gave Riley a pointed look. "You were touching us. Your telepathic skills allowed me to use you as a conduit."

Riley frowned.

"You did not speak to me of this," Logan fumed.

"I believe my memories may have been tampered with," Tyrell said reasonably. "No one else on the ship remembered Anna or the Terran boy and the records do not indicate their presence. I have spent much time in Kiros attempting to reestablish truth. These memories, while still affected, are coming clearer to me, Logan. The Terran girl is correct. Anna is the key."

15

Alec felt dizzy. A trickle of sweat was winding uncomfortably down the centre of his back, constantly luring his attention away from the discovery of the key. Next to him, Erim's sharp panting seemed inordinately loud. There must only be a minute left.

"Help me with this," he muttered. "Hold onto the shield for a sec."

He didn't wait for her agreement. Pulling the energy he'd used for the shield into his search, he pushed as hard as he could into the existence of the door's key. It had to be somewhere... There. No wonder it was so difficult to open once the alarms had been tripped. The sealing mechanism was in several pieces.

Alec re-gathered his strength and mentally shoved with all his might. There was no time to determine how to unlock it—brute force would have to do. He opened his eyes a sliver to see the massive doorway slide up into the ceiling with a sinister hiss.

"C'mon," he urged

The gas around them was already pouring into the corridor beyond—fast. Terribly fast. They had to beat it to the far end and get through the door if they wanted to escape. But Erim was gripping his arm with both hands, barely keeping herself upright, and coughing silently with sharp gasping movements. The gas was seeping up through the shield around their waists.

Alec didn't even think. Without pause he refocused his attention on the shield, firming it up and limiting it to around their heads, where there was still uncontaminated air. He swung an arm to grasp her beneath the armpit and hauled her with him as he ran to the far end. His heart was bursting with the strain. Erim seemed unable to even move her own legs and she was much heavier than she looked. But there was no choice. There were only seconds now.

Alec reached the wall right before the gas did. He leaned up against it, afraid he might slip to the floor because his legs were shaking so hard. Focus, he berated himself. *Get the door open.*

The mechanism for this door was the same as the last and it took him only a second to reestablish the location of the unlocking apparatus. The door slid upwards just as Erim fell unconscious. Alec managed to pull her under the door and immediately reversed the lock. The door slammed downwards, narrowly missing Erim's left foot. A trickle of gas puddled around his ankles.

Alec dropped the shield with relief and dragged Erim with both hands down the long corridor. He gasped at the fresh air. One more door and they were safe.

They were through and into the next corridor in a heart-beat. No gas managed to follow them and Alec dropped to the floor and leaned his back against the doorway at the reprieve. Once he'd caught his breath, he turned his attention to Erim. She looked very unwell. Her face was deathly pale and her lips and fingertips were an unpleasant shade of blue. She was still breathing easily—the coughing had stopped—but something prevented enough oxygen from getting through her body.

He got to his feet and looked around. The metallic floor, ceiling and walls of the station were a bit monotonous, hardly worth the argument with Erim to see them. However, the several doorways on the outer side of the station might hold something worth looking at. He walked over to the closest door, his footsteps ringing hollowly in the silence. He didn't need to use his orb to enter. A small yellow hexagonal button, recessed into the wall on the left side of the doorway, practically screamed Press Me. The door slid laterally into the wall, revealing a huge room beyond. Alec stepped inside.

Why had they kept him in that small chamber when there was this massive space sitting empty? The room stretched far to his right and left. Straight ahead, several huge viewports opened to wide vistas of heaving water, grassy hummocks and swirling pale pink vapour. Several bunk beds lined the far right wall next to two large storage lockers, several shower cubicles and what passed for toilets in Tyon design. The left side of the room was essentially empty but for a ring of chairs without a central table and a small separate area with foam flooring. All the furniture was made of the smooth brown Tyon metal but the floor, walls and ceiling were stark white.

Alec whistled softly under his breath as he reached down and grasped Erim's wrists. He pulled her along the floor and heaved her up onto the farthest bunk from the window. She was still out for the count and her colour hadn't changed, but at least she didn't look any worse. He covered her with a grey blanket and yanked another from the upper bunk to fashion as a pillow. Assured that she looked comfortable, he crossed over to the farthest bunk away from her, jumped to the upper bed and lay down. Cupping his head in his hands he turned to gaze out the window while he thought about what to do.

With any luck, Paran didn't know how to open the corridor airlocks and would have to stay in his section of the station. That was a good thing, as far as Alec was concerned. The bodyguard was a royal pain in the butt. The downside was that Erim was with him. She was no use to him unconscious. It made little difference in her personality, but he didn't want to be stuck with her if she died. He wasn't even sure he wanted to be stuck with her if she got better. Hopefully he wouldn't be trapped too much longer on this station. Anna had said she was coming back for him, just a slight change in plans, so probably any day now she'd...

Bang.

The entire room shuddered. Alec was tossed off his bunk and on to the floor.

Bang.

He grabbed the edge of the bed and hauled himself to his feet. Something was hitting the station from the outside and if he wasn't wrong, very close to the room he occupied. He ran to lean against the window, searching the sky and the sea within viewing distance. The hummocks near the station were bobbing wildly as if something huge had just moved underneath them. Dark navy water sloshed up against the windows. Pinkish gas swirled slowly, ebbing and flowing through the waving grass with each heave and dip of the hummock. But there was nothing else.

Alec pulled his orb into his hand and tightened his grip. If they were under attack, he had only his orb. He had no idea if the station had weapons and if it did, where they were or how to work them.

He caught the movement out of the side of his eye. In the distance the hummocks were rising sequentially, as if something massive was travelling beneath them. He could almost feel the swell against the station as the sea was propelled against the walls. The closest hummocks rose, and then *bang*, the entire station shuddered. Alec was knocked off his feet.

It didn't take a genius to figure this out. There was something in the water, something huge, that didn't like the floating metal building. And from the force of the impacts, it was something that might be able to punch a hole in the metal walls.

If it did, they were literally sunk.

R iley held her breath.

"We are agreed," the lead Councilor intoned. "We must further investigate this issue and pursue the truth. This Terran girl will be interrogated, as well as Darius and Tyrell. Anna must be found and, if alive, questioned. If she is dead, her implant will provide information that might be key."

"I will provide quarters for your comfort and convenience," Logan began.

The Lead Councilor raised her hand to stop him. "The Senate meets in a quarter parton. There is considerable distance between this planet and the Grand Council assembly on Mheeros. We must leave immediately to be present on time." She trained her gaze on Tyrell and Riley. "You will accompany us along with Darius Finn. Logan, you will return to Terra and search for signs of Anna. The implant must be found."

Without another word, the Councilors turned as one and began to climb the stairs in single file. Riley felt Logan's rapid breathing next to her but he said nothing. Tyrell looked at no one and fell in behind the Councilors. Only Martje had anything to say.

"I will contact Dean and Darius and inform them, Logan."

Logan nodded. His jaw was clenched so tightly Riley doubted he'd be able to speak.

"Riley, come with me," Martje said. "I will ensure that you have supplies and brief you on the Council. There are things you should know." Expecting her to follow without question, Martje headed for the stairs.

"Do not think I will forget this," Logan said quietly as Riley passed him.

"Don't think it doesn't work both ways," Riley muttered out of the side of her mouth.

Her mind leapfrogged from one idea to another over the next hour. She was back in the clutches of the Council and whether any of them knew she was working secretly for them, she had no idea. Logan wasn't the mole. She'd touched his skin and felt his thoughts and other than longing for Anna, anger at being second-guessed and frustration at the entire situation with Tyrell, there had been no whiff of a secret agenda. It was looking more and more like Anna was the guilty party. If she was dead, the problem wasn't solved unless Riley could prove it. If by some chance she wasn't, and Riley didn't trust the woman an inch not to have faked her own death, then Logan was probably going to find her. When the Council got their hands on her, they'd sort out this mess for themselves and hopefully that would be the end of it.

Martje's advice to Riley was simple. Keep out of the way of the Councilors and don't show any attitude. Riley didn't let on that she was more acquainted with the Council than she ever wanted to be, and luckily Martje didn't scan her or probe her mind to determine the truth. She was handed a small bag that contained two more uniforms, a smaller Ulat band and a second pair of shoes before she was ordered to head to the central square where they had originally teleported.

Darius was already there, leaning sullenly against a large block of brownish rock, a similar bag at his feet. He looked like he'd rather be anywhere else. He refused to meet her eye or acknowledge her presence but Riley knew he was as aware of her as she was of him. Stifling the urge to kick his shins, Riley dropped her bag to the paving stones and crossed her arms.

The minutes passed in silence. There was nowhere to look and nothing but her own morbid thoughts to occupy her. Her nerves were stretched taut and her stomach churned with uneasiness. She was about to break the silence when Dean appeared. His shoulders were slightly hunched and he was walking with the air of a man going to the firing squad.

"What're you so unhappy about?" Riley asked. Her eyes flicked from Dean to Darius and back again. Darius was studiously ignoring them now and inspecting his fingernails.

"Why do you think I'm unhappy?" Dean's forehead wrinkled. He stopped next to her. "I am following orders. Emotions do not come into it."

Darius snorted quietly.

Dean ignored him. "I wanted to say good bye. I do not know if I will see you again."

"Yeah, well, thanks for being a good Guardian and everything." Suddenly she felt a bit awkward. She watched Dean's eyes and became aware that he might be talking at her but he was speaking to someone else.

"I have found getting to know you illuminating. I wanted you to know."

"Okay," she said.

"I apologize if I was uncommonly hard on you. You are, I mean, you will be an excellent Operative."

Darius gave a short laugh.

Dean looked as if he might retort but was forestalled by the appearance of the Council. Dean stood back and watched them as they silently passed. Darius stood at attention as the Councilors filed by him, but he didn't look directly at any of them. He joined the little procession and walked away without a backwards glance. Dean picked up

Riley's bag and held it out to her. For a second her fingertips brushed his. She snatched them quickly back. She didn't need to deal with his misery on top of everything else. Ducking her head, she swung around and followed the small procession towards the nearest wall of the dome.

She was tempted to say something but the mood seemed to preclude conversation and she hardly wanted to engage any of the Councilors. Darius's rigid back indicated that his previous nonchalance had been feigned.

It was only as they came within metres of the edge of the dome that she noticed a small glass tunnel leaving the dome and heading straight out into the jungle beyond. The procession entered and marched silently forward. Through the glass-like walls and ceiling, Riley marvelled at the vegetation. It crowded against the dome barrier, massive vines and leafy tendrils smothering the glass so thickly Riley couldn't see a glimpse of sky beyond. The Councilors stopped when the tunnel ended in a small circular room. Tyrell was waiting. No one spoke. Riley eased herself around the side of the group to see what they were waiting for, just in time to spot a platform descend from the roof. As it settled to the floor with a slight *whoosh*, she noted a wide tunnel heading upwards, like an elevator shaft. Everyone moved forward and settled on the platform. Riley ducked in on the side farthest from Darius and held her bag in front of her like a shield. The platform began to rise.

It rose past the wild vegetation at a rate of speed that had Riley's stomach dropping into her shoes. There was nothing to hold onto. The platform didn't have a railing so the walls that shot past her nose were that of the shaft. Riley couldn't help it; she leaned against the nearest Councilor and held her breath. Where the heck were they going?

The elevator continued to rise steadily, leaving the vegetation far below. Riley could now see all four domes clustered together, ringing the massive lake. The wildness of the surrounding landscape seemed almost to be pressing in on the tiny settlement as if to suffocate it.

Riley forced herself to look up. In the distance, a huge grey rectangle hovered in the sky. The elevator connected to it at one end. There was a brief impression that she had seen something like it before, on television or in a movie, but that idea left her mind as the platform rocketed towards it. The elevator slowed only at the last second and slipped up through the bottom of what appeared to be a huge concrete building, floating unsupported in the air. There was a moment of darkness as they passed through the floor before the platform came to a stomach-clenching stop.

They were inside a massive hangar. The farthest wall was non-existent and opened to a vast bluish sky. A sharp, cold wind tore in through the open space, whipped around the hangar and gusting steadily out. The most interesting feature of the hangar was not its massive size or the fact that it seemed to be hanging in the sky without assistance, but the handful of small, sleek grey craft that sat in the middle of the floor.

"Oh my God," Riley breathed. The Tyon ships hadn't impressed her much, probably because she had been inside them and so missed the full impact. But *this* was just like *Star Wars*.

She trailed after the procession that was now marching silently across the floor towards the nearest ship. She hardly noticed the wind that tore at her clothes and at the bag she clutched. A flutter of excitement burst to life in her stomach. The closer she got to the ships, the more the excitement grew.

"Are we taking one of these to the Councilor's ship?" she asked Tyrell, who was now walking beside her. "Why not use those huge orbs, like before?"

"Orb travel and power are the purview of the Collective. No one else knows that they even exist."

"Except them." Riley gave a nod towards the Councilors, who were now climbing a steep ramp that led into the largest of the spaceships.

"The Council mandates our secret existence. They can hardly use our powers themselves."

"It seems like an awful lot of people know a pretty big secret," Riley replied. "I'm amazed no one has spilled the beans to the general population yet."

Tyrell ignored her and strode quickly up the metallic ramp. He disappeared inside. Biting her lower lip and stifling an urge to giggle, Riley followed him.

The little ship was clearly a transport vessel, despite its cool sleek lines and shiny metal. Inside there was one large room filled with rows of seats. At one end, she noted a space with a window and banks of instruments that resembled the cockpit of a jumbo jet.

Tyrell indicated that she should sit, buckling her in the instant her backside touched the seat's fabric. Riley heard the doorway slide shut. The floor beneath her feet began to vibrate. She had the sensation the ship was turning but as there was no window in the passenger section and her seat didn't face the cockpit, she didn't have an outside reference point. She only knew they were flying by the sudden, fierce G-force that shoved her back against the seat cushions so strongly she doubted she could even raise her arms.

The trip was rather short and completely uneventful. No one spoke. Darius didn't look at her and even Tyrell seemed occupied with some inner turmoil. The sensation of movement ended without her really noticing; it was only when her seatbelt unfastened and the doorway slid open that she realized they had docked with the Councilor's ship. Immediately the Councilors dispersed.

Riley, Tyrell and Darius stood on the threshold and peered out into the ship. Unlike the Tyon craft, this one was fabricated out of a white and cream material that had none of the creepy smoothness of Tyon metal. The walls rose upwards to at least twice Tyrell's height. Subdued lighting lit the corridor ahead softly. There was a green carpet-like material on the floor. Altogether, it was a far more pleasant vessel than anything Riley had ever been on. She immediately pulled out her Ulat band and settled it into place.

"You won't need that," Tyrell said, looking at the Ulat band. "This ship has Thetris propulsion. There are no distortion fields."

Riley warily removed the plastic glasses but held onto them.

A tall woman wearing a long blue dress that buttoned from floor to neck approached from a side corridor. She stopped and raised her hand, beckoning to them. "I will show you to your quarters. Please rest until interrogation."

"And knowing you're about to be interrogated is so conducive to resting," Riley said with a false smile.

The woman gave her a confused look but didn't respond as she led them down a long hall. Riley followed behind the others and craned her neck to get a good look at the ship. It was certainly much bigger than the one she and Dean had travelled on. The carpet was a slightly spongy material that absorbed their footsteps in an eerie way. All the angles were curved, even where the floor met the walls, and Riley noted that the far end of the corridor curved out of sight as if it travelled in a large circle. All the corridors emerged from the left as they walked, suggesting they were travelling around the perimeter of a sphere. Here and there she saw open metallic stairways leading upwards or downwards, indicating more than one deck.

114

"Please enter here and wait. You will be informed when it is your time for interrogation." The woman pointed to an open doorway.

The room was very spacious but there was no window or viewport. There were none of the posture-loving metallic chairs that the Tyons seemed to adore, only low-slung couches in soft cushy fabrics. The room itself was large enough to hold several sofas and a couple of tables. Large globes on the tables gave off a soft yellow-white light. A wide archway opened to a sizable space beyond. Riley glimpsed several bunk beds and deduced the room was a communal sleeping quarters. The entire space was designed for comfort and rest. At least the Council had a better sense of design than the Tyons.

Riley dropped onto a couch and lay down. "This is much better."

"Wait until they start pulling your fingernails off and see how comfortable you are then," Darius said as he settled himself on the sofa next to hers.

"They're civilized beings, Dare. I would think they'd have much more sophisticated means of torture," she drawled. She should know.

"Interrogation means questions. Answer honestly and there will be no torture." Tyrell leaned up against the wall, eschewing the comfortable option as usual.

"Much you know," Riley scoffed.

"Tyrell is right," Darius said. "Stick to the truth. No second guessing."

"You mean, don't mention Anna." Riley wasn't fooled. She knew exactly what he meant.

"You've always hated her," Darius shot back. "You're prejudiced and just hoping to get her into trouble."

Riley sat up. "You're blind to her faults because you love her. You can't see her for what she really is."

"I've known her for years," Darius argued. Twin blotches of fury stained his cheeks. "My personal feelings have nothing to do with it."

"Oh, please." Riley rolled her eyes. "You're so pathetic. She's been leading you around by the balls for half your life. You have absolutely no impartiality when it comes to Anna." She mimicked him. "'Don't worry, I can trust her. Don't worry, she'll help us.' It's bull, Darius, all of it.

She's manipulated you from the start."

"It's possible," Tyrell interjected quietly.

Riley and Darius swung their heads to stare at him.

"You have got to be kidding," Darius gasped.

"Theoretically, a highly trained Operative can manipulate another," Tyrell mused. "Certainly we do it all the time with civilians."

"I've been trained for the last *fifteen* years to resist Tyon mind control," Darius argued. "I'm good at it. There's no way someone can come in, fiddle with my brain and make me do something I don't want to. No one can do it to you either."

"Technically no, they could not," Tyrell agreed.

"See?" Darius concluded as he turned back to Riley. "I'm right."

"What if the person who trained you was the same one doing the manipulating?" Riley turned to Tyrell. "You might not notice, especially if it started when you were a kid. Before you knew enough to recognize it or fight against it. Right?"

"There's no way—" Darius began hotly.

"She is correct," Tyrell said thoughtfully. "It is possible. Theoretically the best time to begin something like that would be at the beginning of Tyon training, when the mind is most vulnerable. Whether Anna has done this, I cannot conclude without extensive testing. And even then, the notion is only a possibility."

Darius got quickly to his feet and crossed his arms. "This is crazy, not to mention stupid. Anna has never tried to hurt me or manipulate me in any way. I'm warning the both of you, drop the subject. *Now.*"

The door opened and a young man, wearing the same blue, buttoned robe stepped into the chamber. His serene expression didn't give any indication that he had heard them arguing.

"Darius Finn, please accompany me."

"With pleasure," Darius gave both Tyrell and Riley a dark look before sweeping out of the room, the young man following. The silence after the door closed was deafening.

"So," Riley said after several minutes passed and Tyrell seemed entirely disinclined to finish the conversation. "Tell me. What else do you know about mind control?"

"Only that I've heard rumours that it is possible." Tyrell gave a slight shrug of one wide shoulder. "The texts that describe it are off limits to any but the highest officers."

"Like Anna?"

"Possibly," Tyrell agreed slowly. "I have no evidence that she ever studied them or put any knowledge into practice."

"How well did you know her?"

"We trained and had worked on three assignments together. We did not have a close personal relationship. She was pair bonded with Logan for after duty."

"And you thought she was a cold fish," Riley filled in, guessing from the slightly chilled tone in his voice.

"My personal views are exactly that. Personal."

"Okay, fair enough," Riley let it drop. "But getting back to mind control. If the knowledge *is* more than just theory, and *if* she read those texts and *if* she used them…"

"This is a dangerous line of thought." Tyrell pushed himself off the wall and walked over to a cupboard. He opened it with a wave of his orb and proceeded to prepare a bowl of nutritional protein. He spoke over his shoulder. "The Tyon organization functions in a similar pattern to your home planet's military. Orders and information come down the line. Supposition and questions do not go up. You are treading on perilous ground."

He pulled two bowls out of the warmer and carried them back. He sat on the sofa next to Riley and passed her a bowl. Too surprised to say anything, she took it and the offered spoon wordlessly.

"I would strongly suggest that you keep any unfounded suspicion to yourself."

It was clear she wasn't going to get any further. She switched tactics. "Tell me about the Tyon organization. No one ever gave me the rundown on how long this little operation has been going, who started it, and the like." Riley sat back on the sofa and folded her legs lotus-style.

Tyrell gave her a slightly suspicious look. "The Tyons are a relatively recent creation. Kholar discovered that certain individuals were able to sense and fight Rhozan. He petitioned the Council to provide funding to train and operate our missions. The Council agreed. You know that this is secret."

Riley nodded. "Hard to believe that more people don't know about it."

"The secret is becoming more difficult to keep. In the beginning it was a handful of trainees. Logan, Anna, Martje, and a few others. Our mission was far simpler. Now, we have expanded significantly. Currently there are two other missions in addition to your home planet. And the training centre." He scraped his bowl and returned it to the counter. "Finish your meal and rest." Without another word, he left the room.

Riley took another mouthful and swallowed but didn't taste the hated goop. Her thoughts were on double speed. Anna and Kholar were the first of the Tyons. It wouldn't be surprising at all if they were in this together, had special ultra-secret knowledge of Tyon training, and were plotting something completely incomprehensible to the rest of the Operatives. She chewed the inside of her cheek. And if that was true, she had two enemies, not just one.

Great.

Alec sat across from Erim and stared at her. He was gripping the bunk bed posts so hard his knuckles were white. Things were getting worse by the hour. Erim's breathing had slowly changed from normal to rapid to now rasping and weak. She occasionally coughed up blood-tinged spittle, which Alec gingerly wiped from her face with the edge of a blanket. The blue colour had spread from the tips of her fingers up her arms to at least her elbows; Alec couldn't push up the fabric of her sleeves any further to check. Her face was a bloodless white except for her purplish lips. A thin coat of sweat lined her forehead. Even to Alec's limited medical knowledge, she was dying. And he didn't know what to do.

17

He'd broken open all the lockers but his search for any medicines or medical equipment had proven futile. He'd tried to access a computer to search for knowledge or send a distress signal but couldn't get one to materialize. He'd even tried holding his orb over Erim and pushing healing thoughts at her but other than feeling a bit stupid, nothing had happened. He clearly didn't have the healing gift.

The station was still under attack by something in the ocean. He hadn't gotten a glimpse of whatever was doing the smashing, so he had no idea if it was a live creature or another ship. Somehow the thought that a gargantuan sea monster was swimming around underneath him, waiting to bite a hole in the station's outer shell, was more frightening than attack by some other group of aliens. Whatever it was, it rammed the station with regularity and hadn't slackened since it started. If there was any damage, Alec didn't know about it. He didn't dare venture outside the room. He couldn't be sure that the rest of the station wasn't under water. Or maybe another hole had been punctured. Besides, where would he go? Paran was on the other side of the station and Alec didn't know how many barriers he'd have to get through to reach him.

It was strange and worrisome that Paran hadn't attempted to contact either Elim or Alec. Doubtless he had his orb and could send a message or speak to them if he wanted to. Alec could only assume that either the bodyguard didn't want to establish any contact or he couldn't—and mostly likely couldn't was the reason.

He would have paced the floor but the unpredictable ramming had made him fall twice. The second time he'd landed badly on his left wrist. It now felt swollen and tender, but Alec tried to ignore it. He'd been hurt a lot worse, lots of times, and it was the least of his worries.

The station was hit again and shuddered horribly, groaning with the strain. Alec bit his lower lip and held his breath until the last of the reverberations died away. That was the worst so far. Heaven only knew how much of this the station walls could take.

He had to prepare to evacuate. If the station started to sink he was going to have to abandon ship. Could he stay on one of those hummocks of vegetation without it sinking? Were poisonous animals or reptiles out there that would consider him lunch? And what about the atmosphere? He could make a shield, but for how long? None of the cupboards contained anything that might be used to keep him alive outside and there wasn't any food in them. If Anna didn't come back soon he was going to be in serious trouble.

Alec's heart doubled in speed as Erim suddenly

spasmed and gave a strangled, gurgling gasp. He jumped off the bed and leaned over her, unsure of what to do. Her body relaxed as suddenly as it had stiffened and then was completely still.

"Erim?" Alec called. He was almost afraid to touch her but he did reach out with a reluctant hand to give her shoulder a brief shake. Nothing. He moved closer. "Breathe," he muttered beneath his own breath. "Erim, breathe. Don't die on me. Please." He didn't know CPR—he'd seen it done on TV but everyone knew TV was fake. And even if he had known, putting his mouth over hers was too nasty to contemplate. He shook her again. Her head lolled to the side and faced him. Her eyes were open and already starting to glaze.

"Oh man, gross." Alec backed away.

Bang.

The station vibrated from another hit, this time farther away. There was a screeching of metal, as if it was being torn, then the horrifying lurch as the floor tipped slightly. Alec scrambled to grab onto the nearest bunk again. The loose articles he'd dumped on the floor while rooting through the cupboards rolled towards the corridor doorway. More of the sky became visible through the window. This was it. The station was *definitely* going to sink.

He pulled out his orb with his left hand while holding on to a bunk with his right. If he had to, he'd blast the glass right out of the window and climb out. He could make a shield that could protect him from the gas, at least for a little while.

Anna, he thought as hard as he could, *come and get me. Hurry*.

The floor shuddered again and the tilt became even more pronounced.

He really didn't want to break the window.

I'm here. Come and get me.

He truly didn't want to go outside.

I need you. Right now. Hurry.

Bang. The tilt worsened. The walls swayed with the force of the hit. Erim's lifeless figure rolled off the bed and onto the floor with a dull *thud*.

Overhead the lighting darkened to a blood red. Alec could hardly see.

"Anna," he shouted, "hurry up."

Suddenly, his skin sprung to life with goosebumps. Alec froze. *Something* was in the room with him. He raised his orb and pushed the thought at it. Immediately it burst into a powerful radiance that illuminated the entire chamber. In front of his face, only an arm's length away, there was a cloud of sparkling dust.

Oh no.

"Alec, is it time to play?"

The sparkles moved a bit closer.

Alec backed away, holding onto the fixed bedpost and gripping his orb so hard it hurt. Anna hadn't said how to get rid of these things and Alec had no idea of what to do, other than not to let them touch him. The voice was harsh and vaguely familiar. Who was speaking and how did they, whoever *they* were, know him?

"Alec?"

"It's not time to play anything," Alec stammered. The voice was coming from the floor, just beyond the bunk bed, near Erim's body.

"Is it time to play?"

"No."

"Is it time to play again, Alec?"

Another significant lurch of the floor suppressed Alec's shout for the moment. He found himself temporarily hanging from the bedpost. A second later the station righted itself again with a loud, metallic groan and his feet found the floor. A dull thud indicated Erim's body had hit the bed as it rolled back. Alec suppressed the shudder. Keeping his eye on the sparkles he backed up and climbed onto the mattress, putting as much distance between himself and the rip. The lights overhead flickered several times and Alec gave them a brief worried glance. Night was due in another couple of hours. It was hard enough to see with the stupid red

18

lighting. If it got fully dark he wouldn't be able to see the sparkles, never mind anything else. Of course, the station might have sunk by then.

"Leave me alone," he tried to reason with the disembodied voice. "I don't feel like playing anymore."

There was no answer. He took a step back, then another, feeling through the tousled blanket for the edge of the bed.

"I'll play some other time, okay?" he said. "When things aren't so crazy. All right?"

Several minutes passed. He was just getting his hopes up that whatever belonged to that voice had given up and moved on when he heard something stirring on the floor, just out of sight. There was the rustle of fabric and then, just like in a horror movie, a hand rose up above the mattress and reached out, grabbing hold of the bed. It pulled, but had caught hold of the loose blanket that Alec had used to cover Erim. The blanket bunched under the stubby, blue fingers as they clawed at the coarse fabric.

He wasn't sure what made him turn at the last second. Perhaps a second sense he didn't know he possessed alerted him. He glanced behind before moving his foot off the mattress and down onto the floor and came to an abrupt halt. More sparkles—just centimetres from his leg.

Instantly he jerked his foot back onto the bed, just in time to see Erim's corpse pull itself into a sitting position. Her glazed eyes locked with Alec's.

Alec felt his blood turn to ice. He swore loudly, suddenly torn between the animated corpse in front of him and the sparkles behind. Erim grinned.

"I wish to play again, Alec," Erim said. The voice wasn't Erim's but the same entity Alec had heard in China. Whatever it was could travel across the galaxy as fast as they could. This was seriously not good; how would he outrun it? That was, of course, assuming he could get away and into something fast.

"I told you, I don't want to play." This was becoming

124

tedious, fast. He'd had better conversations with himself. "Why are you picking on me anyway?" He darted a glance to his left, noted the coast was clear, and started to shuffle sideways. Erim was pulling herself to her feet. "How do you know my name?"

"You have forgotten, but I have not." The voice from Erim's mouth but her lips barely moved. "You won. We must play again."

"How did I win?" Alec asked as he stepped another metre away, glancing quickly in the direction of his slow flight before making each little move, yet loathe to take his eyes off Erim. Heaven only knew what she might do. Zombies could move fast if they wanted to, he was pretty sure about that. "I can't remember."

Erim's head cocked to one side as if her host was considering what to reply. Before another word was uttered, an impossibly loud screeching cut through the air. The station was being pulled apart. There was another bang as the floor was pounded again from below and a shuddering that didn't stop. The lights grew even darker, soaking the entire room in a burgundy hue that was nearly impossible to see through. Alec was knocked off his feet. Only instinct made him clutch his orb as he fell backwards.

Erim toppled against the bunk bed. He could hear the ringing smack of her forehead as it hit the bracket that held the upper bed in place. He winced reflexively. That would have totally hurt if she'd been alive.

The floor began to tilt, slowly at first, then quicker with each passing moment. Alec glanced at the windows. Sure enough he could only see the sky now as the station began to upend. He'd seen *Titanic*; he knew what was coming.

125

He scrambled to find something fixed to the floor, something to halt his inexorable slide towards the door that led to the outside hall. He had to get to the windows and somehow get himself out before the entire station sunk.

Blankets and chairs rolled past him. He shoved his

orb in his pocket and slammed both hands flat against the metal floor. His palms were sweaty but there was enough traction to hold him.

The floor tipped further upwards. It was now at least at a forty-five degree angle. The shudders were getting stronger, the metallic ripping sound slightly abating. Alec ignored it all. Digging the rubber soles of his shoes against the floor, he pushed himself centimetre by centimetre upwards.

"Alec, play now."

He ignored the voice. The windows were rising further away. He was sliding despite his best effort. Cursing under his breath, he turned his head to look behind him. Erim had tumbled with the rising floor and was lying against the wall just a metre or so from the entry door. Soon that wall would be the floor and if he didn't find something to hold onto soon, he'd end up right next to her.

Desperately he struggled to stay put but there was nothing to hold onto and the floor was now tilted like a playground slide. In the instant he realized that the new roaring he heard was water pouring into the hallway beyond, it was drowned out by a two-toned klaxon, blaring from the ceiling. The door was airtight; it hadn't let the gas in. But how long before the outside pressure blew the door open and the room flooded?

Panting with exertion, Alec considered his choices. Slide down into the vicinity of whatever possessed Erim, break through the window and take his chances in the poisonous air, or wait to drown when the water forced itself into the room or the station sunk beneath the surface.

Cripes.

There was another shudder, stronger this time, and the floor made a sudden lurch. Alec lost his grip. He began to slide. There was no way to stop it.

Below him, Erim's eyes almost glowed in the dark red light and a malevolent smile split her face in two.

"Come play, Alec," she said.

Riley sat in the galley of the Councilor's ship and picked at a ragged bit of skin around her thumbnail. It was *so* boring. The hours passed so slowly it was almost like time was in reverse. Darius was more furious with her than ever. He'd made himself scarce after their last little screaming match. She wasn't sure what had made him even angrier. Everything she said seemed to set him off. And Tyrell was either piloting for the Council or busy somewhere else on the ship, so he wasn't around to referee. The two of them were totally useless.

19

The dreaded interrogation had been a total anticlimax. Maybe two hours maximum of sitting in a chair while one of the insectoid aliens asked her questions about her time with Darius, what had happened on Earth, her relationship with Anna, her suspicions, and Alec. No one had asked about Alec's special, highly dangerous time-travel abilities. In fact, the topic was never mentioned. Which, when she thought about it, was very odd. Anna and Darius had warned them over and over that the Council would go to the ends of the galaxy to find and destroy a time shifter. Alec had shifted time twice. But was there even a whiff of interest in that subject? Even a casual mention of the topic? Nope.

Of course they didn't know about the several weeks she'd been alone with Alec and Darius, which permitted her to skip over a lot of sensitive information. Her inquisitor seemed to think Darius had picked her up and taken her and Alec straight to the underwater facility off the coast of Newfoundland. Riley assumed Darius had woven that shorter version of events and the Councilor was merely confirming his tale. The insectoid didn't even seem interested in Anna's dubious behaviour. Riley had to admit that when she was finished recounting her story and had listed all the facts and balanced them against her suspicions, there was very little evidence against the Ice Queen. The episode on the submersible was really the only clear indication that Anna was evil. Trying to kill someone was a pretty good give-away. But did it add up that she was the mole? Did Anna have another plan that Riley couldn't begin to imagine?

She scraped the last bit of black polish off her thumbnail. There was another seven cycles before they reached someplace called Mheeros and something called the Grand Senate took place. From what Riley could gather it was some pretentious get-together of all the planets' representatives and the overseeing Council. Tyrell had made it sound like there was a lot of pomp and circum-stance surrounding the actual meeting, all of it reported or televised in some alien way to all the planets involved. It sounded hugely stupid.

Her investigation into the mole was at a standstill. She'd exhausted all the questions she could ask Tyrell. He didn't have any more useful knowledge and besides, was as straight as an arrow when it came to his loyalty. She'd been allowed access to the ship's computer system but there was no information there she could use. While some of the languages were readable to her, thanks to her brain implant, many were incomprehensible and the data stores were mind-bogglingly huge. Even with the sophisticated search engines, she could only search so much. And no file was conveniently labelled "secret and highly dangerous Tyon information"—big surprise. The only other person she could interrogate was Darius, but that was less than pointless.

For one, he constantly avoided her. Plus, he couldn't be a double agent; he was too disarmingly open to hide a secret that big.

She'd lost several nights of sleep worrying about Kerry but eventually concluded that the Council knew her search was stalled while she was on their ship and so they knew there was no point in torturing him now.

With that worry lessened, the days had turned into one tedious slog. Maybe she'd learn to pilot one of these ships, she mused to herself as she swung a leg back and forth over the armrest. She'd planned on following her parents into medicine, and she supposed she still could, although now as a Tyon healer. It *would* be kind of cool to be able to just use her orb to save lives, but she'd have to complete the Tyon training program and undoubtedly that would be another absolute yawn. Of course, piloting around the universe would mean Tyon training too.

Across the room, the door opened. Riley didn't bother to look up; a tingling down her spine told her who it was. But she didn't acknowledge him when he came to stop directly in front of her.

"Up and on your feet," Darius ordered.

"Why?" Riley wouldn't look at his face. His arms were crossed and gauging the whiteness of his knuckles, he was annoyed. Good. If he was so blind to choose Anna over her, even after she'd told him about Anna's murderous ways, then the more pissed and miserable he was, the better. "I'm busy."

"Sucks to be you, then," he replied. "We've got work to do."

She nearly smiled at his use of the colloquial phrase. Sometimes he seemed so much more Terran than Tyon.

"Your training has to continue. We're wasting time on this ship. So, on your feet and come with me."

"And just who put that little gold nugget into your brain, buddy boy?" she drawled. "You've ignored me for days. If I wasn't training, who's fault was that?"

"Tyrell reminded me of my obligations." He sounded sulky. "Get up."

"No."

"Don't make me force you."

Riley locked her gaze with his. "I'd like to see you try."

He gave a one-shoulder shrug. "As you're so fond of saying, *whatever*."

Despite seeing him coming, there was nothing she could do to avoid him. Before she could maneuver herself out of the chair, he had her in his grip. He swung her like a sack of potatoes over his shoulder, turned and headed back to the door.

Riley grimaced but said nothing. No one was going to stop him—Guardians had full control over Potentials—and making a scene wasn't going to get either of them anywhere. Biting down a vicious retort, she stayed still.

Darius didn't seem to be in a terrible hurry. He strolled out of the room and turned left, heading down the empty corridor at a steady pace. He took the first stairwell down two levels, exiting into another identical empty corridor. He walked perhaps halfway around the circular perimeter before pausing in front of an unmarked door, where he pressed his palm against the recessed button. When the door dropped silently open, they crossed the threshold. Only then, as the door shut behind them, did he lower Riley to the ground.

They were in a huge room, long and narrow, which curved slightly to follow the outside hull of the ship. The narrow rectangular viewports showed only inky darkness. The glowing ceiling provided a soft and pleasant light. The floor was a spongy, grey material, the same the Tyons used in their sparring areas. Riley poked a toe into the floor. So, orb exercises were out.

She turned around to face Darius. She didn't get a chance to say anything. Like lightning, he was in attack mode. He grabbed her, spun her around and shoved her viciously to the ground. Despite the cushioned floor she hit it hard. The air rushed out of her lungs. He lunged on top of her and before she knew it, both hands were caught together in one of his and wrenched above her head. He threw his leg over her waist and pinned her to the floor.

He loomed over her as she lay immobile and gasping. There was a cold look in his eyes, one she couldn't remember seeing before. It suddenly struck her that she hardly knew him and they were alone. No one would come to her aid or even hear her if she screamed. The happy-go-lucky irreverent guy she'd hung around with was only one facet of his personality. She didn't know the others. And now she realized maybe she didn't want to.

"Get off me," she growled, struggling. He wasn't heavy but she couldn't move an inch. "This isn't funny."

His free hand grabbed her chin. He forced her to face him. "It's not meant to be."

"Okay, you've proved your point," she swallowed dryly, "now get off me."

"You've gone too far with your allegations," Darius ground out. "The Council has had me interrogated three times and they're not above using force to get what they want. I'd show you the bruises but they don't leave any. I've told you before you have a big mouth. Now you'll pay for it."

Abruptly he let her go and rolled off her. He was instantly on his feet. "Get up."

Riley rubbed her wrists. *She* would have bruises. "You're blind, Darius. You've been with Anna so long you can't see what she's really like." She got slowly to her feet.

"I know her better than *anyone*. *I've* known her for years. *You* met her months ago. That hardly makes you an expert."

"Sometimes, a new person can see things someone who is too close can't." She backed away to put a couple of metres between them. "And I only told the Council the facts about what happened to me. What Anna did. How she took Alec. How she tried to kill me."

"You're jealous of her," Darius said coldly. "Her beauty, her rank, her skill. Go on, admit it. You never liked her. You never gave her a chance. You hated her because of me."

"Do you *hear* yourself?" Riley gasped. "The woman told me she wanted me dead and she *actually* tried to do me in, and you're standing there accusing me of being jealous. Are you out of your mind?"

"Your allegations are ruining her career. They'll hunt her down and torture her trying to get some false truth."

"You're furious because you're afraid." Riley took another step away. She'd never outrun him; she had to reason her way out. "Deep down, you know that something about her doesn't ring true. Would the Anna you know and love try and kill me?"

A spasm of uncertainly crossed Darius's face, just for an instant, and then was gone. The cold look of fury replaced it. He noticed her glance at the door and a tight smile curled his lips. "You're not going anywhere. Not for a long time, Riley. I have my orders to continue your training and I plan to do exactly that. But we both know you're never going to be anything more than average with an orb, don't we? So we better ensure you can protect yourself. The old-fashioned way."

Riley's stomach dropped to her feet. She'd watched Darius fight a long time ago. The man was lightning fast and underhanded. He'd bested men twice her size who had years of training. The look he was giving her now indicated he wasn't going to go easy just because she was a novice. She was going to be seriously hurt if she couldn't stop him.

"Darius, listen to me. *Please.* Something is wrong here. We've been friends for ages. You've saved my life. Why are you so angry now?"

He took a step forward. "The first step in physical combat is 'be prepared'."

"Darius, stop. You have to listen to me. You're not yourself. Something is wrong." She backed away as he walked forward.

"The second step is 'know your enemy'."

"You don't want to do this, Dare," she pleaded. She didn't take her eyes off him as she retreated. He had longer legs and each step forward brought him closer. His eyes narrowed to slits.

"The third is 'consider your surroundings'."

She turned and ran.

"I underestimated his ability, Kholar. I will need to change our plans."

Alec came to slowly. He was lying down on something relatively uncomfortable and nothing seemed to really hurt. Anna was talking nearby. Alec kept his eyes closed and feigned sleeping.

"I agree," Kholar's voice came from Alec's left while Anna's came from his right as if they were standing on either side of him. "He has broken your Kira twice now. Impressive."

"It was established too quickly," Anna sounded defensive. "Darius's was woven gently into his mind over years. It will never break or be corrupted. And the seeds of anger I planted are slowly growing. It won't be long before they come to fruition. If they haven't already."

"But this boy," Kholar continued, "is not the same as Finn."

"No. Stronger. Perhaps more obstinate than Darius," Anna paused, thinking. "He's too young for the type of persuasion I used with Darius that sealed my Kira's grip."

That was annoying, Alec thought. He would be sixteen in a couple of months, practically an adult.

"Then how do you propose to accomplish our task? He must be brought on board."

Alec could almost hear the smile in her voice. "Alec greatly values the truth. He fights for what

20

he believes in. I'll tell him our plan and the reasons behind it and—"

"What do you mean?" Kholar interrupted angrily. "It's not—"There was a short pause, then Kholar continued and he too, sounded pleased, "Yes, I see. Well, I will leave it to you. Continue."

There were footsteps as someone left the room. Alec lay still and waited. Anna started humming softly and he heard her move away. Warily, he cracked open one eye and took a quick glimpse.

He was in a small room, Tyon in construction, with no one else but Anna. She was at a far counter with her back to him, looking at something in her hands. He was lying on a raised narrow table and covered with a blanket. Anna must have heard his change in breathing pattern. She turned and smiled.

"Are you feeling all right, Alec?" she asked kindly. She crossed over the few steps and reached out to stroke his forehead with her right hand. She held her crystal necklace in her left.

"Yeah, I guess so." Alec relaxed at the familiar touch. He always felt so much better when Anna touched him.

"You were seconds away from death," Anna explained. "The entire station was nearly under water and most of it had flooded. The emergency beacon reached us just in the nick of time, as you Earthlings would say."

"Yeah, I guess so," Alec repeated. He could barely remember her sudden arrival in the flooded station. His failing air bubble had blurred his vision. Either that or the poisonous fumes he'd breathed. "Why'd you knock me out?"

"I was unsure if the Others had infected you or just Erim. I could not take any chances. Unconscious, I was able to transport you to the ship with the assistance of a transporter and make a full assessment."

"The Others can't control someone with the Tyon gene," Alec reminded her, the words pouring forth without actual memory.

"They can if you're dead," she countered. "And the Others' power seems to be growing. We have no idea what they can or cannot do anymore. I considered it prudent to be careful."

"Okay," Alec sighed as she withdrew her hand. He sat up. "I guess that makes sense."

"Good. I wish to have a serious conversation with you. Are you well enough to walk with me?"

Alec swung his legs over the side of the table in response and tossed the blanket to the end. He hopped down onto the floor. Even his wrist didn't hurt anymore. "What happened to Paran?"

"Drowned," Anna said nonchalantly, as if talking about an inanimate object, not someone she had worked with for ages.

Alec nodded. He couldn't say he wasn't sorry. He certainly hadn't liked the bodyguard, but the gas leak had been his fault and, consequently, so had Paran's death. He should really feel more remorse. Anna led him out into a circular corridor that was familiar. He must be back on board the *Rua*. They walked slowly side by side.

"How did the break in the seals occur, Alec?" Anna asked as she stared straight ahead. "Eu station was constructed to withstand a variety of insults."

"I dunno," Alec muttered. He quickly changed the subject. "What was attacking it?"

"Other than insects, the only life on that planet is below the water's surface," Anna answered. "Creatures that are generally docile and limit any interactions with us. However, when the seal was broken the station emitted a distress signal that was irritating to them. Hence the attack."

They walked on for another minute in silence while Alec digested the information that he was responsible for the sinking of the station, too. It was somewhat sobering.

No one passed by them as they walked. Alec knew everyone must be working on the bridge. They passed the viewport and Alec paused to take a quick look. There was nothing but endless blackness in all directions and tiny diamonds of light so far away it was unimaginable.

"How did the Others find you, Alec?"

Somehow, that wasn't what he had expected her to ask.

"I dunno. He just does."

"You were holding your orb, weren't you? Sending a message to me."

"Yeah. I guess so."

"Do you remember your first interaction with the Others? It was a long time ago. You travelled with a girl from Earth and one of our Guardians, Darius Finn."

Alec nodded slowly. "Sort of. I mean, I have memories of it, but they aren't too clear. Like I was watching a TV show and missed most of the episodes."

"You fought the Others before, Alec, and somehow managed to beat them. We need to access that ability."

"Why? Are they going to attack us here?"

"The Others have a plan to destroy the entire Tyon Collective. You might not remember, but the Tyons are all that stand between the Others and any planet they victimize. Without us, world after world will fall to the same horrible fate as Earth. You don't want that, do you?"

Of course not. Alec hadn't thought much about what had happened to his world. It was strangely settled in his mind, something he knew intellectually but had absolutely no feelings about. But he knew he *should* have emotions. His parents were dead on that planet and the Others were the cause. "So, what can I do?"

"Help us," Anna replied.

"To do what?" Alec reached out and ran a fingertip along the wall as he walked. The metal was cool to his touch and slightly slippery. He didn't like the sensation and dropped his hand to his side.

"Catch and destroy the traitor who is working against us to ensure the Others are successful."

"Do you know who that is? I mean, I'm not a detective or anything. I don't know how I'd find out who it was."

"We already know," Anna said quietly. "We've been following him for a long time now, learning how he operates, watching him turn Potential after Potential against the organization. He's incredibly subtle. No one else has suspected and it has taken us years to gather enough proof. Even some in the upper echelons of the Collective and even in the Council still are not convinced because of the traitor's personality. He seems so innocuous, so likeable."

"So, do I know him?" Alec asked but he had the feeling he already knew the answer.

"Darius Finn is the spy. He recruited you and a Terran girl named Riley to work with him. We think he brainwashed the two of you into believing you were helping your planet. But secretly, you were merely pawns, working to create a situation of terror and destruction on Earth."

Alec stopped walking. He rubbed his forehead. "Are you sure? I mean, I don't remember much about the guy but I never got a sense he was a bad person."

"He isn't," Anna agreed surprisingly. "Even I was convinced for the longest time he was working for us. But I've learned that he truly believes that the Tyon Collective is dangerous and wrong, that the Council is making a mistake. In his own way, he's doing what he believes is the right thing."

"By letting the Others destroy entire worlds?" Alec shook his head. "How could anyone think that's a good thing to do?"

Anna shrugged. "I don't know if you remember, but the Tyon Collective is a secretive organization, developed and supported by the Intergalactic Council for the purpose of invisibly keeping the Others under control. Because politically, the Council cannot be seen to be interfering in the actions of other worlds and species. I think Darius believes that by helping the Others, he can persuade the Council to dissolve the Collective. If that happens, there will be no opposition to the Others. They will decimate world after world. Eventually, the Council will have to openly do something about them. Destroy them perhaps, or confine them to a small portion of the galaxy where they can do no harm. So ultimately, his intentions are good."

"We have a saying back on Earth," Alec said. "The road to hell is paved with good intentions."

Anna raised an eyebrow. "That is an accurate reflection of the situation."

"But didn't you say that this Darius guy was dead? Or did I dream that?"

Anna swung a companionable arm around Alec's shoulder and urged him to start walking again. "You are correct. We did think so. The reason I had to leave you on Eu station was to acquire secret information from one of our contacts. I now know he isn't dead. Nor is the young female you were travelling with. Worse still, they are determined to go through with their plan and stage an assassination at the next Council meeting. We must stop them."

Alec's stomach did a funny little leap. That girl, the one he sometimes dreamed about, she was still alive. All of a sudden, he wanted to see her again, even if she was an enemy. "I thought you were in control of Darius or something?" The words were out of his mouth before he realized.

Anna smiled. "You were listening."

Alec shrugged. "Sort of."

"I did train Darius, that is true, and worked hard to harness his wild impulsiveness to the Tyon way. I did it slowly, over the years, in the same way I train you. I fear I was not wholly effective but certainly some of the edicts

I imparted cannot be broken. Whether it will be enough to prevent his disgrace, I do not know."

That made sense. Anna hadn't done anything wrong, not really. There was nothing *off* about her involvement with Darius. Kholar was talking about something else. Alec was terribly relieved.

"I have a plan for you, Alec. One I hope you have the strength and intelligence to perform. It is absolutely vital for the safety of our galaxy."

Alex's chest swelled with pride. She obviously didn't think he was a kid if she had such an important job for him. "Sure. Anything. You know I can do it."

"It will require stealth and cunning."

"I can be sneaky when I want to," he urged.

"Excellent. I knew I had not made a mistake in selecting you." Anna smiled warmly enough to melt Alec's last reservation. "Listen carefully. You will return to Finn and pledge yourself to him. I will provide you with a plausible explanation for your absence. Once he believes you are willing to complete his task you will, at the crucial moment, thwart his attempt to murder the members of the Intergalactic Council."

"How in the hell will I do that?" he gasped.

Anna swung him around to face her. In the dim light her face held more shadows than usual. "I would think that was obvious, Alec. You will have to kill him."

He was faster than her and far stronger. Riley knew instinctively that running would only inflame his anger but she couldn't stop herself. The cold look in his eye scared her to her core.

She bolted straight for the door but he reached it an instant before her. He slammed his back into the wall, spreading his arms wide. Riley couldn't stop her forward motion in time and barrelled into him. Her breath was expelled forcefully with the impact. She pushed away, surprised that he didn't try and hold onto her. But then, Darius wasn't above being cruel.

"There's nowhere to go, Riley."

She ran anyway, trying to put as much distance between them. She slowed near the far wall and stopped when she didn't hear his breath behind her or his footsteps. Gulping to catch her breath, she turned.

21

He was still leaning against the door. A cold calculating look marred his features. His face was flushed and his eyes over-bright, as if he'd been drugged. Riley rubbed her sweating palms against her legs. Maybe that was it?

"Darius, you aren't yourself," she said slowly, forcing her voice to remain steady and calm. "Something's wrong with you."

A chilling smile spread slowly across his face.

"I'm serious, Dare. You'd never hurt me. I know that. You've been drugged or something."

"You know nothing. You're a child, playing at

being a grown-up. I'm not what you think." Darius pushed himself off the wall and took a step towards her.

"You're sworn to protect me," Riley tried. "As a Guardian. You took an oath. Remember?"

For a second his expression faltered with uncertainty before the smirk replaced it again. He continued to walk with slow and deliberate steps towards her. "I'm training you in hand-to-hand combat."

"I don't want to learn hand to hand combat. It's stupid."

His grin disappeared. "Like me, you mean? Isn't that what you've being saying all along. I'm stupid for loving Anna. I'm stupid for believing her. I'm stupid for spending all this time training with the Tyons, for accepting their ways and joining them. Not like you, Riley. You're too smart for *that*, aren't you? Got it all figured out, haven't you? The entire universe isn't what you thought it was, there's power out there you'd never even contemplated, but you *know*."

There was nowhere to run. He'd demonstrated that quite effectively. And she wasn't going to last a minute putting up a resistance. He'd stop when he realized she wasn't fighting back. Let her go. He had to.

"Darius," she began again, licking lips that were as dry as parchment. "Anna might have done something to you. A long time ago. When you were a kid and she was assigned to train you. There's the possibility, you have to admit it."

Darius was an arm's length away. He said nothing.

"It might not have even been Anna," she gasped in desperation, "it might have been someone controlling *her*. You can't disagree that this behaviour is completely unlike you."

Darius lunged. Riley dropped to the floor and curled into a ball. She wasn't going to make this worse by hitting him back. She felt his hands bite into her right arm, pull and twist. She couldn't help the scream that left her lips as her arm was engulfed in burning pain. She felt the sickening pop as her elbow dislocated with Darius's last sharp wrench.

Then she dropped into the soothing oblivion of unconsciousness.

The medical facility on the Council's ship was much larger than that of Logan's ship, but the technology was much the same. Riley sat on the edge of a meditube and watched as the healer held a portable ultrasound device to her broken left wrist. The pain was already almost non-existent although the pulsing burn from the machine was unpleasant. The bruising they couldn't do much about but the broken bones in her wrist and ribs were easily, if slowly, fixed and her elbow joint restored to function. She raised her eyes momentarily to her assailant.

Darius leaned against the wall near the exit and watched with hooded eyes. He'd been silent since the "lesson" had ended. He'd carried her up to the facility, dumped her on a meditube and waited over the several hours while the medics had quietly gone about their business. Whatever he'd been feeling—remorse, vindication, or something darker—had not been apparent in his words but his expressive face told another story.

The door opened and Tyrell strode in. He took in the situation with one sharp glance then turned and grabbed Darius's neck, shoving him forcefully up against the wall. "Explain this, Finn."

"Get your hands off me," Darius managed to croak as his face turned bright red.

Tyrell's granite jaw didn't slacken but his grip lessened enough for Darius's colour to return to normal. Darius jerked himself out of Tyrell's grip and sidestepped out of reach. "You're breaking protocol."

"Violence towards Potentials is not permitted," Tyrell said. He gave a quick nod of his head towards Riley. "That includes her."

"We were sparring. It got out of hand," Darius said. Riley noted he didn't meet Tyrell's eyes; his gaze was directly focused on her. If there was an unspoken message in his gaze, she couldn't decode it.

Tyrell turned to face her. "Purposeful or accident?"

Riley tried to swallow past the lump in her throat. She stared at her shoes. Somehow saying the words out loud were too painful. Whatever had been between her and Darius was now broken and that thought was far more painful than any bruise. It didn't, mind you, detract one iota from her blazing fury.

"I'll have her removed from your assignment if I so much as suspect mistreatment in the future, do you understand me?" Tyrell had turned back to Darius. "You might not like her suspicions—neither do I. But all facts must be reviewed and contemplated. The Collective is possibly in danger from within. No one is above suspicion. Including you." He stepped back towards the door. "Riley, keep your mouth shut and don't goad him further. You won't turn his affections to you by poisoning his concern for Anna." With that, Tyrell left.

The medical facility was deathly quiet. The medics continued their work as if there had been no interruption. Darius straightened his jumpsuit with slightly unsteady hands. For a moment he looked as if he might say something, then abruptly turned on his heel and dashed through the door. The ache in Riley's throat continued to build until she couldn't stand it any longer and the tears fell.

The medic at her side remained silent; nothing in her actions suggested she even cared. Riley wiped her face on her sleeve and quietly hiccupped. Her emotions were conflicted and no matter what she thought, it only brought pain. Why had she ever gotten off that train in Toronto? She now knew that Darius had used his Tyon persuasion to get her to come with him, but for heaven's sake why hadn't she fought it harder? Run the second she saw him?

She was totally alone now. Her parents were gone; her idiot sister; Alec; Kerry and now Darius too. It was so unfair. What had she done to deserve this? The fury was rapidly burning itself out, quenched by despair.

"I'm tired," she murmured to the medic who was still working on her wrist. "I want to lie down." She settled herself on the narrow tube table and closed her eyes.

The minutes flowed into an hour but Riley didn't notice. The medics quietly went about their jobs and it was soothing, in a way, having this time to be alone with her thoughts and yet not be physically by herself.

The door opened again and she couldn't help glancing up, steeling herself internally to meet aquamarine eyes, but it wasn't Darius. Several medics streamed through the door guiding a floating stretcher. They crowded around it so closely she couldn't see who was lying on it. One of the insectoid Councilors followed them in and stood by the door as it closed.

Silently they lifted the body into a meditube. Riley heard the *whoosh* as the glass covering closed. The tube filled rapidly with white mist while most of the medics held their sensors over the glass and one stared at a computer screen on the wall. The door opened again and several Tyon officers, Tyrell included, filed in. They took their place against the wall beside the Councilor. Riley caught Tyrell's intense look but she closed her eyes, ignoring him. Tyrell was the most intense person she'd ever met—he probably pooped diamonds every morning—and she couldn't face one more second of his scrutiny.

"Report," ordered the Councilor in its mechanical voice.

"The ship was a small, personal vehicle, generally utilized for short interstellar distances," said the man next to Tyrell. He was much shorter and of a slighter build than the pilot, but several decades older. Riley had seen him in the galley. "Its registration indicates it is from the Orion system. We are reviewing its data banks to determine why it is so far from home. There is no information so far on the only living passenger, other than he was placed in deep stasis. The crew of the ship is dead and the ship is badly damaged."

"Indications of attack?"

"Several. Undetermined aggressor, but the laser pattern is consistent with Mheer technology."

The Councilor was silent for a moment. "Have the bodies brought on board. We will determine the cause of death. We must have conclusive proof before we make any accusations, Captain."

"Agreed, Councilor," the Captain began. "But the Mheer grow restless and their ambition is obvious. At the last Grand Council—"

"I was present, Captain. I am most certainly aware of the Mheer delegation and their quest for increased revenues and autonomy. Do as you have been instructed."

The Captain bobbed his head and left. The others stared at the meditube silently. A medic handed a small handheld computer tablet to the instectoid Councilor. Through slitted eyes, Riley watched the Councilor's antennae weave over the tablet, then still.

"This is a Terran male," the Councilor said.

Riley gasped. *Someone from home.* She sat partway up, her fatigue rapidly draining away.

"None of our Potentials are missing," Tyrell said quietly. He raised his eyes momentarily to Riley. "All were taken to Celes."

"This Terran has an implant. It has been rendered non-functioning," the Councilor continued. "This is highly unusual. Medic, initiate the procedure for acquiring all implant information and re-start the device. We must determine who this is. And more importantly, what he knows."

Riley's heart had started beating loudly and her

mouth had gone dry. She didn't need to have the implant's information to know who was lying in that meditube. Slowly she lay back down and averted her face from the crowd. If Alec was now here, and she hoped with all her heart he was, then Anna wasn't far behind. And if Anna *was* around, she'd soon know that the attempt on her life had failed and if *that* happened.... Riley swallowed tightly. Anna didn't give up. She wouldn't let Riley go, especially with everything Riley knew and had told.

A jolt of adrenaline shot through her system. *Darius.* He would follow Anna's orders to the ends of the universe. Would he go so far as to kill her under Anna's orders? Was *that* what had happened in the sparring room hours ago?

Cripes, she wasn't safe on this ship. Who in the world could help her now?

Alec sat at a table and stared out the wide viewport to the universe beyond. Multiple plates of food littered the table along with two beakers of fluid and several types of cutlery, all quite alien. He didn't have much of an appetite; nothing he tasted was familiar or even very pleasant. His head still hurt and he felt odd as if he'd had the flu or something and was just getting over it. He'd only been allowed out of the medical facility that morning (or was it afternoon?) and had spent his first hours of freedom with Darius Finn, touring the massive spaceship. After seeing the comfortable quarters he was to share with other passengers, they'd ended up in the galley, where Darius obtained a variety of foods for Alec to try.

He'd been awake for a day or so before his release, confined to the medical facility while medics probed him and hooked his head up to various machines. He wasn't sure exactly what they were looking for, nor could he answer many of the questions he'd been asked over and over again. How did you end up on the spaceship? *I don't know.* Who gave you the implant? *What implant?* Where is Anna? *Who?*

Darius sat down beside him and set a small bowl in front of him. "Here, try this."

"What is it?" Alec asked warily. It looked like a bowl of worms.

"Mithrus. Sort of like rice noodles on Earth. A bit spicy. You should like them."

"Ew gross, it's moving. Is it alive?" Alec pushed the bowl away.

Darius moved the bowl back. "No. It's a chemical thing. Because it's warm. Go on, try."

Alec paused for a moment to watch the thick pale pink noodles quietly writhe in the bowl before reaching for the utensil that most closely resembled a fork. Carefully, he dug into the bowl, twirling a few of the long slender tubes around the tines and slowly raising them to his mouth. He paused again.

"It won't bite you," Darius laughed.

Alec popped the noodles in his mouth. He froze for a second, then began to chew. A slight expression of relief crossed his face.

Darius leaned back in his chair and linked his fingers behind his head. He gave Alec an appraising look. "It's hard to believe you're here, you know."

Alec shrugged and shoved another mouthful into his mouth. Now that he found something he liked, his appetite was returning with a vengeance.

"What's the last thing you remember?"

Alec sighed. Not again. "Going to the mall with my friends."

"You can't remember meeting me. Is that true?"

Alec swallowed the noodles. The name hadn't rung a bell when he'd been asked about Finn but now, having spent time with the man, there was something clearly memorable about him. Familiar, yet he made Alec feel uncomfortable, almost like the way he felt about his favourite coach after hearing some unsavoury rumours. "I didn't remember your name," he said as he loaded up his utensil with another huge mouthful. "One of the medics told me we've met before. That we travelled together and stuff."

"And stuff indeed." Darius's sly look made the back of Alec's neck prickle. He leaned forward conspiratorially. "And orbs? Do you remember these?" He pulled out a small spherical crystal from his pocket and balanced it in the middle of his hand.

Alec reached out and took it. He held it up to the light. The smooth crystalline sphere was a bit bigger than a golf ball and an opaque pale purple. Alec could see fissures deep within the crystal matrix when he turned it over. He tightened his fist around it without thinking. A warm sensation of comfort mixed with tinges of elation and self-confidence spread through his body. He glanced up to see Darius's satisfied expression.

"You never really forget the orb once you've learned to use one," Darius said. "No matter what happens to your brain. It lives in your bones forever."

"I want one of these," Alec heard himself say.

"Of course you do," Darius agreed. "Keep that one. I have another."

"What does it do?"

"Finish your meal and I'll show you."

"Show me here," Alec said, abruptly pushing the almost finished bowl away. "I want to know now."

"We have an audience," Darius said quietly. His green-blue eyes flicked around the galley. "Orbs are secret just the way the power you hold inside you is secret. I'll let you know who you can trust."

Alec felt the truth in his words. "Let me finish these noodle things and then we'll go."

They left the galley a few minutes later, heading out into the main ship.

In the corridors, they passed individuals who were both crew and passengers. Darius pointed out that the ships' crew wore dark navy uniforms while the passengers, from a range of planets and species, wore their own personal attire that ranged from flowing cloaks and face-covering hoods to absolutely nothing. Alec had to avert his eyes. Nudity wasn't something he was used to, except in his fantasies, and its blatant display made him uncomfortable. And worse, some of the people who passed him didn't seem human at all. It was hard to know where to *not* look—the body parts oozing past him were completely unfamiliar. The scents, too. He'd had to hold his breath more than once.

After several minutes they arrived at a small room with no viewport and a spongy floor. Darius allowed Alec to enter first. Alec turned back just as Darius did something to the controls.

"Why did you lock the door?" Alec asked. He felt a bit nervous. It wasn't as if he really knew this guy.

"I don't want to be interrupted," Darius replied as he brushed past Alec and walked to the middle of the room. He dropped to the floor and folded his legs into a cross-legged position with a fluidity that made Alec's knees ache. He pulled out his orb from his overall pocket and held it out in the middle of his palm. His was the palest pink and slightly larger than Alec's. "Come on, I'll start your first lesson. Again."

"What do you mean, 'again'?"

Darius gave a slight laugh. "We've done this before, you and I. Several months ago I gave you your first lesson on an orb."

Alec sat slowly down across from Darius and mimicked his stance. "I don't remember it."

"Too bad. Fun times," Darius gave a slight snort of derision.

"Really?"

"No." Darius shook his head. "I was just trying out this sarcasm thing Riley always goes on about. We were in serious trouble the first time you did this. Rhozan was on our heels and we kept getting cornered. It's a wonder the three of us weren't killed. Of course, I saved both your backsides."

The word Rhozan gave Alec chills. "Who?"

"Interdimensional invaders intent on sucking your planet dry of negative emotions. Rhozan is one of them, or maybe all of them, we don't know. But a seriously bad dude, either way."

"You said the three of us. Who else?"

"Riley." Darius watched him closely. Alec could almost see the question marks in Darius's eyes.

"Sorry, I don't remember him."

"Her," Darius corrected. "Riley Cohen is a girl. Short, skinny, thinks boys are idiots. Actually, thinks everyone is an idiot. Is it coming back to you now?"

Alec found himself squeezing his orb tightly as he cast his thoughts back. *Riley*, the name didn't ring a bell, but he knew there was *someone* he felt strongly about. Someone small and vulnerable. Someone he'd held in his arms. Someone with navy... "Does she have blue eyes? Like the ocean?"

The edges of Darius's lips curled upwards. "Like the sea on a calm and sunny day."

"I think it's coming back. I mean, there's something just on the edge of my memory. I feel like I might remember her but I don't get any pictures in my head. What happened to her?"

"Nothing," Darius said, a tad curtly. "She's here on this ship. She's been ignoring me, but we can go and find her after the lesson if you want."

Alec felt a frisson of excitement but he shrugged his shoulders. "Sure, if you want to."

Darius only smiled. "The key to using your orb," he started, "is to relax and let your mind do what it is naturally able to do. We'll start with some concentration exercises and work our way up. Hopefully you catch on a lot faster this time."

152   Several hours later Darius was smiling a lot more broadly. So was Alec as he stood and stretched the kinks out of his back and neck. The time had flown as they'd rapidly moved from one exercise to another. Alec was keen to keep going but Darius said he had other things to do. As he followed Darius out of the room and back up the stairs,

Alec was still caught up in his astonishment of the things he could do with the orb—and Darius had promised there was much more.

Absorbed in his new and fascinating power, he didn't notice that Darius had come to a sudden stop. He plowed right into him and almost knocked him over.

"Sorry," Alec muttered with embarrassment. He raised his eyes to see what had caused the hold up and... *She's beautiful.* His brain stopped working.

"Alec, this is Riley. Our previous companion." Darius stood still, his eyes flicking back and forth from the girl in front of him to Alec. Alec only swallowed sharply. Suddenly everything he was wearing seemed to be too tight and he couldn't breathe.

The girl looked shocked too. Her face was pale and her blue eyes were huge, like an anime cartoon. She didn't seem to know what to say either.

"Riley, you remember Alec?" Darius said with a sharp bite to his tone.

The girl nodded. Her lips were pressed into a tight line. She was wearing a grey overall like Darius's except that hers was too big for her, and she'd rolled the cuffs up on the arms and legs. She had a silver stud through one eyebrow. Alec couldn't tell if there was another one as her bangs were cut in a weird geometric fashion that partially obscured the other side of her face. She looked like she could use a seriously strong hug. Without thought, Alec took a step towards her.

Riley bolted. She was down the hall and out of sight before Alec could even blink.

"Man, she's fast," he said to himself.

"Well, that was touching," Darius mused. He half turned to Alec. "That was sarcasm again, in case you missed it."

"Huh?" Alec was still staring down the corridor. Every particle of his being was telling him to go after her. Only his brain refused to comply.

23

Riley leaned her forehead against the viewport and studied her reflection. Her eyes looked wild and glassy, her cheeks were on fire and if her hands hadn't been balled into fists they would have been shaking. Running, running, running. This reaction *had* to stop. Home life in chaos after her mom left? Work all waking hours in a bookstore and rarely go home. Father about to marry the troll who wrecked her parent's marriage? High tail it to Vancouver to stay with her sister. See the man who'd broken her bones and her heart only hours before? Dash down the hallway as fast as her legs would take her. It was time to grow up and face things as they were. Fight back. Stand her ground. She groaned and closed her eyes for a moment. Easier said than done.

And to make matters exponentially worse, she'd reacted to Alec like a thirteen-year-old meeting her favourite boy band. She was *not* going to think about how hot Alec had looked; suddenly older and more experienced than she remembered. She was not going to notice how dark his eyes were or the width of his shoulders or *anything*. She was just caught off guard. It could happen to anyone.

Right. She'd caught Darius's sly look and heard the tone of his voice. He'd seen exactly what had happened between her and Alec and she knew with absolute certainty that the next time she saw him, he'd rub her nose in it.

She took several deep, cleansing breaths. Of

course she'd known Alec was okay and she'd assumed that eventually he'd be let out of the medical station. It was just that she'd been sure it would take much longer for her to run into him, that she'd have a lot more time to mentally prepare herself. Almost bumping into him in a hallway ages before she expected to see him, was what had thrown her off. That and having Darius watch them meet. Darius, who'd turned on her and broken her bones.

She could deal with this. Alec was a lot younger than her, she reminded herself. He'd likely be just as flustered as she'd been. He'd take his cues from her. All she needed to do was figure out how to explain her stupid reaction and play it nonchalant. He'd follow along.

The bigger problem was Anna. If Alec was alive, then she was. Perhaps Alec knew where Anna was hiding? Could she get close enough to him to weasel the information out of his head? Did he even know? He'd been found unconscious; maybe he was brain damaged? After all, he hadn't remembered who she was. Riley shuddered slightly. Alec might not be of any help to her—in fact he might be dangerous. And she couldn't count on Darius to protect her now and somehow, considering Anna's long association with the Tyons, the Collective was not likely to take her side over Anna's. Not without exhaustive proof. That proof, Riley thought ruefully, would likely constitute her lifeless body on the ground in front of them and Anna standing with a smoking gun in her hand.

In the distance, the galley door opened and closed with the peculiar *shushing* all the doors on the spacecraft made, but Riley was too lost in thought to notice. The galley was the busiest part of this ship and since there was safety in numbers, her feet had unintentionally brought her here. She only glanced up when someone slipped into the booth beside her.

"Hi," Alec said.

Riley straightened up and plastered a blank look over

her features while her heart rate doubled. He was a stranger, Riley reminded herself, and she had no idea what had happened to him during the long time they'd been apart. Especially since he'd been under Anna's influence. He could have the same weird mind control thingy that Darius probably had going on, and that was very dangerous. Keep it cool, she reminded herself, tread carefully. "Did you follow me?" she asked, inwardly cringing at the sharp tone.

"Yeah," Alec nodded. He didn't look awkward or nervous to see her. "You looked totally spooked to see me and Darius said you might be upset. Because of before."

"Be...*fore*?" Riley asked as she stared intently straight in front of them and avoided his gaze. Their reflection in the viewport directly opposite gave her a clear image of him. He looked essentially the same, although his hair was slightly longer and there was definitely some dark fuzz on his chin and jaw that hadn't been there when they were on the run together. But that wasn't what had the hair on the back of her neck standing on end. There was something else. Something in the way he held himself that hinted he was now more a man than boy. What had happened to him while they were apart?

Alec leaned forward slightly and dropped his voice. "Cuz, we were, you know, *involved*."

Riley leaned back. Her mouth was dry. She picked at the last remaining bit of nail polish on her index finger. "Is that what Darius told you?"

"Yeah. But I knew anyway." She could hear the smile in his voice and she couldn't help but glance at him. He was wearing his lopsided grin, mischief in his eyes.

156   Riley thought quickly. She knew why Darius had told him that little pearl and even if it wasn't strictly true—and she was not going to admit it anyway—there was a chance that if she played her cards right, she could use Darius's exaggeration to her benefit. Having Alec on her side as an ally was necessary if Anna came back into the picture. That

was, if he was receptive to being on her side. "Well, yeah, sort of. I mean we were pretty busy and didn't get a whole lot time to go out. What with running from Rhozan and the Tyons and everything."

"You'll have to fill me in on it. I can't remember," Alec said. He leaned back in the seat and his thigh pressed slightly against hers. He started tapping his fingers on the tabletop absently. The familiar movement made her grin.

"Really? Nothing? You don't remember Darius kidnapping us on that crappy houseboat? Hiding out in the farmhouse? Nearly getting killed, like, half a dozen times? You've forgotten all of it?"

Alec gave a rueful shrug of one shoulder. "Guess so. Last thing I remember is heading to the mall with the guys. After that, nada."

Riley whistled. "That's a lot of time lost." Not to mention some highly important information, like how to fight Rhozan and win *and* how to move people through time.

"Tell me about it. I have impressions of things but no facts or clear memories. Like for instance, Darius said that Earth got blasted by this Rhozan guy and some group called the Others."

Riley turned her head away and stared out the viewport. "Rhozan *is* the Others. He, she, whatever it is, turns people against one another, releases all their pent up frustration and anger and lets it go. People start fighting, the fights escalate and then boom, there you have it. Nuclear war."

"Are you kidding me?"

"Nope."

"On Earth?" Alec swore under his breath. "Did you see it?"

Riley nodded. She'd never get the vision of cascading explosions tearing across the Earth's surface out of her mind, no matter how long she lived. She blinked quickly to prevent the tears from falling.

"And your family?" he asked quietly.

"Gone," Riley answered around the lump in her throat. "Same as yours. Everyone we know, except Darius, is dead."

There was a long minute of silence. Riley reached up and tried to unobtrusively wipe the tear from her cheek with the back of her hand. She was *not* going to cry. She startled as a warm hand encircled her own and squeezed gently.

"Tell me about your family," Alec said. "You must have told me before, but I can't remember. Who'd you lose?"

Riley licked her lips before clearing her throat. She didn't pull her hand away but she couldn't look directly at him either. "My dad is a cardiologist. I mean he was. In Halifax. He was going to get married this summer. The stepmonster was a complete idiot so it's no loss if she burned to a crisp." Riley paused, almost as if afraid to continue. Alec squeezed her hand again and the floodgates opened. "He and my mom split up a long time ago after he cheated on her. Mom was so angry. She said it was humiliating to have everyone know and talk behind her back. She took off to Africa, joined a humanitarian organization and won an award for her work. Guess I wasn't enough to make her stay."

"How old were you?"

"Twelve." Riley straightened up and raised her chin. "Old enough to manage. My sister Debra didn't care. She had her boyfriends and her acting classes and her dreams of being a big star. I ran the house and stuff. I didn't need my mom for anything anyway."

"It still hurt though," Alec said thoughtfully. "Didn't it?

"What happened to your parents?" Riley changed the subject. "I met them briefly and they seemed as messed up as mine."

Alec took a deep breath. For a moment Riley thought he might not answer. He let go of her hand for a second, then wove his fingers through hers, linking them together, palm to palm. She ignored the butterflies in her stomach.

"When I was a kid, our lives were pretty much perfect. Dad ran a sporting goods company. He had a bunch of stores and was doing really well. Mom didn't have to work. She was home with Peter and me all the time. I remember just generally being happy. You know how it is when you're little. About two years ago, Dad got sick. Mom called it a major depression. He refused to go to the doctor. Said he could beat it on his own. But he started drinking, I guess to feel better, and that just made everything worse. He lost the business. The judge made us sell everything to pay the bills. They even took my bike."

There wasn't much to say. Riley had met Alec's parents under difficult circumstances and hadn't had a favourable impression, but of course, there was more to any situation that met the eye. There always was.

"Your mom was a pretty tough woman," Riley said gently. "She looked after everyone. You're a lot like her."

Alec gave a half smile, "When I was growing up my mom always said I reminded her of my dad. The last couple of years I thought that was an insult, coz he couldn't beat the booze and stuff. But I think you're right." He paused for a moment. "It's hard to believe that they're really dead. I mean, since I didn't see it and everything, it's like it isn't real."

The lump in her throat made talking too difficult. She nodded and glanced down at their entwined hands on the table. They looked good together; her small, pale fingers and his larger, brown ones. She could feel his emotions sliding up her arm and into her mind; deep sadness, frustration and something new and exciting. He was as aware of her as she was of him. He wanted to kiss her.

She couldn't help it. As his face moved closer to hers she held her breath. He reached out and stroked her cheek with his thumb. When he pulled back she noticed his thumb was wet. She hadn't noticed she was still crying.

Alec leaned in even closer. Then he was kissing her. At

159

first it was the lightest of touches, as if he was unsure of her response. She sighed against his mouth. With that, the kiss deepened. His free hand slid across the line of her jaw and around the back of her neck, cupping her head. His lips tasted salty and remarkably pleasant against hers. Soft and yet firm, slightly commanding. It wasn't like kissing Darius, Riley realized with a slight jolt. It was *better*.

"Riley Cohen, you are required to come with me."

They sprang apart as if a bomb had dropped between them. Alec was immediately on his feet, standing between her and Tyrell. Riley had to twist to the side to see around him. Her face felt like it was on fire.

"Who are you?" Alec asked. He had a hard edge to his voice, as if he was ready to take the pilot on.

"This is Tyrell. He's a pilot for the Collective. You knew him before." The words left Riley's mouth in a rush. This new Alec might be as headstrong as the old one. No one needed a wrestling match in the galley as both tried to prove their dominance. Especially since Tyrell would wipe the floor with Alec.

"You work with Darius?" Alec asked.

Riley saw his shoulders slowly drop from around his ears as he waited for the answer.

"Just so." Tyrell gave Alec the once over then dismissed him, turning his granite gaze back to her. "A ship has docked and the occupants request your presence."

Riley's heart shot into her mouth. It wasn't Anna, was it? If she spent one second alone with that woman, she'd be dead. "Who wants to see me?"

"A Councilor."

Riley exchanged a glance with Alec. A feeling of dread was creeping up to settle next to her pounding heart. "What Councilor, Ty? One from Celes?"

"All those travel aboard this ship with us, as you well know," Tyrell said. "This Councilor was travelling in his own ship. We intercepted. He demands your presence.

Come with me."

The bottom dropped out of her stomach. There was only one Councilor in this entire universe who knew her and there was no way she wanted to meet him. She hadn't progressed very far in her assignment, despite her best intensions. Things like her entire planet getting blown up had gotten in the way. A surge of guilt flashed through her. Poor Kerry. He hadn't deserved any of it just for rescuing her from the top of that stupid bridge, which had been Anna's fault. In fact, everything that had gone wrong was Anna's fault.

Riley caught Alec's hardening expression and it occurred to her that he might be able to feel her emotions the same way she felt his. She quickly tried to swallow her anger.

"I'm going with you," Alec said. His eyes were still focused on Tyrell. Riley knew from the tense way he held himself that Alec didn't trust Tyrell, even though she'd vouched for him. She found herself irritated. She could take care of herself. Just because he'd kissed her didn't mean he owned her.

Tyrell looked down his nose at Alec. "She is requested to come alone."

"Yeah, well, I don't think so," Alec said in a tone that telegraphed he was looking for a fight.

"I'm not seeing any Councilor alone, Ty." Riley slid out of the bench seat to stand next to Alec. "I don't know what this guy wants, but I can bet it isn't something good."

"You have no reason to fear the Council," Ty began.

"You know darn well that I do," Riley cut him off. She headed towards the doorway with them trailing behind her. "And I want you with me, too."

Riley strode along the wide main corridor with Tyrell at her elbow and Alec looming immediately behind her. She had no delusions; they might be on a ship and surrounded by dozens of crew and guests but that wouldn't stop one of the Council from ripping her apart if he so chose. She had adequate proof that the Council considered itself above all law, particularly as they apparently made it. Her thoughts were clamouring. What would the Councilor want with her? What did Tyrell know? Would Alec think to run and get Darius the moment the door shut behind her? Would Darius even come to help her, or did *he* want her dead too?

24

The three of them passed through a wide corridor full of passengers. Riley watched Alec out of the corner of her eye, interested in his complete lack of couth. He was staring at the aliens around him as if he'd never seen non-humans before. She snorted. "Open your mouth wider, Anderson. You've missed a couple of flies."

He closed his jaws with a snap and gave her annoyed glance. He was about to retort when he suddenly blanched and nearly stumbled. He stopped abruptly and whipped his head around.

"What?" Riley asked as she craned her neck to see what had him so spooked.

He didn't reply. He was scanning the various individuals around him as if one hid a poisonous asp underneath their clothes—or in the case of the naked couple who'd just passed, in their hair—ready to throw it at him. He was slightly shaking.

"Did you feel that?" he asked quietly.

"Feel what?" Riley eyed him suspiciously. He looked on edge. She glanced quickly around them. Nothing was out of the ordinary. Her own internal monitors reported 'all clear'. It was a sudden reminder. Anna could have done anything to his mind. Riley realized she needed to be a bit more careful around him.

"I dunno," he said softly, as if thinking aloud. "I've felt that before. Like someone is watching me. Someone kinda, um, evil." He blushed slightly and gave his head a slight shake. "It's gone now. Weird."

Tyrell fixed them with a sharp glance that indicated he found the conversation foolish. "You have an overactive imagination."

"Yeah, and you'd recognize imagination." Riley smirked briefly before becoming serious. "Is Rhozan here?"

Tyrell pulled out his orb and glanced down at it. He shook his head. "No sign." He didn't give them another glance as he started walking again. Riley fell into step behind him. "Coming?" she asked over her shoulder.

Alec shivered slightly then quickly caught up to her. He stared straight ahead, his forehead furrowed but his eyes haunted. Riley was tempted to probe a bit further but the tightness of his jaw prevented further thought. She'd talk to him when they were alone.

They turned down an empty side corridor towards the outer part of the ship. Tyrell came to a sudden stop in front of an unmarked door. He raised his right hand. A light at the side of the door flashed twice and the door slid open. Tyrell stood to the side, allowing Riley to enter.

"Riley!" someone shouted from inside the room.

"Oh my God, *Kerry*," Riley breathed. Without another thought she rushed over and threw herself into Kerry's arms. She was neither aware of the smaller man sitting in the corner nor the disturbance in the corridor behind her. All she could think of was Kerry and how incredibly relieved she was to see him alive and well. And he *did* look well. She pulled back from his enveloping hug to study him. There were no dark circles under his eyes, no pallor. In fact, he looked to be in perfect health.

"Wait!" She heard the shout behind her and slightly turned, just in time to see Alec squeeze his way into the chamber as the door shut behind him. She had a momentary glimpse of Tyrell's furious expression before the door closed in front of him.

"Who's this?" Alec demanded.

"I could say the same thing, mate." Kerry stood a little straighter but didn't drop his arms.

Riley twisted inside Kerry's embrace to face Alec. "Kerry's from Earth. I met him in Australia."

A slight cough abruptly interrupted her. She turned around, suddenly annoyed that Kerry wouldn't let go of her, and faced the figure sitting in the shadows. She could make out his features and the hard eyes that penetrated the slight gloom. She straightened to her full height.

"Let go of my girlfriend," Alec growled.

"For Pete's sake, Alec, chill." Riley pulled herself out of Kerry's arms, noting that Kerry was paying more attention to Alec than he was to her. The instant she was free, Alec moved in beside her. He didn't put his arm around her but his facial expression dared anyone to usurp his position. If it hadn't been so serious a situation, Riley would have burst out laughing. She focused her attention on the Councilor. "You wanted to see me?"

164   The Councilor steepled his fingers together. Riley fought the inclination to make a run for it. She wouldn't show any weakness if it killed her.

The Councilor directed his gaze to Alec. "Who are you?"

Riley felt Alec bristle. "Alec Anderson. Riley's boyfriend. Who are *you*?"

The Councilor raised his right hand, palm out. A flash of light flew from his palm towards Alec, but almost instantly Alec had his own hand up, orb glowing within his fingers. The Councilor's flash was rebuffed and dissipated. Riley had never seen Alec move so fast before.

"What is the meaning of this, Terran?" The Councilor hissed. He slowly got to his feet. Riley couldn't help backing up. She bumped into Alec.

"You threatened me," Alec said.

His voice was steady but now that Riley was in contact with his skin, she could detect that he wasn't entirely without fear.

"My sensor determines danger and thoughts. If you have something to hide, Terran, it will not remain hidden for long. As a member of the Intergalactic Council, you must obey me."

"You can't threaten me," Alec replied.

"He can, Alec. Shut up," Riley murmered. She couldn't take her eyes off the Councilor. For such a tiny person he practically oozed menace. Annoying the Councilor was in nobody's best interest. "I've done everything you asked me to do." Her eyes flicked towards Kerry. "You can stop with the *incentive*. I'll tell you everything I know."

"What incentive?" Alec asked but the Councilor's words drowned his out.

"I have reviewed your knowledge and found it wanting." The Councilor waved his hand imperiously in Riley's direction with a dismissive air. "There is nothing conclusive in your investigations and I have found your skill and results sorely lacking."

Riley bristled. "You have got to be kidding. She almost killed me and you find it *inconclusive*. What more do you want? *A signed confession?*"

"Who nearly killed you?" Alec said almost at the same time as Kerry. They glared at each other.

Riley ignored them both. "She's working with Kholar.

He's in on it too; he has to be. They practically shouted it to each other just before the ship got destroyed. Alec was the only thing worth saving. They were willing to break every Tyon rule in the book to do it. And why did they want him? *For the plan.* The plan to expose the whole Tyon Collective."

"There is no proof," the Councilor interrupted her tirade. "You have supposition only."

"You know I'm right." Riley crossed her arms and glowered. Was everyone in this universe *blind? And stupid?*

"What are you talking about?" Alec nudged her without taking his eyes off the Councilor. "Who wanted to save me?"

"Who's Kholar?" Kerry chimed in.

"Silence," the Councilor snapped.

He got his wish. For a second, silence hung heavily in the air. Then the Councilor crossed the short distance between himself and Alec and stopped within a hand span. He craned his neck to peer up into Alec's eyes. Riley noticed how still Alec had become and that the hand that held the orb now clenched it tightly. She didn't want Alec dead, not now that he'd been resurrected. She reached out, put her hand on his arm and squeezed gently. She felt the muscles beneath her light touch relax ever so slightly.

"You are the Terran boy that Darius was training, are you not?" the Councilor mused quietly. His eyes had narrowed as he looked Alec up and down. "The one that disappeared with the Operative, Anna."

Alec rose and dropped one shoulder. "I guess so."

"You guess so?" The Councilor obviously didn't care for Alec's tone.

"I don't remember, so it could be true. Darius says he trained me before but I have absolutely no memory of it. I have to take his word for it."

The Councilor cocked his head to one side. "And your memories of Anna? I understand that those too are missing."

"Guess so."

The beginnings of a cold smile tinged the Councilor's lips and a tingle of apprehension rode down Riley's spine. When this Councilor was happy, no one else was. She glanced at Kerry for some indication of what might be coming. Oddly, Kerry didn't seem afraid of the tiny bureaucrat the way he should be. Weird, considering the Councilor had Kerry tortured for weeks.

"I have read the report on you," the Councilor said as he slowly walked around Alec. "An implant without any record. An unexplained disappearance. Unusual and highly interesting, don't you agree?" He didn't wait for Alec's answer. "And nothing in your mind that answers any of the questions." He finished his examination and stepped back a couple of paces. "And you, Riley Cohen, are so concerned for his welfare and yet you failed miserably to keep your knowledge of him to yourself."

Riley gasped.

"Indeed," mused the Councilor as he gave her an amused glance. "A pathetic attempt but predictable. You really mustn't berate yourself. Highly trained Operatives can't keep secrets from me when I desire information. The implant sees to that."

"What secrets?" asked Kerry. Everyone ignored him.

"Who else knows of Alec's gifts?"

There was no point lying. The creep was just going to pick the correct thoughts out of her head, probably before she could stop thinking them. "Darius knows. I'm sure he told Anna." She couldn't keep the disdain out of her voice. It was Darius's inability to think logically about Anna that had gotten them all in such trouble. Men, Riley thought with annoyance, why can't they think with their brains?

"Ah, Finn, the Terran Operative at the centre of so many thoughts and feelings. I must interrogate him myself. See, as you would put it, what the fuss is about."

"Look, I'm standing right here." Alec raised his voice a

little. "What is it that I'm supposed to know? Or do?" He turned to Riley. "What gifts?"

"An admirable job," the Councilor said quietly as he stared at Alec with mild fascination. "She must be commended on her skill."

"Are you talking about Anna?" Riley asked. That was the only *she* who came to mind.

The Councilor ignored her and spoke to Kerry instead. "This young man before you appears mundane, does he not, Kerry? But so often in life, the most precious of gifts are simple in their packaging and as such, attract so little attention. Only the vigilant or intuitive find them to use for their own purposes. Our young companion is highly imbued with Tyon power. So much so that he frightens those who seek to control him."

Kerry gave Alec an odd look, as if he'd just found a rattlesnake in his knapsack instead of his textbooks. He took a step back and aligned himself next to Riley. Riley barely noticed. She was furiously trying to figure out just what the Councilor knew about Alec and what his rather vague mutterings were really about. Did he suspect that Alec's partial amnesia was not a natural occurrence? And what was he planning to do with them?

"Are you talking about using these orb things?" Alec held his orb up so that they could all see it. "Darius said most people don't know about these."

"Indeed," the Councilor replied. "More importantly, can't use them. The skill you possess, young Alec, is highly desired and worth more than you can possibly know. Put your orb in your pocket and be highly circumspect about divulging this information."

Alec hesitated just long enough for it to appear that he wasn't following orders, that he'd simply decided himself to put the orb away.

"You haven't answered my question," Riley said.

"I do not waste my time with those who fail my orders,"

the Councilor said cuttingly. "Your Tyon power is merely moderate. My need for you is limited. Take Kerry and assist him to assimilate to his new life. Dismissed."

Face burning, Riley turned on her heel, grabbed Kerry's hand and literally hauled him behind her. It took an instant to realize that Alec wasn't leaving. She paused, turned her head and snapped, "Alec, coming?" Without waiting she stalked out of the room. Alec followed a moment later. She thought she heard the Councilor say something to Alec but the words were indistinct and she was both too furious and too embarrassed to listen. She thought she heard Alec say "Sure" before the door closed behind him.

Marching down the corridor at a speed that had Kerry almost jogging to keep up, she grit her teeth and vowed to never do anything for that weasel-faced creep as long as she lived.

"Man, that was rude," Kerry said behind her. He tugged her arm.

"You should know what an absolute ass he is," Riley replied as she let go. "You've travelled with him for weeks."

"Nah, I didn't. I mean, I guess I was with him, but I hardly saw him or anything. I had my own room on his little ship and he kept pretty much to himself. It was really lonely. There was no one to talk to."

They turned a corner.

"Didn't he torture you?"

"Are you crazy?" Kerry snorted. "Torture? Seriously?"

Riley glowered and picked up the pace. Of all the insufferable, smug, condescending creatures, the Councilor took the cake. She'd lost entire *nights* of sleep over Kerry's suffering.

169

"Where are we going anyway?" Kerry asked blithely.

"Might as well take you to our room," Riley muttered. She was barely paying attention to either boy at her side now; far too many important things had just happened, not the least of which was that the Councilor disagreed that

Anna was the traitor. She wove her way through a myriad of beings to the main door of their quarters and absently waved her hand across the small control panel. The door opened.

"C'mon in."

Kerry gave a low whistle as he entered. "Nice place you got here, mate," he breathed.

"What? Oh, yeah, thanks." Riley patted one of the sofas. "Take a load off. Relax."

"You know, this travelling across the universe is hardly what I expected," Kerry began as he flopped on the sofa and stretched out. "I mean, sure, this is how it's done on television and stuff, but crikey, I rather thought the real thing would be a lot more, you know, *science-y*."

Riley ignored him. "Alec," she asked pointedly, "what was the Councilor saying to you? Just as we left."

Alec had chosen to sit across the room from Kerry and was staring at the Australian with barely disguised dislike. Without looking at her he answered. "Nothing."

"It wasn't nothing," Riley pushed. "You said 'sure'. What'd he ask you?"

"Jeez, what's got in your craw?" Kerry gave a short laugh. "Leave the kid alone, Riley."

"Who are you calling a kid?" Alec got to his feet.

"Don't tell me what to do," Riley snapped.

"Seriously, Riley, chill." Kerry pulled a small cushion towards him and then settled it behind his neck as he slid down into a lying position. "The Councilor hasn't any weird plan going on. He's just a guy who works for the government. Sure, he likes to throw his weight around a bit, but honestly, what's he doing that's got you so worked up?"

Riley was too unsettled to sit. She paced across the floor in front of Kerry's sofa like a caged tiger. Alec took a step back to get out of her way, but he stayed on his feet too and his eyes never left Kerry's face.

"That little government flunky, as you think of him, put a device inside my brain that gave me severe pain whenever I didn't do what he asked." She ignored Kerry's gasp of outrage. "He flooded my mind with images of you being tortured in the most horrible ways as incentive to do what he wanted. You might think he's innocuous, but I know better. A lot better." She stopped and crossed her arms in front of her.

Kerry ran his fingers through his hair. "Jeez, I had no idea."

"How long did that go on?" Alec asked quietly.

Riley pulled a face. "Weeks."

Alec looked like he was about to leave the room and charge back to the Councilor with more on his mind than a friendly chat. Riley put out her hand and touched his arm. "Don't," she said.

"Don't what?" Alec didn't return her gaze.

"Don't do whatever you're thinking of doing. It won't help."

"I should have been there for you," Alec muttered. "That's my job."

"I fight my own battles," Riley pulled her hand away.

"That's telling him," Kerry laughed.

"Shut up," Alec growled.

"Yeah," Riley scowled at both the boys, "both of you, shut up."

"Hey, what'd I do?" Kerry rested his hand over his heart and assumed a wounded expression.

"Leave her alone." Alec gave Riley a slight shove to the side and stood directly in front of Kerry. He was practically flexing his muscles.

"Oh, for Pete's sake," Riley snapped. "That's enough. I'm sick of this. Kerry, stop goading him. It isn't funny. And Alec, quit the 'me Tarzan, you Jane' routine. It's pissing me off, big time. Either the two of you act like civilized beings or I'm out of here."

"She's cute when she's mad," Kerry remarked.

Alec nodded. "For sure."

"Arghhhhh." Riley turned on her heel and stomped towards the door. "Don't wait up."

Three hours later Riley was still wandering through the darkened ship. For the first hour or so she'd been so angry she'd barely even noticed where she was going. Now the worst of the fury had melted into nothingness and she was left with underlying worry. Partly too embarrassed to return to her quarters and partly needing time to herself, she let her feet lead her. The ship was on rest time now; the crew used the pattern of approximately twelve Earth hours of work time alternating with twelve of rest, the same as the Tyon training station. It had crossed Riley's mind that sleep and work were universal constants and that all the aliens on the massive vessel seemed to be familiar with it, although from the number of people who had passed her, lots of people had things to do and places to go despite the late hour.

25

She rubbed her wrist absently. It didn't actually hurt anymore. The medics on board had done a thorough job but the mental ache hadn't subsided. She still found it hard to believe that Darius, of all people, could have injured her. She'd have bet her life on him. But now, *everything* was turned upside down. If Darius could turn on her, who in the rest of this godforsaken universe could she trust?

Her footsteps echoed quietly in the empty curving corridor. The doors to her right were all closed and for the last few minutes or so all the narrow passageways that branched off to the left and the inner portion of the ship had been empty. The overhead lighting cast faint shadows to either side of her. It wasn't creepy, just lonely. Someone had mentioned that these big intergalactic ships could carry a thousand passengers at a time. Riley had no idea if it was that full now—it hardly seemed so, even during work hours— and this section seemed deserted. She wished she could find a viewport. Perhaps staring out at the endless vista of empty space would cure the restlessness that had infected her.

Something startled her. She stopped in her tracks, trying to figure out what had pricked her subconscious. She looked behind. The corridor was still entirely empty and the light hadn't changed. She turned back. There was no one there either. Where was she? Was this the same level as her guest quarters or had she gone up and down more stairs than she thought? Suddenly it became abundantly obvious just how alone she was.

Frowning, she started walking again, this time with her attention focused on her surroundings and at a faster pace. Now her steps seemed too loud in the empty silence. A tiny tingle of unease rippled down her spine. It almost felt like she was being watched. She squared her shoulders. Her imagination was getting the best of her.

She was almost jogging when she heard the voices. She came to such a jarring halt she nearly tripped. Were they coming from behind her or ahead? She paused, listening attentively. The voice was a woman's and getting louder with every passing second. It seemed mildly familiar. Someone replied to the inaudible question the woman posed but whether male or female—or considering the occupants of this ship, another gender altogether—Riley couldn't tell. For no reason other than instinct, she ducked out of sight into the nearest narrow interconnecting corridor and hugged the wall.

The voices grew louder and so did the footsteps of more

than two people. They had been walking toward her. She had hidden just in time.

"I want this matter sorted out," the woman was saying. Whoever she was, she wasn't happy. "You have this entire ship's instrumentation at your disposal. Surely any form of communication can be decoded."

Riley frowned again. That voice was definitely familiar.

"The communications expert aboard can only confirm deep space broadcast towards this ship. The contents of the message cannot be unscrambled. We cannot discern whom the message was intended for. If so, I would have that individual interrogated." That was a man, Riley decided. His voice was unusual; so low it rumbled and crackled with each word.

"That is unacceptable, Keerscrip. This is the third communication between this ship and some unknown party. With the recent attack on Trovis and Heliothe, we cannot take any chances. Kholar was convinced that a rogue faction had infiltrated the Organization. The destruction of two planets within this section of the galaxy and Terra, gone as well, indicates significant hostile activity."

The identity of the female speaker came to Riley just as the small party passed the corridor she was hiding in. The head Councilor, the one that had questioned her on Celes. Riley bit her lip. The group passed so quickly she didn't have time to count how many there were. Fortunately no one glanced down her passageway, and Riley didn't stick her head out to watch them leave. If anyone turned around and saw her, she'd have a lot of explaining to do. But the conversation *was* highly interesting.

She could always say she was just walking the same way.

Ducking back into the hall she quickly began to jog, only slowing when the group came back into sight. There were only four of them. Riley could identify the lead Councilor from behind as well as another female Councilor from Celes. The inlaid jewels in the lead Councilor's head glinted under the lights. The other two were unknown to Riley, although maybe if she saw their faces, she'd recognize them. As silently as possible she moved as close as she dared to hear the conversation. The head Councilor was still speaking.

"... The ship he was found in."

"Definitely Mheer, Madame Councilor. The weapon marks are classic for Mheer strategy and technology." This speaker was a short male with very wide shoulders and skin the colour of an arctic iceberg. Riley could see his large rubbery lips as he turned his head to speak to the Councilor.

"And all aboard were dead except for the Terran boy," the Councilor mused. "A remarkable coincidence wouldn't you say, Keerscrip? The very child who was the centre of the Tyon mystery?"

"It does seem implausible." Keerscrip was the owner of the bone-rattling voice. He was a very tall humanoid with a gleaming skull and an extra set of arms. He was walking closely to the lead Councilor and holding something Riley couldn't see in his upper set of hands. The second set was hidden in what looked like pockets of his long jacket. He was nodding his head at her statement. "As does the fact that the female Terran is trailing behind us at this very moment."

Riley stumbled. She looked up, plastering a totally nonchalant look on her face. The group in front of her came to a complete stop. The lead Councilor had a sharp look of dislike on her face. The rubber-lipped alien was staring too, although his three eyes all seemed to stare in different directions.

"Why are you following us?" the lead Councilor demanded.

Riley raised her chin. "I was out walking because I couldn't sleep. I'm not following you."

"This section of the ship is restricted to members of the

Council and their attendants. You are not permitted here."

Riley lifted one shoulder. "I didn't see any signs and the corridor wasn't blocked off. I've been walking for ages. No one tried to stop me or anything."

For a couple of heartbeats the little group in front of her was silent. Riley fought to keep her gaze steady. She had a right to walk anywhere she wasn't literally barred from doing so. Tyrell had told her so. If the stupid Council didn't put up a sign that everyone could read or erect a barrier of some sort, then it was their problem if unsuspecting visitors wandered in.

Keerscrip leaned over and murmured something to the Councilor. She nodded as the stork-like assistant straightened up.

"Come with us," the Councilor ordered.

Riley couldn't think of a good enough reason not to obey. "Sure," she replied neutrally. She walked over to them and stopped when she was within touching distance. She avoided looking at the rubber-lipped alien. His eyes were totally creepy.

Silently the group began to walk again. Riley followed behind. No one looked to see if she was complying with orders, she noticed. Arrogant bunch of weasels. The group marched for another minute before coming to a halt in front of door. Keerscrip placed his hand on the sensor to the right. The door slid open without sound and the group entered. Riley hung back for a moment, assessing the situation. The room ahead of her was huge. Several large viewports dotted the farthest wall. The interior of the room was lavishly furnished with cushions and clusters of chairs and sofas, upholstered in soothing pastel shades. Filmy curtains hung from the ceiling, sectioning the space into multiple areas. The air was scented with something floral but not familiar and blew gently across her face. The curtains wafted gently in the cross breeze. Overall, it was an incredibly appealing chamber and surprising for all its opulence. Riley entered and the door shut silently behind her.

"Sit and be comfortable," Keerscrip beckoned to her with one right arm and indicated a squashy chair beside him with his other.

"Would you care for refreshment?" the rubber-lipped person asked.

Riley stopped herself from agreeing to something to drink. Heaven knew the kind of drugs the Council had at their disposal. She could be knocked unconscious and tossed out the nearest airlock in the blink of an eye. She swallowed against a suddenly dry throat. Why had she willingly entered this room?

"Sit, girl," the lead Councilor ordered. Riley glanced to her left. She hadn't heard the woman come up beside her. Slowly she lowered herself into the chair and immediately regretted it. All the others remained standing. She was now at a significant psychological disadvantage. She tried to unobtrusively lift herself up but the chair was too squishy and easily defeated her.

"Okay, I'm sitting," Riley said. She couldn't help the tinge of annoyance that coloured her tone. "What do you want to talk to me about?"

"The Terran boy," the Councilor said.

Riley's eyebrows disappeared into her fringe. "Alec? Or Kerry?"

The Councilors and their attendants exchanged a look before the lead Councilor replied. "The tall one with brown skin."

"You want to talk about Alec? Why?"

"I will ask the questions," the lead Councilor admonished. "You will answer."

Remember the airlocks, Riley reminded herself. She took a deep breath and pasted a cooperative look on her face. "Okay. What do you want to know?"

"The Terran boy, Alec, as you call him, was found on a

ship almost completely destroyed."

Riley nodded. "I was in sick bay when they brought him in."

"You have spoken to him?"

"Sure," Riley shrugged. "He's staying in the same guest room. I've spoken to him a few times."

"And you knew him before. On Terra."

Again, Riley nodded. She glanced at the others briefly before turning her attention to the other female Councilor. "We travelled together. Alec, Darius and me. You should know that. I think it was in the report that Logan gave you."

It was the Councilor's turn to nod. "That report was significantly limited in detail."

"Well, I can't help that," Riley replied. "I didn't write the thing. I can fill in the blanks if you want." She quickly amended her statement at the Councilor's puzzled expression. "I'll add any details you need. Just ask."

"My reports indicate that Alec's memory is faulty and that he cannot remember anything of his Tyon training or experiences. Is that your impression?"

"Yeah. That's what he says."

"But do you believe it?"

Riley felt her brow crinkle at the question. She hadn't thought to question Alec's statement that he couldn't remember. The Alec she knew had been unfailingly honest. But now, with the small group in front of her, all eyes peering intently at her, the question brought an uncomfortable thought to the foreground. What if Alec had a reason for lying to them all? A dark, horrible reason? But if she raised that possibility with this group and Alec was innocent, she could get him into serious trouble.

"I don't have any reason not to believe it," she answered carefully. "I've known Alec for months. We've been through a lot together. He's always been a pretty stand-up kind of guy." At least he *had* been.

179

Suddenly it hit her. She'd known the Alec *before* the time shift. The boy that had disappeared with Anna after moving back in time, she hadn't known as well. Was it possible that the shift in time had somehow changed him? Was that why Darius was different too? Was that why Anna had saved their lives before the shift and was out to kill them after it? Good grief, what else had changed?

"You've thought of something," the lead Councilor said as she leaned over Riley. Her dark eyes pierced Riley's with an intensity that held all her power and command. No wonder the woman had reached such lofty political heights.

"Alec left Darius and I for a while. He was travelling with an Operative named Anna." Riley broke the gaze as her eyes started to water. "I can't vouch for him after that. I don't know what Anna might have done to him. But the Alec *I* knew wouldn't be working for enemies."

"And you don't trust Anna," the other Councilor stated Riley's unspoken words.

"No, I don't." Riley gave the Councilor the benefit of her own sharp gaze. "I never did. I can't say why in the beginning, but when she pulled out a honking big crystal around her neck and told me she was going to kill me with it, yeah, my suspicions were kinda confirmed."

"I have reviewed the records of this Operative," the other Councilor said in her hissing voice. Riley was startled to note that the woman's mouth and the words she spoke didn't match. It took a moment to realize that this was the first time she'd truly been aware of the implant in her head doing its job. It was really disconcerting. She had to force herself to focus on what was being said. "She has the highest commendations and has provided exemplary service to the Tyon Collective. Yet you accuse her of heinous crimes. Where is your proof?"

Riley sighed with impatience. "I went through all of this before with you guys on Celes. Remember? I don't *have* any proof. The ship's logs are bogus. No one else heard her say anything. No one else on the ship except Tyrell has any memory whatsoever that she was even there. It's my word against hers."

Both the jewelled Councilor and the head Councilor straightened up, their facial expressions almost non-existent.

"Is there anything else you want me for?" Riley asked as she faked a yawn. "It's really late."

"Have you been in communication with any person not aboard this ship?" Keerscrip asked. Both his sets of arms were folded in front of him giving him the unfortunate semblance of a praying mantis.

"No." Riley returned his gaze and held it. "I haven't. I wouldn't know the first thing about contacting anyone who isn't on this ship and there isn't anyone out there," she waved at the viewport with a free hand, "that would be contacting me. Except Anna, if she's even still alive, which I don't know for sure, but would bet money on it. And if Anna decides to look me up, trust me, I'll be running for help so fast you won't see me for dust."

Riley looked at the four of them and waited for the verdict.

The Councilors and their aids turned to look at each other. Riley had the impression of a silent communication between them that went on for what seemed like a very long time. Suddenly Keerscrip held out one of his hands towards her. Reluctantly Riley grasped it. He pulled her up from the chair to her feet. The instant she was upright, she let go of him. She squashed the motion to wipe her hand against her leg.

"Come with me," Keerscrip said.   181

There seemed nothing else to say or do. Riley gave a minute shrug and followed the tall aid to the doorway. He released the mechanism with a hand-movement and with-out another word Riley was outside in the hallway with the door sliding silently closed behind her.

For a moment, she merely stood there. How odd. And how rude. She had nothing they wanted and was tossed out without even a thanks for your time. She blew a puff of air through pursed lips and made a slight face at the door before she realized they were probably still monitoring her. Slightly embarrassed, she turned on her heel and strode away.

The hallway seemed even more deserted now. Riley purposefully picked up her pace and marched along. These halls didn't go on forever, she reminded herself, even if they didn't look familiar. Somewhere along here there'd be a main corridor or something. The silence seemed even more ominous now and the shadows a bit longer than they had before. The sounds of her rapid footsteps seemed to echo eerily.

A wide entrance to another long corridor opened to her right. Riley braked, paused and then abruptly turned into the hall that headed towards the interior of the ship. She almost gasped when a door unexpectedly opened on her left and a heavily robed individual stepped out right in front of her.

He was huge, both bulky and extremely tall. Riley couldn't see his face. The cowl of his dark brown robe was pulled so far forward that his face, if he had a face, was completely hidden in shadow. Both his arms were at his sides and the sleeves were so long there was no indication of hands. He blocked her way and stood completely still. Riley couldn't get past him without squeezing; the hallway wasn't all that wide and the person, whoever he was, seemed disinclined to move to one side.

Riley came to a stop. A cutting phrase hovered on her tongue but something stopped her from speaking. The same something erupted into goosebumps all along her arms.

Her heart sped up. She took a step backwards. The creepy feeling was growing inside her. This was wrong, somehow. She couldn't put her finger on it but it was vaguely familiar. Her hand hovered over her orb in her pocket. If he made one threatening move...

The massive, robed person suddenly turned away from her and without a sound strode off down the hallway. Within a few moments he had turned a corner and disappeared from sight. Riley's knees felt weak and a slight shivering stole through her. This was silly. She was overly tired, that was it. She was seeing danger in every shadow like a five-year-old. She gave herself a mental shake. Whoever he was, he wasn't interested in her.

Riley waited a moment for her heart to settle then resumed her journey. She found herself pausing at the corner the man had taken and staring down the now empty hallway with a sense of relief, regardless of what her rational mind was thinking.

A good night's sleep would end this kind of stupidity. She just had to get back to her quarters and bunk down as soon as possible. This would be the last time she wandered around this stupid ship alone, she decided.

26

Alec lay on his bunk and listened to the deep and steady breathing of his roommates. The overhead lights were off and the wide room was bathed only in the pale glow of a transparent, floating computer screen that Darius had neglected to dissolve before he'd fallen asleep on the couch. Alec had opted for the upper bunk next to the door. Consciously he wanted to stay as close to the exit as possible, but the subconscious reason was locked away and try as he might, he couldn't remember anything that had happened to him since going to the mall with Stevie and Chin.

Things had certainly become complicated since that shopping expedition. In the last several days he'd learned he was an orphan, met the few remaining Earthlings, fought on and off with two of them, kissed one of them, and learned that he had skills and abilities far surpassing anyone else. Facts, opinions and impressions crowded his brain. It was almost too much.

According to Darius, who may or may not be lying, the entire world Alec had known had been annihilated. Riley had corroborated Darius's story, and while it felt right to believe Riley, the truth was he had no real reason to believe *anything* she said. Why either of them might lie, Alec didn't know, but something in the back of his mind urged caution. The tall guy, Tyrell, who was presently snoring lightly in the bunk below, seemed like a straight shooter type of guy, but again, Alec had nothing to go on but his instincts. Tyrell hadn't offered to talk and Alec had the impression that the hulking officer found his presence an annoyance.

Kerry, on the other hand, was definitely untrustworthy. *No one* was that sunny and happy all the time, Alec reasoned. He had driven Alec up the wall with his constant comments of "get a load of this" and "fair dinkum, that's amazing" about everything he saw, touched or tasted. And besides, he had arms like an octopus, always groping Riley and patting her shoulder and such. Alec should get a medal for the restraint he'd shown; Kerry seemed to have no idea how close he'd come to having his nose broken into eighteen pieces.

Riley was just as bad. Maybe they'd had something in the past—and if they had, he dearly wanted to remember it—but she lit up like a Christmas tree whenever she spoke to Kerry and you'd have to be blind, deaf and incredibly stupid not to notice it. She didn't light up when *he* was around. In fact, he got a variety of reactions, as if she was see-sawing from love to hate and back again, all within seconds. Alec had been sure she'd enjoyed the kiss in the galley a couple of days ago; she'd been pretty responsive. He knew *he'd* really enjoyed it. But there'd been that odd sensation of knowing how she felt *while she hugged Kerry*, which was truly weird. Riley stirred up emotions so intense he found it difficult to think around her. There hadn't been any time to be alone with her in the last day or so, so nothing about their relationship had progressed.

He frowned. There was just too much going on right now that he didn't understand. He felt like he was going to explode with frustration. And while Darius initially had been helpful, giving him some background information, he'd also been incredibly annoying, asking the same questions over and over again while they'd practiced with the orb. So too had the medics in the sick bay and the two senior officers who questioned him after he got the all clear from the doctors.

185

Then there was the orb. Having such fantastic power was an amazing bonus in an otherwise unsettling situation. The possibilities were unbelievable. Darius had demonstrated how to levitate things using the orb and how to create a type of protective force field. He'd hinted there was a lot more to learn and Alec wasn't surprised. Despite having no memory of ever using a Tyon crystal before, manipulating the power that tingled underneath his skin felt entirely natural. He was tearing through the lessons at light speed. Tomorrow, Darius had said they might try teleporting.

He heard someone turning over in bed and raised his head to peer through the semi-darkness. It was Riley again. He doubted she was asleep. She'd disappeared a fair bit over the last day and had managed to dodge both him and Kerry, an admirable act since the Australian tried to stick to her like a leech. She'd returned to the communal guest quarters only a little while ago, briefly visiting the bathroom before heading to an unoccupied bunk on the far wall. He had the sense that she was upset, probably from the way she stalked around the room, and he considered climbing out of his bunk and trying to talk to her. But any noise might wake Tyrell or Darius or worse, Kerry, and Alec figured he hardly needed an audience if Riley reamed him out. Why she would do that he didn't know, but girls were totally unpredictable and a guy never knew when one was going to yank his guts out with a stick.

As usual, his hand mindlessly stroked his orb while he thought. Maybe once he knew how to teleport himself, he could send Kerry to another part of the ship–it stood to reason he could learn to move someone else, too. Then he could grab some private time with Riley. Have a conversation, make her laugh, maybe even get his arms around her for a minute. He smiled to himself. *That* image was a lot more pleasant than any of the other thoughts passing through his head lately.

A sharp vibration shuddered through the bunk bed.

Alec's heart flew up into his throat. Without thinking he jumped out of bed and landed on the floor, orb tightly held in his hand. "Lights," he shouted.

The room was suddenly glaringly bright.

"Hey, what're you doing?" Riley scolded from the other side of the room. Any answer was forestalled as Tyrell leapt from his bunk and stood next to Alec.

"Finn, on guard," Tyrell shouted.

Darius gave a groan and rolled off the couch. He snapped to attention as he pulled his orb from his pocket.

"What's happening?" Riley asked.

"Get out of bed," Tyrell ordered. "We're under attack. Finn, guard the Potentials." With that he dashed through the door into the hallway beyond. Alec had a glimpse of several people moving quickly past the door before it automatically shut. He turned to Darius in time to see a flicker of distaste cross his face. Babysitting obviously didn't suit him.

A second, more noticeable shudder passed through the room. Kerry's snoring didn't change a bit.

"Who would attack us?" Alec asked the room.

Darius had crossed the room and was already using his orb to modify the glowing screen between him and Alec. Without answering, he pointed at it. Alec moved up behind Darius to look over his shoulder. A model of the ship they were on was depicted in space. It was a far larger than Alec had thought: a massive donut surrounding a red pulsing light inside the donut hole. The ship was spinning very fast. Alec had a moment of vertigo as he realized that he must be spinning inside the ship but it instantly dissipated. Their ship was surrounded by several very small and fast moving craft, darting in and out of the screen like wasps coming in to sting.

"The Mheer," Darius muttered almost under his breath.

"Who are they?" Riley was yawning. She stood well behind Darius and, too short to look over his shoulder, peered around his arm. She didn't meet Alec's eye.

"Our hosts for the Senate," Darius said, a wry tone infusing his words.

"Guess they've changed their minds about having the Council's party," Riley observed.

"Mheeror never wanted it. No one ever does. They were brought into the Galactic Consortium kicking and screaming and they've caused untold trouble since they joined."

"Then why did they?" Alec asked, as one of the little ships zipped into the view screen and out again, immediately followed by a mild shudder through the floor.

"When the Council shows up at your door, there's no such thing as saying, no thank you. You just hope they leave you alone enough so you can get on with your life."

"Isn't there a benefit to being part of the alliance?" Riley asked. "Strength in numbers, all that sort of thing?"

"That's part of the marketing campaign," Darius moved his orb a bit and the picture changed to show a close-up of one of the little ships. It was silver and shaped like a cigar. Weird swirling designs in black and red covered the entire hull. There were no windows and no obvious form of propulsion. "But the truth is, every planet gets less back from the Council's Alliance than they put in. For some civilizations, it becomes a form of slavery." He glanced away from the screen to Riley and back again. His expression was cold and unfeeling. "But you didn't hear that from me."

Riley took a small step backwards and glanced over at Alec. He didn't understand the concern that crossed her face. She quickly dropped her eyes from his and focused on the computer screen. Kerry gave a loud snort and rolled over.

"Better wake him up and have him on his feet. Just in case." Darius turned to Alec and gave a nod in Kerry's direction.

188

"Are we in danger?" Riley pointed to the screen. "They don't look like they could do much damage."

"You're small and you pack quite a punch," Darius replied. "But in this case, they're only trying to assert their displeasure. It should be over in a minute." The crease between his eyes belied his casual tone.

Alec ran lightly across the room and gave Kerry an unnecessarily hard shove on the shoulder. "Wake up. There's trouble," he snapped before quickly returning to Darius's side. Despite the explanation he felt uneasy. Something, somewhere, was wrong.

"How can we see this?" Riley was asking. "Are there cameras outside this ship or—"

"It's a simulation based on sensor readings," Darius cut her off abruptly as four of the tiny ships suddenly darted into view. There was a slight flash of light around the hull of the massive interstellar craft. Almost instantaneously they felt a deep and thorough shudder. Riley almost lost her balance and grabbed instinctively at Darius's arm to keep upright. She gasped and tore her hand away the moment the floor stilled. She stared at Darius with wide eyes.

"That's not 'asserting displeasure'," Alec said as he let go of the sofa that had stopped his fall. "They're pissed."

"Yeah," Darius murmured, "it does seem that way." Outside their quarters the sound of many running feet and a distant klaxon cut through the silence. Across the room, Kerry was slowly getting to his feet and rubbing his eyes. He didn't seem to realize that something important was going on. "Get your orbs out," Darius instructed quietly. "Keep them ready." He waved his in front of the screen and the picture dissolved. It was replaced by a series of symbols, some glowing in red. Darius waved at the screen and the symbols rapidly scrolled downwards. He pointed a finger at one red symbol before it disappeared off the screen. "Hull breach, deck 11."

Alec knew next to nothing about physics and interstellar travel but a hull breach in the vacuum of space could not be a good thing.

"How far away from us is it?" Riley was peering at the screen intently. Alec didn't know if she could read those symbols or not. He wished he could.

"Opposite side, two decks below. It's sealed. Don't panic."

"I'm not," Riley snapped. "I never do, no matter who turns on me."

Darius didn't answer but his body language spoke volumes. Something had gone on between those two, Alec realized, something very bad. As Riley's boyfriend, he was obligated to take her side and protect her against Darius if need be. He hoped it wouldn't come to that. Darius was pretty cool and the number of people who knew him before he'd lost his memory was exceedingly few. He didn't want to lose any of them.

"Any chance of a coffee?" Kerry yawned at his elbow.

"No," Alec barely noticed him.

"No need to be so touchy, sport," Kerry replied. "I can go and get one myself."

"You don't have time for food or drink at the moment." Darius was frowning at the screen more thoroughly now. "You might not have noticed, but this ship is under attack."

"Really?" Kerry's wide eyes scanned the room. "We're in a space battle?"

"Really," Riley replied.

"Now that is cool," Kerry breathed. "Any chance we could find a viewport and watch it?"

Darius waved his orb and the screen changed back to the outside view again. Now there were more, many more, of the tiny Mheer ships surrounding them, and only three or four were darting in and out of the screen. Most were lingering around the hull in an ominous manner.

"That doesn't look good," Kerry remarked as he leaned

forward to get a better look. "Aren't we defending ourselves?"

"It doesn't look like it, does it?" Darius said quietly. He held his orb up in front of his face and closed his eyes for a moment.

"What's he doing?" Kerry whispered as he gave Alec a slight nudge.

"Orbs work like private radios," Alec replied just as quietly. As he spoke, he remembered that Kerry didn't have an orb and that Darius had warned him to keep quiet about them around those who didn't have the talent. But Darius wouldn't have used his orb in front of Kerry if he really didn't want him to know about them, Alec reasoned. So it must be okay.

"You use them to control these weird holographs, don't you?" Kerry was eyeing the computer screen that hung transparently in front of them.

"Yeah, I guess so." Alec focused back on the scene unfolding before them. More of the little ships were arriving. Several seemed to have attached themselves to the hull of the ship like barnacles. The red glowing sphere in the middle of the Council's ship pulsed brightly, then dimmed.

"We're being boarded." Darius opened his eyes.

"By the Mheer?" Riley spoke up. Alec noticed she was paler than usual and her arms were crossed protectively.

"Ty thinks so," Darius replied. "He's near one of the entry doors. He says they look like Mheer but that something's off. He doesn't know what yet."

"Should we hide or prepare to fight?" Kerry asked.

"Good question," Darius turned to face him. "Any other options?"

"We don't have weapons," Riley pointed out slowly. "So, we couldn't launch any sort of offensive. And besides, we're clearly out numbered. And if we, by that I mean the captain of our ship, hasn't fired back, then maybe we shouldn't either. This ship has sensors everywhere so there's no place to hide they wouldn't find us. Tyrell said this transport doesn't have escape pods or anything we can run away in. We can't transport to the surface of any nearby planet without a ship or those special orbs you guys have." She was looking at Darius now, instead of the screen. "I don't see that we have any other option but to go wherever they take us and hope we have a chance to escape."

"Logical and succinct," Darius answered. He too was staring at Riley with an odd intense look on his face. "I suspect you are correct. We'll be prisoners of the Mheer."

Riley sat in a booth in the packed galley and watched her surroundings with little attention. Kerry and Alec crowded against her, one on either side, both stuffing their faces as if the containers full of food were suddenly going to disappear into thin air and never appear again. Darius sat with his back to them and watched the galley door. His orb was tightly held in hand just under the table.

Riley couldn't eat. She'd grabbed a bowl full of Tyon protein, because it was the first thing she saw, and shovelled half of it down her throat without tasting. Darius said they were prisoners and prisoners often didn't get fed, so it made sense to try and get something into her stomach. But her guts were too churned up to finish the bowl.

27

Riley's worries had intensified during the rush to the galley and the hour since they'd arrived to wait for the Mheer. She wasn't so much worried about the impending captivity, although that was scary enough, but about the feelings and thoughts she'd come in contact with when she accidentally grabbed Darius's arm back in the guest quarters. He was filled with rage. Exactly where that burning anger was aimed wasn't clear. Riley had only the instant impression of unadulterated fury. It had scorched her soul. She hadn't been able to let go of him fast enough.

Darius had never been that angry before. His emotions tended to run like quicksilver; amorous one instant, reckless the next. This was similar to what she'd sensed when he was in the sparring room with her and had broken her wrist. Except that had been mild in comparison.

The door opened. Everyone in the galley swivelled to see but most went back to whatever they were doing with an audible sigh of relief as they recognized Tyrell. Darius's back stiffened and he half rose out of his seat.

"They're searching the ship," Tyrell said without preamble.

"For what?" Darius asked. Riley noticed his knuckles whiten around his orb then purposefully release.

"Unknown. No demands, no orders. They silently move from room to room." Tyrell stated. "I will obtain nourishment and join you. You were wise to bring them here."

Darius appeared slightly surprised at the faint praise and slowly sat back down in his seat as Tyrell crossed over to the food section and strode down the rows of edibles. Riley watched as he selected a bowl of Mithras noodles and another of Tyon protein. He returned to them and slid in beside Kerry. Without speaking he began to eat.

Kerry dropped his utensil onto his finally empty plate. "That's better," he sighed. He turned slightly to look at Tyrell. "Darius says you're a pilot."

Tyrell nodded but didn't stop eating.

"What sort of propulsion system do the Mheer have? What kind moves this ship? Do we have any weaponry and if so, why didn't we use it? What's the purpose of stopping this ship under threat and what do you think they're looking for?" Kerry hadn't taken a breath.

194

Darius looked like he was about to tell Kerry to shut up, but surprisingly, Tyrell placed his spoon on the table and answered. "The Mheer use a combination of ion and gravitational propulsion. It has an unpronounceable name in our language. Generally inferior and for short range only. The Councilor's ships all use standard propulsion. If you have seen a model of this ship you'll notice a small star in the centre of the ship's hull. That's the Thetriston. The ship's computers have the technical manuals imbedded for access. Darius could obtain one for you. As for weaponry, we naturally have the most advanced in the galaxy, but using it towards a member of the Councilor Protectorate is unadvised. Currently, the Councilors are meeting with some of the Mheer. Negotiations, I assume, are ongoing."

Riley felt her eyebrows rise into her bangs. She'd never heard Tyrell speak so much before.

"And they're searching for…?" Alec prompted.

"Currently unclear, as I said. I was not privy to their discussions with the Councilors." His frown indicated exactly what he thought of that. "Whether it is for something, or someone, I do not know. We will find out if and when they find it." Tyrell returned his attention to his meal.

"Maybe they're not really dangerous," Alec ventured.

"The ship you travelled on was damaged by Mheer weapons and everyone aboard it other than you was dead," Tyrell said. "They are definitely dangerous."

"Oh," Alec muttered. The colour in his face deepened.

"What are we going to do if it's us they want?" Riley asked into the heavy silence.

Tyrell glanced up at her with a slight frown. Darius also swivelled around to watch her. For a second she felt foolish that she'd even given voice to the thought. "Well, it's possible," she protested.

"Why?" Tyrell asked.

Riley licked her lips. At least he was willing to listen. "I don't know. I mean I don't have any real information, but you have to admit a lot of strange things have happened lately and Darius, Alec and I always seem to be somewhere near the middle of it."

195

Darius pursed his lips but said nothing. Alec merely looked a bit puzzled.

"What kind of things?" Kerry leaned forward. His eyes were sparkling.

"Nuclear war, for one." Riley shot Kerry a sharp look.

"You started a *nuclear war*?" Kerry gasped.

"Don't be ridiculous," Darius sneered. "We didn't start anything. The Others did. We just happened to be there at the time." He turned to Riley. "Your overstated sense of self-importance has this all wrong. We aren't the target. The very thought is ridiculous."

"Yeah," Riley leaned forward and hissed at him angrily. "Then why are the heavily armed goons who just came in on their way over to our table?"

Alec couldn't help the sudden lurch of his stomach as he took in the approaching Mheer. They were shorter than Riley by a hand-span but broad and heavily muscled. They wore form-fitting one-piece suits with a hood that curved low over their foreheads. Their skin was nearly black and their eyes a jarring pale grey under jutting brows. They were clearly humanoid but their facial features were blunted and heavy. None of them looked remotely friendly and all seven of them were marching towards them. Everyone else in the galley was slowly backing away.

"Don't get up," Tyrell muttered out of the side of his mouth. "Standing is considered aggressive."

Alec swallowed the instinct to bolt. His eyes never left the array of what he assumed were weapons that hung on the Mheer's waists. He reached over and grasped Riley's hand under the table. She didn't pull away.

28

The Mheer surrounded the table. For a long moment no one said or did anything. Alec shivered slightly. There was something about these aliens that made him acutely uncomfortable. He couldn't put his finger on it, but it went beyond their menacing appearance. The feeling was familiar but the memory was nonexistent. What had happened during the time he was missing? Why did the Mheer affect him this way? Or was it something, no, *someone* else that was giving him this uneasy sensation in the pit of his stomach?

The Mheer closest to Darius pulled a small, hand-held tablet off his belt and peered at it for a moment. He then raised his eyes and stared at the group. He turned the tablet around so Alec and the others could see what was on it. The pictures were small but the images clear enough. The Mheer had the right people. Riley's fingers tightened around Alec's as she gave a tiny gasp. Alec squeezed back.

Two of the Mheer pulled ugly grey metallic objects off their belts and aimed directly at them. No one needed words. The Mheer took a step backwards.

"Do exactly as I do," Tyrell said evenly. "They frighten easily." Crouching in a half upright position, Tyrell slowly eased his way out of the bench seat. He placed his hands upon the top of his head and, keeping his eyes focused on the floor, stepped towards the Mheer. Kerry gave everyone a look that mixed excitement with terror before he too, doubled over and slid out from the seat. Alec gave Riley an encouraging squeeze before letting her hand go. She slid out behind Kerry and followed him.

Several of the Mheer were walking backwards towards the door, their weapons trained on Tyrell, who acted as if he didn't notice them. Three others waited for Darius and Alec to take their places in the line before marching silently behind them.

Alec tried to slump his shoulders and appear sufficiently cowed but inside he was growing angry. What the hell did they want them for, anyway? It wasn't like he knew any state secrets or anything. Riley's statement that he could be a target because of something he couldn't even remember made him distinctly uncomfortable. What on earth could they have done to piss off the Mheer so much they'd attack an intergala tic ship and chance getting blown out of existence? *Or was this entire thing staged to look like trouble?*

That odd thought stopped dead centre in his brain and seemed to lodge there.

It almost made him stumble. Was *that* why Riley had said what she'd said? Was she just pretending ignorance? Was Darius? Could he trust either of them? Could he trust *anyone*? He was so deeply caught up in his thoughts his hands drifted from the tip of his head to his ears. He only realized as the Mheer rushed towards him, weapons level with his face.

"Put your hands on your head," Darius almost shouted. "Don't look them in the eyes."

Quickly Alec complied. He kept his gaze firmly on his feet and tried not to flinch when one of the Mheer struck him across his shoulders. The blow hurt, but not terribly. He heard Riley cry out in defiance behind him before her voice was abruptly stopped. He didn't turn around. He didn't dare.

The Mheer indicated they should continue walking. Alec tried to keep up the appearance of subservience but snuck a peek here and there when he thought he wasn't being observed. There were Mheer leading and following other small bands of people. Everyone, like him, was walking eyes downward and hands/appendages clasped to the tops of their heads. Everyone else looked as concerned as he felt. They all didn't seem to be heading in the same direction, however. One group passed him going the other way entirely. What was going on? Why were the Mheer moving people to various parts of the ship? Weren't they going to either take them off the ship or lock them up?

They trudged through several corridors and down one flight of stairs in silence. The twisting and turning through a myriad of corridors didn't make much sense to Alec. From Darius's grim expression, not to him either.

After what seemed to Alec to have been a walk all over the ship, they halted. Alec raised his head enough to look around. They were in a functional corridor that lacked all the polish and glamour of the main ship. This was the sort of place that would have holding cells, Alec thought to himself; the general passenger population would probably never venture here. One of the Mheer waved his weapon at them. Alec's heart zipped into his throat in anticipation. He didn't know what they wanted. How could he obey their commands when they didn't even speak to them?

"Turn around and face the wall," Darius whispered, just loud enough for his companions to hear him.

"Are they going to shoot us?" Kerry hissed. He sounded more excited than scared.

"They will if you don't shut up," Riley muttered. Alec smiled despite his fear.

"Just do as I say," Darius ordered. "And keep your hands up."

They turned as one and faced the wall. Riley's shoulder bumped against Alec's arm as she moved into position. For a split second he caught her eye. He winked.

He was shoved from behind. His forehead slammed into the wall. In the split second before the pain blossomed, he nearly forgot himself and dropped his arms. His self-control snapped into play at the last moment, stopping him from swinging around and decking the closest Mheer guard.

The sound of boots on the metallic floor caught his attention through the pain. He twisted just enough to see. Another group of captives was heading their way. He goggled slightly at the woman heading the procession; the shiny jewels embedded in her skull dazzled with each overhead light she walked under. They were past in seconds, heading further down the hall. No one made any sound except Riley, who gasped slightly. When he glanced down at her, she was biting her lip but had an odd little smile.

A door opened a metre or so to Alec's right. He caught a whiff of cold, stale air, which had a metallic tinge that lingered on his tongue. The Mheer closest to the door beckoned in a gesture that no one could misunderstand. Grimacing slightly, he moved towards the doorway. Just as he'd suspected, the cramped interior of a small spaceship was visible at the end of a short, utilitarian hall. The Mheer waved his weapon. Alec was not inclined to see what exactly the weapon did; he hurried forward.

He managed to keep his hands on his head despite having to duck almost in half to enter the tiny quarters. It was obviously a storage compartment of some kind, about a metre in length and two metres high. The walls were bare metal and there wasn't a viewport of any kind. Reluctantly he crossed to the farthest wall and waited. He heard indistinct voices outside the ship and leaned over to see back out the corridor but Darius blocked his view. A moment later Darius ducked his head and squeezed in beside him. Before Alec could open his mouth to speak, the metallic walls groaned slightly and a sliding wall moved into place, sealing the doorway. They were smothered in near blackness.

"Oh, this is great," Darius muttered. Alec could feel Darius's breath on his ear but there was no space to move away.

"Where's Riley?" Alec asked. His voice seemed inordinately loud in the confined space. "What'd they do to her? Where are they taking us? What're they going to do?"

"Relax, Alec," Darius sighed. Alec felt him shift as he tried to get comfortable. "She's fine. Probably being loaded into another ship like this at this moment. Wherever they're taking us, I think they want us all together."

"How do you know?" Alec's voice took on the worry he'd tried to suppress while they were marching under guard. "Is Kerry with her?"

Alec could almost hear Darius's smile. He couldn't see the orb in Darius's hand but felt the coolness of the crystal when Darius tapped him on the wrist with it. "If you remember our orb lessons, you'll know that I'm a pretty experienced telepath when I have one of these in my hand. I've been trying to listen to their thoughts as they gave us the grand tour. Their brains are harder to access than humans, and there's some weird distortion going on, but I think I've got the gist of it. They're under orders to bring us to their planet. None of them know for what reason, but then Mheer aren't known for their ability to think beyond the next ten minutes. Don't worry. They might wave their guns around a bit and aren't above a good slap or two, but they aren't planning on seriously hurting us. At least not now. And Tyrell is with Riley and Kerry. Relax. She's safe."

Alec digested that information with a deep sigh. He didn't like it, but he could hardly do anything about it now. "So now what?"

Before Darius answered, the entire ship began to vibrate and a deep throbbing noise filled the air. Alec quickly ran his hands over the nearby walls but there was nothing to hold onto.

"We sit back and enjoy the ride," Darius yelled over the engine whine. "And hope that you don't get space sick."

Riley was going to throw up. Wedged in beside Tyrell on one side and Kerry on the other, she barely had room to take a deep breath.

The Mheer had locked them into a space the size of a linen cupboard aboard one of their ships. Other than pointing with the business end of their weapons, there'd been no instructions and nothing in the way of threats. Riley had taken her cues from Tyrell. He'd shown no resistance and climbed into what Riley had figured was a small cargo hold without a word. Riley had scuttled in behind him, and Kerry had been shoved in after her. The wall had slid back into place with an ominous grinding sound, cutting off most of the light and a fair bit of the ventilation. The cell quickly grew too warm. Claustrophobic. To add to the misery was the constant roller coaster movement. Clearly a tiny ship like this hadn't the kind of stabilizers the giant intergalactic vessels did.

29

The tiny ship rolled again to one side before righting itself. Riley's stomach lurched. She wasn't aware of groaning but she must have.

"If you can reach your orb," Tyrell yelled above the din of the engine, "touching it will allay some of the sickness."

Riley couldn't nod; she was afraid that any further movement of her inner ears would be too much for her stomach. She forced herself to concentrate. She hadn't had time to locate her orb or pull it into her palm while they entered the ship.

She forced her attention to shift from her heaving guts to her orb. She could feel it in the front right pocket of her overalls, jammed into her hip between herself and Kerry. Maybe if she shifted to the left, the orb would be freed up and she could get her hands down to it?

She doubted that Kerry would mind if she twisted around to get at it. He still seemed fascinated at being captured by aliens and didn't appreciate the seriousness of the situation at all.

"Ignore what I'm doing," Riley said to him.

"Why?" Kerry asked. Riley would have kicked him, but her legs were squashed under one of Tyrell's and she couldn't move them.

"Because," she ground out, "I can barely breathe in this position. Shift over."

"Which way?"

The deep sigh coincided with another of the Mheer vessel's stomach-emptying drops and for a minute Riley was far too preoccupied with desperately trying not to heave out the entire volume of the protein supplement she'd eaten a short time ago. Vomiting in such an enclosed, unventilated space would be the absolute worst. Eventually the waves of nausea diminished to a dull roar. Without bothering to answer Kerry, Riley tried to squirm towards Tyrell, moving so that her right hip rolled away from Kerry and the opening to the pocket was unobstructed. The orb had worked its way deep into the narrow pocket. The pocket had gotten twisted. Grimacing, she tried rocking to and fro but it didn't seem to be helping. In fact, if anything, the orb seemed to be pushed further away.

"What are you doing?" Kerry asked. "I can't see."

"Of course you can't. It's almost entirely dark in here." Riley shot a venomous look in his direction and wished he could see it. He was seriously getting on her nerves. "Shut up."

"If I knew what you wanted, maybe I could help,"

Kerry snapped back.

"The walls could have listening devices," Tyrell warned.

"I thought this was just a cargo hold," Kerry hissed back.

"Mheer generally transport live cargo," Tyrell replied.

"Well how they'd hear anything with the engines blasting like this is beyond me," Kerry groused. "Haven't these aliens ever heard of mufflers?"

"My overalls are twisted and really uncomfortable," Riley said slowly. "Can you reach my right leg, just above the knee and give it a tug to straighten it?"

Kerry shifted a bit. Riley suppressed the grunt when his elbow dug into her side as he wriggled until he was able to reach her knee. The tight space didn't allow him to bend but there seemed to be enough room to slightly squat. A couple of brief tugs pulled the material straight.

"Thanks," she sighed. She twisted her shoulders again and tried to slip a hand into the pocket. Slowly and carefully she pushed the crystal upwards, easing it past her hip. The ship rolled again and the three of them were slammed to the left wall. For a moment Riley lost track of the orb. It was only as the ship righted that her hands were free again to find it. Unfortunately, it had fallen to the bottom of the pocket again. Riley started all over.

"Where do you think they're taking us?" Kerry asked.

"Mheeror," Tyrell replied.

"That's their home planet?" said Kerry.

"Yes. I have not visited Mheeror before. Most off-Worlders would be actively discouraged from visiting. The Mheer are not known for their hospitality. And with all the volcanic activity, their planet is hardly the most pleasant or scenic."

"So why do you think we're going there?"

"These are short range vessels. There is nowhere else they could travel to safely."

Kerry paused. "Why have this big Council thing on

their planet? If they don't like people visiting it seems kind of crazy to host some massive party. Darius was saying that the Council Senate is the biggest shindig going. People from every section of the galaxy show up for it."

"I doubt the Mheer offered," was all Tyrell replied.

"Finally," Riley muttered. Her orb was clutched tightly in her hand. Already the nausea was rapidly abating. Feeling stronger, she turned her attention. "So Mheeror has active volcanoes? Like, just how many and how close will we be to them?"

"Hawaii has active volcanoes," Kerry said placated. "Don't worry."

"Don't tell me what to worry about," Riley snapped. "I've travelled a whole lot more in space than you have. I can make up my own mind when to worry. Ty?"

"Mheeror is a relatively young planet, colonized centuries ago for its strategic position and exceptionally high mineral content. The main commercial enterprise is mining. The gravity is higher than you have experienced elsewhere. However most Mheer now live above the planet where the gravity is not as troublesome. Volcanic activity, while persistent on the surface, has little impact above the clouds. You should not be in danger from that."

"But we are in danger, aren't we?" Riley asked quietly.

"Most definitely," Tyrell agreed.

"Why?" Kerry asked. "I mean they haven't hurt us or anything. They've waved their weapons around but no one's been shot. We've been rounded up and dumped on this little ship but for what purpose? If they wanted to kill us they could have done that already. Easily. They haven't. So, are we really in danger or do they want us for something else?"

"That's the stupidest thing I've heard in ages," Riley scoffed.

"It isn't." Tyrell said. "You have an excellent point. My data suggests that no one on board the Council's vessel was harmed. The threat is more implied than demonstrated. The question is, *why?*"

"The question is, *who?*" Riley amended.

"Huh?" Kerry gave a short laugh.

"Who, you idiot," Riley said. "It's the *who* that's important. Once you know *who* is behind this, the *why* will fall into place."

Tyrell was silent, likely thinking hard.

"Yeah, who wants *us?*" Kerry asked the two others. "I can count on one hand the people in the universe who know I'm alive and I can't think of a reason why they'd want me."

"I know someone who'd be glad to see me dead," Riley muttered.

The little ship changed pitch again. The engine roar exponentially increased in volume and the metal around them started to hum and vibrate. The ship dropped, faster and faster. Kerry tried to bring his hands up to brace himself but the space was so tight he couldn't manage it. Riley gave a strangled cry as Kerry's arm dug viciously into her neck. Tyrell shouted something but his words were inaudible above the screaming metal. Riley struggled. She couldn't breathe with Kerry so close. His shoulder was pressed tightly against her mouth and his arm cut across her neck like a vice. She desperately tried to move her head but the G-force held her immobile.

Another sensation slithered into her awareness. Something malevolent and familiar. Something just outside of her conscious mind and she couldn't quite put her finger on…

She couldn't breathe. She couldn't move. If this didn't stop in seconds, she was going to die.

30

Until an hour ago, telepathy was only a word in a dictionary. Now, Alec had a new and decidedly interesting form of communication at his disposal. It was fast and incredibly clear. Darius had managed to dump a colossal amount of information into Alec's mind, complete with mental images that he would never have been able to communicate with words. Best of all, it was unnoticeable to the Mheer, whom Darius had warned were likely observing them from outside their holding cell.

The ship was now heading towards the planet for docking. The docking station was in the stratosphere of the planet, Darius had informed him, and these puny cigar-shaped ships were only capable of entering the atmosphere at a particular angle. Which explained why Alec had the uncomfortable sensation of having his brains pushed out his ears in the headlong rush. Fortunately, Darius managed the continuous contact that permitted communication and the steady flow of information helped take Alec's mind off his discomfort.

He hadn't had much time to worry about Riley. There wasn't any time to lose, Darius urged him. They had to be prepared for anything to happen on the planet once they got there. What exactly "anything" was, Darius hadn't explained. And to be frank, Alec kind of didn't want to know.

Keep your orb within touching distance at all times, once we land, Darius's thoughts came through.

Should we try to make a run for it?

No point, Darius replied, not without a touch of wry amusement. *The planet's covered in lava flows and the lower atmosphere is poisonous. You can't fly one of these ships and even if you could, where would you take it? The nearest planet is two light years away. This ship doesn't have enough power to get out of this solar system.*

Then what do we do?

Watch and wait. I'm assuming they'll let us know once we arrive.

Waiting around for the axe to drop wasn't Alec's forte. *Are you sure? I mean, maybe we can break into their command centre, read their plans or something.*

Alec, you watch too much TV.

Stung slightly, he changed tack. *What about Riley?*

What about her?

Even Darius's tone was a bit sulky. Time to find out what was going on between those two. *Is she okay? Can you use this telepathy thing on her too? Can you get a message to her from me?*

She's too far away. And don't ask me, Alec.

Ask you what?

Alec, telepathy works differently from speech. I can sense what you are going to say well before you say it, even in your head. You want to know what's going on between Riley and me. I'm telling you to butt out.

Did you do it with her? Alec couldn't believe he'd asked so bluntly, but really it had been at the back of his mind for ages now. He had to know. *While I was gone. Is that why you're fighting?*

He could feel Darius's amusement. *No. There's never been anything like that between us. Riley might have, at one time, had a bit of a crush on me, but it never progressed into anything but a couple of chaste kisses. I love someone else. Incidentally, so does she. She's just too stubborn to admit it.*

And she hates the woman you love.

Darius pulled away for a second. Not an easy thing to do when the force around them was making it almost impossible to breathe. Then his hand re-connected with Alec's wrist and the connection was reestablished. *True.*

But it's something else, isn't it? Alec pushed. He could feel something. Something uneasy, infusing Darius's thoughts with just a subtle tinge of darkness.

Your imagination is working overtime. It's simple annoyance, Alec. Riley was pretty uncomplimentary about Anna and it pissed me off. Nothing more. Now get ready, the ship is leveling off. Slowing. As soon as we dock we'll be sprung from this box. They might try and separate us. Stay as close to me as possible without making it obvious. I can maintain a link with your mind if you concentrate on hearing me and we're physically not too distant.

Alec agreed as a shiver of apprehension ran through him.

Almost immediately he felt the ship rapidly decelerate. They were slammed into the forward wall, which fortunately was very close so the impact was merely uncomfortable. There was a juddering halt and the sudden reduction in the engine's whine to silence. Alec had been concentrating so intently on Darius he had forgotten how noisy the flight was. Something outside the cargo hold banged several times, then a pale yellow light flooded the compartment. Almost immediately the doorway started to open and a flood of cool air, tinged with something burnt and metallic, hit them.

Alec lifted his hand to shield his eyes while Darius dropped his hand from Alec's wrist. He started to scramble out before the first weapon was pulled from the Mheer guard's holster. Alec immediately followed suit, holding a hand over his eyes to protect them from the sudden glare.

The door opened into a small, low ceilinged area that looked like a drunken handyman had thrown it together from scraps. There were two Mheer guards standing next to the opening. Both wore the same all-over bodysuits and the same belligerent expressions as those who'd boarded the Intergalactic vessel. Naked square light bulbs dangled between the piping that zigzagged across the ceiling. There was no viewport so Alec had no idea how big the station was or how many ships might be docked. He didn't have much time to wonder about it, either. Almost immediately he and Darius were shepherded towards another door and out into a busy corridor.

They joined the streaming crowd. It seemed the Mheer had emptied out the entire contingent of the Councilor's vessel and everyone had landed at once. Mheer were everywhere, jostling the crowd forward, urging stragglers with the butts of their weapons, pointing towards some distant target that Alec couldn't see and grunting orders that even with his imbedded translator made little sense.

The trek down the corridor went on for some time. Here and there doorways opened and more people spilled out. Alec kept his eyes peeled for Riley but there was no sign of her.

She's around somewhere, Darius's thought popped into Alec's mind. *Don't worry. Pay attention to your surroundings, in case we have an opportunity to escape.*

I thought you said we wouldn't escape?

I said we wouldn't make a run for it until we knew what the situation is. Look around you. All these people didn't come here under force. Most of them don't have guards. They might have ships we could hide on.

Alec realized that what Darius said was true. Many of the beings jostling against him as the crowd grew thicker were not under any type of supervision and only a few had weapons trained on them. Odder still, those without guards didn't even seem to notice those who did.

The corridor suddenly funnelled into a glass-doored entryway. Several Mheer were allowing people into a small chamber one cluster at a time. Alec and Darius had to wait for several groups to pass through before they too were herded in. The doors behind them closed, an overhead light flashed several times and the doors ahead opened. Alec stepped out into a massive hangar with a ceiling far above them and various small ships parked here and there. There was a sharp, cold breeze rushing through the space and an unpleasant smell of smoke and rotting eggs. Alec couldn't stop a sudden shiver as he raised his hand to cover his mouth and nose. He looked around. There were openings in the walls that allowed craft to fly in. Alec wanted to go look out an opening to see how high above the planet they were, but the smell was too disgusting. The crowd continued to surge forward and he lost sight of Darius when a group of extremely tall aliens with mottled, purplish skin pushed in between them. Alec fought his anxiety, let them brush past him while he slowed down. Almost immediately he saw Darius again, but he had to push against the tide to make his way to Darius's side.

Are all these people here for the Senate?

Darius nodded, his eyes scanning the crowd while he spoke aloud. "Must be. There are delegates from all the planets in the Home Galaxy that are part of the Senate Collective. Attendance is mandatory." Suddenly Darius grabbed his head and cried out. Alec turned to look. The Mheer behind Darius was dropping his arm to his side. Obviously, he hadn't liked Darius speaking.

Are you okay? Alec thought urgently.

Will be, came Darius's reply as he rubbed the back of his head. *Avoid annoying them, Alec. These idiots don't know their own strength.*

What's that smell?

Sulphur. Poisonous gas from volcanoes. You noticed we passed through the decontamination airlock to come in here. We'll go through another to get into the safer part of the station on the other side of the hangar.

Alec held his breath and tried not to look scared about

what those gases were probably doing inside his lungs. Without trying to seem panicked, he hurried forward. The crowd was funnelled through a huge doorway and into another, larger airlock. Alec bumped shoulders with Darius and several others as the decontamination procedure ran its course. The farther doors opened and they stepped into a long corridor. Alec took a deep breath of relief.

The crowd again surged forward. There were far fewer Mheer in the crowd now, though the two that had them under guard hadn't left their sides. There was little conversation but he picked out the occasional phrase or word. Nearly everyone had the same subject; the Senate and the proclamations that were due to be voted on. No one expressed any annoyance at having to attend, which Alec thought was rather strange considering Darius's previous comments. Perhaps the delegates were being very careful?

The corridor eventually opened into a wide hall. Like the rest of the station, it looked to be cobbled together of odds and ends. There was a fuzzy material on the ground, like a carpet, and several archways leading out into a number of narrower corridors. The crowd was dissipating in different directions. Alec came to a halt. He had no idea where to go.

A shove to his shoulders made the decision easy. He turned briefly to make sure Darius was beside him before reluctantly moving in the direction he'd been instructed. Only those with Mheer guards were travelling this way, he noticed. And no one looked familiar. No sign of Riley or Kerry.

Where do you think they're taking us?

Probably to be locked up again, Darius replied. He gave Alec a tight smile.

Hope they feed us, Alec thought morosely. *I'm starved.*

After walking what seemed like kilometres they finally stopped in front of a pair of massive doors. There was an uneasy murmur among the prisoners as guards moved to pull back bolts that were thicker than Alec's waist. The bolts shot back with a hollow *boom* and the Mheer applied their muscles to opening the doors. They swung open with a loud grating noise, as if the hinges had rusted. The crowd was ushered forward with Alec and Darius near the rear of the procession.

The room was about the size of a school gymnasium and like the rest of the station, low ceilinged and without windows. Pipes crisscrossed above their heads and here and there the square bulbs dangled on thin cords. The space was about half full of beings who looked expectantly at the newcomers. Alec quickly scanned the crowd but didn't see Riley.

He received a shove against his shoulders when he slowed crossing the threshold and bit his tongue on the retort. Darius was at his side and almost immediately the doors closed behind them.

Alec turned and spoke aloud. "Now what do we do?" There was no need for telepathy. None of the Mheer had stayed.

Darius gave a one-shouldered shrug. "See if Riley, Tyrell or Mr. Enthusiasm are here somewhere. Find out if anyone knows what's going on. You take the right side of the room, I'll go left."

Walking around, Alec craned his neck trying to spot a distinctive dark head among the crowd. It wasn't easy. Riley was pretty tiny. He had a feeling that she'd find him first. He listened attentively as he walked, letting the translator from his restarted brain implant do its job. He heard snatches of conversation; most were anxious at being segregated and locked up, a few angry at the imposition. No one seemed to have any idea why this had happened to them. He slipped his hand into his pocket and gripped his orb but the telepathic connection he'd had with Darius didn't seem to work with any of the people that surrounded him. Maybe it was Darius who made it happen? Or maybe it only worked between Operatives?

Someone tapped his shoulder. Alec whirled around.

"Glad to see ya, mate. We were starting to get worried." Kerry was wearing his usual grin but there were signs of strain around his eyes.

"Where's Riley?"

"Over there," Kerry gave a nod to the far corner. "I think she's sick or something."

Alec rushed off in the direction Kerry had indicated, pushing his way through the crowd, not noticing the indignant looks he engendered. He arrived at the corner of the room but there was no sign of Riley. He grabbed Kerry's arm the instant he appeared.

"This way," Kerry pointed to their left before Alec could open his mouth. "Follow me."

Kerry led him a short distance away. Riley was on the floor, her head in Tyrell's lap. She was fast asleep. Tyrell had his orb in his large hand, almost hiding it completely, and had pressed it up against Riley's forehead. Alec dropped to his knees.

"What's the matter with her?"

Tyrell looked up and met Alec's eyes. "She passed out as we entered the atmosphere. She should be fine."

Alec interpreted the slight pause in Tyrell's speech. "But you're not sure."

"Since she shouldn't have become unconscious in the first place, then no, I'm not."

"Maybe she's sick?" Alec reached out and stroked an errant lock of hair off Riley's forehead. She wasn't feverish, if anything her skin was rather cool. "Or maybe she got hurt and you didn't notice?"

"She was wedged in between us like ham in a sandwich. If anyone was going to be injured it would have been Ty or me," Kerry spoke up. "I think this whole thing has been too much for her. Girls are like that, you know.

Fainting for no reason and stuff."

Riley had hardly struck Alec as the swooning type and he was about to say so when Darius appeared at Kerry's elbow.

"Riley's tougher than you are." Darius also dropped to the ground and whipped out his orb, pushing Tyrell's out of the way. He closed his eyes for a moment. Alec could almost feel his concentration. After a moment he opened his eyes and sat back on his heels, removing his orb. He dropped it into his pocket. Before Alec could ask, Riley's eyelids fluttered open. She blinked several times in apparent concentration. Alec watched comprehension flood across her face. She struggled to sit up.

"What are you looking at?" she snapped.

"You," Alec grinned. "You fainted."

"I did not," she responded avoiding his eyes. She straightened up a bit shakily, pulling her arm away from Darius who had reached out to steady her. "I'm fine. Stop staring."

Darius was frowning and staring at Riley with a type of concentration that made Alec distinctly uncomfortable.

Riley pierced Darius with a sharp look. "What?"

"You've been in contact with the Others," Darius said.

"*Whaaat?*" Riley gasped.

"Impossible," Tyrell said at the same time.

"I can still feel the lingering touch," Darius replied. "Did you see a rip or anything?"

"Of course not," Tyrell responded for her. "If we had encountered a rip we'd be dead now."

"What's a rip?" Kerry interjected, but no one paid any attention.

"I felt something," Riley said slowly as she tried to recall the moment just before passing out. "But it didn't feel like it has in the past. You and I have been in a rip before. I know what that feels like. This was something else. I can't describe it."

"I suggest we maintain a high alert from now on," Darius said. "If the Others are here and if they can move among us without a rip, then it goes without saying that we are in serious trouble."

Everyone but Kerry nodded. They stood for a moment quietly, contemplating this new and very troubling situation. Alec almost wished Darius hadn't put so much information into his brain—he'd prefer Kerry's ignorance just now.

"Who are these Others?" Kerry asked again.

"Aliens. Really, *really* bad ones," Riley answered shortly. "Where are we and what's happened?"

"Mheer holding cell on the station above the planet's surface," Tyrell reported. "We are still prisoners, as are many of the passengers of the Councilor's ship." He got to his feet as he spoke. "As you will notice, many of our fellow prisoners are the staff of the Council. Curious."

"Why curious?" Alec asked before Kerry could.

"Because I do not understand its implications," Tyrell said.

"When is the Council meeting?" Riley asked.

"A cycle or two maybe," Darius replied. "I don't know exactly. Why?"

"Because it gives us time to see if we can figure out why they've brought us here," Riley said. "And time to plan what we're going to do once we know."

Despite Riley's optimism that someone, somewhere in the crowd would know something more than they did, the ensuing hours were, in Alec's opinion, a waste of time. They'd split up at Tyrell's suggestion and moved through the crowd, asking everyone with whom they could communicate their ideas. The answers ranged from outright terror (two non-humanoids with muscles as big as Alec's legs) to nonchalance (the undersecretary to a Councilor who thought answering questions was beneath her). Tyrell had been the least successful. Something about him intimidated fellow captives and most just moved out of his way as he approached. Darius had probably wormed his way into more conversations than any of them, but even he hadn't come up with a solid piece of intel.

31

The hours passed. With nothing to do and no new information to mull over, Alec found a spot against a wall and slid down into a sitting position. No food was forthcoming and worse still, there weren't any bathrooms. Alec imagined that some of the aliens didn't need to use one but the humans in the crowd did. It seemed odd that they'd be confined to a place without the most basic of accommodations.

Riley was curled up asleep next to him, her head pillowed on his leg. She was still overly pale and her eyes ringed with dark circles. He was secretly happy that she was out for the count. She'd been unhappy, to say the least, with the lack of information and eager to share her disappointment with anyone in earshot. But she'd wound down faster than he'd expected and had fallen into a deep sleep hours ago. Contact with these Others was clearly not good for one's health.

Darius was sitting on Alec's other side, rolling his orb around in the palm of his hand and saying nothing. Alec had the impression he was worried but Darius hadn't confirmed that one way or the other. The lines of telepathic communication were down, at least for the moment.

Tyrell stepped out of the crowd with Kerry at his side. He squatted in front of Alec and Darius. "Several of our fellow prisoners are growing restless. We must brace ourselves for trouble."

Alec sat up a little straighter but Darius didn't seem to respond.

"What kind of trouble?" Alec asked, looking around.

"Revolt, perhaps. It is unclear."

Kerry chimed in. "See those big sloth-type guys over there?" He pointed down the room to where two furry quadrupeds were circling each other slowly. "Apparently, they're claustrophobic. Rumour has it they walk around in circles just before they go ballistic."

"I've seen Reasurui lose control before," Darius muttered. "It isn't pretty."

Tyrell ignored him. "The Denovian Councilor's entourage is at the door. They've been working on the hinges for the last couple of hours. They could have the door off in minutes. If that happens, there will be a rush for freedom."

"And then the guns come out," Kerry added.

Darius nodded and slowly got to his feet. "We're in the direct line of fire. We should move to the side, preferably near the door so if we get a chance to run for it, we do. I don't think Mheer weaponry goes around corners."

"What about Riley?" Kerry asked.

"I'll get her," Darius said. But before he could move close enough to pick her up, Tyrell moved in front of him and reached for her. Alec saw Darius's face contort into rage for the briefest of seconds. In a blink, a composed, uninterested expression was back in place. Tyrell hadn't noticed.

Tyrell smoothly picked Riley up in his arms. She didn't stir as they quietly began to move around the periphery of the room. The unrest was becoming clearer. Here and there pockets of people were talking animatedly, arms and other appendages gesticulating with increasing force. Voices were raised. Alec had a momentary glimpse of two people shoving each other before the crowd around them closed ranks. Goosebumps broke out on Alec's arms and across the back of his neck. The unpleasant feeling in the room was palpable, and vaguely familiar.

He didn't have time to think about it. Tyrell led them to wait against the same wall as the doors. He lowered Riley carefully to the floor and stood with his back against the wall, protecting her with his body. Darius took up a position directly beside him and after a moment of contemplation, Kerry did the same.

"Alec, stand apart a little from us. Tell us what's happening at the door," Tyrell ordered.

Alec moved slightly away and rose on tiptoes to get a clear view of the door. Tyrell was right. A tight crowd was actively engaged in some activity in front of the massive doors. Several of them had climbed up onto the shoulders of their comrades and were using their hands and in one case, claws, to attack the hinges. Two out of the three hinges on the far side were destroyed. It was only a matter of minutes.

He returned to the others. "They're on the last hinge." He glanced down at Riley. "We should wake her up, just in case we have to run."

"Kerry?" Tyrell gave a brief nod in Riley's direction. Kerry squatted down and began to shake Riley's shoulder. The crowd around them was talking so loudly Alec couldn't hear what Kerry was saying.

"Have you noticed how angry people are with each other?" Darius asked Tyrell quietly.

Tyrell gave Darius a long look before answering. "You're thinking the Others, aren't you?"

Darius nodded. "I didn't see any rips anywhere but it just feels wrong. I don't know. Maybe it's knowing that Riley was contacted and now everyone here seems too short tempered, too quickly. I could be reading more into this than I should."

"Stay alert," Tyrell advised.

A sudden roar of voices indicated victory. Alec quickly dashed to Tyrell's side as the crowd around him surged forward, almost sweeping him up in its wake. Tyrell's hand grabbed his upper arm to hold him steady. Riley stood upright but she looked confused and not quite herself. Kerry had his arms around her and was speaking quietly into her ear. Alec fought the sudden impulse to punch Kerry's lights out.

The crowd was a lot faster leaving the enclosure than they'd been entering it. Within seconds only the slowest moving were still inside.

"Keep Riley close, Darius," Tyrell ordered. "Let's go."

Joining in with the last of the captives, they ran outside. While most of the crowd seemed to have gone back the way they had come, Tyrell turned in the opposite direction and sprinted down the corridor without a backwards glance. Darius and Riley ran hand in hand right behind him and Alec and Kerry took up the rear. Alec shot rapid glances behind them but no one was following.

They rounded one corner after another. Tyrell led them down a short flight of stairs and doubled back the way they'd come. Finally after several minutes of unrelenting running, he called a halt.

Alec gripped his knees and waited for his breath to return. There was a time, he knew, when he could have run like that for hours. He glanced at the others; everyone was short of breath. Then it hit him; the altitude.

"Where now?" Darius asked. He'd let go of Riley's hand and she'd moved away from him to lean against the wall.

"Use your orb," Tyrell instructed. "There may be a schematic of this station we can tap into."

"While you're looking for an escape route," Alec spoke up, "find a bathroom. And a kitchen. In that order."

"Good idea," Riley added. Her eyes met Alec's and she gave him a quick grin.

"I think I saw one just back a few metres," Darius said. He waved his orb back the way they'd just come. "Open doorway, has two triangle symbols above it. You won't be able to mistake the smell. Be quick."

Riley led the way, Kerry and Alec right on her heels. Sure enough within seconds they had found it.

"You go first," Alec offered Riley with, he considered, a great deal of chivalry.

"If I pass out from the stink, come in and get me," Riley muttered as she pinched her nose and darted inside. She was out in double quick time and somewhat green in colour. She waved the boys in and headed back to Darius.

Alec took a deep breath and entered. It looked remarkably like a bathroom at home—at least he could figure out generally where he was to do what. Kerry had that rapt expression on his face that indicated he was in the throes of geek ecstasy and probably had forgotten why he'd entered in the first place. Alec ignored him and quickly went about his business. A second later he heard Kerry say, "This is just so cool." Alec rolled his eyes but didn't respond.

When they returned to join the other three, they found all of them with their orbs out and their eyes shut. Riley cracked open one eyelid for a moment, then immediately resumed her concentration.

"Found anything?" Alec couldn't wait.

Tyrell shook his head. "Not yet. The Mheer don't use central computer banks like us. Specific information is harder to uncover."

"But the benefit of that is one group has no idea what the others are doing," Darius opened his eyes. "That means a less coordinated effort to find us."

"So if any of them come across us, they won't necessarily know that we shouldn't be out and about, right?" Kerry had joined the group again. "Technically we could bluff our way out of this."

Darius shook his head. "If we're in a section of the station we shouldn't be, then no. If we're mixed in with the other delegates, it's possible. Hiding down here is not a good idea."

"Can't we find a ship and make a run for it?" Riley asked. "There were lots of people the Mheer weren't guarding. They arrived on ships. Who would question if one of those ships left?"

"People are coming to the Senate, not leaving," Darius reminded her. "A departing ship will stand out. There'll be questions. Then big guns trained on us when they don't get the answers they like. Then lots of very annoyed Mheer pulling the triggers."

"So what do we do?" Alec asked.

"Avoid getting recaptured, for a start," Tyrell answered. "Find somewhere to hide and monitor the situation. Prepare to act, if and when it becomes clear that we must."

They looked at one another. No one had a better suggestion.

"Okay then," Riley sighed. "Hiding places. Anyone got a good idea?"

But no one had a chance to answer.

The ceiling panels right above them suddenly slid back and two Mheer dropped to the floor. Tyrell and Darius flung their hands up and used their orbs to create a force field that repelled the first several shots from the Mheer guns. But it wasn't enough.

Several other Mheer appeared from the other end of the corridor and open fired. Energy beams sliced through the air. Another two Mheer soldiers dropped from the ceiling a little further back and rushed Riley and Kerry. Alec managed to pull his orb and start the process to create a shield but he was too late.

An energy beam hit him directly in the centre of his chest. There was a horrible sensation of bees crawling over his entire body. His lungs constricted. He couldn't find the breath to scream.

Alec stood with his hands in the air. The Mheer had their weapons trained on him and Darius.

This was the weirdest attack he'd ever seen. And after playing video games like a fanatic for years, he'd seen *a lot*. The Mheer had poured out of the ceiling and around corners so fast he'd barely had a chance to grab his orb from his pocket. When they'd fired, he'd seen Kerry fall to the ground and not move again. He'd tried to erect his own barrier but it hadn't been effective enough. Riley had been shot next. She dropped. Tyrell and Darius had managed to throw up an orb-created barrier between them and the main group of Mheer, which had deflected most of the weaponry for a while. An energy beam had managed to penetrate and had hit him, and while the sensation was horrible, it had done nothing but paralyze him for a few seconds. There wasn't even an after effect. While that was happening, two Mheer had created a whole in the wall directly behind Tyrell and had shot him. He dropped to the floor too and didn't move.

Then the firing stopped. The paralysis ended. Darius and Alec quickly moved back-to-back and waited. Now Darius stood panting and Alec was staring at the Mheer, puzzled. Alec leaned backwards and whispered. "Why'd they stop?

"No idea," Darius murmured. "Stay prepared."

Alec had no plans to drop his shield. He faced the Mheer who stood several metres away, their

32

guns dangling from their thick fingers. The Mheer stared back. No one said anything.

"If I keep the barrier up can you check Riley?" Alec asked quietly. "I think she's hurt."

"No offense, Alec, but your barrier isn't strong enough. If I drop mine, we're done."

"I don't know how to do that healing thing, though. Maybe she's hurt really badly." Alec couldn't help glancing at Riley. She was deathly pale and barely breathing. What exactly did the Mheer's weapons do to humans and why were Riley and Kerry hurt far worse than he'd been?

"I won't be able to help her if I'm taken out next. Wait— something is going to happen."

"What makes you think that?"

"They aren't acting on their own, Alec. Someone is telling them what to do. So now that they have us, they'll get fresh instructions."

That wasn't reassuring in the least. Alec tried to steady his ragged breathing and calm his heart. He'd fight better with a cool head. He needed Riley to move or something. A groan would be better than this terrible silence.

"They want us to move," Darius informed him.

Alec twisted to see what Darius was seeing. Indeed, the closest Mheer was beckoning with a free hand. None of the others had dropped their weapons and every face that stared at him was distinctly unfriendly.

"What do we do?" Alec asked.

"They have the guns. Guess."

"We can't just leave them," Alec hissed, indicating his companions at his feet.

"We can't pick them up and carry all three of them with us," Darius countered.

That was true. Tyrell alone would need both of them to even lift him. Alec stared at the Mheer again. They still stood entirely still, not even blinking. None of them had hung their weapons back on their belts. Darius hadn't lowered his orb either. It was a weird sort of stalemate.

They didn't badly hurt you or me, Alec. There's a reason.

Alec was a little startled at the telepathic communication but he allowed it to flow through him and responded in kind. *You don't think it's an accident, do you?*

No. In my experience, accidents are just planned occurrences arranged by unknown forces.

So?

Who wants us alive, Alec?

I dunno. Who?

Think. It's inside you. I know she'd have put it there.

Alec suddenly stood up straighter. The emotions emanating from Darius were building in strength and starting to get uncomfortable. There was excitement and an odd kind of revulsion intermixed with anger. It was the anger that was growing stronger with every second. But, anger against whom? Alec almost took a step backwards.

Think, boy.

I am thinking. *And don't call me boy.* Alec focused on Darius's words. He couldn't think of anyone who would spare him and hurt Riley, except maybe the weird Councilor guy on the ship. But he'd only met him briefly. And why hurt Kerry? The Australian had travelled with the Councilor for weeks and the guy hadn't laid a hand on him. Why transport him all the way across the galaxy just to mow him down in laser fire? It must be someone from his past that he couldn't recall, Alec decided. Right now he'd give his right arm to remember.

He looked up at the sound of footsteps. He raised his orb a little higher in a defensive stance. A small, compact human wearing the same overalls as Darius and Riley was striding towards him. He had a salt and pepper goatee, tight eyes and the kind of swagger that made Alec think of the gang members in his old high school. There was something about him Alec instantly didn't like. Two tall, blank-faced men that reminded Alec of Tyrell flanked him on either side.

There's a reason you don't like him.

Alec turned sharply to stare at Darius. He was standing straighter and had a look on his face that seemed at first glance to be respect and admiration, but on closer inspection wasn't.

You don't like him either, Alec realized with surprise.

He covets what is mine.

It took Alec a second to understand what Darius meant but then he reacted with surprise. Alec turned back to the man. The guy was at least twice Darius's age. Who on earth were they fighting over?

The man stopped a couple of metres away and surveyed the carnage with satisfaction. One of his hands came up to stroke his beard. "Are they still alive?" asked the man.

Darius nodded. "Yes, Commander Kholar."

Recognition struck Alec squarely across the shoulders. That name was *very* familiar. He peered closely at Kholar and wracked his brains for a memory.

"Was it necessary to use Immical force beams on them, sir? The Australian boy was hit three times. I doubt he'll recover."

"He's no use to me alive, Finn. He has no Tyon power and therefore no purpose." Kholar indicated with a sweep of his hands that the Mheer should move forward. "Take them to the Senate chambers," he ordered, waving his hand at Riley and Tyrell. "If I can't have Logan here then I would have his first-in-command witness the end of this. And Anna wants the girl."

Alec startled. *Who's Anna?*

Darius didn't answer. The connection between them was broken again. He wasn't sorry to have it end. The waves of anger and distress emanating from Darius were getting stronger and more uncomfortable by the minute.

"What does she want her for?" Darius asked. His voice was tight with strain.

"Still care for her, Finn? A moderately talented, whiny Terran child who will never conform to our ways? Really? You grew soft among them. It was a mistake to send you back to Terra for the collection phase." A sly smile crossed Kholar's face. "In retrospect I should never have given in to her, but as you know, she has ways of persuasion."

Darius stiffened and held still. A battle raged silently inside him for a second until he got his emotions under control. Kholar seemed to notice and he smiled as he watched Darius slightly drop his shoulders. "You have learned some degree of control, Finn. That is good. I can use that."

The Mheer moved forward and pairing off, picked up Tyrell and Riley under the armpits and began to drag them away down the hall. They merely stepped over Kerry.

"Hey, be careful with her," Alec said sharply as one of the Mheer gave Riley an unpleasant yank. The Mheer ignored him.

"She isn't worth your concern, Alec," Kholar almost purred. He had stepped closer to them while Alec's attention was on Riley. He was now standing uncomfortably close. Alec had the uneasy impression that the man found him inordinately desirable. Alec took an unconscious step backwards. "Soon you will have much more important things to occupy your mind."

"How do you know me?" Alec asked uneasily.

"I trained you for weeks to obey my commands, Alec, so that our mission could be accomplished."

"I don't remember it."

"No, of course you don't. We saw to that. But you will." Kholar's gloating smile was too creepy for words. A shiver rode down Alec's spine.

"Look, I don't know what you think I'm going to do for you, but I won't do anything that's going to see Riley hurt. So if you think that I will, you're wrong. I mean it."

"But Finn would, wouldn't you?" Kholar fixed Darius

with his probing gaze.

Darius stood very still for a moment and his facial expression was entirely blank. Then he gave a sharp nod. "If Anna tells you to slit Riley's throat, Alec, you'll do it. You won't worry about wanting to or not when the time comes." He faced Kholar. "Isn't that right, Commander?"

Kholar's smile widened even further. "Just so, Finn. I see you completely understand the situation. I am pleased to hear it. Your life, although you did not know it, was hanging on your willingness to help us with our task."

"My loyalty was never in question," Darius murmured.

Alec couldn't believe what he was hearing. Darius was working for this guy and was willing to do *anything* they told him to? This didn't make sense at all. The Darius Finn he'd come to know in a short time was not someone who could kill an innocent person without a qualm. How could Alec have been so wrong about him?

"Good. All is in order," said Kholar, apparently oblivious to Alec's distress. "We will proceed to the Senate and play our part in the proceedings. Pay close attention, Alec. You will see the history of this galaxy change tonight. Soon the Council will be no more and the chronicles will hail *you* as the instrument of destruction."

The first thing Riley noticed was that her armpits hurt. Which was odd. Why not the rest of her? The answer slowly became clear. Someone, or in fact two someone's, were dragging her, their hands gripping her cruelly under her arms, letting her feet trail on the ground. She was facing downwards and could only see the scuffed metallic floor and the black clad boots of her captors. She squinted for a moment. Those boots looked familiar.

It came back in a rush. The Mheer. The bolted-together station above their home planet. Getting shot in the corridor with Alec and the others. Riley would have shaken her head to clear it but whatever she'd been hit with interfered with motor function longer than it did with conscious thought. Her body wasn't responding, not a twitch, to the signals she was sending it.

33

Okay, she'd think now, act later. What she could see of the corridor seemed fairly wide. Here and there other feet came into view and passed her. There were sounds of many people moving around and talking in quiet voices. Various smells assaulted her nostrils. The pervasive aroma of overheated metal was the most prominent, but other odours, most unpleasant, came and went. Riley associated those with the people or creatures that passed her. The familiar scents of Darius, Alec and Kerry were missing. Her guts spasmed with worry. She couldn't remember them being shot but it was highly likely. She could only hope their injuries weren't more serious than hers.

Where were the Mheer taking her? It seemed that most of the people around her were walking in the same direction. The logical conclusion was that the Senate was going to start soon and she was being taken to participate. Why? The Council had no need of her; they'd made that abundantly clear. They could be taking her to lock her up again, she supposed. That was sort of reasonable. But again, *why*? How was she a threat to anyone? This didn't make sense and the longer she thought about it, the less sense it made. Someone was going to an awful lot of trouble for no reason.

Riley realized that she'd just licked her lips. Motor function must be returning. She decided not to let her captors know—if they thought she was incapable of running they'd be a lot more likely to relax their vigilance. The instant she had a chance, she would take it.

The crowd was thickening and the speed her captors were dragging her slowed. No one said anything about the Mheer carrying a young, obviously unconscious woman around, but then perhaps this sort of thing was common on Mheeros or at Council Senates? For a moment all movement stopped. Riley forced herself to stay limp. Then her captors started moving again.

The muted conversation suddenly changed. Riley was sure they had now entered a much larger space; from the echoing of voices and the airiness of sound around her, she guessed they were in an amphitheatre of some sort. She was dragged a short distance before the stairs started. Her captors grunted at people in their way, and most hurried to the side as Riley was dragged down metallic steps. The stairs went on forever, her feet striking each one with a jarring sensation that ran up her legs. Riley focused on counting. She lost track after she hit one hundred and seventeen.

It seemed to take forever, but finally the floor levelled out to a flat surface. The metallic sections of flooring had been bolted together just as haphazardly as the rest of the station and here and there were small gaps through which sunlight poured. The slight sizzle of a force field—probably all that protected them from the majority of the poisonous gases—hummed barely audibly. It dawned on her that there was probably nothing between her and a sea of molten lava but the thin metal planks, a thin layer of electromagnetic energy and kilometres of air. Focus on something else, she advised herself sternly.

Suddenly the hands under her arms pulled away and she was dropped unceremoniously. She managed to twist somewhat and hit the floor on her side. Luckily gravity pulled her onto her back. Keeping her eyes closed she forced her breathing to remain slow and steady, prevented the twitching of an eyelid by summoning all her will.

Her booted captors walked away. It was only when she was absolutely sure they had left her alone that she stole a quick glance at her surroundings. She was on the bottom floor of an incredibly massive spherical structure, created entirely of metal struts that were woven together. While the floor was essentially solid, the walls and ceiling that rose at least ten storeys high had gaps here and there, like latticework, allowing beams of light and cold gushes of smelly air to filter through. Row after row of balconies ringed the walls. They were filling up with delegates but the sound was oddly muted. The place looked like it had been thrown together at the last moment and none too carefully.

Footsteps near her grabbed her attention and she closed her barely opened eyes to feign unconsciousness. The footsteps stopped right beside her. Riley could feel the shadow across her face. Stay still, she ordered herself.

"I know you're awake." Riley's heart literally stopped. *Oh no oh no oh no.* She *knew* that voice. "There's no point acting like a child, Riley, pretending that if you ignore me long enough, I'll go away. I won't."

Every fibre of her being was screaming but Riley refused to make an audible sound. She would not give that *creature* the satisfaction.

The voice moved closer and dropped in decibels. An intimate sound now, between two people who were very close. "You have lost. You know that, do you not? I held all the cards from the very beginning, to use one of your quaint Earth phrases. You never stood a chance against me." Riley could almost hear the smile. "Letting you think you were searching for the traitor in order to spy on the Collectives' progress in learning my real agenda, sending the Mheer out to segregate you until we had arrived and set up our plans here, all of it my design and my triumph. How does it feel to be so ignorant and outsmarted, Terran child?"

Riley steeled herself. She was NOT going to lie on the ground, weak and pathetic and giving up before the fight had even started. And, she was NOT going to run. Not now. Not ever. Taking a deep breath, she sat up and faced Anna. The insipid, almost colourless eyes were the same as ever, although at this close range, Riley saw they lacked any semblance of a soul. The ash blond hair was pulled back in a seamless ponytail that hung over one slim shoulder. Anna was wearing a white shimmering gown of a material that almost floated in the air currents. The air of physical perfection was complete. Shame it was wasted on a monster.

"Where are your Tyon goons?" Riley said.

Anna's smile didn't reach her eyes. "Mostly dead. Anyone who is not useful to me is dead, Riley. As you should know."

"*I'm* not," Riley said before she could rethink it.

"Merely a matter of time. What you do not appreciate, but I will be kind enough to demonstrate for you, is the importance of timing."

"What?"

"Timing. Ensuring that you reap the most from your actions by ensuring that the timing is perfect. For example, to seal the heart of your slave you must spurn his affection until he is desperate. Then any kindness has greater weight. You can bind him to your will forever if you use the right bait."

"You mean Darius?" Riley swallowed against a dry throat.

Anna gave a short laugh. "Among others. Pretty much everyone is under my control: Logan, Dean, and yes, in particular, Darius. Even from a distance I control his actions and his desires." She paused to let that sink in. "By the way, how is your wrist?"

Riley's stomach hit the floor. It made sense now. Darius's crazy behavior, his growing dislike, the anger that burned through his skin. As Anna exerted her control, Darius had been less and less able to fight her. She felt sick. "Alec too?"

Anna's head tilted slightly to the side while she examined Riley's face. It was like being under a microscope. "I had a shorter time with Alec. I couldn't weave an unbreakable binding upon him. It is a more fragile hold." She smiled cruelly as she saw the glimmer of hope cross Riley's face. "You mistakenly believe the bond can be broken and Alec returned to you. That is not so. To break with me is to break his mind. It will destroy him."

Anna straightened. Her smile was glacial but that was nothing compared to the coldness in her gaze. She raised her arm and waved someone over. Riley could barely tear her eyes from Anna but managed a quick glance. Two Mheer guards were dragging someone between them down the same steps. Tyrell. It seemed to Riley that he was struggling ever so slightly.

"Tyrell was resistant. A shame really, as he's strong with Tyon power and could have been useful."

"Could have been?" Riley said.

"He's dead. Or will be shortly."

The Mheer carried their captive over beside Riley and at Anna's signal dropped him to the ground like a sack of potatoes. Tyrell groaned. Blood dripped down from a gash on his forehead and from his nose. He didn't seem to notice anything around him.

Anna watched Riley's expression of horror and her smile grew. "Everyone who cannot help me attain my goals dies," Anna repeated. "It is a practical and logical approach to success."

"You've been dead," Riley hissed. "Before. Darius told you what happened. Not everything goes your way."

Anna smiled. "Silly girl, are you absolutely sure? Did you check my pulse yourself?"

With a toss of her head she turned and began walking away. Riley barely saw Anna's trek across the floor as her memories replayed; the tunnels underneath Newfoundland; Dean hitting them with killing beams; Darius's anguish. Had that been feigned or had her brainwashing made him believe something that wasn't true? Had Dean been under Anna's control too? Was everything that had happened before just an elaborate set up?

Several metres from Riley, the floor ended and a floating stage started. Anna stepped up onto the stage and crossed its wide expanse without looking backwards.

Riley began to shake. Anna had confirmed her worst fears and increased them ten-fold. The men she held most dear were lost to her. Darius would never be free of Anna's hold over him no matter what she did. He wouldn't even want to break it. And while Alec could potentially break her grip, to do so would cost him his sanity.

And *both of them* would kill her without hesitation. Anna only had to ask.

n the hour since Anna had delivered her devastating news, the entire auditorium had filled nearly to the brim. Three Mheer soldiers, weapons in hand, had come to stand behind Riley and Tyrell. Tyrell had pulled himself to his knees but hadn't managed anything further. Riley had tried to speak to him once but she'd received a sharp blow and hadn't tried again. She'd opted for holding her orb tightly in her hand and sending healing thoughts in Tyrell's direction. Whether it was doing any good or not, she had no idea—she'd only tried healing with direct touch before and the Mheer forbade that now—but it was better than doing nothing but fretting. There was no sign of Kerry. He might be locked up somewhere or lying in the corridor where they'd all been shot. She could only guess. Wherever he was, she could only hope he was alive. If she got out of this situation alive herself, she'd find him.

34

Anna had disappeared a short time ago. She and Kholar had spoken briefly then walked behind the Councilor's chairs, then stepped down off the stage and out of sight. Riley had no doubt they would return soon. It looked like the show was about to start.

The Councilors trouped silently onto the stage while the crowds in the stands rose to their feet. Without fanfare, they took their seats in a semi-circle of gilded chairs, facing the spectators. The crowd maintained a respectful stillness. The lead Councilor turned her hawk-like gaze onto the spectators and swept over the crowd briefly with a slight look of contempt on her face. If she noticed Riley off to the side, a gun pointed at her neck, she gave no sign. Riley ground her teeth. No one seemed to think it wrong or even unusual to have hostages at the Senate meeting. What went on at these things? What sort of twisted galaxy was this Council running, anyway?

Riley remained still, kneeling beside the others and waiting for whatever was going to happen next. Her knees were sore but she dared not move in case the trigger-happy Mheer behind her got the wrong idea. Tyrell was breathing heavily and shifting slightly next to her. Blood still dripped from his nose to the floor with a steady rhythm. Already a small crimson pool had formed around his knees, with a rivulet of his blood draining down an uneven channel in the metal and falling through a crack in the floor plates. His face was nearly as white as the marble dais under the Councilor's chairs, Riley noted with worry. He was concussed or something worse; neither of his eyes seemed to focus on anything though they were both open.

Alec and Darius arrived. They trouped in behind Kholar from a doorway on the other side of the stage, coming to a stop just in front. Both knelt. Darius was staring upward in rapt attention. Alec, on the other hand, kept glancing in Riley's direction, then back at the stage. He looked confused and worried. Unlike her, neither of them had guards.

The Councilors straightened their robes and ceremonial outfits. The lead Councilor began to stand. She hadn't quite risen from her chair when Anna strode onto the stage. Riley heard Darius's gasp but she didn't look at him. What was happening on stage was far more important.

Kholar and Anna crossed the stage quickly. When they were only a handful of metres from the Councilors, they rose their right hands in unison. Both held orbs.

"What is the meaning of this intrusion?" the lead

Councilor began angrily. She never got the chance to say anything further. There was a brilliant flash of blue-white light. The lead Councilor froze in position, as did all the others. Only their faces were capable of movement. Several opened their mouths to shout but there wasn't a sound.

Anna took centre stage. The massive Council chambers echoed with the buzzing of thousands of beings, eyes and sensory appendages all focused on the free-floating dais. The light filtering through the vast latticework overhead struck Anna's hair, making it glow in a sickening parody of a halo. The calculated effect was superb. Even the Council members couldn't seem to tear their eyes off her. Anna raised both her arms into the air. Something flashed from around her neck but Riley couldn't get a good look at it. The drone of the crowd rose slightly for a moment then died. Only when there was silence did Anna drop her arms.

"Welcome, delegates of the Home Galaxy, to the official Senate." Anna's voice carried to the farthest reaches of the hall without echo. The audio transmission was excellent. "This will be the most important Senate meeting in history. You are fortunate to participate in the occasion that will change life as you presently know it."

Anna walked slowly towards Alec and Darius. Her long white flowing robes billowed around her feet with every step and the light caught in the iridescent threads woven through the fabric, glistening. Behind them, the members of the Council stared at Anna with expressions of growing outrage from their ring of chairs.

Anna stopped at the edge of the raised platform and looked down at Darius and Alec. She reached up towards her neck and pulled a long chain out from under her dress. At the end of its links, a huge opaque crystal twisted in the light. The reflected shards darted outwards to the farthest reaches of the grand chamber. Anna clasped the crystal in her left hand, smothering the reflections, and raised her fist to shoulder height.

239

"Darius," she said so quietly Riley could barely hear. "Come to me."

Darius scrambled to his feet in the only awkward move Riley had ever seen him make. He vaulted up onto the floating platform and launched himself towards Anna. Riley couldn't make out his muffled exclamation as he'd buried his face against Anna's neck. His arms were flung around her. Anna used her right hand to stroke his forehead. His shoulders shook. Perhaps he was crying, Riley considered. A sick feeling built in her stomach.

"Darius, first of my weapons," Anna said clearly. "Prepare to do my bidding."

Distaste crossed Kholar's face but Anna didn't see it, nor did Darius. They were now looking into each other's eyes while Anna continued to stroke his forehead. There was something *wrong* about her gesture. It made Riley's skin crawl. Finally Anna stopped and dropped her hands to her side.

The small Councilor, the one Riley hated, suddenly rose from his chair behind Anna and Kholar. The other Councilors, still frozen in their ornate chairs frowned. Several struggled, but to no avail. He crossed the wide space quickly and came to stand beside Anna. At the swelling noise of the crowd, he lifted his hand. Immediately the noise dimmed.

"I am Xo, Councilor for the Itthraxi Star system," the Councilor said. His voice was magnified and echoed slightly.

At least the idiot has a name, Riley thought to herself.

"I bring greetings from my people to you all." Xo pivoted so that he could face the crowd behind him for a moment. "And also release from the tyranny of the Intergalactic Council."

At that a huge roar went up from the crowd. Some were angry, some pleased, Riley noted. Arms and appendages were waving everywhere. Only a few sat quietly in their seats. The other Councilors looked even angrier, if that was possible. The lead Councilor's imbedded jewels flashed with each small twitch of her head. She was struggling to reach her knife but her arms were not obeying her. Her eyes had narrowed into glittering slits of malice.

"Hear me, people of our Home galaxy." Xo was facing Riley again, although he gave no indication that he even noticed her presence. "For immeasurable time you have been subjugated by the Council, whose rules and tariffs strained your very existence. Secret dealings have swirled around you, out of your control. Agreements and counter transactions formed out of your sight, so that you, the very foundation of our galaxy, have been made to look like fools. For many partons, I too, took my place at the Council chambers and partook of the secrets. But unlike my fellow Councilors, I did not rejoice in the enslavement of others. I did not condone the creation of a clandestine power—a power that threatens to destroy you all."

The crowd went mad at this. Riley watched how Xo encouraged their outrage with his silence. He was a master manipulator; she'd give him that.

He finally raised his hands again for silence. "But the time for complacency is long past. For those of us who wish to change the future, to embrace a freedom long denied us, the time has come. The power created by the Council for their use alone is here revealed." He swung his arm to indicate Anna and Kholar.

Anna smiled slightly. Darius still gazed adoringly, as if she was the centre of his universe; if he was aware of Xo's monologue, he gave no indication.

Kholar stepped forward to stand beside Xo. The smarmy creep looked so smug he could almost burst, Riley noted sourly. Kholar looked expectantly at Xo as the Councilor continued talking. "This power, hidden from all but the highest officers in the Council, is silent and unseen. It can move objects by only thought, can propel a craft through the depths of outer space without engines, can determine another's most secret thoughts and is strong enough to control minds." Kholar was beaming but the crowd was lapping up Xo's diatribe with increasing anger. Kholar obviously thought he was being praised, the stupid fool. Riley waited for the penny to drop.

"This power is hidden. Not one of you can detect who has it and who does not. None of you could contain it or control it. Only a select few know how to create those who have it." Xo's voice grew louder and louder, galvanizing the crowd. Most were on their feet now. "Should one small group of beings be so privileged? Should the Council control power that is unlimited and unchecked? Should this be allowed to continue?"

A spasm of uncertainty crossed Kholar's face. Xo pointed at Kholar. "This is the man who discovered and controls that power. His Tyon Collective is hidden among you, dispersed throughout your civilizations, gathering information, spying upon you, using you for their own purpose. Who knows what unknown deeds his spawn has wrought. What power he has over you."

At this the crowd's roar became deafening again. Xo didn't smile but he was pleased nonetheless. "Commander Kholar, is the Tyon Collective under your control?"

"I oversee the operations, true," Kholar said slowly, carefully. His puzzled expression indicated that things were not going as he'd planned.

"And your operations are secret, known only to the Council."

"Well, yes, because we—"

Xo cut him off. "And the Operatives are highly trained in the use of mind control and telekinesis, are they not?"

"Among many other talents, some Operatives do have—"

Again, Xo did not let him finish. "Talents that can result in death."

"My officers are trained to avoid harming others. We work to protect the citizens of—"

"But they do kill civilians, don't they?"

Kholar's face was reddening. The trap was now clear. He looked up at the surrounding sea of unhappy faces and found few, if any, allies. "Which is why we approached you in the first place," Kholar said quickly. "We wished to readjust the balance of power. End the secrecy of the Tyon Collective."

"It was I who approached you, Kholar. *My* suggestion that the Tyon tyranny end. *You* are the traitor to your ranks. It is you who has broken the trust with the Council, the very ones who gave you the power in the first place." Xo turned to the remaining Councilors and gave them a slight bow. "The traitor you created seeks to destroy you. As you see my fellows, treason has a dangerous edge."

At that remark, Anna whirled around and grabbed Darius's hand. She wrapped his hand around the unpolished crystal and raised it high, uttering a short command to Darius that Riley couldn't make out. Before Kholar could even raise his eyebrows in surprise a brilliant beam of blue-white light shot from the crystal and struck him directly in the centre of his chest. The light surrounded him for a moment, like a sickly aura, then appeared to be sucked directly through his skin. His eyes started to glow. He opened his mouth to scream and the light poured out. His hands grasped at nothing. Then suddenly, Kholar's body seemed to *bulge*. Without a sound it grew and grew, then suddenly, exploded into a million shards of light.

Riley's heart was pounding so hard it almost blocked out the cheering crowd. She had never even imagined that something like that could happen or that Darius would be the one to do it. It was as if Kholar's very atoms had been annihilated. She glanced around her. The Councilors were outraged. Tyrell's eyes weren't focusing but he was facing the stage. Alec was staring at Anna intently, his expression unreadable.

"Alec," Riley shouted. "Don't look at her."

Alec didn't seem to hear. The crowd was still cheering so loudly it well might be impossible for him to make out her voice. But she had to try.

"She'll do the same to you, Alec," Riley tried again.

Xo raised both his hands for quiet. It took nearly a minute for the crowd to settle.

"I have brought with me tonight a new order. A new plan." Xo continued. He stepped over to Anna's side. "Bring the Others," he said to her in a lower voice.

Anna pushed Darius gently to her side. She held out her right hand to Alec and again clutched her neck crystal.

"Alec, come to me."

"No!" Riley screamed. "Don't listen to her."

A cold smile curved Anna's lips. She didn't break her gaze with Alec as she spoke. "He is far beyond your pathetic influence, Terran girl. His mind belongs to me." Her voice became soothing

35

again. "Alec, obey me."

Alec slowly got to his feet.

"Alec, please," Riley implored.

Alec's dark eyes swung towards her. For a second Riley was sure she saw uncertainty. But then it was gone and he was clambering up onto the raised dais without a backwards glance. He walked over to stand in front of Anna. She reached out with her free hand and in the same repulsive way she'd done with Darius, stroked Alec's forehead. Alec's eyes glazed over. His shoulders dropped and he swayed slightly.

"Alec!" Riley shouted desperately. Between Alec and Darius, Anna could take over the galaxy. Or worse.

"Take your orb in your hand, Alec. Concentrate. Bring the Others to us," Anna ordered.

Riley gasped. Summon the pan-dimensional beings that destroyed *everything* in their wake, right into the middle of the Council Chambers? Was Anna *out of her mind?* No one could control Rhozan. No one. They'd all be killed.

Alec pulled his orb out of his pants pocket and held it in front of his chest. He looked down at it. All his movements were sluggish, as if he were moving inside a vat of cold molasses. His forehead creased with concentration. Anna didn't stop her stroking. Darius too was frowning. He watched Alec, then turned his gaze to Anna's face before returning to Alec.

"Darius, stop him," Riley yelled. "He'll destroy us all."

"Do not listen to the Terran female, Darius," Anna said. She didn't drop her gaze from Alec's nor did her hand falter. "She is inconsequential. Pay no attention to her."

"She's using you, Dare. I warned you and you refused to believe me. But this is proof. She has control over your mind. Fight her." Riley stopped shouting as the cold metal of the Mheer's weapon jammed into the back of her

245

neck. Cripes, she'd forgotten all about the goon with the gun.

"I'm letting you see just how much you've lost, Riley. It gives me pleasure to let you suffer. But speak again and you will die," Anna warned.

Think, Riley admonished herself. She had to do *something*.

Nothing came to mind. With the Mheer soldier jamming a gun into the back of her neck, even if she had telekinesis or mind control, she wasn't powerful enough to reach Darius or overcome Anna. Alec was a possibility, if only she could get him to listen to her, but right now, he seemed totally lost in concentration on Anna's task. Which meant time was seriously running out.

A collective gasp rode through the crowd. Riley looked up. A contingent of heavily armed guards, wearing the green and gold of the Council, ran onto the dais. Several looked dishevelled and at least two had crimson stains on their uniforms. They immediately took a protective stance, ringing the Councilors and pulling out weapons. Their leader, a tall human with dark hair pulled back in a ponytail, quickly conferred with the head Councilor. He turned back to face Anna.

"Drop your weapons," he shouted at her. Anna merely smiled.

Xo took a step towards the guard. The sounds of several weapons being brought to readiness reverberated throughout the auditorium. Xo raised both his hands in a peaceable gesture. "Lay down your arms. The Council is not in danger."

"None of them can move. Remove your control over their bodies and we'll discuss the terms of your surrender," the lead Guard shouted back. The dangerous end of his weapon didn't waver a millimetre.

Riley gnashed her teeth in frustration. The guards didn't know who they were dealing with.

"I'm afraid that is impossible," Xo replied pleasantly enough. "You see, they aren't under my control. They are under hers."

At those words, Anna and Darius again raised the uncut crystal. Again, a bright beam of light—so bright Riley had to close her eyes for a second—streaked from the crystal. It enveloped all the guards and the Councilors. There was a pulsing, as if the light was alive, then it dove inside each of its victims. Just like Kholar, the light inside them shone brilliantly out of their eyes and mouths. Riley imagined there was screaming, but in truth it might have been her horrified mind that created the sound. Again, each of the guards and Councilors seemed to swell in size until, in unison, they burst apart as miniature explosions of light. When the brilliance dimmed enough for Riley to see properly, there was no sign any of the Councilors or their guards had ever been there.

Darius dropped his hand to his side. Anna retained hold of the crystal.

The crowd was now panicking and fighting to reach the exits. Anna craned her neck to watch for a moment before settling her gaze on Xo. He nodded in return. Neither of them seemed overly concerned that their audience was departing. The reason became immediately clear.

"Stop them leaving, Darius," Anna ordered. She pulled the chain over her head and handed her crystal to him.

Darius licked his lips once and frowned slightly before he raised the crystal high in the air and shouted, "Stop!" His voice echoed around the chamber, growing stronger and stronger. The louder his voice grew, the slower the crowd moved. Riley couldn't help but put her hands to her ears as Darius's command became painfully thunderous. Just as she thought she couldn't bear it any longer, it stopped. The crowd was frozen in position as the Councilors had been moments ago.

"Impressive," Xo said to Anna.

"I told you he was worth keeping alive," she responded. She leaned back to Alec and spoke in a quiet voice. "Alec, concentrate on your task. Bring the Others to me."

"Now that I have your attention," Xo said to the auditorium, "let us proceed with your instructions. As you can see, I have weapons at my disposal that none of you have ever seen before. None of you will be able to fight us. My servants here," he pointed at Darius and Alec, "cannot be corrupted or turned from their course of action. I assure you they are quite infallible.

"Perhaps by now you have wondered as to our true purpose? Most of you are intelligent beings. You will see the destruction of the Council and begin to think that freedom is within your grasp. Sadly for you, this is not the case." Xo walked to the edge of the stage. It was now hovering about a metre above the floor where Riley knelt. Riley had to crane her neck to see his face. His expression had turned from gleeful to ugly. Here it comes, she thought.

"There will be a new order. The Council is dissolved and will not be reinstated. However, we all understand that order and control is required, lest we fall into chaos. Many of you are incapable of leading your own worlds and civilizations. I will lead this galaxy."

It was worse than she'd thought. A madman was setting himself up as Dictator right in front of her eyes. And Anna had the power to get him whatever he wanted.

Alec was standing on the edge of a precipice. One wrong step and he would hurtle to his death. At least, that was what it felt like. He was having trouble concentrating on what was happening around him.

Over and over the phrase, *Alec, obey me* ran through his brain. He knew the voice; it was Anna, a face from his dreams now come to life and standing next to him. The imperative to do what she told him was overwhelming. He understood that if he disobeyed her, he'd tumble off whatever pinnacle she had him standing on—and that he'd fall and fall forever. It made him shake inside with fear.

At the same time, a movie on fast-forward was running through his mind and the scenes were riveting. Nearly getting shot at the mall but saved by a handsome stranger who whispered in his ear; meeting a navy-eyed girl who stole his heart; swimming in an angry sea, salt burning his mouth as he drowned; the cold, clinical efficiency of the underground training facility. Then blistering summer days hidden on a farm while his heart grew heavy with longing but jealousy ate him alive. Running, fighting, fearing; scene after scene of terror, with Darius, now both admired and hated, at his side. Then a confrontation with an invisible enemy and the battle for his life in a place that wasn't his world, wasn't *any* world. The cycle of running and fearing repeating itself over and over, in different places but this time, the beautiful blond woman at his side, constantly whispering in his ear, soothing, terrible words he couldn't quite remember but words that had woven themselves into his mind, his heart and his soul. Some of those words repeated now. *Obey me.*

The fog around him was difficult to penetrate and the scenes flashing across his eyes were so absorbing that he paid little attention to what was going on outside of his head. He vaguely understood he was standing on a dais surrounded by a crowd of people. He was holding his orb in his right hand. The crystal sphere was warm, not uncomfortable but different from usual. Part of his mind wondered if that had any significance. He heard Anna's voice in his ear.

"Call the Others. Bring them here," she ordered.

Alec didn't want to. He remembered the Others. He feared them. There was someone here he didn't want the Others to hurt. But Anna was now touching his forehead. She ran her fingers lightly over his skin and with every pass across his brow, the precipice near his feet got closer and deeper. He wanted to obey her, he really did. But what if the Others hurt Riley? His fingers tightened on his orb.

Anna's hand dropped away, reducing the compulsion to obey her. His vision cleared enough that he could see the auditorium. He cast his gaze around quickly, searching for Riley among the throng. He breathed a sigh of relief. She was still where he'd last seen her. Kneeling beside Tyrell, the Mheer guard behind her, she looked tiny and defenseless and scared. She was mouthing something and staring straight at him, but strangely, he couldn't hear her words. At least she was all right. The Mheer would protect her if anything went wrong; Anna wouldn't hurt her.

Satisfied that she was okay, he turned his attention to the rest of the auditorium. The stage was empty except for himself, Darius, Anna and the unpleasant Councilor Xo, who had travelled with Kerry. The ornate chairs for the rest of the Council were vacant. Alec wondered briefly where the other Councilors had gone, but it didn't matter. What was *really* interesting was the entire crowd in the balconies and stairways above them were standing—in some cases, hovering—completely still, as if they had turned into statues. Darius was holding Anna's uncut crystal on a chain in his hand and his face was laced with strain. Alec understood: Darius was using Tyon power to hold everyone in place and the power needed for that was formidable.

Xo was speaking. "And therefore, you will sign agreements on behalf of your worlds to pay tribute to me and to obey the edicts that I will distribute to you. You have seen the power I wield. You have seen that I do not hesitate to use it." Xo crossed over to the Councilor's chairs and reached behind the one he'd been sitting on. He picked up a very large folder with gold embossed wording across the front and carried it reverentially back to his place at the edge of the stage. Anna waved her orb and the folder floated out of Xo's hands and hovered, waist height, unaided. Xo opened the cover. Inside there were several pages of parchment, each about a metre in length, covered in scribbling.

"Darius," Xo said, "bring the delegates to me, one by one. Ensure they sign the documents."

Darius nodded once. He was pale and sweating but moved energetically enough up the closest stairway to the first of the frozen delegates. The humanoid's face was contorted with rage as Darius's hand gripped his upper arm and practically tossed him down the stairs. Still unable to move to protect himself, the man rolled down the steps and landed on his face. There was an unpleasant *crunch*. When Darius pulled him to his feet, an unfettered stream of blood poured from the man's nose. Darius didn't seem to notice. He dragged the delegate to the edge of the floating stage, which had lowered somewhat. Anna waved her hand and the top piece of parchment floated over to the delegate and hovered in front of his chest.

"Let him speak, Darius," Anna said.

The delegate began yelling the instant Darius's hold over him wavered. "This is an outrage. The Council will pay for this."

Xo gave a little snort of laughter. "The Council is no more, Pedric of Unas Minor. You saw my power. Or did you think I merely conjured them away?"

"The Council is greater than any individual member, Xo. This galaxy will not sit idly back and watch you destroy every success we've worked so hard to attain!"

"Listen to him," Xo spread out his arms as he faced the upper reaches of the auditorium, his voice booming across the vast space. "See the defiance so displayed, a defiance that burns inside many of you. You think to yourselves, what can one man do to an entire world? How can these four before me match the power and might of a collection of planets? Watch how your new leader quells this fire." Xo walked over to where Alec was standing and stopped right in front of him. He reached out and placed his hands on Alec's shoulders. The pressure from the grip bit into Alec's muscles but he knew enough not to flinch or pull away. Even without Darius's skill at picking up psychic messages, Alec knew Xo was frightened, elated and very much on the edge. "Alec," Xo said quietly so his words could not be heard by the crowd, "hold your search for the Others for a moment. Darius, join hands with Alec. Hold Anna's Tyonic orb between you."

Darius shuffled closer and placed the uncut crystal in Alec's hands, folding Alec's fingers around it, then wrapping his own hands over Alec's so that his fingers touched the crystal surface in between Alec's. The crystal was bitterly cold.

"Darius, search out those delegates who refuse our offer," Xo ordered loudly so that the entire room could hear. "Using the Tyonic orb, the two of you must destroy half of them."

Alec inhaled sharply. Kill people? He couldn't kill anyone. He wouldn't. He opened his mouth to refuse but before he could utter the words, he was flooded with panic and fear. His heart sped up, his skin goose-pimpled and broke out into a sweat. He could barely get his breath. He was hanging over the precipice, the ground under his feet gone, about to fall and fall and fall. His tongue stuck to the roof of his mouth. "Help me," he croaked.

Darius's words ricocheted inside his head. *Do what he says, Alec. It's the only way to survive.*

I'm gonna fall, Alec could barely form the thoughts, *help me.*

It's a mental projection. You're still standing on the stage.

I'm not, I can't feel it, I'm gonna die.

You will die if you don't obey Xo's orders. Focus, Alec. Follow my lead.

The fear was almost overwhelming, but there was something calming in Darius's words. Alec grabbed on to the hope that Darius was right even though everything inside his mind screamed at him in terror. It wasn't easy to follow. Alec had never done anything like it before. It was fortunate that Darius's mind was so easy to find, as if a shining beacon in a tunnel of darkness. Alec didn't bother to consider that the Tyonic crystal he held between his hands might be helping; he latched onto Darius's thoughts and clung tenaciously. Together they travelled across the width and breadth of the auditorium, touching the mind of every delegate. Some had mental defenses and it took longer to probe for thoughts of rebellion, others were weaker and crumbled before the onslaught. Alec was overwhelmed with the impressions of the people; their thoughts, emotions, experiences, all laid bare before him. Some weren't human and entering their minds was both terrifyingly alien and beyond interesting. But there was no time to linger. Alec could feel Darius tiring; the effort to both hold the entire population of the hall in place as well as enter their minds and search put a heavy burden on him, even aided by Anna's special orb. Most were angry and their hatred and fear burned slightly when Alec touched it. There were very few who were openly willing to capitulate to Xo's new regime.

I need you to boost my power, Alec.

How?

Focus on the crystal you hold. Will your power to grow and flow through me.

We're not going to kill everyone here, are we? Alec couldn't help the revulsion that crossed his mind. It wasn't right. Killing was never right.

We may hold the Tyon power to do this or not do it, Alec, but you know as well as I do that we'll do anything Anna tells us to do. Don't you feel the compulsion to obey her? Isn't that the most important part of us now?

Alec couldn't deny it. The words Anna had woven into his brain and his soul felt unbreakable. A part of him he could no sooner remove than his own heart. It was stronger for Darius. Anna's touch had saturated Darius's mind. There was hardly a place she hadn't entered and altered. Alec fleetingly wondered if she was there now, inside both of them, knowing their thoughts.

Alec did as he was told. The Tyonic orb between his fingers grew colder and colder as he focused on it, pushing his thoughts deep into the crystal matrix. The cold burned. It inched up his wrist and into his arm, consuming the warmth of his flesh. Alec shivered, though not just from the temperature. The crystal was like nothing else he had ever experienced. While the orbs he'd touched before were merely conduits, having no discernable feeling, this Tyonic orb did. It almost felt malevolent, as if the crystal was an entity in and of itself. As if it was alive.

The wild electricity that lived under his skin began to grow. It tingled and snapped at his nerves and blood like a live creature. He'd never felt it this strong before and it kept growing.

Pay attention, came Darius's sharp rebuke.

Sorry, Alec automatically replied. He focused on Darius as hard as he could, ignoring the increasingly uncomfortable sensation between his hands and under his skin. Darius had now identified all the delegates who were opposed to joining Xo's list of subjugated planets. His mind was running through the list, determining the strongest and those who could be a serious threat to Anna and Xo. Some delegates ruled civilizations with extensive military power; others had long histories of resistance to domination. Those were high on his list to remove first; it would send a strong message. Alec could feel the increasing outrage and fear among those whose minds he'd invaded.

Darius gave a single nod to Xo, indicating they were ready.

"By now you know that my power is infallible," Xo addressed the crowd again. "I have been able to reach deep within your minds. I know which of you will fight, and who will yield to domination. There are no secrets from me. I have no use for those who resist and I destroy that which I have no use for." He looked at Darius and gave a nod. "Now."

Darius took a deep breath. He stared for a moment into Alec's eyes, the aquamarine irises now clouded with pain. Then he squeezed his lids shut and his hands, slightly trembling, tightened around Alec's.

No, Darius, don't, Alec tried. But it was too late. The overwhelming compulsion to obey swamped Alec's mind at the same instant that Darius's forceful control took over. The power quadrupled and shot through Alec's brain, down his arms, through the Tyonic orb where it seemed to multiply tenfold, then flowed backwards into Darius. Alec felt Darius's internal scream as Tyon power, stronger than Darius had ever imagined, ripped through his psyche and into the minds of hundreds of victims. Alec couldn't stop it. The pain of each individual mind, still connected to his,

255

was beyond bearing. He could feel each entity; their fear, their pain, their disbelief and then their final thoughts. It was beyond horrible. He felt himself drifting away in a desperate ploy to be free. Then it was over.

He opened his eyes as a drop of water splashed against his intertwined fingers. Then a second warm tear fell. Alec didn't hear Xo's resumed speech to those still alive. He was concerned only for Darius.

"Hold him up," Anna whispered fiercely beside him. "And don't make it obvious. Appearing weak will destroy our position."

Alec quickly moved in closer to Darius to prevent him from falling. Darius was as white as a sheet, the freckles standing out in sharp relief against his bloodless skin. His eyes were half closed and unfocused, his breathing ragged and uneven. His forehead fell forward and came to rest against Alec's. Darius's skin was as cold as ice.

"What's the matter with him?" Alec whispered back.

"He's not as strong as you," Anna replied quietly. "More disciplined and conditioned to obey me, but lacking the innate power. If I'd had as long to train you as I wished, I wouldn't need him."

"But you love him," Alec gasped.

"Don't be so stupid," she snapped.

Alec slipped his left hand under Darius's armpit to hold him up as Darius teetered. The mental connection between them was now gone and he had no idea what Darius was thinking, or if he even *was* thinking. "Is he going to recover?"

Anna didn't answer. "Did you follow what Darius did?" she asked so quietly he had to strain to hear her. "Could you replicate his ability to violate another's mind? To destroy them?"

"I don't know," Alec stammered. "I don't think so."

Anna swore under her breath and Alec cringed. He didn't want her mad at him, or worse, disappointed, but it was the truth. He couldn't replicate Darius's ability, even if he'd wanted to. Besides, if she needed Darius, she'd help him to get better.

"Don't move," Anna ordered. "Don't let him fall. Any appearance that we aren't as strong as they fear and they'll be on us like Telothian Creyotes on a Larma. There are guards outside with weapons. If Darius falters further, the hold on the doors will be dropped. Understand me?"

"Can't you heal him?" he asked

"I don't have that particular power." Anna's jaw tightened. "It's only the weakest, the *sympathetic* that have it, like Darius." Her eyes widened and began to gleam. "And your Terran girl." Anna smiled coldly.

"Leave her alone," Alec whispered frantically. "Please, Anna, just leave her. She's no good at healing either. She didn't learn it very well."

"Liar." Anna reached up and stroked Alec's cheek with one finger. "You can't hide how you feel for her from me. I've shifted through your mind more times than you could count, boy, and I know what she can and cannot do, and more importantly, what you'll do to protect her."

Anna flicked her fingers at the Mheer guard behind Riley. Alec's heart skipped a beat as he watched Riley being pulled to her feet and dragged over to them. He wanted to say something to her but he couldn't make a sound.

"I've found a use for you, Terran girl," Anna said quietly. "Obey me and you'll live."

"What do you want?" Riley answered. Her gaze didn't waver from Anna's.

"Darius is weakened. He must be healed. Take your orb and do it. Make no sound and do nothing that catches the attention of the crowd."

"And if I won't?" Riley asked, a belligerent tone tingeing her response.

"Then I will have Alec kill you."

As incentives went, it was a doozy. Riley counted to five before she spoke. She wasn't going to ask how high when told to jump. But on the other hand, she wouldn't put it past Anna to knock her off, just for the fun of it. And besides, apparent capitulation could camouflage her real goal.

"Fine," Riley muttered.

She gave Alec a quick, probing look before she stepped up onto the dais. She moved in as close to Darius as she could. He was breathing quickly and his eyes were only partway open. He was standing upright but now that she was closer, she could see that Alec was holding him up. He looked very unwell, like someone who was about to faint. Alec didn't look much better; sweat beaded his upper lip and his eyes were huge, but he was the one holding Darius so he must have been in better shape. So much for Xo's unbeatable weapon, Riley smirked to herself. She moved as near as possible and touched Darius's neck with her orb, hiding it from view by leaning her face against his ear.

She willed herself to concentrate on the task at hand, but Anna's presence, so close and so deadly, was a distinct distraction. *Heal*, she commanded. She felt nothing, as if she and her orb were impotent. Then she remembered Darius's words from long ago. *Relax, let the orb work, don't force it.* She smiled to herself. She took several slow and careful breaths, willing herself to unwind and let

37

the power inside her do its work. *Heal.* This time the warm sensation that indicated the healing power began.

Darius, what has she done to you? How can I help you? Please, please answer. Riley didn't know if Anna would know that she had established the link with Darius's mind the way he'd taught her, but she had to take the chance. She might not get another opportunity to convince him to side with her and even if the chance was infinitesimally small, she had to try. *Darius, please answer me. I only have a short time. I need you.*

He didn't form words. Perhaps he couldn't. But he could let her into his thoughts and did. Wave after wave of emotions slammed into her mind. Despair, desire, guilt, fear, pride, embarrassment. He knew what he was doing and whom he was doing it for. He wanted so desperately for Anna to love him, to fill the void from his needy childhood. He'd been a sitting duck for her, Riley understood with a shock. She hadn't known much about his early life, had hardly bothered to ask, but it was all there now; the depravation, the longing to be loved, the endless days of being ignored in a family with too many mouths to feed and not enough money or willingness to feed them. The Tyons had been his salvation in a way, Riley realized, bringing order and structure to his life on the streets. Regular meals, education, and discipline instead of chaos, starvation and victimization. He'd rebelled of course, his nature would never have easily acquiesced, but secretly, he'd craved the acceptance and the approval of his superior officers. Anna had noted this early and used it. Riley couldn't help but hate her even more.

It was now totally clear that Darius loved Anna in a way that was thoroughly unbreakable. It was in every thought, every fibre of his psyche. It wasn't a true love—how could it be when Anna had created it for her own purposes?—but the result was the same. He would never refuse her orders, never deny Anna's desires. Riley knew it now. There was no

259

way he could help her. She pulled away mentally, ending the connection.

She stood there for a moment, gathering her thoughts and forcing the crushing disappointment out of her mind. She'd heard what Anna had told her and knew that Anna delighted in creating despair. Despite that, a tiny part of her had maintained hope that Darius would rescue the day, just the way he had so many times before. Now that hope was gone. She quickly rethought her situation. If Darius couldn't be a help to her, then she'd focus on those remaining: Alec and Tyrell. Tyrell hadn't improved since he'd been brought into the amphitheatre; he was still on his knees and while he was facing her direction, his eyes remained unfocused. He was probably off the rescuing cavalry, too.

That left Alec and her to fight.

Anna's face suddenly loomed so close, Riley could smell the smug arrogance off the woman, like a cheap perfume. "Finished trolling Darius's mind, looking for loop holes?"

Riley refused to answer. She defiantly closed her eyes and worked on healing.

Xo began speaking again.

"Now that you all understand the power I truly wield and the impossibility of defying me, I suggest that you willingly come forward, one by one, and sign the declaration of allegiance to me. Destroying the rest of you is wasteful and I do not crave waste. Temper your defiance. It will go easier on your world if you do."

"Release Darius's hold on the delegates," Anna hissed to Alec. "Keep the doors locked and protected. At the first sign of defiance, kill them all."

Riley felt shock run through Alec's body and the turmoil Anna's instructions created inside him, but her contact with Alec's mind wasn't fully developed yet. She hoped that Alec could read her concern and dismay in the brief glance she gave him. There was nothing else she could do but return to the task Anna had ordered her to complete, for her own sake and Darius's.

She heard footsteps as the delegates began to traverse the stairs and come closer. There was murmuring as each delegate stepped forward and the sound of something scratching across parchment. Riley didn't bother to look. The faster Darius was back to himself the better, even if it meant that he might turn his considerable power against her. It crossed her mind to harm Darius further; render him incapable of furthering Anna's aims, but she didn't know how to mess with his mind and part of her didn't want to do it. Her father had said, over and over as she was growing up: a healer must first do no harm. The words had ingrained themselves into her psyche. If she did try and harm Darius—and there was no way she could even be sure that she could—wouldn't that make her as bad as Anna?

There was no real choice.

She opened one eye. Anna was standing closer to Xo now, supervising the signatures and facing away. Riley shifted herself slightly, moving closer to Alec. She stopped when the bare skin of her arm contacted his.

Alec. Can you hear me?

There was no response.

Alec, please, listen to me. You've got to break free of her. She's going to kill us all and destroy so many worlds.

Nothing.

Alec, I know you. You're better than this. I couldn't love a man who would kill innocents. You know I couldn't.

There was no reply. Abruptly, Alec pulled back, ending the physical link between them. For a second their eyes locked. Then Riley gasped and wrenched her gaze away.

Alec's eyes were empty. The boy she'd known was gone.

A lec watched Riley as she leaned into Darius and went to work on healing him. A nasty, jealous feeling burned in his stomach when he saw how close she stood, practically snuggling up under Darius's chin. Her eyes were closed. He recognized the slight flush to her cheeks and her rapid breathing. One more second of this and he was going to punch Darius's lights out—no matter how important it was for the illusion of strength to be maintained.

She's not worth your affection.

Alec was startled at Anna's mental intrusion on his thoughts. She so rarely used telepathy with him.

She never cared for you. It was all a cruel game. She desires Darius. You would be wise to hate her.

Alec's thoughts were muddled for a moment before becoming crystal clear. Anna was right. Riley didn't care for him at all; she'd only led him on, making him believe that he was special to her. Any romantic feelings Riley had were for Darius. Anna had warned him to be careful—the thought flowed through his mind and permeated all his memories—and he was wise to heed her advice. Let Finn have Riley, he decided, he had better things to do. He had Anna and she loved him.

Alec purposely turned his face away in distaste. The second Finn could stand on his own, he'd let him go and move as far away from the two of them as possible. He turned his attention to Anna and Xo.

The former Councilor was talking again to the delegates but Alec hardly paid attention. That man liked the sound of his own voice far too much and Alec was getting heartily sick of it. The delegates didn't like him either. You could see it on the faces of those who approached the stage to sign the declarations. The subservient scraping barely masked their contempt. Soon that would all change, Alec thought smugly. He wasn't privy to Xo's most secret of plans, but he soon would be. Anna would see to that. Hadn't she promised that he'd be the most important person to her? That Darius would be gone, Xo too, and it would be just the two of them?

Another supplicant warily approached Anna and Xo. This one was covered in a dark, glossy fur, with beady eyes and long, wicked looking claws. It crept forward until it was within reach. Anna handed the parchment to the alien along with a writing utensil. Xo stood slightly to the side, watching with hooded eyes. The alien took the paper in one set of claws and stooped to make whatever constituted a signature. It held out the parchment for Anna to take.

Alec knew an instant before it lunged what the alien planned to do. Before its claws could reach Anna's neck, Alec's orb power ripped the alien's arm out of its socket. There was a high-pitched keening sound as dark blue blood pumped quickly into a pool at Anna's feet. The creature keeled sideways at the second blast, then dropped to the floor, dead.

Anna turned and gifted Alec with a rare smile. "You react quickly, Alec. Well done." She turned to face the rest of the delegates, now huddling in a sorry group on the lower stairs. "And if any of the rest of you are planning to slit my throat, I'd suggest you consider restraining yourselves. I grow weary of this foolishness."

Alec felt rather than heard Darius take a deep breath. He looked to see Darius blinking rapidly and giving his head a slight shake. When Darius stood up straighter, Alec

263

immediately dropped his arms and took a step away.

He felt a sudden mental tug: Riley. He gave her a dark glance of loathing and turned his back. She'd shown her true colours. He wanted nothing to do with her.

"Alec, come to my side," Anna ordered. She'd noticed Darius's improvement.

Alec needed no second invitation. He felt Riley's anguished mental cry but he ignored her as he walked across the stage to be closer to Anna.

The last of the delegates, a humanoid female with quivering antennae, was signing her parchment. The female glanced up with terror as Alec approached and practically dropped the parchment at Anna's feet in her haste to get away. Alec watched her back away with a vague feeling of satisfaction. They knew who wielded the power, he thought to himself. They're as much afraid of me as they are of Anna. He smiled. It felt good.

Anna looked over her shoulder as he approached. "I have a task for you."

"Anything," Alec replied.

"You must show me your loyalty, Alec. Before we go further, before I permit you to take your position at my side, as my equal partner, I must know the depth of your willingness to do what must be done. Without question."

He knew what she was offering. To take Darius's place, maybe even remove him from her affection altogether. He shivered with anticipation. Mentally he squared his shoulders. She wanted a man as her partner, not a boy. Well, he was a man now. Hadn't he proved that already?

"Just say it," he urged.

Anna reached out and stroked his cheek once with her finger. The need to obey her doubled in strength. "Kill Tyrell."

For just a second, Alec felt doubt, even a twinge of revulsion. Then it passed. If that's what it took then so be it.

Alec turned on his heel and marched across the stage.

He jumped down to the floor and crossed the short distance to Tyrell. The pilot was on one knee, trying valiantly to get to his feet. Alec saw that he knew what was about to happen. He raised his eyes to Alec and stared hard at him. Alec hesitated for a moment.

"Alec, don't hurt him."

Alec glanced at Riley over his shoulder. Inside him a growing sense of anger surged at the sound of her voice. How dare she order him around? Wasn't that how she'd treated him the whole time he'd known her? Like a kid. Never letting him show her what he was capable of.

"Alec, she's manipulating you. Don't let her." That was rich, coming from Riley, Alec thought. An ugly sneer crossed his face. He'd show her who was boss.

Do it, Anna's thought hit him broadside.

He redoubled his resolve. This would be easy. The power built inside him quickly.

Tyrell had managed to pull himself to his feet but was swaying as if drunk. His eyes, however, were clear, icy grey and trained on him. Alec had a sudden unbidden memory of his father, looming over him when he'd done something wrong. For an instant he was flooded with shame. Then he remembered Anna and the memory melted from his mind along with the emotion.

"You've corrupted the boy," Tyrell said. His words were slightly slurred. Whatever he'd been hit with back in the corridor clearly affected motor function for a long time, but he was lucid and thinking.

"Of course." Anna walked over to the edge of the stage and stared down at them. "I would have taken your mind as well, if I hadn't been so busy with Kholar and Logan."

"You were pair bonded with Logan," Tyrell spat. "Did that mean nothing to you?"

"No more than the oaths we took when we trained together, Tyrell. I congratulate myself that none of you ever suspected. But then, none of you were as strong as I."

"The Collective was worth something," Tyrell said slowly. "The mission to protect was noble. You've corrupted everything."

"The Collective was created by the very force it was designed to thwart. Have you not realized that yet? Where our power comes from? How we can sense them and resist them and use these," she held up her orb and the one on the chain, "against them?"

"Rhozan controls you?" Tyrell gasped.

"I am a conduit. His power flows through me." Anna's smile was colder than ice. "I control him."

Alec tried to understand but it was beyond him. Hatred and power were pounding through his veins with every beat of his heart. He was having trouble even hearing their conversation. Not that it mattered. What could such an insignificant creature say that would make any difference at all to the plan.

"You're in league with the Others?" Tyrell's face twisted in disgust. "Are you that stupid? They cannot be trusted and they cannot be controlled."

"You grow tiresome, Tyrell. Alec, kill him."

Alec heard her order and raised his orb for the killing shot. He was too slow. His orb suddenly flew out of his hand and shot towards the rafters so fast he lost track of it almost instantly. Tyrell's orb glowed in his hand. Alec only saw it for an instant before the pilot was off and running. He bounded up the stairs three at a time. Clearly, he'd been faking his weakness. Alec was momentarily impressed; he'd never thought Tyrell could be sneaky.

"Stop him," Anna shouted angrily.

"How?" Alec asked. He couldn't do anything without an orb.

"Get your orb back, stupid boy and stop him." She turned to Darius and Riley. "Darius, kill him."

Cringing, Alec held out his hand and willed his orb to return to him. It took a moment for the orb to zoom back into his grip. Darius was blinking rapidly and leaning on Riley's shoulder as he tried to focus on Tyrell's disappearing form. A shot of weak white light flew from his orb but hit only the stairs. Alec tried too but Tyrell was out of sight. The slam of a door echoed throughout the amphitheatre.

Anna was furious. "If he gets into a ship and leaves this station he could destroy everything I've worked for." She rounded on Xo, who was still staring upwards at the last place Tyrell had been. "You should have killed him."

Xo gave a short, nasty laugh. "I will not dirty my hands over some insignificant Tyon officer. That's what we have these two for."

"We need time for our tools to grow in strength. You know that. It was the reason for starting here on this ridiculously remote planet and having the Mheer under Rhozan's control." Despite Anna's urgency, Xo seemed unconcerned. "After all our work to dismantle the station's communications, we cannot allow Tyrell to leave here and communicate with someone off this station. Tyrell is second in command only to Logan. His record is impeccable. He will be believed."

"Don't be stupid. He's only one man," Xo said derisively. "He won't get out of this planetary system. I am well prepared. When my minions see his ship leave they'll destroy it. You forget, I am in charge."

He turned his back to her. Alec saw that was a mistake instantly. He heard Anna's sharp intake of breath and felt her fury across the stage. She grasped the Tyonic crystal in one hand and grabbed Darius's hand with her other. Darius was nearly pulled off his feet as she yanked him close enough to clasp his hand over the crystal. The brightness of the beam hit Xo squarely between his shoulder blades. He stumbled slightly, turned partway to face her, disbelief spreading across his face. Then he collapsed in a heap and didn't move again.

There were gasps from the remaining delegates. Several

267

began to run towards the upper doors. Alec remained rooted to the floor as if he'd become cemented there. She'd been Xo's partner and she'd cut him down without a second's hesitation. Thank heavens she needed *his* power. She'd hardly turn on him.

He shivered. Something was coming.

He caught a flicker out of the corner of his eye and at first, didn't comprehend. Then recognition surged through him and he backed away. Several large glittering clouds of sparkles were descending from the ceiling.

Rips were appearing out of nowhere. Dozens of them and all at once. Riley could barely believe her eyes. *Things are getting worse?*

Riley heard a scream, a wild plaintive sound that was abruptly cut off. She saw the humanoid delegate cut directly in half as a rip hit him dead centre on its way past. Greenish blood splattered the floor and the seats on either side. What was left of the body fell to the ground.

Retching, Riley turned and stumbled away. She had no idea why the alien hadn't fallen into the rip; she couldn't remember rips tearing people in half before, but there wasn't time to contemplate it. She had to get out of the amphitheatre, although she had no idea where exactly she'd go. She had to get off this station before the whole thing fell apart and dropped into the boiling lava below. There must be a hangar where they docked the ships, but she didn't know where it was.

39

She forced herself to her feet and swayed for a moment. Her head was spinning. Healing Darius had drained her. Gasping for breath, she turned towards the closest stairway. The exit wasn't too far away but between her and there was a massive hole in the floor where an entire metal panel had been eaten away by a rip. A cold blast of foul air was pouring upwards. Xo's parchments were being picked up and tossed by the currents. They swirled around the dais like a paper tornado, smacking up against the few Council chairs that were still upright and sticking to them like wallpaper.

She had two options. Take the shorter route around the massive hole and come far too close to Anna, Alec and Darius or take the longer route, which meant climbing over multiple bodies. Instinct made her choose the latter.

Anna was screaming something at the top of her lungs but Riley couldn't hear her above the wind and the shrieking of those being literally ripped to shreds. Ignoring her, Riley struck out, launching herself with unsteady steps. Her head was spinning and there was nothing to hold onto. Carefully stepping over the first body, Riley tried to avert her eyes from the sickening picture at her feet. Another victim of a rip, his head was gone. The floor was slippery in places with blood and other unidentifiable fluids. Riley caught herself before she fell once, but missed the second when she turned to glance quickly backwards. Losing her balance, she fell to her knees, onto the chest of what had been a young woman. Riley threw out her hands to break her fall. Horribly, both plunged through the woman's chest wall up to her wrists. Riley couldn't stop the scream that tore from her lips. Yanking her blood-covered hands out of the woman's body, she jerked away, not allowing herself to contemplate why the woman's ribs had dissolved beneath her skin. Riley overbalanced and fell backwards. Her head spun sickly. Don't throw up, she admonished herself. Just keep moving.

She twisted around and pulled herself to her feet, wiped her gore-covered hands on the nearest piece of clothing, the young woman's pants, and wrenched her eyes away from the sickening sight at her feet just in time to see a rip sail by her head. Her heart slammed into her ribcage. Oh Jeez, that was close.

She pulled her orb from her pocket and gripped it tightly as she began to jog towards the stairs. A gust of wind, pungent with volcanic stink, struck her briefly.

She gasped and held her breath. Her eyes began to water. She clambered over another two bodies, resolutely refusing to even look at them, then rounded the corner and headed straight for the stairs.

She was nearly there. Another rip, this one large enough to swallow her whole floated towards her. Riley had no choice. She dropped to the ground and flattened herself as close to the floor as possible, pressing her face against the warm metal planking.

"Alec, come and play."

The mournful voice from inside the rip could barely be heard above the screaming of the wind and the cacophony of the dying around her. The rip slowed for a moment, right above her, sensing her presence. Mouth dry with fear, Riley held her breath. She had to let go of the orb. Careful not to attract any attention, she let her fingers slide off its surface. The floor wasn't even. The orb, free of her embrace, rolled a little along the metallic struts. It stopped against an outstretched arm. Just out of reach.

"Crap," Riley muttered to herself. She couldn't bring herself to turn her head. What was the rip doing? It shouldn't be able to sense her now that she wasn't touching the orb.

"Alec," the rip moaned.

"Go away," Riley mouthed the words silently. Out of the corner of her eye she could see Alec and Darius. They were holding their orbs up into the air and the crystals were glowing with an eerie pale blue light Riley had never seen before. She had no idea what they were doing but at least they weren't paying any attention to her.

The creepy sensation rips always gave her eased a tiny bit. There were so many around that goosebumps covered her arms and the back of her neck. Mentally crossing her fingers, she turned her head a minuscule amount to look upward. The rip was moving away. She let her breath out with profound relief, a sob escaping her despite her attempt at control. She slithered forward and grabbed her orb.

"Such a tender moment. I'm quite sorry to interrupt it."

Riley gasped. She looked up. Anna stood only a metre away. Darius stood beside her. His eyes were slightly glazed, as if he was caught up in another world altogether, seeing something no one else could see. Considering what was happening, perhaps he was. Alec was still standing on the stage, watching in fascination as the rips swirled around, punching holes in the walls and floor. He seemed mesmerized.

"You bitch," Riley hissed.

Anna only smiled as she jeered, "Have you noticed how everyone you touch falls prey to disaster and horror? Have you ever thought, Riley, that maybe it's *you*?"

"That's rich. *You're* the megalomaniac, not me."

"Big words from such an insignificant being. You have seen that I am invincible. You know that you've lost. I don't need your possible distraction. We have more work to do." She pulled the chain with the Tyonic crystal over her head and held it out. "Alec," she called out. "Take this. You will need it to kill Tyrell; he is too strong for a simple orb. Then locate the command centre of this station and set our bomb to destruct in fifteen of your minutes. Return to me immediately so that we can vacate this miserable station."

Alec didn't say anything and his expression didn't change at all as he jogged over to her and accepted the crystal. He slipped the chain over his head and turned without looking in Riley's direction. Perhaps he didn't even see her. Silently he ran up the same stairs Tyrell had taken
a few minutes ago.

Riley shivered as she watched him go. There wasn't much she could do. Her moderate Tyon gift against Darius's extraordinary one? Not a chance. And now her one possible hope was disappearing. She focused on the stairs. Only metres away; could she manage it?

"There is nowhere to go. If you have a god, I suggest you make your peace now." Anna's smile stretched from ear to ear.

"You'll lose in the end," Riley tried. The longer she was talking, the longer she lived. Some brilliant idea might pop into her head to save herself if she only had long enough. She was *not* going to lie down and die. *No way, no how.* "Eventually they'll overthrow you. No one has enough power to hold an entire galaxy in control. It's crazy."

"You underestimate me," Anna replied smugly. "I control nearly all the Tyon officers you know. The Tyon power grows exponentially between my two servants here. The longer they use the Tyonic crystal, the stronger Rhozan's hold is over them and the deeper they become enslaved to me. Within four cycles I will have the power to control all space flight within this solar system. Within twelve partons, this section of the galaxy will be mine. It's only time before I become completely invincible."

"So what?" Riley argued. "You have the entire universe bowing and scraping. Who cares? What are you going to do with it? There's only so much money and stuff anyone can use. And eventually you'll just get old and die anyway."

"You are so limited," Anna gave a short laugh. "You haven't thought this through, have you? I have the power to control time in my hands now. I can change anything, merely by shifting time and setting things in motion. You are such a pathetic child, you cannot fathom the exhilaration of being a god."

Riley gasped. "That's what you need Alec for!"

"Yes, now you understand" Anna murmured. "But it is not solely Alec's gift as everyone believes. It is more rare than that. It is the combination of Alec and Darius that creates the key to shifting time. Individually, neither can do it. Together, they can. It is the true reason I've kept Darius alive."

What? Riley's mind rushed into rewind, replaying the

273

memories of when they'd moved in space and time. It was true. Darius and Alec had always been together—even in that first rip, they'd both been holding on to her.

"I thought you loved Darius?"

"He's a tool for me to use. As is Alec. It would be akin to you loving a pen or one of your cellphone devices."

Riley was sickened. It was even worse when Anna told the truth.

"But—" she started.

Anna interrupted her. "Enough chatter, Riley. You haven't thought of a way to defeat me and I have let this go on long enough. Thank you, by the way, for healing Darius enough for him to kill you." Anna reached out and touched Darius's cheek with one slim, pale finger. He turned towards her, eyes opening wider. An expression of dismay crossed his face then the blank look of dominance replaced it almost instantaneously. Anna dropped her hand to her side.

"Do it," she ordered.

"Oh God, no, Dare don't!" Riley scrambled up onto her feet in horror. Darius took a step towards her.

She couldn't face it. Panicking she ran. There was nowhere to go but back the way she'd come. She leapt over a body without thinking and streaked across the floor, around the edge of the massive hole, ducking a rip that sailed in front her. She'd managed only a handful of metres before the energy caught her.

The force of Tyon power slammed into her, paralyzing her legs. There was no way to stop her forward momentum. She hit the floor hard, knocking the air from her lungs and numbing her wrists and knees. Pain as she tumbled over and over. It was a miracle she didn't let go of her orb. She rolled onto her back and her right shoulder ended up at the edge of the hole. The wind grabbed at her hair, blowing it into her eyes.

Darius walked over slowly, stepping deliberately over

the littered bodies. He came to stop at her side. He looked down.

"Don't, Dare, please," Riley whispered.

He stared at her. His eyes were bright and his cheeks flushed. He was almost quivering, but his fingers were white with the grip he had on his orb.

"Please," she begged.

She couldn't move. The power he wielded held her legs immobile. He moved his right foot and placed it on her knees. Suddenly she knew exactly what he was about to do.

"Don't push me over," Riley cried out. Waves of fear swamped her. He knew her fear of heights. This was the worst way she could die. A cold sweat broke out instantly soaking her clothes. "For God's sake, Darius, don't make me fall."

He didn't listen. With the gentlest of pressure, he moved her legs an inch, then another, closer to the gaping maw.

She couldn't breathe. Her heart was pounding like a jackhammer. *I don't want to die.*

Another inch. Her ankles moved beyond the edge of the floor, feet dangling over the nothingness below. The bitterly cold wind caught at the cuffs of her overalls and flowed up her legs. The slight energy barrier sizzled. The sweat froze to her skin.

"Darius, don't!" she screamed.

Anna appeared at his shoulder. She leaned over to watch.

"Clever of me to employ your greatest fear, wasn't it, Riley? The greater the terror, the sweeter its taste. Perhaps this is how I'll spend my unlimited fortune—glorying in the absolute dread."

Riley tightened the grip on her orb with one hand and reached out and grabbed at Darius's ankle with the other. She couldn't get a solid grip but she managed the contact.

She almost yanked her fingers away in pain. His mind

was on fire. Pain, loathing, love, desperation, fear, desire; a maelstrom of emotions so powerful she couldn't hope to make herself heard above it.

You don't want to do this. She forced the thought desperately at him. *Darius, listen to me. You can fight her. She doesn't love you.*

Nothing. No response.

He pushed her knees out over the edge.

Darius, please, try and listen. She's doing this to you. I know you don't want to hurt me. I know you never did. You can't love someone who makes you do these kind of things. You just can't. Stop.

He nudged her again.

She was going to fall. Her hips were almost off the edge of the floor. She twisted. Swung her other arm around his leg. Held on tight. Her legs dangled over the abyss.

Darius pleeeese…

I have to. The words formed inside her mind. They were faint and tinged with incredible pain. It was killing him to even try and communicate with her.

You don't. Fight her, Dare, fight her. Don't let her use you like this. You can fight it.

I can't.

The words dissolved into despair. Anger took its place. A wild, conflagration of hatred, aimed at himself, at her, and at the puppet master that controlled his mind and his body.

He kicked at her gripping arms, breaking her hold against him. She screamed and scrabbled her sweat-covered hands against the floor, desperate to get a purchase, to hold on for one more second. It was no use. There was nothing to grab. She began to slide further.

"Nooooo," she screamed.

Alec jogged along the wide corridor. Around him, people and creatures fled, panic in every gesture and every sound, but he was focused on his task. His inner eye, the one powered by the Tyonic crystal he held in his left hand, led him forward. One corridor and then another.

He felt nothing inside except a vague sense of embarrassment. All his emotions seemed to have been syphoned off. Anna was busy. The mental connection between them wasn't quite severed but her attention was clearly elsewhere. Alec didn't like it. It felt wrong for them to be apart, as if he was suddenly missing his legs or something. He hoped she'd put her focus back on him soon. He could use her instructions.

He turned another corner and stopped. The airlock and decontamination corridor. He must be near the hangar and the docking centre for the station. Excellent. It was the most likely place for Tyrell to be.

40

Alec ran into the decontamination corridor and skidded to a stop as the doors ahead and behind him swooshed shut. A red light began to blink. Alec paced. "Hurry up," he muttered under his breath. He stopped in front of the long window that overlooked the landing bay. It was pandemonium, creatures of all types were running, floating, and hopping to their ships, thrusters flaring red as ship after ship dashed out the opening to freedom. Alec growled. Tyrell could be among them, if he hadn't already made his escape. He banged a fist against the door but the procedure continued on its own timing.

His eyes continued to scan the scene as his blood boiled. Anna would be furious so many were escaping. They'd all raise the alarm.

Wait a minute, he knew *that* figure, the young man limping between a tall alien with many antennae and a crab-like creature the size of a refrigerator. His arm was around the tall alien's shoulder and the crab had a claw around his waist. They were slowly making their way up a steep ramp.

Kerry. The Australian human octopus. And he was getting away.

"No way," Alec snarled. He gripped the rough crystal tightly and raised it in the escaping trio's direction but stopped just in time. The walls of the decontamination chamber were solid metal—the killing blast would have bounced off and straight back at him.

That was close.

"Hey!" he yelled, banging on the window with a fist. "Kerry, wait for me." If he could catch his attention, just slow him for a moment...

The trio had made it to the top of the ramp. Alec kicked the door. It looked like Kerry turned to look back. Alec started to smile in triumph. Another three seconds and he'd have him. Kerry looked right at the decontamination corridor, opened his mouth. But the taller of his companions pulled him into the spacecraft. The ramp rose up quickly to fit seamlessly against the hull. Even inside the chamber, Alec could hear the roar of the big ship's engines.

278

"No, you loser. Wait for me to blast you!"

The cycle completed. The door ahead opened. Alec dashed out into the stink of the landing bay.

Coughing, he focused his power. Raised the crystal as he ran. Unleashed the killing beam towards the ship—and at the same instant, slipped on some oily substance. The beam hit the rafters as Kerry's ship lifted off the ground and gunned it for the entry portal. Alec swore. He righted himself. Raised the crystal again.

"Not so fast," he shouted.

But the ship was fast. Faster than was safe, clearly. It wobbled slightly as it dove through the portal. Alec's beam grazed the port side but most of its power hit the structure. There was a tremendous bang. Debris and fire flew everywhere.

Alec stood inside his protective sphere and cursed a blue streak as fire blew around him. He could just make out the glowing thrusters as Kerry's saviours banked to the left and disappeared from view.

Damn.

He would hunt him down, he decided. No one escaped from him when he wanted them dead. *No one.*

He raked his gaze around the landing bay. No sign of Tyrell, so he must have gone too. But Alec could stop the rest of them from getting away.

Job finished, Alec left the burning hangar and headed back into the depths of the station. Anna had ordered him to go set off the bomb that had been placed in the command centre. Trouble was, he had no idea where that might be.

The stupid Tyonic crystal was of no help. It wasn't guiding him now and he had no idea how to reestablish it. It was just a heavy lump of bitterly cold rock. He hung it around his neck and headed down a wide corridor. Why didn't Anna give proper instructions instead of just demanding he do things? It wasn't like he was trained or anything.

Aware that with every passing moment, Anna's annoyance was sure to be growing—and he'd just seen firsthand what she did to those who pissed her off—he turned another corner. He ran quickly down the length of the corridor, peering into every room he passed. He didn't dare contact her mentally, at least not yet. She was still emanating waves of satisfaction; something she was doing was very pleasing, and he hardly wanted to interrupt her unless he absolutely had to. Besides, he wasn't a kid who had to go running to a grown-up the minute something got too difficult.

He passed another cluster of Mheer as he ran. Like all the rest, they were huddled in a corner, aimless and terrified now that their mental hosts were gone. It was funny that he hadn't identified the weird feeling the Mheer gave him as the presence of the Others. And odd that only Riley had been affected. Either it was because he'd been protected by Anna or just because Riley was so weak. Alec didn't give the Mheer a second glance. They were no longer useful and as good as dead.

He rounded another corner and came to an abrupt stop at a dead end. Cursing fluently under his breath, he turned around and headed back the way he'd come. Why didn't this stupid station have a map he could access?

The sound of running feet caught his attention. He quickly pulled out his orb and waited, almost holding his breath.

A small group of Mheer came into view around a corner down the hall. They were wearing very different clothes than the ones that had boarded the Councilor's ship. None had weapons on their belt. When they caught sight of Alec, they came to an abrupt halt. For a second they stared at him before one spoke—too quietly for Alec to hear. Then they all turned back the way they'd come and disappeared. Alec chased after them. If they weren't guards or soldiers, then maybe they were officers. And officers manned command centres.

He caught up with them effortlessly. Short, squat individuals couldn't run as fast as tall, lanky ones even if they had the advantage of being used to the lower oxygen level. Within seconds he had them cornered in a small room. It was only as he raised his orb, preparing to demand to know where the command centre was, that he realized he must be in it.

Riley was hanging over the chasm with one hand splayed against the slick floor, her orb still clutched in her other. The gusts from the nothingness below her buffeted her legs. She had only seconds left.

She glanced up at Darius. The link between their minds was abolished but Darius met her eyes for a searing moment. Time seemed to stop and she was suddenly *aware* in a way she'd never been before. She took in the scene before her; Darius, standing above her, his eyes awash with tears; the irises, such an incredible blue in the brightness of the light pouring through the gaping hole at his feet. His golden hair, mussed as always; the carved cheekbones and the freckles, standing out in the pallor of his distress. For an instant Riley was overcome. *This* was the Darius Finn she'd fallen for; the irresistible beauty, the indomitable spirit, the mischievous devilment he'd approached life with—all before her, still there, somewhere underneath. Then his eyes lasered into hers and his message hit her.

Forgive me.

There was no time to stop him. He moved so fast she barely saw it. Whirling around, he yanked Anna's orb from her hand and hurled it to the farthest reaches of the amphitheatre. Then he flung his arms around Anna, pulling her tight against him in an unbreakable bond. Disbelief flashed across her face, warring with anger. Anna opened

41

her mouth to berate him but it was too late. With a last, fleeting look at Riley he pitched forward into the chasm.

Anna screamed.

It took ages to fade into nothing.

The entire world around Riley became soundless. Parchment still flew overhead. Delegates still fled. Rips still relentlessly moved throughout the amphitheatre. Her heart still beat.

She couldn't hear it. Couldn't feel it. Couldn't care.

Her grip on the floor slipped slightly. Panic at falling took over. Summoning an inner strength she hadn't known she possessed, Riley pulled herself up and onto the floor, collapsing as far away from the hole as she could get before her strength gave out. She lay on the floor in a violently shivering heap, utterly spent.

He was gone.

He was gone.

He'd saved her. Darius had managed to momentarily break free of Anna's strangling grip on his mind and had sacrificed himself to save her. She couldn't believe it.

She couldn't bring herself to crawl back to the edge and peer over. Even though it was kilometres to the planet's surface and there was no possible way she'd see his broken body on the ground, she wouldn't look. She dissolved into tears, unable to rally any concern for her own safety, unable to even focus what was going on around her. Sobs racked her body so hard it was impossible to breathe. How could he have done that?

How in the world could he have done *that?*

Forgive me.

His words came back out of time to haunt her, something he'd said so long ago. *That he was too important to die for someone else.* He'd been joking then.

If it hadn't been for the rip she might never had moved. Something inside her noted the moving cluster of sparkles, zoning in on her like a homing beacon. Self-preservation pulled her disjointedly to her feet and started her running. She was halfway up the stairs before her mind connected with her body. She glanced behind. The rip was still coming though she'd lengthened the distance between it and herself. And there were others floating around, some quite close. Don't *think*. She forced herself to focus on the task at hand. She would fall apart when this was over.

Gripping her orb tightly, she sprinted up the stairs. She dodged another rip, this one much smaller but still deadly. The ghost of Rhozan's voice wafted eerily out behind her.

"Alec, come back."

Emotionally numb and barely thinking, she tore through the open doorway at the top of the stairs and out into the hall. She came to an abrupt stop. There was something she had to do, something vitally important, but her heart hurt too much to try and remember it.

"Darius," she moaned. Another sob blocked further speech. How could she go on without him? She sank slowly to the floor with her back against the wall. She rested her forehead against her upturned knees.

Darius was dead and Alec too far gone to reach. Riley was alone.

Hang on—maybe not. Tyrell had probably vacated the station like a rat from a sinking ship. Even if he had gone for help, he'd never get back in time. But Kerry was still somewhere on this pathetic station. He could be dead for all she knew; he'd been unconscious before she was shot. But she'd woken up, so maybe Kerry had too. Maybe he was wandering around this station looking for her right now? She scrambled to her feet. She had to try and find him.

A memory tickled her subconscious. There was something else, something important…

It struck her like a slap across her face. Alec had gone to set off a *bomb*.

She had to get off this station—*now*. It might already

be too late. Her heart slammed against her ribs as another surge of adrenalin poured through her. Her brain switched into high gear again. She'd have to find the docking bays, search for someone who could pilot a ship and convince them to take her with them. She glanced around her, taking in her surroundings for the first time. The corridor was entirely empty and there were no signs anywhere to indicate which direction to run. Damn.

Wait a minute, she smacked her palm against her forehead, Anna was dead. How could she control Alec if she was gone? Maybe without Anna's hold on his brain, Riley could break through and get Alec to listen to her, to see where Anna had twisted everything, convince him to escape together. Riley wiped her tears with the back of her hand. She might not have been able to prevent Darius's death but she sure as hell wasn't going to give up on either Alec or Kerry without a fight.

There might be only minutes left before the station blew up. No time to lose.

42

The entire room was filled with rows of computer banks. There were counters littered with equipment, though Alec hadn't the faintest idea what any of it did. At the far end of the room, a massive window overlooked the hangar deck. Flame still engulfed the collapsed wall. Alec quickly scanned the chamber but there was nothing that resembled a bomb either on the surfaces or below them. There was no storage cupboard or desk where one could have been hidden, either.

He grabbed the Tyonic crystal with both hands and, ignoring the cluster of frightened Mheer, focused his attention on finding the bomb. An uneasy feeling crossed his shoulders. The sensation of the Others hovering just on the edge of his consciousness, the same as he always felt when he held Anna's crystal, was stronger now than it had ever been. He shuddered internally. He pushed them out of his head and focused.

But it didn't work. Again. Alec dropped the crystal with disgust. It was less useful than an orb and heavy, too. The chain cut uncomfortably into his neck. He couldn't see why Anna liked it so much. It was useless talking to the cringing Mheer. They'd hardly know where Anna had hidden an explosive device and even if they did, he doubted they'd willingly tell him. Of course, he *could* torture them to find out. His heart leapt a little at that thought. A vision of the Mheer officers, on their knees, cringing before him, swam across his eyes.

The corner of his lips turned up. He could make them do anything he wanted, he remembered. The Tyonic crystal would see to that. His hand reached up to clasp it.

Perhaps the Mheer had correctly read his expression or maybe they had mild telepathic abilities, Alec didn't know. All he was knew was that the instant his hand clasped the cold surface of the crystal, the Mheer scattered like leaves in the wind. Three ran to his right, another two headed left and the last two ran directly towards him. He was surprised but not frightened; what could any of them do against his amazing power?

Quite a lot, as it turned out. Alec didn't expect the energy bolt that hit him from the left and numbed that arm. He threw up a protective force field but it was almost too late. Another bolt partially got through, this time on his right side, hitting his shoulder and blasting it with a sudden burning pain. His hand was paralyzed for a second and his grip on the crystal slipped.

Anger blossomed in his chest. Where the hell had they hidden weapons? How dare these insignificant creatures even try to hurt to him? Didn't they know who he *was*? He could feel Anna's gloating presence in the back of his mind, pleased with his attitude and anger. Fueled by her emotions, his burned hotter.

"Think you can hurt me, you pathetic scum?" he shouted.

The Mheer didn't respond. In fact they kept on running, none of them interested in turning to fight. Alec threw a mental shot at them, catching the last through the door squarely between the shoulders. The Mheer arched his back with pain then crumpled lifeless to the floor. None of his companions even slowed. They were gone by the time Alec was finished blinking.

The numbness slowly wore off. Alec gripped the crystal in frustration. He marched over to the dead Mheer and gave him a sound kick. A twinge of remorse was drowned by the overriding wave of frustration and anger. Totally useless alien; he couldn't even die without a decent fight.

Alec swore loudly and surveyed the room. Like everything else on the station it looked like it had been found in a recycling dump and put together by blind mechanics. There were multiple instrument panels and blinking lights by the score but not a word or number or symbol near anything that would let his translator decipher what did what. Were there controls for gravity and thrust and whatever was keeping this hulking pile of crap from falling into the fields of molten lava below? Some mechanism for purifying the air of all the poisonous gas? If he couldn't find the bomb then he'd destroy the station in another way. Anna wouldn't care in the end. As long as everyone died, she'd be happy. In fact she'd probably be pleased with his creative initiative.

He crossed the short distance to the biggest control panel, hefted the crystal in his left hand and spread his right onto the grey metal console. A slight vibration travelled up his arm. He took a slow and cleansing breath before beginning. Focusing his attention on the machine beneath his skin he slipped into it mentally, following the wires and paths of electricity the same way he had searched for the locking mechanisms on Eu station. This time, perhaps because he had a more focused task, the Tyonic crystal was helpful. He swam through the tangled wire mentally, tracing the most important circuits easily. He could visualize the destruction he wished to cause. The energy beneath his skin built quickly, coming to a flashpoint in less than a heartbeat, urging release. Alec didn't bother to control it. He focused his concentration on the engines and stabilizers and let go. The power was sickening in strength. There was a blinding flash and the sudden acrid smell of burnt metal. He yanked back his hand with a cry. The control panel was glowing with heat.

Alec staggered back and dropped the crystal. He stuck

his sizzled fingers in his mouth and backed away. Jeez, that hurt. Why hadn't he thought to protect himself?

Alec stood in the middle of the control centre, sucking futilely on his fingers, and waited. For several long moments nothing happened. He frowned. Surely he'd broken *something* important? He was about to kick the nearest console in frustration when his ears caught a distant groan. He pulled his own orb out of his pocket to amplify his hearing. There it was; metal, slowly and tortuously being pulled apart. It was far away for the present, but Alec smiled to himself. Whatever it was sounded big and important.

He turned on his heel to leave. That's when it hit him. So hard, so unexpected that he actually fell to his knees and retched.

Anna.

It felt like she was inside his mind and was being ripped, millimetre-by-millimetre, from every living cell of his brain. He screamed in agony. She was fighting it, he was aware of her anger and fury, but he was unable to do anything to either grab hold of her with his mind or stop the brutal assault. He was aware of her in a way he hadn't been before: the ugly hatred that had corroded her from youth; the overwhelming desire to control at all costs. He had a sudden glimpse of her memories. He saw her with a boy who could only be Darius. He watched through her eyes as she stroked his forehead until Darius's lids drooped with pleasure. Alec felt her emotions, the mild disgust and intense pleasure at her dominance as she wove the spell of binding through the boy's soul. He saw her repeatedly punish Darius then take him as a lover; twisting his emotions over and over until he'd been too confused and distorted to understand what was real and healthy. Alec felt her triumph and her abhorrence. She'd never loved him; it had all been a twisted deception.

He saw her planning with Xo, obtaining the Tyonic crystal in an alien black market where the seller had no idea what he was selling. He felt her attraction for Logan and saw scenes from their clandestine affair. He didn't have time to cringe at the exposed intimacy; it was gone in a microsecond. She hadn't felt love towards him either, he realized, only a sense of gratified domination at his ever-increasing capitulation to her control. Alec felt sick.

The pain built. He couldn't stand it. His head would burst. She clawed at him, raking his mind with her desperation, but he didn't know how to help her. He was uncertain he even wanted to. The last impression was of unadulterated fury and surprise; as if bitten by a pet she'd assumed she'd beaten into total submission. Then it was gone.

Gone.

All of it.

Everything.

He was free.

Alec lay on the cool metallic floor and shivered. For a long while he couldn't straighten out his thoughts. Anna's were mixed in with his, the visions he'd seen too vivid and disturbing to easily purge. He panted and rolled over onto his back, staring for a long time without seeing the bulbs that hung haphazardly from the ceiling as the realization sunk slowly in. She'd done such terrible things. Tricking him, lying to him, making him believe that she loved him. Making him do things to prove his loyalty. Horrible things.

He saw the Chinese peasants in front of him, their sightless eyes glazing into death. The Mheer he'd just attacked without a second thought. The delegates in the auditorium he'd destroyed. The bile rose in the back of his throat. There were more, too. He knew it. His memories were sketchy—Anna had fiddled with his brain too much for it not to have some damage—but he knew in his soul that there had been other deaths. Other horrors he was responsible for. It was all coming back to him.

A tear slipped from the corner of his eye and ran across his temple before dropping to the floor. Never in his life had he wanted the soothing, forgiving embrace of his mother as he did now. A sob tore from his lips. She was gone. Dead like the rest of his family. Incinerated to ashes or maybe killed even before the bombs; it made no difference. He'd never see her again, never have the chance to tell her how much he loved her. To thank her for everything she'd done for him.

The weight of his grief was crushing, made exponentially worse by the guilt. Why had everything gone so spectacularly wrong? Why, why, why had he ever let himself be taken in that way?

His memory came back in waves, still spotty in places, but mostly there, and stronger with every passing minute. The fights with his brother, the failures at school because he'd been so wrapped up in his own self-pity, the guilt that he couldn't help his dad and that he'd hated him for what he'd become, even though he knew his father had a sickness. God, he'd made so many mistakes. Even when he'd learned of his Tyon gift, he'd acted like an immature kid. He'd bought into the glory of unlimited power without evening starting to question the burden it posed, the consequences of his actions. He'd played enough video games over the years to know better. Didn't responsibility come with power? Wasn't that what Darius had been trying to teach him? Why Riley had scoffed at him?

Darius. Riley. Alec sat bolt upright. Where was Darius? What had happened to him? The last thought Anna had was of Darius. She'd been beyond furious with him. And Riley had been with them, laying on the floor, looking terrified and angry; an odd combination but one typical of her.

What had they done to Riley? Heart in his mouth, Alec staggered to his feet.

He had to find her. Not pausing to think, Alec ran towards the door just as a stabilizer beneath his feet blew apart.

43

Riley slid across the floor and slammed into the wall. She grasped her shoulder and cursed out loud. In the last few minutes the floor had started tilting precariously and she'd dropped to her knees to prevent an injury. The sound of heavy running footsteps made her cringe against the wall as if to disappear. Several Mheer, their boots more suited to sticking to the metal floor than her Tyon footwear, ran past in frenzied terror. They were oblivious to her and eerily silent. But then she really didn't need an explanation. Even an idiot could tell something was terribly wrong with the station. What they were doing heading down this narrow side corridor she didn't know; everyone else was running, screaming, and shoving in the opposite direction.

Another dull explosion rocked the base. It seemed to be coming from underneath and a considerable distance away. There had been six so far. How many more were needed for the entire structure to lose power and go spinning out of whatever orbit it was in and plummet to the boiling ground? Riley grimaced. Looks like Alec had been a resounding success at his mission. A little more incompetence would have suited her, though.

A rip floated past and Riley managed to duck in time to avoid it. There were fewer rips in this passageway than in the wider corridors, one of the reasons she'd chosen this one, but there were still a fair number. Five minutes ago she'd nearly put her hand right into one; a sickening moment that had turned her legs to jelly and one she was determined not to repeat. Muttering under her breath about the stupidity of the entire universe, she began to crawl. She had no idea if she was getting closer to the command centre where Alec was working on his evil task—she had no idea where the command centre was, but sitting still wasn't an option. It was possible she reasoned, that with all these bombs going off, he'd completed his assignment. And if that was true, he was likely heading back to the amphitheatre to meet up with Anna. Did he know yet what had happened to the two-faced traitorous scum?

Riley stopped her progress to think. There was no point going to the command centre now. Alec was no doubt done there, and since she didn't speak or read Mheer, Riley doubted that she would be able to fix anything that had been blown up. Her best bet was to turn back and see if she could head Alec off. There was no sign of Kerry either. She found the corridor where they'd been shot. At least she thought it was the same one. He wasn't there. Someone had either taken his body somewhere else, which was unlikely, or he'd come to and left under his own volition. That meant he could be anywhere on the station or, better still, off it and safe. Fingers crossed.

She looked in both directions. She was pretty sure she'd turned right into the present corridor, which meant she should turn left to go back the way she'd come.

She pulled herself up to the junction of another corridor. Pausing to catch her breath, she looked around. Something about this floor seemed very familiar. She had a twinge of recognition, maybe from the pattern of the metallic plates. Whatever. There was nothing to lose—she either tried this hall or another one—and time was running out. With a grunt, she pulled herself to her knees and began a sideways shuffle.

There was another explosion, this one closer than the

others, then a heart-stopping minute of heavy vibration. The station tilted back towards normal.

"Jeez, Alec, quit with the bombs would ya?" she shouted at the walls. She pulled a face. Now she was talking to herself. Any minute she'd be babbling and drooling.

An acrid smell pervaded the air; something—something probably important—was burning. The floor dropped again as the metallic walls moaned with the strain. Riley fell over; she couldn't stop herself. She hit the floor, not overly hard, but her orb was pocketed between her hipbone and the unyielding floor and it hurt like the devil. "Ow," she cried.

Ohmygod my orb! Cursing her stupidity, she rolled onto her back and jammed her hand into her pocket, pulled out the crystal. Her shaking fingers spasmed around the warm surface.

"Alec, are you there? It's me, Riley." She dared not close her eyes to facilitate concentration. A rip was sure to zero in her while she used the orb and she had to be prepared to get out of its way. "Alec, can you hear me?"

He was out there, somewhere. She could almost sense him. "Alec," she pushed as hard as she could mentally. "Where are you?"

Still nothing. She glanced around warily. There were two rips about three metres away but stationary. Another, large and pulsating, was much farther off but might be moving in her direction, it was hard to tell. Keeping her eye on the bigger rip, she tried again. *"Alec."*

"Riley, is that you? Where are you?"

She almost collapsed with relief. She turned slightly to lean against the wall; it was easier to see all the rips. She was about to answer him when a horrible thought hit her; he might still be under Anna's control. Just because Darius had managed to temporarily break free didn't mean Alec was as strong or as lucky. Anna's grip on his mind just might stretch beyond the grave.

"I'm okay, *but are you?*"

She could hear the distress in his answer. "Yeah, I guess so. Riley, I *remember*. I know what happened to me. What I did. What she made me do." She could almost feel his sob. "I didn't mean for any of it to happen, but I didn't stop her. I didn't even *want* to stop her."

She groaned internally. She hated this kind of mushy stuff. "Look, Alec, pull yourself together. You never had a chance. She fooled everyone she encountered. The entire Tyon Collective thought the sun shone out of her ass."

"You didn't."

Riley sighed. "Yeah, and look where that got me. Blasted and nearly dead. It hasn't exactly been a picnic."

"You haven't killed anyone."

Riley leaned her head back against the wall. He sounded like the weight of the entire galaxy was on his shoulders. They didn't have time for him to wallow in self-pity. "Look, you can feel sorry for yourself later. This station is on its last legs. I need to find you and we need to get off this rust bucket before the entire thing plummets to the ground. So, where are you?"

There was a long moment of silence.

"Alec?" *Oh for heaven's sake, was he sulking?* "Alec, answer me."

Nothing. The bigger of the rips was clearly moving in her direction. Crap. She had to get going. "Alec, listen to me. I'm in a corridor near the big auditorium and I'm heading towards it. There's a huge rip following me and if I use my orb much longer it's going to zero in on me and I won't be able to get out of its way. So please, get your ass in gear, and *come and get me!*"

She didn't hear if he replied. There was a massive *BOOM* below her feet. The air around her seemed to suck inwards for an instant before everything blew apart. The floor splintered and panels flew off in all directions. There was a sudden intense pressure in her ears. She screamed but her breath was pulled out of her lungs. It felt like millions of tiny shards of metal had pierced her skin. Flying debris clouded her vision and foul air choked her. Wildly she thrust out her hands. Her orb fell from her fingers. She grabbed at it in desperation but instead her fingers closed around a jagged metallic strut, almost too hot to hold.

The roar of breaking metal subsided only to be replaced by the screaming cacophony of an icy wind. Riley opened her eyes a slit. The corridor behind her was gone; a gaping chasm of at least ten metres lay between her and the main hallway. Bright sunlight flooded the passageway, illuminating in stark reality the devastation around her. She was merely inches from falling into the sky.

She could see the vast nothingness below; thick greyish clouds lay between the station and the boiling landmass— and that was more frightening than knowing just how far down the ground actually was. Riley shivered violently and turned her head away. She was *not* going to fall into that hole: no way, no how. She quickly scanned the corridor around her but it was no use. Her orb was gone. Cursing herself for letting it go, Riley pulled herself up the hallway, inch by inch. She only let go of the metallic strut when she firmly had a grip on a doorway frame. She had to peel her cramped fingers off it one by one.

There was no going back now. She could only hope that Alec was on her side of the chasm and that he was on his way to get her. If that huge hole was between them, he'd have to find another way to the auditorium and that would use up precious time. Or it would be impossible.

A coughing fit seized her. She had to stop moving for a moment. The air rushing into the station now was disgusting and bitterly cold. It was hard to take a deep breath; her head was spinning slightly. The atmosphere was thin up this high and with the massive holes in the station, it was clear that the energy shield was gone. She wiped her chin on her shoulder and tried to ignore the blood-tinged sputum. Great, now she was being poisoned.

There was a horrific grinding noise, as if all the gears in the station had suddenly lost their oil. It started somewhere ahead of her and rapidly moved in her direction. The walls began to shake. The floor buckled. Riley was thrown upwards. It was only her vice-like grip on the doorframe that kept her from being tossed backwards. Another explosion, this one larger, blew the corridor ahead to smithereens. Black smoke engulfed her. She was pelted with debris. She couldn't breathe. A flash of fire singed her hair and skin. She managed to duck her head and missed the worst of the flames as they flared overhead before extinguishing. She slammed back onto a metal floor plate but it tilted the second it felt her weight. *Oh God*, she was sliding downwards. Scrabbling, she grasped the edge of the floor plate. It was jagged and hot but she didn't dare let go.

The entire corridor ahead was gone. Stopping to catch her breath had saved her life. Twisted metal and wires protruded at odd angles around the edges. It was as if an entire section of the station had blown off. If she'd been another metre or so further along she would have gone with it.

Shivering violently, she looked backwards, almost too afraid to see. Her worst fears were realized. She was lying on a wide section of flooring that was barely attached to the wall on her left, like a dock hanging out over the water. Everything to her right was gone. Through what was left of the doorframe, Riley saw the room beyond was impassible; the ceiling had collapsed and sparks flew here and there from exposed wiring. The chasm behind her had increased in size and her left foot hung over it. Part of the roof above her was gone. Her little dock of metallic plating was shivering with the strain of her weight and any second it would detach from the wall and plummet to the ground below.

Riley screamed her head off.

44

Alec shoved his orb in his pocket and backed up as quickly as he could. He scanned the corridor left then right. It was no good. There were six Mheer on one side of him and four on the other and all had the blank look of someone taken over by Rhozan. But none were holding their weapons. Yet. Alec swallowed painfully. His mouth was parched like the Sahara and his limbs had that unpleasant, quivery feeling that precedes total panic. He was trapped.

Wherever Riley was and whatever was happening to her would just have to wait. He wouldn't be able to outrun the Mheer. The floors were tilting all over the place, thanks to whatever it was he'd done.

"Look, I don't want to hurt you. Just get out of my way," he said loudly in what he hoped was a commanding voice.

"Alec, play again." The disembodied voice was as creepy as it had ever been. Alec suppressed a shiver. He was not falling into a rip again and he was *not* going to get entangled inside Rhozan again. *No matter what.*

"No. I'm not playing. Leave me alone. I have things to do." He swung his gaze back and forth between the two groups of Mheer. They were both inching forward, waiting for his attention to shift from one to another, moving when his gaze was elsewhere. While he looked at them they remained still. It was beyond creepy. The floor rumbled again and the vibration travelled up his legs. He placed a palm against the wall. It was unnaturally warm. Alec didn't want to think about what that meant. Almost as if the Mheer recognized that his attention had wavered, they collectively stumbled forward, waving their arms and grimacing.

There was nowhere to go. Alec swore. He had no choice. His hand rose instinctively to grasp at the crystal around his neck. His fingers tightened against the rough stone. The power surged through his skin, as if he'd stuck his finger in an electrical socket. There was a fleeting sense of something *other*, then, the deep pleasure of allowing the painful tingling to release as the power flew out of his body. He felt rather than heard the wild *sizzling* that engulfed the Mheer.

A ghostly moan filled the air as each of the Mheer called his name. *Aleeecccc...* His blood ran cold.

He backed away, unable to tear his eyes from the sight. I don't want to kill them, the thought flitted across his mind, but he was unable to do anything about it. The power, once so easily controlled, was literally out of his hands. The Mheer twisted and screamed as the force flowed through them. They fell to the floor, almost in unison. Lay still. None were breathing.

Alec didn't move. Waves of guilt and disgust washed over him, twisting his guts, making him want to throw up. He'd done it again, but this time Anna hadn't forced him. He'd murdered those beings all by himself. She'd been right about him. He needed protection from himself. The universe needed protection from him. He didn't deserve to live.

Riley clung to the edges of the floor panel. Her bleeding fingers burned with the strain. Around her, the icy wind tugged and pulled at her, sudden gusts lifting her off her precarious perch only to suddenly disappear and drop her back. The floor plate groaned with the strain. Inch by inch it was tilting. The attachments to the wall creaked. Any minute now they'd break.

Riley moaned. Where was Alec? Wasn't there anyone left on this vile lump of stupid metal who could be *useful*? It was so unfair she could just *spit*.

She didn't want to die. Maybe being alone in the universe *totally sucked*, but where there was life there was hope, wasn't there? She didn't want her life snuffed out at seventeen.

45

"Alec," she cried. It was futile but she had to try. "*Alec.*"

A sound caught her attention. Ringing footsteps. An indistinct shout.

She twisted her head.

Alec appeared across the chasm. He was holding onto the wall and trying to get his breath.

Riley blinked away tears of relief. "Find something to make a bridge."

Alec wildly scanned around him. "There's nothing here."

"What about a rope?"

"Nothing."

"I can't jump that far, Alec," she screamed.

A piece of metal bracketing snapped underneath

her. The plate tilted a bit more.

Oh God.

"This floor is pulling away from the wall. It's going to break off any minute."

Alec turned and ran off.

"Alec!" she screamed. "Don't leave me." She couldn't believe her eyes. What the hell was he doing? Tears of anger ran down her face. The wind whipped them away. The floor tilted a bit more.

Alec came back into view. He was tugging a long cable of some sort. He wrapped the cable around his waist, then curled one arm around a piece of exposed girder. He widened his stance and began to swing the free end of the cable in circles. "Hold on!" he shouted.

The free cable swung in increasing arcs. One. Two. Three. He let it go. It sailed through the air. And fell halfway between them. Too short by a long shot.

"Isn't there anything longer?"

Alec shook his head. "Everything's been blown off." He squinted at her. "Can you climb up onto the doorframe and maybe over it? That part of the wall is still connected to the station."

"I can't even get myself up on this floor," Riley called back. "I lost my orb. The wind's too strong."

"Maybe I can boost you?" Alec pulled out his orb. It began to glow inside his hand. "I'll send this over to you," he yelled. "You climb up and over the wall there. I'll help you from here."

There was no other option. "Be fast. He'll track you."

No need to explain who *he* was.

Alec's power hit her. It was like being swatted by a train.

"Jeez, Alec, not so hard," she gasped. She doubted he heard her. The power hurt, like burning ants crawling all over her. She forced herself to ignore it. Disregarded the wild wind, the horrific distance below, the sick feeling in her stomach.

Inch by inch she pulled herself up. Carefully she slithered over to the wall edge. Mentally measured the distance. Reached over and grabbed the doorframe with one hand. It was hot, but not impossible to hold. The plate tilted again, now almost at a forty-five degree angle, worse than a slide at the park. Hurry, she told herself. *Hurry.*

She pulled one knee up. Then the second. Little by little she rose to kneeling. Grabbed the frame with the other hand. Turned to glance at Alec.

Oh no.

A massive rip was closing in on him.

"Alec, let go," she screamed. "He's found you."

Alec whirled around.

The rip was taller than him and as wide as the corridor. It pulsed with sickening irregularity. The centre was opaque. His skin crawled. He couldn't duck under. He couldn't get away.

It was closing in fast.

"Alec," Rhozan's voice eerily echoed. "Come to me."

Time seemed to stop.

"You destroy my Emissaries but you cannot destroy me. You know this to be true. I have won this game."

Alec froze with terror.

He was *not* going back into a rip. There was no way.

46

A horrific cracking sound rent the air.

"My agent prepared you. You use my source to guide your power. It comes from me, Alec. You are mine."

Alec mutely shook his head. What was Rhozan talking about? What source? What agent?

There was no good choice. Let go of the orb, and perhaps reduce Rhozan's ability to find him *but* allow Riley to fall off. Hold onto the orb and have the rip engulf him. Or...hold onto the orb and jump.

"Play again, Alec."

Certain death either way.

"Your power comes from me. You do my bidding. I have won."

Alone or with Riley.

He jumped.

R iley was hallucinating. She had to be.

She could see the massive rip. Knew Alec had nowhere to go.

Felt her blood turn to ice. Waited for the horrible vision of him being engulfed by the rip. Gasped as he locked his gaze with hers.

Then watched in absolute astonishment as he backed up slightly. Took two rapid strides.

Leapt.

Orb power carried him across the chasm.

She realized at the last second.

"Alec, you'll break the—"

He landed. Mostly on top of her.

His arms encircled her, his fingers biting deep into her skin.

She cried out.

"Hold on," he yelled.

The floor broke free.

Oh. My. God.

We're falling.

Riley couldn't breathe in deep enough to scream. She buried her face in Alec's neck. She swung her legs around him. Held on so tight the massive crystal between them dug cruelly into her skin. Alec was shouting but the wind was screaming so loudly his words were lost.

I don't want to die.

This isn't fair.

Her mind flitted nonsensically. She was five and her father handed her the puppy. She waved good-bye to her mother at the airport. The boy she liked kissed another girl in front of her. Alec's hug melted her heart. Running from Rhozan. Running from Anna.

Darius's blue eyes. The mischief in his smile. The unwillingness to give up.

The air was getting hotter. The choking fumes thicker.

The unwillingness to give up.

She couldn't get her breath. Her lungs screamed in agony. Her skin stung with volcanic debris. Too paralyzed with terror to move.

Do something.

She might not have her orb but Alec was holding his and she was holding him.

Alec, teleport us.

The instant she connected with his mind she was overcome with his fear. It melded with hers. Overwhelmed it.

Alec, listen to me. Break us out of here. Now.

Any second they'd hit the ground. Burned to a crisp. Boiled into vapour. Smashed to a pulp.

I mean it, Alec, stop being a wimp and save our skins.
Do it NOW!!!

She didn't see the rip forming underneath them.

Alec blew apart.

He was suddenly everywhere at once, multi-dimensional, in time and out of it, in a place and yet not.

On the smoking remains of Earth.

On the Mheer station.

In the Councilor's intergalactic vessel.

On too many alien worlds to count.

He heard the voice of the Others, of Rhozan; felt his desire, hunger, gloating superiority. Knew him. Was him.

And yet, he was alone. So separate, so friendless, so crushed, that he could never be a part of anything again. It hurt. Hurt *so* badly.

49

He saw millions of people. Few he recognized. They stood out, their images sheered into his consciousness in the split second he was aware of them. All looking at him, knowing he was the cause of their destruction. Hating him.

It was all his fault. He deserved to die. Alone. Hated. Despised.

Alec, now.

The words were hazy and came from everywhere at once. They stirred his heart. Touched a memory. Pulled him back from the madness for a moment.

Use the orb.

Who spoke to him? What was a dream? What was reality? The voice was familiar.

Use it now.

The voice was insistent. Persistent. Demanding.

He drifted. His mind fractured into a million pieces. He was losing. Losing.

Alec, use the orb.

The voice urged him. Nudged him. Forced him.

His body had ceased to exist in his own mind. His sense of self was splintering. The pain was all-consuming.

Alec, I love you. Save us.

Love.

Someone loved him.

The crystal burned. He would have screamed if he'd remembered how.

The voice echoed over and over. Someone loved him.

Loved him.

He had no recognition of his hand moving. No realization of action. No real thought.

Someone loved him.

EPILOGUE

They winked into existence and landed in a heap of arms and legs. For a moment neither moved other than to gulp in great lungfuls of clean, faintly scented air and then convulse with racking coughs. Riley was unable to unclench her fingers from Alec's arms. Her nose was buried in the vee of his jumpsuit. Beneath the soft material she could feel the heat of his skin and the rapid thudding of his heart. Slowly she pulled back, allowing her breathing to calm. Her pounding heart eased to normal. Alec stayed still.

She raised her head but couldn't meet his eyes. Her cheeks burned with her new knowledge of him. She'd felt everything that he had; the overwhelming fear, the isolation Rhozan had created to break his spirit, the way his soul had leapt when she'd told him how she felt.

As she moved backwards slightly, the massive crystal around Alec's neck was freed from between them. Riley felt something fall into her lap. Anna's crystal had shattered. Silver shards and powder were all that was left. Amazed, she reached down and ran the silt through her fingers.

"What did you do to it?" she croaked.

"It was Rhozan's." Alec's voice was rough, as if he'd screamed for hours. He reached down with trembling fingers and picked up the largest piece.

"And you broke it?" Riley murmured. What kind of

311

power did it take to destroy orb crystal? She glanced up. Met his eyes. Was surprised at what she saw there.

Alec gave a slight, one-shouldered shrug before breaking her gaze and turning his head away.

"Yeah," Riley sighed. "I was inside your head while all that," she waved her hand to indicate the trip inside the rip, "was happening. I know what you felt. What Rhozan was yakking about."

"He was gloating that his crystal could control me. Like it controlled Anna. The Tyon gene gave Rhozan access to us. I guess you heard all that, how he was going to use me to destroy the universe." Alec let go of her and lay back in exhaustion. He closed his eyes against the bright overhead glare and groaned. "Where are we?"

"Good question," Riley murmured, almost to herself. She got slowly to her feet. Wherever they'd landed was not familiar. They were situated on the edge of a huge open field that seemed to end in the silver shimmer of a river. Tall field grass waved in the cool breeze and scents Riley had never smelled before wafted past. Behind them, the trees were impossibly tall, like the redwoods of the west coast, but thinner and with light green instead of brownish red trunks. Across the river, the land rose gently upwards, dotted here and there with massive round bushes that were more blue than green. In the farthest distance, a city's lean, delicate spires rose gracefully, crystalline beauty reaching towards the heavens. The sky overhead was an odd pink-tinged blue, like at sunrise, yet it seemed to be daytime. Riley figured it was daytime because the suns were high in the sky.

312 Wait a minute. *Suns?*

"Oh my God, Alec," Riley breathed. "We're on a planet with two suns."

Alec sat up. He looked around him. He rubbed a hand over his face and took a deep breath. "I have no idea how we got here or where this is."

"Me either," Riley murmured.

They were silent for a long moment while the implications percolated through their brains. In the distance, some type of flying craft crossed the sky.

"I thought an orb couldn't bring you anywhere you didn't know?" Riley said. "Have you been here before?"

"No…" Alec said slowly. "But I'd guess Rhozan has. I must have seen it when I was him."

"You were never him," Riley corrected. "You've always just been you."

"And you love me," Alec replied quietly.

Riley hugged herself and turned away. "Maybe."

"Coz I'm totally hot," he continued. She didn't see the beginnings of a smile.

She nudged something on the ground with her toe. "Yeah, well, don't get too hung up on it, Anderson."

He couldn't help but laugh. She hadn't changed a bit. Nearly died, fell into a rip, and came out just the same as always.

"Okay, you've brought us to wherever the heck this place is. Good job defeating Rhozan's mind control thingy, but minus ten points for getting us lost on some alien planet."

"I was lucky I could teleport us *anywhere*."

Riley considered that.

Alec brushed the shards of crystal from his clothes as he got to his feet. He looked around him and whistled. "This place is amazing."

Riley was shading her eyes and staring where a large bluish planet was visibly cresting the horizon. "Totally." She paused as sadness hit. "I wish Kerry could have seen this," she said softly.

"Yeah, well, he's probably seeing something just as weird right now." Alec replied as he turned to face the other way and peer at a single massive mountain in the distance.

Riley whirled around. "What? He's alive? You know that for sure?"

313

"I saw him leave." Alec turned to face her. "On a ship. With some huge crab and another weird tall thing. Kerry is probably so enthusiastic right now he's turned inside out. He'll drive everyone nuts. I bet they'll throw him out of an airlock any day now."

Tears of joy streamed down Riley's cheeks. He'd made it. "I thought he was still on the Mheer station."

"Nope. He escaped while I was, um, blowing things up."

"Well you could have told me earlier." She wiped the tears from her face. A frown of annoyance was already creeping into place.

"Like when?"

"Like, when we met up. I was worried sick about him."

"Riley, I was *trying to save your life*. I didn't have time to fill in all the details of who I'd seen and what I'd done." Alec couldn't believe it. "And you didn't *ask*."

"That's not the point. The point is, you *could* have told. It would have saved me a lot of worrying. And what about Tyrell? Did you see him escape or did you blast him?"

"I didn't get him. I don't know what happened to him."

"Okay, he probably got away. That's good. We can use that."

"Use that? How?" Alec was frowning. Sometimes Riley thought as fast as she ran. "What...?"

She cut him off. "And I'm pretty sure these little orbs won't get us off a planet. We need really big ones just to transfer from a spaceship to a planet's surface. And you just blew that one up."

"Hey, that's not fair," Alec managed to interject. "I saved us by getting rid of Rhozan's big crystal. You wanted to stay in that stupid rip with him for the rest of your life?"

"Don't be stupid. Of course not. But we can use the little orb to contact Tyrell."

"From another planet? Are you kidding me?"

Out of the corner of her eye, Riley noticed one of the

sleek flying craft heading in their direction. Already it was lowering its altitude. They probably had only minutes of true privacy left. Better now than never. She turned around and poked his chest with her finger. She looked him straight in the eye.

"Alec," Riley said. "See the little spaceship? They're coming to get us. Who knows how intelligent these aliens are, if they like visitors or have ever even seen humans before. With our luck they haven't had interplanetary contact and we're going to be grabbed, interrogated, locked up and maybe even killed. So hang on."

"Hang on?" he started to question. He didn't get any further. Riley stepped forward, reached up and threw her arms around his neck. She paused only for a second, meeting his astonished gaze with a raw intentness he'd never seen before, before closing her eyes and pressing her lips to his.

Wow.

ACKNOWLEDGMENTS

No author lives in a vacuum. Countless people influence our work and give us immeasurable support. Sometimes, a friend emails to say they love the series, or a teen at a convention names their favourite character, or your editor sends along a note of encouragement. Those words, seemingly simple or offhand, make a world of difference to a new writer. So a warm "thank you" to everyone who's ever expressed admiration and encouragement for this series.

As always, a huge thank you to my family. My mum, who always believed I could; my husband, who said I should; and my kids, who were pleased I did.

In particular, a big thanks to my superb editor, Leslie Vryenhoek, who was both very encouraging and super helpful in polishing this manuscript; Rhonda Molloy, the very talented graphic artist who brings the covers to life; and of course, James Langer and Rebecca Rose, at Breakwater, for taking a chance on me.

SUSAN MACDONALD's *Edge of Time*, the first book in
The Tyon Collective series, won The Moonbeam Award (US)
for best young-adult science fiction. Book two, *Time of Treason*,
was shortlisted for the Bruneau Family Foundation
Children's/YA Literature Award. She's married, has two
children, three dogs, a cat, and lives in St. John's.